A NICE REBELLION

A NICE REBELLION

By

Artemus Root

Copyright © 2019 Artemus Root

ISBN: 9781797555492

Dedication

To my brother Col

CHAPTER ONE

The market town of Bridgeford dates back to medieval times. For a small town, it has more bridges than you can shake a heavy, medieval cudgel at, thanks to the river Brid that runs right through the middle. On a 1980s industrial park on the outskirts of town, strings of multi-coloured flag bunting wave above Frank's Auto Sales in the warm summer breeze. The rows of gleaming cars in every shape and colour are adorned with red and white balloons to entice potential car buyers.

Among the shiny cars Ford Wilkinson, a tall, slim, suited 29-year-old man, was standing in front of a blue hatchback. A middle-aged male customer was chatting away to him, but Ford wasn't really listening. His attention was on the hand-written poster that had been placed inside the car's windscreen:

Shop mileage only! Left forgotten in garage by little old lady with dimensha!!!

Ford audibly sighed and briefly wondered if he was in a coma and this was all a bad dream. The poster was the work of Frank's son-in-law, Blake. He had been put in temporary charge of the business and was more insufferable than ever now he was the manager. Ford had already spent hours over the last few weeks with this customer, who insisted on being called Aldo. Ford had never been questioned so much about a car and even asked for his own opinion of other makes, old and new. Blake, had called Aldo, 'A fucking time-waster' and instructed Ford, to tell him to 'fuck off and use up someone else's time!'.

1

Despite Aldo wasting his time, Ford quite liked him; he was friendly, and they shared an interest in classic cars. The more time he spent with Aldo, the less time he had to spend in the company of Blake, who was becoming power-crazier by the day.

'What do you think I should do, Ford?' asked Aldo. 'Should I buy this car?'

'If you're not in a desperate hurry,' said Ford, 'it might be worth waiting a couple of weeks.' He glanced around to make sure Blake was not in earshot. 'I found out that a newer model is due out very soon with an extremely generous part-exchange scheme.'

Aldo shook Ford by the hand and gave him a beaming smile. 'I'll do that, Ford. Thanks for your help.'

'My pleasure. Would you like to take a balloon with you?' Ford hated the balloons. They were another of Blake's stupid ideas, and Ford deliberately gave them away to annoy him.

'I have grandchildren; they love balloons,' said Aldo, looking around as though searching for someone.

Ford untied a couple of balloons. 'Let's get you a few. How many grandchildren do you have?'

'Just the eight!'

Ford thought he looked a bit young to have eight grandchildren, but then again he might be a Mormon or something like that. 'Let's give them two balloons each!'

Blake stood glaring out of the showroom window. The dark grey pinstriped suit he wore had been a perfect fit three years ago, but now, its Third World stitching was at full stretch. His jaw dropped as he watched Ford untie some balloons.

'The fucker...' was all he could mutter, as he watched most of his balloons bobbing off the sales lot with the fucking time-waster. Stumbling to the showroom door, he stuck his head out and shouted, 'Wilkinson! The office. Now!' Blake could not understand why his father-in-law still bothered employing

Ford; it could only be out of sentimentality because Ford's father and Frank had once been partners.

Ford's farewell smile to Aldo faded with a heavy sigh. Ever since Frank's heart attack, he'd had Blake moaning at him all day. With a feeling of dread, he trudged over to the showroom office, not noticing a large white multi-purpose vehicle parked across the street. As Ford reached the showroom, the MPV's engine started and the vehicle crawled away.

The office was executive grey with framed photographs of cars from different eras on the walls. Blake was leaning back in his chair with his feet on the desk that had recently been moved to the centre of the office to show he was now in charge. Ford reluctantly shuffled in. 'I know what you're going to say…'

'You're a mind reader, are you? Well, let's hope you do that better than you sell cars.'

Ford tried to hide a half-smile. 'It's the balloons, isn't it?'

'Of course it's the balloons!' screamed Blake. 'Every customer you talk to goes away with balloons instead of buying a car!'

'They might come back and buy one,' said Ford, knowing that they probably never would.

'That fucking time-waster will be back all right. He's more than likely got a market stall where he's selling my balloons for a tidy profit as we speak.'

Ford could not help, but chuckle. Blake was obsessed with the balloons. 'I thought it was a nice thing to do.'

'You've hit your problem on the head with a fucking big hammer… You are too, too nice.'

'Too, too nice?'

'Too, too nice,' repeated Blake with a sneer. 'What's the saying? "Nice guys come in last".'

'Is that a good thing or a bad thing?' wondered Ford.

Blake stared at Ford in disbelief. 'It's not fucking good, is it?! It means you are a big loser, a loser with a capital L.'

Ford, whose self-esteem was on the low side most of the time said, 'That's a bit harsh.'

Blake reclined further back in his chair and glared at Ford with disgust. 'Look at you; I don't know how you have the nerve to call yourself a car salesman. You don't even own a car. If that doesn't say loser, I don't know what does.'

'Kate had a car so I didn't need one. Anyway, there aren't enough parking spaces where I live.'

'You make me sick, Wilkinson. You're an embarrassment to the noble trade of car sales.'

Blake's words cut deeply. Ford was a third-generation car salesman who had never quite matched the successful sales records of his father and grandfather. His life had revolved around cars ever since he was a baby; even his first word had been 'car'. By the age of five, he could name all the makes and models of every British car in production. His teenage years were not spent playing sports, but reading up on cars, studying their history and design. All this knowledge had not necessarily made him a good car salesman. Some customers found him just a bit too knowledgeable. They preferred to be flattered and lied to, rather than being told they should buy a sensible hatch back rather than a sports car as it would be more practical for their weekly food shop.

'Do you know how I came to be manager?' asked Blake, springing forward and thumping the newly moved desk.

'You live with Frank's daughter after getting her pregnant, and he reluctantly put you in charge while he's recuperating.'

'Don't say it like it's a bad thing! Anyway, I earned my position by not being nice. I sold cars, hundreds of them. Before I moved upstairs, I was my last showroom's top salesman for four months in a row, and that is an official record. Look, I've got a special badge to prove it!' Blake proudly displayed his lapel badge, which looked suspiciously like a racing car from Monopoly glued to a safety pin.

'Nice badge,' said Ford, who had it pointed out to him at least three times a day. 'I take my tiny top hat off to you.'

'Okay, smart-arse, how many cars did you sell last month?'

'Let me see,' said Ford counting on his fingers.

'I'll save you the trouble. A fingerless man could count them on both hands and if he had no toes, he could count them up on his feet as well!'

Ford sat down at his small desk that Blake had pushed into a dark corner and pretended to look for something in a drawer. 'I'm having a dry spell,' he mumbled.

A big grin spread across Blake's spray-tanned face. 'A dry spell! One of those things… the ones with the humps… You know? They live in the desert…'

Ford looked up. 'Do you mean a dromedary?'

'Cows don't live in the desert do they?'

'No, not dairy…'

'I mean a camel! You have more dry spells than a camel.' Chuckling at his own cutting wit, Blake picked up a pen and wrote a few words on a notepad. 'I'll put that joke in when I write my biography…'

'Autobiography,' interjected Ford, unable to stop himself correcting Blake.

'No, it's not about cars, it's just about me,' gloated Blake, throwing the pen down.

'I look forward to burning it,' muttered Ford, under his breath.

'When you're a boss like me, you have to make tough decisions,' said Blake with a smug smile. He leant back in his chair again, caught sight of his own reflection in the glass of the door and gave himself a wink. 'In your case, it was an easy tough decision. If you don't sell three cars by the end of the month, you are fired… History… On your bike, sacked.'

Whatever Blake lacked in compassion or empathy, he made up for with brimming confidence that could never be dented. His personal life was a mess of failed relationships and a failed marriage. How he found himself at Frank's Auto Sales at this time was pure chance as he saw it. He had picked up a young woman at a nightclub, and despite being married with two children under six, he started an affair with her. The young woman was Frank's daughter, Jane. After having regular sex in Blake's garden shed on his days off from his job before Frank's Autos, she fell pregnant. He was now living in Frank's house with his only daughter and the icing on the cake was that Frank had a dodgy ticker, was nearly sixty and would surely soon be dead. Jane would inherit it all, which meant he would as well. After a couple of years, he would marry her, get everything signed over to him and then dump her for a younger model.

It took several seconds for Ford to take in what Blake had said. 'That's only two weeks away. You can't do that!'

Blake puffed out his chest until it was the same size as his spreading midriff. 'Frank put me in charge of everything while he gets better.'

'No, he said mind the shop for a couple of months!'

'That's what you think he said,' explained Blake. 'But what he really meant was "Get rid of the dead wood," meaning you.'

Ford could not quite believe the conversation he was having. 'Let's check with Frank, shall we?'

Blake gave Ford a self-satisfied smile. 'You won't be able to get hold of him because he's taken a last-minute cruise. So, I suggest you pull your finger out, loser.'

'That's not fair! I'm away next weekend, and they're the best two sales days of the week.'

'Well, that's just tough.' With a final sneer, Blake said, 'People like you always finish last. Even your girlfriend figured that out and dumped you... What did she say you were again?'

'The wrong shapes,' mumbled Ford.

Blake burst out laughing, as he watched Ford squirm. 'What a fucking loser you are. Finishing last and the wrong shapes.'

Ford had been going out with Kate for three years, and he had thought they were both happy. Then, to his shock, she dropped the bombshell and told him that his shapes were all wrong. This was devastating. As an artist specialising in abstract art, Kate looked on every object as having what she called 'shapes'. Kate became so obsessed with this idea, she believed all shapes had a unique character of their own. On the fateful day, Ford was acting as a life model for Kate at her studio. He was wearing only boxer shorts and holding a red umbrella over his head. She was at the top of a stepladder, wearing her paint-splattered white overalls. She applied a small dash of paint to the mess of colours already haphazardly arranged on the huge canvas in front of her.

'Will you stop moving the umbrella?!' she screamed. 'I can't work like this, I need shape order to express… the… the…'

'Umbrella shape?' suggested Ford helpfully.

'It's not umbrella-shaped!' snapped Kate. 'You just don't get it, do you?' She threw down her paintbrush and theatrically put one hand to her forehead. 'I can't do this anymore.'

'Is it finished then?' queried Ford, who was keen to put his clothes back on and get warm.

Kate pointed to some smudgy green colours on the canvas. 'Do you see these shapes here?'

Ford couldn't make out distinct shapes in the smudges, but he said 'Yes.'

'That is my shapes,' said Kate, as though she was pointing out the obvious.

'Your shapes?' said Ford, squinting in an effort to see a form.

Kate pointed to some yellow smudges. 'These shapes here,' she said bluntly, 'are your shapes.'

Ford craned his neck and tilted his head. 'My shapes?'

With an icy stare, Kate said, 'Well?!'

'Well, what?'

'The shapes!' screeched Kate. 'Our shapes are incompatible! I can't spend my life with someone whose shapes are all wrong!'

Ford was baffled. 'Which shapes am I again?'

Kate had secretly been thinking it for several weeks while sleeping with an art dealer in London, but now, she came out and told it like it was: 'You're the wrong shapes.'

By the time Ford opened the door and walked into his apartment, he was feeling downright depressed. Even though Kate had only stayed over a few nights a week at most, the place still felt emptier. Ford stared at the framed movie posters that lined every wall and wondered if she might still be with him if he had thrown them away as she had asked. Feeling sorry for himself, he headed for the kitchen to find a bottle of wine. Just as he was deciding whether to drown his sorrows in red or white, the doorbell rang.

'Kate?' exclaimed Ford hopefully. He ran over to the door and opened it. The smile fell from his face; it was only his friend, Dave Simpson, standing there. 'Oh, it's you.'

'Thank you for the warm welcome,' said Dave, as he pushed past Ford.

Dave and Ford had been best friends since their first day at primary school. Both had lost a parent in their teenage years, which had made their bond even closer. Dave was very different from Ford, he was extremely good-looking and made friends easily. Whereas Ford was quite plain and did not easily make new friendships, confirmed by the fact that all his friendships dated back to his schooldays.

Ford's glimmer of hope faded completely. 'I thought it might have been...'

'Kate? Forget about her,' insisted Dave, as he walked into the kitchen and picked a bottle of white wine out of Ford's fridge.

'I never liked her anyway; she was too weird and selfish. You deserve someone better than her.'

'Really? Because I'm sure you said Kate and I were soulmates.'

'Did I say that?'

'Yes, you bloody did!'

'Was I drunk at the time?'

'Maybe,' sighed Ford. 'I can't remember.'

Dave opened a kitchen cupboard, pulled out two wine glasses and filled them to the brim. 'Drink this; I know you're hurting at the moment, but she wasn't right for you.'

Ford took a slug of wine. 'It's all right for you. You never have trouble getting a date. Kate was only my second proper girlfriend, and it took me three years of constant rejection till I found her.'

Dave sipped his wine and said, 'Five ninety-nine?' After another sip, he frowned, puzzled. 'Who was your first girlfriend again?'

Ford stared at Dave, poker-faced. 'Don't start; I'm not in the mood.'

Dave tried to keep a straight face, but couldn't help giggling. 'Any news from Gina? Is she still a nun?'

Ford knocked back the rest of his wine. 'No idea. Ever since she went back to Italy, I haven't heard a thing. I was having a shit day as it was without having that dragged up from the past.'

'She never seemed the nun type.'

'Going out with me must have been so bad that she decided to marry God instead. It's no wonder my self-esteem is in the gutter.'

Dave sat down at the small kitchen table. 'Come on then, sit down and tell me all about your shit day. Bring the bottle with you.'

Ford grabbed the wine bottle and sat on the chair opposite. 'Because Frank is still too ill to come back to work, that bastard

Blake is in charge, and he's given me an ultimatum. I have to sell three cars by July, or I'm out of a job.'

Dave took a sip of wine. 'Quit. You're only doing that job because you think you have some kind of legacy to uphold.'

Ford pointed to a framed newspaper cutting on a bookshelf. The headline read, *Like father, like son*. The photograph underneath showed a teenage Ford standing with his father in front of a car showroom. 'I was named Ford! I'm a third-generation car salesman. I can't break the chain! My dad and granddad would turn in their graves. If their ashes hadn't been scattered at Brands Hatch.'

'Sometimes, you just have to face the facts,' declared Dave. 'You're too nice to sell cars.'

Ford poured himself another glass. 'I'm not nice! I'm fed up with people thinking I'm nice. Blake even said I was too, too nice.'

They both looked toward the front door as a latchkey fumbled into the lock.

'Kate?' murmured Ford in anticipation.

The door opened to reveal the unkempt figure of Jason, another of Ford's friends from primary school. Jason described himself as a transcendental beat poet. Ford described him as a work-shy layabout, still living at home with his doting mother who subsidised his lazy lifestyle. Jason held up a full shopping bag. 'I've got the beers!'

Ford was disappointed it was not Kate, but also perplexed. 'How did you get in?'

Jason went over to the fridge. 'I used my key.'

'How come you let him have a key?' asked Dave.

Ford was mystified. 'I didn't.'

Jason began to stack the beers in the fridge. 'I had a key cut, I knew you wouldn't mind.'

'Well I do mind! In fact, I mind quite a bit,' argued Ford.

Dave took a sip of wine. 'Jason, back me up... Is Ford too nice to be a car salesman? He has to sell three cars by next week or he's sacked.'

'He's way too nice to do that,' agreed Jason. 'He thinks he has to keep up some legacy...'

'I do!' interrupted Ford. 'Selling cars is in my blood!'

Having completed the stack of beers in the fridge, Jason took one back out and cracked it open. 'Dave... how is the wee lovely bride–to-be, Morag... I mean wee Evie?'

'She's still hates you for calling her Morag and saying "wee" all the time.'

Evie and Dave had met at a business conference a couple of years before and were very much in love. Evie Henderson had been born on the Isle of Skye; consequently, she had a sweet Scottish accent. Jason, for some reason, could not stop himself constantly saying 'wee' in her company. No one knew how he had managed to confuse Evie with Morag, but he called her that all the time as well. Even Ford had begun to call her Morag and say the odd 'wee'. It was contagious.

'I can sell cars!' protested Ford, ignoring the change of subject.

Dave topped up his own glass and took a sip. 'Maybe it was six ninety-nine? Anyway, Evie and I have managed to find another venue for our wedding.'

Jason took a swig of beer and burped. 'I thought you were getting married at that posh place, The Grange?'

'I've sold plenty of cars,' mumbled Ford, deep in troubled thought.

'Don't you read the papers?' asked Dave. 'The Grange burned down. A rogue scented candle exploded.'

Jason smiled. 'Now you mention it, I did hear about that! What was the scent again?'

Dave held up his glass to peer at the wine. 'I'm not saying.'

'Go on. What was it?' urged Jason.

Dave gave a sigh. 'Okay, according to the newspaper it was called "Home Fire Essence".

Jason burst out laughing. 'Brilliant!'

'It's not funny! We really wanted that venue. Anyway, to cut a long story short, Evie's Auntie Stella said we were welcome to use her place, the Queen's Head.'

'Hold on,' said Jason. 'You mean that old run-down pub?'

'It's not a run-down old pub. It's a sixteenth-century coaching inn. Charles Dickens stayed there… Or was it his mum?'

'I have repeat customers,' said Ford, still sulking. 'I've sold Mrs Watson three cars over the last few years.'

'Hold on!' said Jason. 'Isn't Morag's auntie…'

'For Christ sake, it's Evie! How many more times?' moaned Dave.

'Hold on,' said Jason again. 'You said Evie's aunt was a… What was it? A fucking power-crazy-psycho-bitch-maniac.'

'And leased loads of cars,' muttered Ford, still in his own little world.

'I might have said that,' confessed Dave. 'But for a power-crazy-psycho-bitch-maniac, who is now running for mayor, she is a very generous woman.'

Jason swigged his beer. 'Is your brother, Conrad, still going to be your best man?'

'Seeing as Evie thinks you're both fucking halfwits, it's just as well. But I did man up and tell her that I want you both to play a part on the day. So she's agreed to have you as ushers.'

'Ushers!' marvelled Jason. 'I've always wanted to be an usher.'

'I don't care what anyone says,' Ford said firmly. 'I'm going to sell three cars by next week just to prove my point! And save my job.'

Jason briefly looked at Ford before turning back to Dave. 'Can you just confirm that I will be number one usher?'

Ford looked puzzled. 'What was that about ushers?'

Dave was just saying,' explained Jason, 'that we can be ushers, with me being number one usher.'

'I never said that!' said Dave, quickly.

'Ushers are equal, aren't they?' asked Ford.

'Dave mentioned ushers to me first,' insisted Jason. 'So I probably am number one usher.'

'I've known him longer than you,' argued Ford. 'So, really, I should be number one usher!'

'You'll be dead ushers if you fuck things up,' stated Dave. 'Evie took a lot of persuading; she thinks you're both useless idiots.'

'She's warming to us,' pointed out Ford. 'She used to think we were hopeless morons.'

Jason finished his beer and returned to the fridge for another. 'Dave, are you staying to watch the football with us?'

'Wait a minute,' chimed in Ford. 'You are not watching the match here. I had my evening planned: a takeaway and a film.'

Jason ambled over to a huge stack of shelves full of video cassettes. 'I cannot believe you still watch stuff on these old things. What were you going to watch?'

'*Casablanca*,' declared Ford. 'And I will be watching it!'

Jason browsed the box filled with more cassettes beside Ford's clunky video recorder until he found the *Casablanca* case. 'It only lasts an hour and forty-two minutes, so you can watch the footie first. Right, let's get the TV on.' Jason grabbed the remote, flopped into an armchair and flicked through the channels.

Dave picked up his wine and sat down on the sofa opposite Jason.

'If you're ordering Chinese food,' called out Jason, 'get a set meal for two. I'll pay you next week.'

'That'll make a change,' said Ford in his most sarcastic voice. 'You never pay me back.'

'I might as well eat here with you guys,' announced Dave. 'I'll have a chicken curry with special fried rice.'

'I'll pay for Dave's meal!' offered Jason generously.

'Thank you, number one usher,' laughed Dave.

13

'I don't want to appear childish,' said Ford childishly, 'but if he's number one usher, why isn't he going to judge your company's annual fancy dress party for you?'

'Because he's not as nice as you.'

'Nice,' said Ford glumly. 'I hate being known as nice.'

Jason sipped his beer and burped again. 'What is Morag dressing up as?'

'It's fucking Evie!' bellowed Dave. 'And I'm not telling you.'

Jason could feel another burp coming, but managed to keep it down. 'Does it involve a wee kilt?'

'No! And as it happens, Evie is away with work, so she can't make it.'

'Anyway,' said Jason, carelessly, 'on that particular night, I will be on a date. I met a woman online. I might be meeting my forever soulmate.'

Ford shook his head in despair. 'You mean another depraved sex mate, courtesy of *No-strings-bonking-dot-com?* I suppose.'

Jason turned toward Ford, a hurt expression on his face. 'It's a very respectable website.'

'Paying by direct debit doesn't make it respectable,' argued Ford. And with a feeling of moral superiority, he picked up the phone and called the Chinese takeaway.

Jason took another swig of beer and turned to Dave. 'He'll never sell three cars by next week.'

'I know,' agreed Dave. 'He's way too nice. Oh, I nearly forgot. I have news about the stag arrangements for next weekend.'

Over-excited, Jason leapt into the air. 'I'm looking forward to a boys' weekend! One last big piss-up before you tie the knot. Where are we going? Barcelona? Prague?'

'The food will be here in twenty minutes,' said Ford, hanging up the phone. 'What was that about the boys' weekend?'

'It's going to be extra-special,' said Dave.

'I must admit,' said Ford, 'a weekend with the boys might just do me the world of good. I'd better check my passport.'

'No need for a passport,' Dave assured him. 'We are going…
you'll love this… to an old hotel in the Yorkshire Dales.'

Ford and Jason gazed at each other with matching frowns.

'Do they have strippers in the Yorkshire Dales?' asked Jason.

'There's bugger all but sheep in the Yorkshire Dales!' moaned
Ford.

'Let me explain,' said Dave. 'Evie and I want to do things
differently. Neither of us wants a same-sex stag or hen party,
so we decided to have a joint party. We're hiring this fantastic
old hotel in the Dales. The two groups can have a wing each
and go on hikes together in the day. It'll be great fun.'

'Hikes?' asked Jason. 'Do you mean like walking hikes?'

'With boots on?' added Ford.

'Exactly! It will be a chance for all our friends to bond…'

'Bondage!' exclaimed Jason.

'No! A chance for our friends to get to know one another
before the wedding.'

'I don't have any boots,' revealed Ford, 'or a proper
waterproof coat.'

Dave held up his hand to stop any more questions. 'Don't
worry, the hotel hires out boots, clothing, the works. All you
have to do is bring yourselves; it's all been paid for.'

'Is the bar free?' asked Jason, crossing his fingers.

Dave nodded. 'The bar is free.'

Jason danced around the room. 'We're going to Yorkshire!'

'Please don't make me sit with strange people and make small
talk,' pleaded Ford. 'You know I can't do small talk.'

'It's all going to be very relaxed and informal,' Dave assured
him.

'I promise you, you'll enjoy every minute of the weekend.'

CHAPTER TWO

The Movie Poster Shop on Gutter Lane sold a few original posters along with many reproductions. It was squeezed between a hairdresser's and a tattoo parlour in the oldest part of Bridgeford. Above the shop was a shabby two-bedroom flat with classic movie posters covering the walls to disguise the fact that it could do with redecorating. In the sitting room, twenty-eight-year-old Nina Summer wiped her nose with a tissue. Her blue eyes were red and getting redder by the minute, as she sat in front of her TV watching the final scenes of the film *Brief Encounter*. She was not the type of girl who wore a lot of make-up. However, tonight, because she was going out to celebrate her best friend's recent promotion at work, she had made an effort and applied mascara and lipstick. Her cat, Petal, recognised sobbing noises from her owner and decided to make a dash for it. The cat's yawning stretch gave Nina enough time to reach over, pick her up and give her a mighty big hug.

'It's so sad,' bawled Nina. 'They should have got together.'

Poor Petal was being squeezed so tightly that she had no means of escape. Thankfully for her, the doorbell rang, and she managed to wriggle away. Nina blew her nose and opened the door.

Trixie Clarke was met with the full effect of Nina's movie viewing. Smeared lipstick and tear-fuelled streaks of black mascara covered Nina's face. Deadpan, Trixie just took in the mess and said, 'Are you ready to go? I booked the restaurant for eight.' She would have made a great poker player.

Trixie was tall with beautiful looks that she had inherited from her Trinidadian mother. She and Nina were more than friends, they were like sisters. Nina's parents had died in a motorway accident when she was seven, so she had gone to live with her grandmother, on the same street as Trixie's family. The girls soon became best friends, and Trixie's parents treated Nina like another daughter.

Trixie strolled in and saw the movie credits playing on the TV. 'Nina... you need to get a life and stop watching soppy old movies.'

'They make me happy,' she insisted, wiping tears from her eyes and blowing her nose.

'I worry about you,' confessed Trixie. 'You spend too much time watching weepy old black and white films, with a fat cat.'

'Petal's not fat! She's big boned.'

'You need to get back out there. It must be a year since you and Edward split up.'

'Ten months and twenty-six days.'

'It's good that you're not letting life pass you by, sitting here, counting the days,' said Trixie, with a wry smile.

'I had someone who was really good-looking,' sighed Nina. 'Good-looking men don't grow on trees, especially rich ones.'

'You never really loved him!'

'I did love him,' protested Nina. 'He had a lovely face.'

'That is not love. I promise you there is someone out there who is perfect for you. Someone who will make you truly happy.'

'Do you really think so?'

'I know so.'

'As long as they're good-looking,' insisted Nina.

Trixie felt shaking some sense into Nina. 'Looks aren't everything!'

'Of course they are!' snapped Nina with a puzzled expression.

'I give up with you,' sighed Trixie, checking her watch. 'Come on, we're going to be late.'

17

'I'm ready,' said Nina, flicking her blonde shoulder length hair. 'How do I look?'

Trixie once again kept a poker face, as she inspected the ruined make-up on Nina's face. 'You look really beautiful!'

A faint glint in Trixie's eye made Nina suspicious and she went over to the wall mirror. Her own reflection made her gasp in shock. Her black mascara had runs all the way down to her neck, and her bright red lipstick was smeared right across her cheeks.

Trixie giggled and stealthily backed toward the door.

Nina burst out laughing, pointed at her retreating friend and screamed, 'I'm going to kill you!'

'You'll have to catch me first,' laughed Trixie, already running down the stairs to the street.

Nina went back to the mirror and stared at her reflection. With a smile, she said, 'I'll teach you Trixie Clarke,' and dashed after her.

The Three Olives restaurant was the latest in place to be seen. The chefs had worked at Michelin starred kitchens, and the waiting staff were second to none, especially for Bridgeford. The rich and the pretentious were drawn to it like bees to honey. Trixie was a high-flyer in a company that organised luxury corporate events for multinational companies and had managed to reserve a table through one of her contacts. Her promotion was just the excuse they needed to give the place a try.

The ambiance, the lighting and the wonderful service were only bettered by the delicious food and wine.

A half-smile on her face, Trixie said to Nina, 'We've been here two hours now; you've proved your point and got your own back.'

Nina still had mascara runs down her cheeks and lipstick smeared across her face. 'Why would I need to get my own back when I look really beautiful? You told me so yourself.'

Nearby diners occasionally peered over, passing comment in hushed tones.

'It doesn't bother me what you look like,' laughed Trixie. 'No one knows me here.'

Nina childishly stuck her tongue out. 'No one knows me either, so I don't care.'

'Nina!' said a male voice.

'Edward?' Nina recognised her ex-boyfriend's voice straight away.

Edward was twenty-nine, blonde and handsome, with a chiselled jaw that was too good to be true. On his Savile Row, tailored arm, was an attractive manicured woman whose age could have been anything between twenty and forty.

'Hello, Edward,' stuttered Nina.

'Are you okay?' he asked, a look of concern darkening his tanned face. He circled his own face with an index finger as a hint.

'She's fine,' replied Trixie, who did not have a lot of time for Edward. He was too much of a control freak for her liking, even if Nina couldn't see it. 'Nina was just saying how really beautiful she is.'

An uncomfortable silence followed.

'The food's very good here,' muttered Nina.

The manicured woman on Edward's arm glared down at Nina and Trixie as if they were guttersnipes and whispered, 'Let's go to our table; people will think we're with them.'

'It was nice to see you again,' said Edward, before being pulled away.

Nina put her hands over her face and sighed, while Trixie burst out laughing.

'Oh, no,' whined Nina. 'What must he think?'

'It doesn't matter what he thinks,' chuckled Trixie.

A smart young waitress approached the table and asked, 'Would you like to see the sweet menu?' before handing over two handmade paper menus.

'I'll just go and wash my face first,' said Nina despondently.

'No, don't!' said Trixie adamantly. She picked up a glass of water from the table and splashed her eyes before smearing her lipstick across her face with the back of her hand. Mascara was soon running down her face. 'I'm proud of you!' she said. 'Not many people would keep a joke going that long.'

Nina peered closely at Trixie's face and managed to say, 'You look really beautiful!' before collapsing into peals of laughter alongside her.

Ford had managed to drag himself out of bed as soon as the radio alarm kicked in, cutting off the chirpy middle-aged disc jockey before he could start going on about how wonderful his life was. Ford had not slept that well. He was hoping that the late night he had eventually had would send him off to sleep quickly, but the words, 'You're too nice' would not stop echoing in his thoughts and kept him wide awake until the early hours. After a quick shower, he stood looking at himself in the bathroom mirror while he removed the previous day's stubble from his face. The buzzing of the electric razor seemed louder this morning, mainly due to his pounding headache. The sudden silence after he switched the shaver off made his ears ache.

'Oh, God,' groaned Ford, as he examined his face closely in the mirror. His eyes were red, and his skin looked pale and dry.

'Come on, Ford! Pull yourself together; you've got to look your best if you're going to sell cars. Get focused!' The slight rise in his own voice made his headache worsen, so he opened the bathroom cabinet to search for aspirin. With a relieved sigh, he picked up a small blister pack, popped out two tablets and swallowed them without water. A little jar at the back of the cabinet caught his eye, and he pulled it out. It was a present that his Auntie Bess had sent him for Christmas; he had forgotten all about it. She usually gave him chocolate Brazil nuts, which he could not eat because of a food intolerance he had since he was a child. Ford opened the jar and gave it a sniff, it smelt vaguely of pinewood and Earl Grey tea, but he could not really tell what it was. He inspected the label, it was a make he had never heard of before. The reassuring description said, *Soothing face cream for real men.*

'I'm a real man,' said Ford, putting on a deep, manly voice. He spread the cream on his face and gently rubbed it in. 'That is soothing!' he admitted to himself. Ford suddenly stopped massaging in the soothing cream. His face began to itch. He quickly picked up the jar to check the ingredients. He had to remove a *Buy one get one free* sticker to see the tiny words at the very bottom of the list: *May contain Brazil nuts.* Ford jumped in the shower and scrubbed his face with a flannel and every soap product within reach, while yelling, 'No! No! No!' in a much less manly voice. After several minutes of scrubbing, his faced stopped itching and he quickly went to check it in the mirror. The face staring back at him was his, but a version with both cheeks puffed up and a bright red rash all over it.

Ford usually cycled to work, but the strap of the cycle helmet was too painful on his face, so he took the bus. On several occasions, he heard audible gasps when other passengers and even passers-by caught a glimpse of his scarlet face. One elderly lady with a walking frame offered him her seat out of pity, and he took it, rather than stand and draw attention to himself. The bus driver obviously had ambitions to beat his personal best time for the journey, and Ford felt a bit guilty when the elderly lady nearly fell over a couple of times.

When Ford finally walked into the car showroom office, Blake took one look at him and began to heave.

'Oh, come on!' pleaded Ford. 'It's not that bad!'

Blake put his hand over his mouth and retched again.

Ford went to the restroom and checked his face in the mirror. It seemed even more swollen than earlier and was now aching, making it painful to talk. When he walked back into the office, Blake was drinking water from a paper cup.

'Shouldn't you be in hospital or in an isolation ward or something?' Blake was worried that Ford might have Ebola and be infectious.

'It's a skin allergy to Brazil nuts,' Ford assured him. 'I've had it before, it goes away after a while.'

'Brazil nuts?' queried Blake. 'If that's what they do to you, why did you eat them?'

'I never ate them,' explained Ford. 'It was in the face cream I used this morning.'

'If it doesn't go away,' smirked Blake, 'you could always learn to play the trumpet. Louis Armstrong had cheeks that size when he played.'

'I've been thinking about that face cream,' mused Ford, deep in thought. 'It was a present from my Auntie Bess. I think she's been trying to get her own back on me for years because I kicked her two chihuahuas when I was four. It all makes sense now. Every year, she's been sending me chocolate Brazil nuts as a Christmas present. She must have found out I wasn't eating them, so last Christmas, she sent me face cream with Brazil nuts in instead!'

'Your fat face is making you paranoid,' reasoned Blake. 'Seems a long time to hold a grudge.'

'You don't know her,' argued Ford. 'She was always a bit odd. Her house is full of stuffed animals, including the chihuahuas I kicked. Now I think about it, there was a sticker over the list of ingredients so I couldn't read it. I bet she put that sticker there!'

'Revenge is a dish best served with Brazil nuts,' laughed Blake. 'What if she did do it on purpose, what are you going to do about it?

'Nothing, I suppose,' sighed Ford. 'I'll probably just wait for her to die and then go and kick her chihuahuas again.'

'Revenge on a dead person,' pondered Blake, 'that has to be a first.'

Ford put his shoulders back and straightened his jacket. 'Allergy or no allergy, I'm going to show you that I can sell cars and be assertive.'

Out on the forecourt, an old car pulled up. A young woman climbed out and started to explore the cars on display.

'Okay, Mr Assertive,' Blake goaded Ford, 'here's your chance to get off the mark.'

Ford stared out at the young woman. 'I think she might just be browsing.'

'You make me mad when you talk about a potential client like that,' snarled Blake. 'Now, get your fat face out there and sell her a bloody car.'

Ford took a deep breath and headed toward the young woman with a determined stride.

Nina had been driving past Frank's Auto Sales in the old Ford Fiesta her grandmother had left her when it began to splutter. This was not new behaviour. She had even paid to get it fixed several times, but it still spluttered and sometimes even refused to start. Knowing the car was on its last legs, and not being in any hurry to go anywhere, she pulled up on the forecourt and went to check out a Mini Cooper that had caught her eye. She opened the driver's door of the Mini and sniffed the interior; it had that reassuring new-car smell. Slipping behind the wheel and leaving the door open, Nina imagined herself driving it.

'Can I help you?' said a male voice.

Nina looked up to see a large, red, puffed up face staring down at her. 'Oh, my God!' she screamed. 'Somebody help! Please!'

Ford took a step back. 'It's okay, it's okay, I work here. I'm sorry I made you jump.'

Nina clambered out of the car and pressed her back against it.

Ford pointed at his face. 'I didn't mean to startle you; I had an allergic reaction to a face cream this morning.'

'A face cream did that?' said Nina, trying to avoid pointing at his swollen red face.

'It had Brazil nuts in it,' explained Ford. 'My skin reacts to them.'

Nina stared at Ford's face, the initial repulsion had worn off and she now felt sorry for him. 'Does it last long?' she asked.

'It goes down after a few hours,' answered Ford. 'It's something in the nuts that makes my face swell, then I just have these bright red cheeks for a day or so. Looking like I'm…'

'The Red Skull,' said Nina before he could finish, 'from the movie *Captain America,* his head was bright red.'

'The Red Skull? Is it that red?' asked Ford, checking his face in the Mini's side mirror. 'I was just going to say, "Looking like I'm blushing".'

'I meant blushing!' added Nina quickly. 'In fact, it's hardly red at all.'

Ford laughed. 'Don't worry, I think it's funny.'

'Can we start again?' said Nina nervously. 'Can you tell me about the Mini and what you would give me for my old car?'

Across the road, overlooking Frank's Auto Sales, the white MPV was parked up. The driver was holding a phone to his ear, as he stared over at Ford talking to Nina.

Later that afternoon, the swelling on Ford's face had finally begun to finally reduce, but the bright red rash lingered. He finished filing some paperwork in a metal cabinet drawer. 'Sale number one went through quickly,' he said proudly.

From his desk, Blake scowled at Ford. 'I'm not surprised you sold it! You gave her a huge discount and offered too much in part-exchange! It's a wonder you didn't just give it to her to save yourself the paperwork.'

'It was just the boost I needed. I feel confident that I can reach the target now.'

'Just out of interest,' queried Blake, 'do you get a hard on when you sell a car?'

Ford had to repeat the words in his head before saying, 'No!'

'If you were a true car salesman, you would. Every time!'

Ford thought he had heard all of Blake's absurd ideas about selling cars, but this was a new one. 'I can't see how getting an erection defines you as a true car salesman.'

Blake shook his head in pity. 'That's why you'll never be any good in this business; you're too nice to get a stiff one when you close a deal. When I sold all those cars to win my special badge, I was rock hard for weeks. Happy days.'

Ford stared blankly at Blake and wondered whether this was all a bad dream.

'Just thinking about it again gets my huge knob twitching,' sighed Blake, smiling dreamily.

Ford was now sure he wasn't having a bad dream, he was living a nightmare.

Nina met Trixie later that afternoon at Brad's Gym. To describe it as a gym was being generous. It wasn't the best-equipped sports facility, but seeing as it was only option for twenty miles, it didn't have to try too hard.

'You bought a car!' exclaimed Trixie, as she pounded away on one of the two tatty running machines. 'Well, it's about time. It was costing you a fortune to keep that old banger on the road.'

'The salesman gave me a great deal: trade-in and a discount,' explained Nina, as she slowly strolled on the other shabby running machine. Unlike Trixie, who was wearing Lycra leggings and a matching sports bra, Nina wore jogging bottoms and a large tee shirt. To complete her sporty

25

appearance, she was munching on a large packet of cheese and onion crisps.

Trixie picked up the pace of her running. 'What are you doing eating crisps? You'll never lose any weight scoffing them.'

'I've been busy,' protested Nina, who was still happily strolling on her treadmill. 'I didn't have time for lunch today; anyway, this machine says I've used five calories already.'

A door opened, and the spray-tanned figure of thirty-six-year-old Brad, namesake of the gym, strutted slowly toward them. He had to walk slowly because his white shorts were very small and tight-fitting. As soon as he saw there were some attractive women, he whipped off his white tee shirt, holding his paunchy stomach in.

'Ladies… Looking good!' Brad complimented them. He proudly showed off his six-pack, which looked suspiciously like it was tattooed on to his portly midriff. His brilliant white teeth glistened in his orange-tanned face, as he fixed Nina and Trixie with a flirty gaze.

Nina hid the crisps behind her back and said, 'I'm waiting for Trixie to catch up, I don't want to get too far ahead.'

'What's your name again?' asked Brad. 'You keep telling me… I remember… Tina!'

'Nina,' she said coyly.

Brad winked at her. 'Yeah, Tina, that's what I meant.' With a final pose to show off his tattooed six-pack, he said, 'If you need anything, and I mean anything, you come and see Brad, the owner. That's me.' He liked to make sure everyone knew he was the owner. He wasn't the actual owner. His father still owned the place but was letting his idiot son run it until he could sell the site to a property developer for a big profit.

Brad strutted away as fast as his tight shorts would allow. His slow pace gave Trixie and Nina time to read the tattoo across his back, *Rich gym owner*.

Trixie continued to pound away on the treadmill. 'What a fucking arsehole!'

'I think he's cute,' confessed Nina, as she resumed eating her crisps.

'You worry me,' said Trixie, now perspiring quite heavily. 'How can you not see he's a twat?'

'All I know is he's good-looking, successful, rich and single,' pointed out Nina. 'In my book, that makes him a catch.'

Trixie set her machine to walking pace and wiped the sweat from her brow. 'Why can't you be attracted to normal people? To someone who isn't a… isn't a twat?!'

'Brad is normal!' argued Nina. 'He's as normal as me.' Glancing down at the display on her machine, Nina screamed, 'Yes! Ten calories, get in there!' To celebrate, she poured the remaining crisps into her mouth.

Trixie shook her head. 'I despair of you, I really do.'

'I've decided what outfit I'm going to wear tonight,' said Nina, as she tore open the crisp packet and licked the inside.

'Good, as long as it isn't the Dorothy outfit again. The last time we went, there were so many Dorothys, my eyes went funny from all the blue gingham.'

'That's where I'm being clever,' smiled Nina. 'Because of last year, no one will wear that outfit again, so I'll be the only one.'

'I wouldn't be so sure,' muttered Trixie.

CHAPTER THREE

The annual fancy dress party was held by the Luxury Corporate events company Trixie worked for, along with Ford's friend Dave. This job of organising this year's event had fallen to Dave. The planning had all gone to schedule, apart from the judge for the fancy dress cancelling after being arrested for corruption. Luckily, Dave knew he could talk Ford into being a replacement judge at short notice because he was too nice to say no.

The event was held at the prestigious Black Swan Golf Club, which prided itself on having a six-year pre-waiting list, just to get on to the four-year waiting list.

Ford opted to cycle the couple of miles to the golf club as it was a lovely summer's evening. Dave had offered him a lift, but that would have meant arriving three hours early so, rather than sit around, he said he would make his own way. Ford reflected that he should have accepted the lift as he puffed his way up the long, steep drive to the clubhouse.

As Ford struggled up the narrow driveway, a traffic jam began to form behind him on the one-way road. Car horns and irate voices berated him for not getting out the way. Climbing one of the six-foot fences that hemmed in the road did cross Ford's mind, but the bicycle was very old and made of cast iron, and there was no way he would have managed to heave it over on his own. He eventually stopped in a clearing near the clubhouse to let the cars pass. He was sweating, gasping for breath and his face was now even redder than ever. The still air of the summer evening was filled with the voices of drivers calling him every name under the sun as they passed.

Ford had just finished locking up his bike beside the clubhouse when Dave appeared wearing a creepy-looking clown outfit. 'Why didn't you get a cab? Whoa! What the fuck have you done to your face?! Did you come off your bike?'

'Didn't I tell you? My skin allergy has flared up. The face cream my Auntie Bess sent me had Brazil nuts in it. I think she did it deliberately because I kicked her…'

'Shit, shit, shit! Why didn't you tell me about your face?'

'I didn't want to let you down at short notice,' explained Ford.

'You know what will happen, don't you? No matter how good the party is, after all my efforts, the talking point will be, "Did you see the judge with the big red face?". I don't want that.'

Ford touched his face and winced, the rash still sore. 'Is it that bad?'

'Yes, it's that bad,' moaned Dave. 'And it's too late to get another judge. Hold on! I have an idea… There are some spare costumes. Follow me.'

Ten minutes later, Ford was in the club changing room, standing in front of a full-length mirror. The masked figure of the Phantom of the Opera gazed back at him.

'I must admit,' confessed Dave, 'you are the best looking Phantom I've ever seen.'

Ford was still feeling self-conscious about his face, but even he had to admit he looked quite good. He started to sing *The Music of the Night,* attempting a tenor voice, until he forgot the words, which was immediately after he sang, 'The music of the night'.

'Good,' enthused Dave. 'Once everyone has arrived, I'll announce you as the fancy dress judge. Then you mingle with the partygoers and judge their costumes.'

'I think I can mingle with the best of them, now I'm in disguise,' said Ford, swishing the costumes cape.

Dave handed Ford a notepad. 'Remember, home-made costumes get extra points.'

'Don't worry, no one's going to buy first place with an expensive shop-bought outfit,' promised Ford. 'Not on my watch!' He raised his left hand and put the other on an imaginary Bible.

'Oh, I forgot to mention,' added Dave, 'make sure my boss wins. I'll point her out to you. She's wearing a Dorothy outfit.'

Ford was stunned. 'What? A rigged fancy dress party?! I won't do it! No way!'

'Don't go all Mother Teresa on me. I found out today that I'm in the running for a promotion! This just might give me an edge.'

'I… I don't care!' stuttered Ford. 'I have my principles.'

Dave eyed Ford up and down. 'A bottle of whiskey.'

'How old?'

'Three years, it's only fancy dress.'

'Fifteen years, because my principles have taste.'

'Okay, a fifteen-year-old bottle, but not one of those overpriced rare labels.'

Having quickly pondered the deal, Ford reluctantly shook hands on it.

'Guess what?' said Dave, with a big smile. 'I would have stretched to a twenty-five-year old bottle.'

'Hey! Don't tell me I've sold my own integrity too cheaply.'

Dave checked his watch. 'Don't let me down, I need this promotion.'

With a luxury corporate events company in charge, no expense was spared in making the party at the golf club a success. The catering and the service were well above par. A talented jazz trio played catchy music at just the right volume so people could still speak to each other without shouting.

Dave stepped on to the small stage as the band came to the end of a song. 'Ladies and gentlemen, thank you for turning up in some incredible-looking costumes for our annual charity fancy dress competition. The judge for this year is… the Phantom of the Opera!'

Ford acknowledged the enthusiastic round of applause as he stepped on the stage. Several people commented approvingly on the time and effort it must have taken for him to put all that make-up on.

After holding up his notepad and receiving another round of applause, Ford went in to mingle mode and joined the party crowd.

Trixie and Nina arrived a little late because Nina insisted on giving her gingham dress another quick iron before putting it on. Trixie had no choice but to wear a costume Nina had brought in a charity shop after the Cat women outfit she was going to wear was suspiciously ruined by Nina using a very hot iron. As soon as they entered the room, guests were handed a welcome glass of champagne by smartly dressed waiting staff. Nina promptly slugged a glass down in one go, gave back the empty glass and held out her hand for another. The waitress had orders to give out one glass per guest and attempted to back away. Undeterred, Nina dashed forward and wrestled another one from her tray. Nina's eyes were suddenly drawn to a middle-aged woman surrounded by attentive listeners, who laughed in the right places as she told them some tale. To Nina's horror, she was wearing a Dorothy outfit.

Nina tugged Trixie's arm. 'Some old bat has the same outfit on as me.'

'That old bat, as you call her, is my boss. Hey, I might get some brownie points because I'm the lion.'

Trixie skipped over to the other Dorothy, who howled with laughter when she saw Trixie's outfit, and made her promise to stay close for the rest of the evening.

Swigging back her champagne, Nina gave Trixie and the other Dorothy a disapproving stare, before going over to the bar area.

Ford went through the motions of taking the names of the people with the most interesting outfits, but his heart wasn't in it, now he knew it was fixed. He had just noted down the details of a man in his sixties dressed as Groucho Marx when he spotted Nina at the bar. Unsure on whether to tell her that he was the salesman who sold her the Mini, Ford opted to be anonymous and went over to her.

Nina gave a startled yelp as she turned to find The Phantom of the Opera, looming over her. 'You startled me, that's the second time today.'

'Second time?' said Ford, with a smile.

Nina took a sip from a fresh glass of champagne she had managed to get hold of. 'This man with a big ugly red face crept up on me when I was looking for a new car. He nearly gave me a heart attack, his face was so big!'

Ford felt his self-esteem dropping past the hem of his cape, so he tried to coax something positive out of Nina. 'Did he make up for it by having a great personality?'

'He was nice,' admitted Nina. 'I think he had special needs because he kept going on about Brazil nuts.'

Ford had never been the type of person to hold a grudge and didn't want to start now, so he changed the subject. He held up his notepad and said, 'I'm judging the costumes. What have you come as? Let me guess. Baby Jane?'

Nina was halfway through a swig of champagne and spluttered it over a nearby barman. 'Dorothy!' coughed Nina. She pointed to various parts of her outfit. 'Red shoes, ribbons on pigtails, blue gingham dress and a basket with a stuffed dog. It's an exact copy of the costume Judy Garland wore in the film.'

Ford made meticulous notes on his pad. 'Dorothy had blue socks, and we have another Dorothy with the correct clothing, but seeing as it's all for charity, I'll put you down as Baby Jane.'

Nina set down her glass and tried to wrestle the notepad out of Ford's hand. 'I spent ages making this outfit and went to a lot of expense, so I'm not going in your book as Baby Jane! Anyway, who are you supposed to be?'

'I'm the judge, that's who I am!' blurted Ford, as he managed to snatch back his notepad.

'Well,' complained Nina, 'if that other woman is Dorothy, with shoes that are more pink than red, then I should qualify as well!'

Ford had the feeling he was never going to win this one, so said, 'Okay, Baby Jane. I'll put you down as a Dorothy.' With a quick stroke of the pen, he crossed out *Baby Jane* and scribbled *Dorothy, white socks*.

Nina peeked over his shoulder and watched him write *correct clothing* next to the other Dorothy.

'She is not wearing the correct clothing!' thundered Nina.

Ford noticed that the little disagreement was drawing attention from some of the partygoers, so he thought it would be best to pacify her. 'Okay, okay. I'll change it so they are both the same. Happy now?'

'Yes,' said Nina, feeling that justice had been done at last.

Heading off to do some more judging, Ford paused and turned to Nina. With a big smile on his masked face, he said, 'I hope you enjoy the party, Baby Jane.'

Nina felt like throwing her drink at him. The smile he gave seemed a little familiar, she had seen it somewhere recently.

Trixie arrived just as Nina was racking her memory bank. 'I saw you talking to the fancy dress judge. Did he like your outfit?'

'He thought I was Baby Jane,' moaned Nina.

Trixie giggled. 'You should have just said you were.'

'It took me ages to source all the right material!' declared Nina defensively. 'Everything I'm wearing is an exact copy of what Judy Garland wore in the film. The gingham fabric was imported from Kansas City!'

'You never told me you went to that much trouble and expense. No wonder you want to wear it all the time.'

'I don't wear it all the time.'

Trixie shook her head. 'I've caught you three times wearing that outfit sitting in front of the TV. It's a bit weird.'

Nina mumbled, 'I don't remember that,' and knocked back her champagne.

'Did you tell the judge it was an exact copy of the film outfit?'

'Yes,' said Nina sheepishly, 'and he said the socks should be blue.'

'Is he right?'

Nina nodded. 'I think they were blue.'

'How do you like that?' said Trixie, shaking her head. 'Someone who knows more about a movie outfit than you.'

'All I know is I don't like him,' whined Nina.

Meanwhile, Dave was feeling pretty happy with himself. The fancy dress party was turning out to be a big success. Even his boss, Melinda, had assured him it was the best yet.

Near the end of the party, Dave went back onto the small stage. 'Ladies and gentlemen, we have come to the part of the evening where we award the prize for the best fancy dress costume.' He smiled humbly as he was given a round of applause.

Nina had been drinking steadily all evening and was now beginning to get a bit unsteady on her feet. She was still annoyed about being called Baby Jane and would tell anyone who would listen what the so-called judge had said about her Dorothy outfit. In fact, she had also told some people who were reluctant to listen. She assured them that the judge was an idiot because her gingham had come from Kansas City!

From the stage, Dave pointed to Ford. 'Let me invite our Phantom judge onto the stage to give his verdict.' The party crowd gave him a big cheer as Ford joined his friend on stage.

A loud 'Boo!' from a lone female voice made the partygoers giggle, and a couple more 'boos' joined her.

Ignoring the heckles, Dave put his arm around Ford. 'Phantom… I know it's been a tough decision, but do we have a winner?'

'We do have a winner,' replied Ford earnestly. 'Can I just say that I think everyone here in this room, raising money for charity, is a winner?' He applauded the crowd who generously applauded him in return.

A tipsy female voice shouted out, 'I'll have to remember that little speech next time I wanna be sick!'

Ford recognised Nina's voice, but opted to ignore her. 'I will announce the top three costumes that I have humbly selected.'

Ford waited for the gentle applause to stop, only to hear Nina's loud voice again.

'You're an idiot!'

Choosing to make a joke of it, Ford said, 'I didn't realise charity fancy dress competitions were so competitive. Now, in third place… Edward Scissor-hands, a.k.a. Bob from accounts.'

Bob from accounts was in his late forties and overweight, and his scissors were made of brown cardboard. Apart from that, he looked just like Johnny Depp in the film. He made his way to the stage and was handed a bottle of champagne, which he gratefully received with a beaming smile.

Nina took one look at Edward Scissor-hands and shouted, 'You've got to be kidding! How can that costume be better than mine? My gingham was imported from Kansas City!'

Trixie was standing beside her boss when she heard Nina heckling the judge.

'Who is that woman?' asked Melinda. 'She seems to have had one too many.'

Momentarily pondering how she prided herself on being true to her friends, Trixie said, 'No idea, I've never seen her before in my life.'

'And in second place,' announced Ford, 'is the Lion, a.k.a. Trixie Clarke…'

Trixie have a shriek and eagerly rushed to the stage to accept her prize of a bottle of champagne.

Nina was now utterly incensed at the injustice of the fancy dress world, especially since she had only paid five pounds for Trixie's outfit. All she could do was stare with her mouth open like a dead fish.

Ford asked the drummer of the jazz trio to give a drum roll. 'The winner of this year's charity fancy dress ball is…' Seconds passed in silence as Ford built the tension.

'Get on with it!' shouted Nina.

'The winner is…' continued Ford, 'Dorothy with the correct clothing! A.k.a Melinda!'

Melinda received a great big cheer from the partygoers, not because she was popular, but because she was the boss, and to be seen not cheering might well damage your career.

The rapturous applause Melinda received while accepting the large trophy was too much for Nina to take. She marched onto the stage, pushing Edward Scissorhands out of the way so she could address the crowd. 'This fancy dress competition is a farce!' she declared, only slurring slightly. 'That… That outfit is not better than mine! The dress isn't gingham, the basket's the wrong shape, and her shoes should be red, not pink!'

Dave whispered in Ford's ear, 'Let's get her off stage.'

'And another thing,' continued Nina, 'Dorothy wasn't fat like her. She was skinny. That Dorothy,' stated Nina, pointing at Melinda, 'has had too many fry-ups!'

Dave and Ford attempted to ease Nina off stage.

'Come on, Baby Jane, it's only a bit of fun,' muttered Ford, but Nina refused to budge.

With a swing of her basket, Nina whacked Ford. 'Stop calling me Baby Jane! I'm Dorothy. The gingham material came from Kansas City!'

Dave and Ford had to resort to carrying Nina off stage, with Ford holding on to her flailing legs.

'Dorothy had blue socks,' Ford reminded her, unable to stop himself.

'I'll sock you in your stupid masked face!' ranted Nina, as she was carried out to the changing rooms.

'I'll make sure that deluded young woman is taken home,' Trixie assured Melinda with the saintliest expression she could muster.

Melinda gave a Trixie an admiring, thankful look. 'What a caring person you are. I'm very lucky to have you on my staff.'

By the time Trixie entered the changing room, Nina was back on her feet and had Dave and Ford trapped in a corner, brandishing her wicker basket at them.

'Calm down, Baby Jane,' giggled Ford, who found it all very amusing.

Nina swung at Ford. 'Stop calling me that!'

'Stop antagonising her,' begged Dave, who now had a basket weave imprint on his forehead.

Trixie wrestled the basket out of Nina's hand. 'What the hell are you doing?'

Nina wiped her hair from her sweaty brow. 'Did you see?! I was manhandled, humiliated!'

'Be fair, Baby Jane, you did go a bit nuts,' reasoned Ford.

'I'll kick you in the nuts,' promised Nina. 'Nuts?' Nina had heard that voice before… when she had bought her car. 'You!' The sudden memory of her earlier conversation made her groan.

Trixie was confused. 'Do you know each other?'

'He's the car salesman with the big red face,' explained Nina.

'Baby Jane here thinks I have special needs,' added Ford.

'I apologise,' said Nina with feigned sincerity. 'I should have said EXTRA special needs!'

Dave held Ford by the shoulders. 'I think it might be best to keep you two apart.'

'Agreed,' said Trixie, pulling Nina away.

'If I had some nut cream,' continued Nina, who liked to have the last word, 'I would rub it in his stupid fat face.'

Unfortunately, Ford was just as determined to have the final word. 'If I had some blue ankle socks, I would shove them in your big, Baby Jane mouth!'

All Trixie and Dave could do was shake their heads in despair and drag their friends away.

CHAPTER FOUR

It was the early hours of the morning by the time Ford arrived back at his apartment. He had chosen to cycle home rather than go back to the golf club for his bike the next day. The driveway out of the golf club was even longer and narrower than the one coming in. Once again, Ford had to put up with hooting car horns and verbal abuse, as he rode as fast as his legs would let him. He had expected it to be all downhill, seeing as it was such a climb going in, but somehow, the road out of the golf club was also uphill and, if anything, even steeper.

Despite his late night, Ford was up bright and early the next morning. Apart from his face feeling tender, he was relieved to see that the swelling had gone and the red rash had disappeared as quickly as it had arrived. Feeling a lot more positive with a sale under his belt and his face now back to normal, Ford let the alarm radio play and even smiled at one of the chirpy presenter's jokes. Sitting at the small kitchen table in his boxer shorts and a tee shirt, Ford checked his phone while tucking in to a bowl of cornflakes. A female voice caught him by surprise.

'Have you seen an earring? I've lost one.'

The voice belonged to a red-headed woman in her forties, who, despite being a fully rounded shape, was wearing skimpy red lingerie with baggy black fishnet stockings.

Ford's jaw dropped as he set eyes on this woman; he had never seen her before in his life.

The mysterious woman went to the sitting room area and poked around the cushions on the sofa. 'Found it!' she said with great relief and put it back into her right ear lobe as she hurried into the bathroom and shut the door.

'Who are you?' asked Ford, knowing it was pointless because she would not hear him. Still, he thought he should at least say something. 'What are you doing in my apartment?'

The spare bedroom door opened and Jason lumbered out, wiping the sleep from his eyes. To Ford's disgust, he was completely naked.

'Good morning. What's for breakfast?' asked Jason, with a big yawn. 'If you have any bread, I'll make us some toast.'

Ford stretched out a hand to shield his eyes, blocking the view of Jason's genitalia. 'What the fuck?!'

Jason noticed Ford's hand half-covering the mortified expression on his face. 'Does my naked body offend you?'

'Of course it offends me! I don't want to see your bits!' exclaimed Ford. He threw Jason a tea towel to cover himself up with.

Jason reluctantly held it over his privates, while Ford made a mental note to burn the tea towel later.

'What the hell are you doing in my apartment?' demanded Ford. 'And who is that woman?'

A lecherous smile crossed Jason's lips. 'That woman is my *No-strings-bonking-dot-com* date. We couldn't go to her place to... you know, do the no-strings bonking. My mum was binge watching a box set of *Downton Abbey*, so I couldn't go to my house. Then I remembered I had that key.'

Ford stared at the spare-bedroom door. 'No, no, no! Not in the bed my mum sleeps in when she stays over!'

'Don't worry,' said Jason, who had it all planned out. 'My mum will clean the bedding and I'll turn the mattress.'

'Turn the mattress?' enquired Ford.

'Let's just say,' explained Jason with a wink, 'that things got quite moist.'

'Moist?'

'She was dripping like a tap,' said Jason proudly. 'I've never had sex like it.' He lowered his voice conspiratorially. 'Have you ever had a woman shove two fingers up your bum?'

Ford stood up and covered his ears. 'Don't give me details. I don't want details.'

'I think I might be in love,' declared Jason, staring at the bathroom door.

'I want you and drippy woman out of my apartment,' commanded Ford, pointing to the front door.

'Jenny X,' said Jason with a sigh. 'She's Jenny X.'

'I don't care who she is!' shouted Ford. 'I want her out, you out, and I want that key back!'

'You're just saying that because you're always a bit grumpy in the morning.'

For the first time in years, Ford was shaking with anger. 'You're supposed to be a mate, but you just take advantage of me all the time. Well, I've had enough!'

'Am I sensing that you're annoyed with me, maybe just slightly?' asked Jason, who had never seen Ford this animated before. 'You're too nice to get angry.'

'Being nice was the old Ford. I'm seeing a professional therapist who's going to purge me of niceness forever, so get your clothes on, get your… your drippy girlfriend, and get out!'

Jason put his hands on his hips and stared at his friend aghast. 'I don't think I'm going to like the new Ford very much!'

Once again, Ford used his hand to shield his eyes from the sight of Jason's genitalia. 'No more nice guy from this sucker, no more being trod on by so-called friends who just use him.'

'Now, that's just not true,' insisted Jason.

The bathroom door opened and the woman Jason had named as Jenny X strolled in and pulled a small diary out of her handbag. Licking a finger, she flicked through the pages and said bluntly, 'I can do Wednesday night. Same time, same place?'

'No problem,' confirmed Jason. 'And I'll have those things I mentioned,' he added, mysteriously.

'Well, make sure you charge them right up first,' grumbled Jenny X, and without a second glance, she marched to the front door and left.

If there had been a high horse in the room, Ford would have climbed on to it. 'You are not having another sordid bonking session in my apartment, and especially not in the bed my mum sleeps in.'

Jason had already given this some thought. 'I'll make sure I turn the mattress over before we start, and after, I'll…'

'No!' stormed Ford. 'I won't permit it. And when you go, make sure you leave that key here.' Ford scrutinised Jason's confused face and felt confident that he had at long last made his friend take notice.

'I might have some cereal with my toast,' said Jason, as he began to search the kitchen cupboards.

That same morning, in the Movie Poster Shop, Nina was slumped over the counter beside a computer keyboard. Her pounding headache was just bearable if she did not move. Any customers who had the audacity to approach her with a view to buying something were told, 'Go away! Can't you see I'm dying?'

Fortunately for the customers, Nina had an assistant, twenty-one-year-old Ava, who liked to dress in 1940s clothing like her movie heroines. Ava would take the customers to one side and explain that her boss was an alcoholic and like this every day. Ava had worked full-time for Nina since she had left school, having been a Saturday girl for several years before that. She had been invaluable in helping to set up the online poster sales, which now accounted for ninety percent of the turnover. She was very different from Nina. For someone so young, she knew what she wanted in life and had a plan for the next ten years. She and her childhood sweetheart, Bertie, would live in the flat above the shop while they saved enough money for a deposit on a house. Nina would often find Ava measuring for curtains or holding up paint chart samples. 'I'm not going anywhere!' Nina had protested on numerous occasions. 'I don't know why you think I will.' Ava would just say, 'You're nearly thirty, you won't want to keep going up and down stairs at that age.'

Nina shuddered as the bell over the shop door gave a gentle ring. Ava had opened the door for the latest departing customer as she wished them a good day.

Nina managed to raise her head from the counter to call out, 'I'm only a social drinker!'

Ava strode around the counter and moved Nina's head further away from the keyboard so she could tap away.

'It's too loud,' moaned Nina, holding her hands over her ears.

'Did you know that alcohol is a poison?' asked Ava, ignoring Nina's sobs. Being teetotal, she had no sympathy for overindulgence.

Nina lifted her heavy head. 'Ava, I am really dying, I need an ambulance, I need help.'

'You do need help, you need your head examining. There is nothing worse than a drunk thirty-year-old. How embarrassing!'

'I'm only twenty-eight! Anyway, I had a good reason for drinking too much.'

Ava continued tapping away, not really interested in her excuse.

'The Phantom of the Opera,' sobbed Nina, 'said my Dorothy socks were the wrong colour!'

Ava stopped typing. 'Phantom of the Opera?'

'The fancy dress judge… he said my socks should be blue,' wailed Nina. 'Then he said he would put me down as Baby Jane instead.'

'Baby Jane,' giggled Ava. 'Classic!'

43

'It's not funny,' whined Nina, feeling even sorrier for herself.

Ava snickered, as she typed with a flourish while peering closely at the computer screen. 'Yep, Dorothy's wearing blue socks. Not many people would have spotted that.'

'To make matters worse,' sniffed Nina, 'the woman who won the fancy dress contest was dressed as Dorothy and her dress wasn't even proper gingham, not like mine...'

'I told you it was a waste of money, buying cloth from America,' pointed out Ava. 'You wouldn't listen to me though. "It's all in the detail," you said. Well, putting on the wrong socks serves you right. Anyway, you're too old to be Dorothy, she was sixteen.'

Nina groaned. 'That's what makes it even worse; the other Dorothy was twenty years older than me.'

'Oh, good!' exclaimed Ava, still staring at the computer screen. 'We have a bidding war for the *Vertigo* poster.'

'Ava... I don't look like Baby Jane, do I?' whimpered Nina.

'You do this morning. But normally, no.'

'That fancy dress judge said I looked like Baby Jane. I always thought I was pretty. I am pretty, aren't I?'

'Of course you are. You are what I call classic pretty.'

'Classic pretty?' pondered Nina. 'What does that mean?'

Ava shrugged. 'You know, a bit too old to be pretty, so you're more classic pretty. Someone who is a bit older.'

'It's no wonder that I can never meet anyone new, with this old, classic pretty face.'

'Oh, come on,' argued Ava. 'Since you broke up with Edward, you've had plenty of opportunities. You're just too fussy.'

'I'm not fussy,' protested Nina.

'What was wrong with Bob? He was a nice bloke.'

'He wasn't quite good-looking enough,' responded Nina, quickly. 'His ears stuck out a bit.'

'Larry!' shot back Ava. 'He had the hots for you, and he was good-looking.'

'He had hairy nostrils, I can't stand hairy nostrils! Edward never had hairy nostrils.'

Ava shook her head. 'There you go again, comparing every man you meet to Edward, who, I must keep reminding you, dumped you for another woman.'

'But he was perfect,' whined Nina.

'No man is going to live up to your rose-tinted view of Edward, who, I'll say it again, dumped you for another woman.'

'Stop saying that like he was bad,' protested Nina.

'I give up with you,' declared Ava. 'Unless you come to your senses, you'll end up an old maid just like… Baby Jane.'

'I'm beginning to think I will end up an old maid at this rate,' sulked Nina. 'I can feel my biological clock getting ready to set an alarm off! Maybe I should get my eggs Captain-Birds-Eyed.'

'Oh!' exclaimed Ava. 'Guess who I saw queuing up outside that new club, the Orifice, last night?'

'I'm too ill and too sad to guess.'

'It was the gym owner, Brad. Apparently, he goes there all the time.'

'I'm too ill to think about going to a club,' mumbled Nina. 'What was it called again?'

Ford's morning was uneventful with regard to selling cars. The few customers that he had approached were just killing time while waiting for a bus. Ford witnessed one of Blake's attempted, hard sells. It was on a man in his eighties. Despite the pensioner explaining that he had a bus pass to get around and his poor eyesight meant he couldn't drive, Blake lay down on the tarmac, clutching the old man's leg and pleading with him to make an offer on any car. The whacks on the head from the geriatric man's walking stick did eventually loosen Blake's grip, allowing him to get away.

'If that bus hadn't turned up,' moaned Blake as he got to his feet, 'I reckon I would have sold him one.'

Ford was always amazed by Blake's optimism. 'He was half-blind, had no driving licence and owned a bus pass. He was never going to buy a car.'

'That is loser talk and the reason you're going to finish last in life,' pointed out Blake. 'You probably would have helped him get on the bus, put a rug over his knees and given him a kiss goodbye!'

Ford could not deny that Blake sold more cars than him and knew deep inside that he needed help in being more assertive. Like it or not, he would try to learn from him and do things his way. His mother had used a hypnotherapist, Cedric De Mange Tout, to help her stop smoking. The office he used was only a few streets away, so Ford made an appointment for that lunchtime, confident that his life was about to change for the better.

The hypnotherapist's office was in a shabby Victorian building next to a bookmaker's, where the punters stood outside between horse races, smoking cigarettes and cursing their luck. Inside the lobby, a noticeboard informed the reader of the four practices that shared the building. On the ground floor were an osteopath and a chiropodist, and on the first floor, an aromatherapist and Ford's destination, the hypnotherapist Cedric De Mange Tout. Ford's mother had told him that Cedric was a bit extrovert, so he was expecting someone with exaggerated mannerisms. After trudging up the flight of stairs, he was just about to knock on Cedric's door, when he heard a faint male voice from inside the room. 'You love it!' The voice was followed by a whacking noise. A faint female voice called out. 'Tangerines, I said tangerines…'

Ford went ahead and knocked on the door. There was a five-second silence before the male voice shouted out, 'Who is it?'

'Ford! I made an appointment for one o'clock.'

'Hold on. Don't come in!'

Ford thought he heard a zip being zipped and a laptop being closed.

Several seconds later, the door opened to reveal a plump middle-aged man wearing a bright yellow baggy suit and a pink flowery shirt. To top off the clashing hues, he wore a bright green fedora set at a jaunty angle.

'Come in, my dear boy,' grunted Cedric, mopping his brow with a red silk handkerchief. 'I was expecting you... Todd was it?'

'I'm Ford... Tippi's son? I spoke to you earlier.'

'Ah, yes, of course, of course,' beamed Cedric. 'Your delightful mother attended one of my "stop smoking" group sessions. How is your dear mother? Still off the cigarettes, I hope.'

'She is off the cigarettes, just vapes and the odd cigar every now and then.'

Cedric led Ford into his wood-panelled office while wiping non-existent tears from his eyes. 'Forgive me, my dear boy; I still get very emotional, knowing that I've helped someone kick the habit.'

Cedric sat down at his large oak desk. 'Take a seat, my dear boy, take a seat.' Ford sat down on a red leather armchair. 'Now, my dear boy, what can I help you with? Have no fear, anything said in this room is completely confidential.'

'I do have a problem,' said Ford nervously. 'I can't stop myself...'

'Porn addiction can be a problem,' interrupted Cedric, rubbing his hands and opening his laptop. 'What sites of human degradation have you been looking at?'

Ford was a confused. 'Sorry? Say that again.'

'That's a new one on me,' smirked Cedric. 'BDSM, is it? Very popular at the moment.'

'No, no,' stammered Ford. 'I want you to stop me being nice.'

'Safe word,' said Cedric, tapping the side of his nose. 'If you hurt them too much, they say the safe word. That way, you can

47

stop being nice and give them a bloody good thrashing. Here, I'll show you.' With a quick tap on his keyboard, a female voice began screaming in ecstasy, 'Oh, my God! Oh, yes!' followed by the sound of a whip on flesh. 'Yes! Yes, yes.' The whip-cracking sounds became very loud. 'Tangerines! Tangerines!'

'See?' said Cedric licking his lips. 'When she said "tangerines", I stopped... I mean he stopped thrashing her.'

'No, sorry, there's been a misunderstanding,' explained Ford. 'Everyone tells me I'm too nice, I need to be more assertive to keep my job.'

'Oh!' said Cedric, disappointedly.

'I was hoping that you could use hypnotism to help me. I don't want to be nice anymore.'

'Well, you have come to the right place,' said Cedric, pointing to several framed diplomas on the wall. 'By the time you walk out of this office, you will no longer be nice. Sit back, Ford, close your eyes and listen to my voice.'

Ford did as he was told and listened to Cedric's calming voice, telling him to imagine lying on a warm, sun-drenched beach and assuring him of his relaxed state. Cedric told him he was now in a dreamlike state and to listen carefully.

'You are strong and assertive,' Cedric assured him, in a calming voice. 'Repeat after me... "I am not nice."'

'I am not nice,' responded Ford.

Cedric was staring intently at his laptop screen while Ford had his eyes shut. The sound of a loud slap made Cedric hurriedly search for the laptop's volume control.

'Slap!' said Ford, following orders to repeat the word.

'You want your bottom spanked harder, don't you?' said Cedric's voice from the laptop. Cedric began to panic, searching for the volume switch.

Ford repeated the words, 'You want your bottom spanked...'

'Stop, stop, stop!' shouted Cedric, as he tried in vain to stop the video he was watching.

'Stop, stop, stop!' repeated Ford.

A female screamed out over the sounds of slaps. 'Oranges! I know it's citrus. Satsumas! Clementines! Stop, stop! That really hurts. Tangerines! I mean tangerines!'

'Slap,' said Ford before letting out a scream and shouting, 'Oranges! I know it's citrus. Satsumas! Clementines! Stop, stop! That really hurts. Tangerines! I mean tangerines!'

Cedric pulled every lead out of the laptop and closed it down. He gave a sigh of relief, knowing it was now off.

Ford gave a similar sigh, before Cedric's reassuring voice said, 'Ford, you are a self-assured assertive man who is no longer nice. When I count to three you will awake and feel refreshed. One… two… three.'

Ford slowly opened his eyes.

'How do you feel, Ford?' asked Cedric, hoping he would have no recollection of what had happened.

'Have I been hypnotised?'

Cedric smiled. 'Yes, and I have embedded in your subconscious the tools you need to handle life's situations without being nice.'

'So, I'm not nice anymore? Are you sure, because I don't feel any different?'

'I can assure you, you are no longer nice,' confirmed Cedric, in his most professional voice.

'Brilliant!' marvelled Ford. 'This is going to change my life. How much do I owe you?'

'Two hundred pounds.'

Ford's jaw dropped. He glanced at his watch. 'Two hundred pounds for twenty minutes? That's daylight robbery. I'm not paying that much!'

Cedric gazed at Ford with pride. 'See? You're not being nice already.'

After paying Cedric his two hundred pounds, and admitting that his initial response hadn't been very nice, Ford headed back to Frank's Auto Sales with a skip in his step and his heart full of optimism. This optimism had the edge taken off it as soon as he strode into the showroom office and saw Blake filling in a car sale form.

'Another car sale,' beamed Blake. 'And another full erection. Happy days!'

'You don't need to share that information,' said Ford, repulsion etched on his face. 'Who have you sold a car to this time?'

'Some old biddy,' shrugged Blake. 'She wanted a little runaround because her dead husband had a company car.'

'Which car did she choose?' asked Ford, gazing over the forecourt.

'I chose for her,' chuckled Blake. 'I managed to flog her that old Jaguar that was sitting around for ages.'

'The gas guzzler?' queried Ford. 'You sold her that?'

'I found out she likes cats,' smirked Blake. 'She's got half a dozen of 'em. I told her ten cats a day are getting flattened by traffic around these streets, but Jags have a built-in sensor that avoids running over them.' Blake signed the form with a flourish.

'That's misleading,' protested Ford. 'It's against the law, I think.'

Blake glanced at Ford as though he was a half-wit. 'Listen up, goody two shoes. If you want to reach the top in this business, you have to use your wits. You don't have any wits, so that makes you a loser.'

Ford reminded himself that he was no longer nice. Why should he worry about an old lady driving around in a car that was totally inappropriate? Despite what he told himself, he still worried.

Blake stood up and went over to one of the filing cabinets, making no effort to hide the bulge in his trousers.

Ford averted his eyes because the bulge was making him feel ill. Especially after seeing Jason's bits earlier. He stared out to the street where the large white MPV was parked across the road again.

'Do you ever get the feeling that life is pointless?' pondered Ford aloud. 'You know, just a waste of time?'

'Are you kidding?!' laughed Blake. 'Life is bloody brilliant; I'm shagging the boss's daughter under his own roof, rent-free! And when Frank kicks it, I'll marry her, take over this place and ship in a real dirty Thai wife after I get a divorce.'

'It seems as though you've hardly given it any thought,' said Ford in his best sarcastic voice.

Blake had a dreamy expression on his face. 'And you know what? I deserve it!'

Ford had to give Blake ten out of ten for being positive. In a strange way, he envied that attitude. 'I want to be as good a salesman as you,' he found himself saying. 'I'll do whatever it takes to be the best.'

Blake put his hands on his hips and scrutinised Ford. 'Okay, if you want to be the best, you need to think like the best. You should come out with me and the Rat Pack.'

'The Rat Pack?'

'The top car salesmen! We call ourselves the Rat Pack, and tonight, we are going out on the pull. If you want, you can come along and absorb our greatness.'

Ford shuddered when Blake said the word 'greatness'. 'On the pull? Why would you go on the pull? You're in a relationship.'

Blake shook his head in disappointment. 'Lesson number one, the Rat Pack are not mono gag… mono… gog…'

'Monogamous,' suggested Ford.

'That's right, we're not what you said,' agreed Blake. 'We're too much of a catch for just one person. So don't forget to bring your condoms and get ready for the night of your pathetic life.'

Ford began to wonder if he should have just kept his big mouth shut. Despite no longer being nice, customers were thin on the ground and he didn't manage to sell a car that afternoon. Blake was feeling uncharacteristically generous after his sale, and suggested that Ford watch him the next day so he could learn how to hard sell and save his job.

Later that evening, standing in front of the full-length mirror in his bedroom, Ford thought for the first time in his life that he could see a confident, even arrogant man staring back. He practised a snarling glare, but decided it made him look as if he had a wonky mouth.

'All you have to do,' he told himself, 'is be like the top salesmen, learn from them, absorb their mannerisms. Simple.' With a final glance at his sharply dressed reflection, Ford headed out into the night, feeling that his life was finally going to change for the better.

Trixie's apartment overlooked the River Brid, that ran through Bridgeford. The block had only been built two years ago and was now one of the most sought-after residences in town due to its proximity to the best shops and restaurants. Trixie had been looking forward to a quiet night in after a busy day sitting in endless meetings. She had her evening planned: a glass of red wine, catch up with her soap operas, followed by a soak in the bath and an early night.

The buzzing of the door intercom disturbed the calm of her pastel-coloured apartment. Trixie was tempted not to answer it, but it buzzed again. And again. The incessant buzzing could only mean one person. Reluctantly pressing the intercom button, Trixie said, 'Hello, Nina.'

'You never replied to my text messages,' said Nina's distorted voice.

Trixie buzzed her in and went to find her phone. Because of all her meetings, she had turned it off. As soon as the phone had powered up, it bleeped several times. Trixie opened the apartment door for Nina's arrival, and read the texts.

Nina was slightly out of breath when she tottered in on high heels that matched the tight-fitting red mini dress she was wearing. 'Why aren't you ready?' she asked.

Trixie looked to the heavens and felt her life force drain from her body. 'I've been in meetings all day, and I am not going clubbing because you want to meet some bloke.'

'Why didn't you text me back and say so? I've spent hours getting ready?'

'Nina! I'm not at your beck and call twenty-four seven. I have a life of my own and I want a night in.'

'Oh,' said Nina, giving Trixie her best sad-eyed gaze. 'I'm sorry… It's just that you said I need to get back out there. Never mind, I'll just go on my own.'

Trixie had seen Nina try this on lots of times. 'I am not falling for your sad eyes, so go, clear off, goodbye.'

Nina cast her eyes down to her feet before staring at the door. 'You've been busy, I understand. I will go on my own.'

'That's right, you go on your own then,' agreed Trixie.

Nina managed to get her bottom lip to tremble a bit before saying in her most pathetic voice, 'I'll just have to hope no one slips a ruby in my drink when I'm not looking.'

Trixie burst out laughing. 'It's roofie, not ruby, and your bottom lip makes you look like a lost fish.'

Nina struggled to get down on her knees. 'I'm begging you! Please just come with me. I'll never ask a favour ever again.'

Trixie shook her head in despair. 'All right, I'll come with you, but only for a couple of hours, and I mean a couple of hours! I'll just get ready.'

'I love you,' beamed Nina. 'But can you hurry because this new club is very popular and gets full very quickly? Like in half an hour.'

'What club are you on about?' asked Trixie, as she went into her bedroom.

'It's a new one, the Orifice!' shouted Nina as she struggled to her feet.

'Are you telling me,' moaned Trixie, 'that you are dragging me out of my cosy home to go to a club called the Orifice? Isn't that a hole?'

'I think it means a Greek god or something.'

Trixie strolled back into the room. 'Greek for shit hole, more like.' With a quick straightening of her black mini dress, she said, 'I'm ready!'

Nina stared at Trixie with envy. 'How come it takes me hours to look as good as this, and in just five minutes, you look fabulous? I really hate you sometimes.'

'Come on, the quicker we go, the quicker I can come home.'

CHAPTER FIVE

It was half past seven on Thursday night and already a neon *Full up* sign flickered over the entrance to, the Orifice nightclub. The name Orifice had come about by accident. It was meant to be called the Orpheus nightclub, named after a great musician from Greek mythology, but the owners had ordered the sign over the phone, and the sign makers weren't big fans of Greek myths so cocked up the spelling.

Outside the wrongly spelled club, two heavily built, pugilist-faced doormen, dressed in black dinner suits with bow ties, stood stony-faced in front of a queue of eager clubbers.

As Nina and Trixie approached the entrance, they took in the queue of twenty or more people. Trixie said bluntly, 'I'm not queuing, I'm going home.'

'Hold on,' implored Nina. 'Just because there's a little queue, it doesn't mean there's going to be a long wait.' After taking their place at the end of the queue, Nina leant forward and spoke to the young couple in their early twenties before them. 'Excuse me, do you know how long the wait is?'

The young woman glared at Nina, suspecting that she had eyes for her spotty-faced boyfriend. The spotty-faced boyfriend smiled and said, 'About an hour, I would say.'

'I am not waiting for an hour!' declared Trixie.

Nina peeked over the heads in front. 'Wait a second, just hold my place, I'll have a word with the doormen.' Nina pushed her shoulders back and wobbled to the front of the queue. 'Excuse me, sir!' she said with a flirty smile, to the widest doormen. 'Is there a first-class entrance I can use? See, I'm supposed to meet someone here.'

The wide doorman glared at her through the scar tissue around his eyes and bluntly said, 'No.'

Nina took an instant dislike to the wide doorman, but decided to try another tack. 'You must reserve spaces for VIPs.'

'Are you a VIP?'

'Yes, I am,' confirmed Nina, sensing a way to get into the club.

'Where's your pass?' asked the wide doorman, impassively.

'I believe it was left for me... for me to pick up. Yes, it was left for me to pick up.'

'What name?' inquired the wide doorman.

Nina had made a judgement that the wide doorman had been thumped in the head quite often, by the look of his boxer's face, and was therefore a bit slow. 'What names do you have?'

The wide doorman opened the club door and disappeared within.

A further twenty people had now joined the queue behind Trixie. Nina waved her arms to attract her attention and gave her a thumbs up. She joined Nina just as the wide doorman came out of the club door and said, 'We don't have any VIP passes put aside.'

Having gambled and lost, Nina went all in with a raised voice. 'Well, this is not good enough! I want to see the management. This so-called system you have makes a mockery of... of systems!'

The other stony-faced doorman, with even more scars on his face, stepped over to them. 'What's going on, Leslie?'

'This lady says a VIP pass has been put aside for her,' grunted Leslie, 'but there ain't any.'

'Are you really called Leslie?' interrupted Nina. 'Isn't that a girl's name?'

'Please don't say Leslie is a girl's name,' said the other stony-faced doorman, in a deep, low voice. 'My colleague is very sensitive about his name. Anyway, a girl's name is spelt differently.'

56

Nina was not really listening, still getting her head around the fact that this bull dog of a man had a girl's name. 'But Leslie is a girl's name! Trixie, 'isn't Leslie a girl's name?'

'Does it matter?' said Trixie. 'Anyway, the club's full up, I'm going home.'

'Please, miss,' pleaded the other stony-faced doorman in his deep voice, 'don't keep saying it's a girl's name.'

But Nina was still trying to understand and couldn't let it go. 'Leslie is a girl's name, why does he have a girl's name?'

Leslie had a flashback to the schoolyard when he was a skinny eight-year-old child and a gang of kids were chanting, 'Leslie is a girl's name! Leslie is a girl's name!' Tears began to run down the scar tissue on his cheeks. 'It's a boy's name!' he sobbed.

The other stony-faced doorman put an arm around his colleague's shoulder. 'Go and take five minutes, I can manage.'

Leslie pulled out a handkerchief, blew his broken nose and dabbed his eyes, before stepping inside the club.

The remaining stony-faced doorman glared at Nina. 'We do not tolerate bullying in this club.'

'All I said was that he had a girl's name,' stated Nina. 'And he does have a girl's name! Leslie is a girl's name!'

The glowering doorman recognised Trixie as she began pulling Nina away. 'Are you with her?' he rumbled.

Trixie wanted to say no, but muttered, 'Yes, I'm sorry to say I am.'

'It's me, Joe!'

Trixie was puzzled. 'Joe?'

'We do the same Zumba class at the gym!'

Trixie gave him a big smile. 'Joe! I didn't recognise you with long trousers on.'

Joe smiled modestly. 'Seeing as it's you, you can go in.'

'Does that include my friend? She's not really a bully.'

'Okay,' agreed Joe, 'because we're Zumba buddies.' He opened the door to the club and ushered them in. Just as the door began to close, he heard Nina's voice.

'Zumba? Isn't that dancing for girls?'

Joe sniffled; his eyes began to redden. 'Zumba is not just for girls.'

Ford had met up with Blake and his car salesmen friends in a pub close to the Orifice. His first impression was that the so-called Rat Pack looked more like a fat hamster pack.

Blake introduced them to Ford using their Rat Pack nicknames. 'This is Muncher!'

Muncher was in his forties, and Ford thought he might have got his name for eating a lot of pies. 'I've got a double garage at home,' announced Muncher with some swagger.

Ford was also introduced to fifty-year-old Donga, who had managed to fit his forty-two-inch waist into a thirty-four-inch pair of skinny trousers by fastening their straining material under his gut.

'He's got two extensions,' explained Blake with deferential respect.

Donga took a shallow breath, because that was all he could manage, and said, 'Three extensions!'

Ford was introduced to Big Dog, who was in his late thirties, bald, rounded and short. Ford wondered if he should suggest they call him Sausage Dog.

'He's got electric gates,' stated Blake with envy.

'Top-of-the-range electric gates, and CCTV,' boasted Big Dog.

The last of the Rat Pack to be introduced to Ford was Bongo. Bongo was in her late forties, smiley-faced and with a beer gut that protruded over her skinny trousers.

Pulling a squashed wallet out of her back pocket and opening it up, she showed Ford a photograph. 'Guess how old he is,' urged Bongo.

Ford took the wallet and peered closely at the photograph. It was a young Asian man dressed in a dark suit with a flower in the jacket buttonhole. 'Fourteen?' guessed Ford.

'Nineteen, and as randy as a rabbit,' bragged Bongo. 'He's Filipino.'

'Does he have a name?' asked Ford.

'Of course he has a name, it's Bri... Biryani or something like that.'

'Is his family still staying with you?' queried Blake. 'There's quite a lot of them.'

'Yeah, still staying with us. There was some mix-up with visas,' explained Bongo, rolling her eyes. 'Biryani's uncles and aunts are having to stay as well, until it gets sorted. Anyway! Nineteen and randy as a rabbit, ker-ching!'

With a smug smile, Blake turned to Ford, and with open arms said, 'You could become one of the Rat Pack if you try hard enough. And stop being useless.'

Blake ushered the Rat Pack over. They grouped together in what seemed like a well-rehearsed move, posing like action heroes, before shouting 'Rat Pack!' Unfortunately, they said 'Rat Pack' at different times, ruining the effect.

'We're still working on that,' explained Blake scratching his head, 'Right, let's do tequila shots before we go to the club. We'll show you how the Rat Pack can party!'

Ford eagerly tossed back two shots in quick succession, hoping they would numb the embarrassment of being seen out with the Rat Pack. After four shots, he started thinking that they were not as obnoxious as he had first thought and even smiled a couple of times at their corny banter. By the time the group left for the nightclub, Ford was even beginning to enjoy himself. When they eventually strolled over to the Orifice, the queue was forty people long.

'This way, Rat Pack,' instructed Blake, as he led them to the entrance.

Joe, Leslie's stony-faced colleague, gave a sigh when he saw Blake strutting toward him with his entourage. He really disliked the smug little twat for always talking down to him and would have loved to punch him in his arrogant face. However, being the professional that he was, Joe just forced a smile and said, 'Good evening sir.'

Blake flicked open his wallet to reveal his gold VIP pass. 'Good evening, my good man. The Rat Pack are back and ready to party!'

Blake had been given a VIP pass by Gino, the club's owner. Blake had sold him a top-of-the-range BMW at a big discount before working at Frank's Auto Sales. Actually, it had not been a big discount, but by the time Blake had woven his lies, Gino was convinced Blake had sold it to him at a huge loss.

Joe nodded to Leslie, to let the Rat Pack in. Ford noticed that this doorman's eyes were red, as if he had been crying.

'Wait!' ordered Joe. 'The VIP pass is for you and four guests, not five. One of you will have to go to the back of the queue.'

Blake moved his Rat Pack friends aside and stepped over to Joe. With the most condescending scowl, he informed him, 'The Rat Pack always stick together, all for one, one for all!'

'Then I suggest that you all go to the back of the queue,' responded Joe, 'because the pass is for four additional guests only.'

Blake pondered the ultimatum for a good five seconds before turning to Ford. 'You're not technically in the Rat Pack, so you'll have to go to the back of the queue.'

Ford turned and gazed at the long queue. 'What about all for one, one for all?'

Blake patted Ford on the shoulder. 'We'll all be waiting for you, one and all. These queues move quickly at this time of night. You'll be back with the Rat Pack before you know it.' Without a backward glance, Blake and the Rat Pack strode cockily into the Orifice.

As Ford reluctantly made his way to the back of the queue, he checked his watch. It was 8:37pm. 'I'll give it twenty minutes at the most,' he thought to himself.

Trixie's visit to the club was turning out as she expected: terrible. As soon as they had walked in, Nina had clasped her hand to drag her around the club in search of her male conquest.

'Let me get a drink first!' protested Trixie.

However, Nina was in determined mood. Finally, she halted and pointed to a figure on the dance floor. 'There!'

Trixie gazed in the direction of Nina's pointing finger and saw Brad the gym owner, posing and dancing in front of a group of uninterested women.

'You have to be fucking kidding!' groaned Trixie. 'If I'd known what you were up to, I would have stayed at home. I know I said you need to start dating again, but him?'

Nina seemed to be mesmerised by Brad's dancing. 'Don't be like that, he's gorgeous.'

Trixie checked her watch. 'I am going for a drink now, and in one and a half hours, I'm going home.'

'Don't look! I think he's seen me. Is he looking?'

Trixie felt like she was back at a school disco. 'I don't know, you told me not to look.'

'Well, look to see if he's looking, but look like you're not looking.'

'He's not looking,' answered Trixie.

'Look again to see if he's looking, but still look like you're not looking,' urged Nina.

Trixie rolled her eyes. 'You go ahead and look because I'm getting a drink.'

Nina had a choice: keep her friend company and buy her a drink for coming out with her, or go over to Brad and let him know she was there.

'I'll see you later,' she said, and danced over to Brad, whose shirt buttons were struggling to keep his tattooed six-pack from breaking free, as his hips gyrated to the music.

Nina's dancing style could kindly be described as unusual. If you were not kind, you would say she had about as much rhythm as a six-year-old child who had no rhythm whatsoever.

Brad gawked at the female body dancing oddly toward him. After checking her legs, her butt and her boobs, he finally glanced at her face. 'Hey, Tina! It's me, the gym owner.' He unbuttoned a shirt button before the tension broke it free.

Nina pretended to be shocked to see him. 'It's Nina! Hi, Brad, I didn't know you came here.'

'It's my way of letting off steam,' gasped Brad. He was getting out of breath and feeling hot. 'Being a wealthy gym owner is stressful, but this... this I could do all night.' Unfortunately Brad couldn't do it all night and felt that if he did not stop dancing, he would collapse in a heap, just like he had the week before. 'I would buy you a drink,' wheezed Brad, holding his left side, as he felt a stitch coming, but trying to make it look like a pose in front of Nina. 'But I left my designer wallet with a wodge of fifty-pound notes inside it at home.'

'I'll buy you a drink, if you like!' said Nina, eagerly. 'What would you like?'

Brad wiped the sweat from his brow. 'I'll have a lager shandy, but with tonic water instead of lemonade.'

'Lager with tonic water? That doesn't sound very nice.'

'Believe me, it's delicious,' Brad assured her, taking deep breaths. 'It's my own invention. I spent three years inventing it actually. I call it a lager-onic. Just you wait and see. Everyone will be drinking lager-onics soon. I've written to the *Oxford Dictionary* so they can add it to their new book.'

One of Nina's faults was her tendency to be easily impressed. 'Wow! You invented a drink, I'm going to have one of them as well.'

When they reached the bar, Brad was still sweating and catching his breath.

'Are you okay?' asked Nina, as she heard his chest rattle.

'Asthma!' lied Brad. 'But I don't let it stop me relaxing.'

Trixie had bought herself two large glasses of wine to make the evening bearable and sat down at a table on the mezzanine floor overlooking the whole area below. Her glare dissuaded any male from approaching her, as she indulged her favourite hobby: people watching. There were a mixture of ages enjoying themselves in the Orifice; some very young, probably underage, and some a lot older, like the obnoxious middle-aged morons by the bar.

It was just after 10pm when Ford finally entered the club, minus twenty pounds for the entry fee. His mood was now glum, verging on pissed off. It was the first time he had ever been inside the place, and he found it was just one huge room. At one end was a dance floor and at the other a bar that stretched the width of the room. Seating booths of various sizes hugged the walls, with a balcony on a mezzanine floor overlooking the whole area. The music, to Ford's relief, wasn't deafening, and a raised voice was all that was needed to be heard.

'Wilkinson!' shouted the familiar voice of Blake. Ford turned to see him and the Rat Pack at the bar. 'We're over here on the pull!'

Ford was feeling a bit like Billy-No-Mates, so was happy to join them. Blake's version of being on the pull meant accosting women and making lecherous remarks. That even went for Bongo, who put a few young men off sex for a while by grabbing them by the balls and giving them a good grope.

Blake and the Rat Pack were half-cut and even louder than before. When Ford explained that he had had to queue for an hour and a half, they fell about laughing with the arrogance of practising bullies.

Keeping one eye constantly on Nina, who was now flirting with Brad at the bar, Trixie had noticed a man in his late twenties, ordinary-looking, nothing special, wandering about like a lost sheep. His facial expression said, 'I wish I was some-place else.' That made her smile; it described exactly how she felt about being there herself. Whatever empathy she had for him evaporated quite quickly when he joined the group of loud-mouthed, middle-aged morons. Whatever he looked like, he was obviously an arsehole like the rest of them.

Nina was feeling elated; things were turning out better than she had hoped. Brad was the perfect gentleman. As soon as his asthma had subsided, he apologised several times for leaving his designer wallet full of fifties at home.

'Thanks for the drink,' said Brad. 'I'll pay you back because I'm old school.'

Nina wasn't sure what that meant so just said, 'Okay.'

Brad gazed deep into her eyes. 'I'm going for a slash.'

While Brad dashed off, Nina's eyes searched the club for Trixie. They caught sight of her up on the mezzanine floor, waving down at her. She ran up the nearby staircase to see her friend, pausing only to grab her lager-onic from the bar.

Trixie shuffled into the next seat so Nina could slump down beside her.

'Brad wanted my phone number and let me buy him a drink!' she said with a big smile.

'He's a real gentleman,' replied Trixie, with not an ounce of sarcasm, but about a ton's worth.

'I think so to,' agreed Nina. 'He invented this drink.' Nina took a sip and winced. 'Do you want to try it?'

'What is it?' asked Trixie suspiciously. She would not put it past Brad to slip something into Nina's drink.

64

'It's lager and tonic water. Brad calls it a lager-onic.'

'Lager-onic? Isn't that just a tonic shandy?'

'It can't be. Brad said it took him three years to invent it.'

Trixie worried about how gullible Nina could be. 'Where is the Thomas Edison of the drinks world?'

'He's just having a slash, as he calls it,' said Nina, sipping her lager-onic and screwing her face up.

'He invents, and has the vocabulary of Shakespeare as well. What can't he do?' said Trixie, as she checked her watch. 'Nina, I said I would come out with you for two hours. I have an early start tomorrow, so let's go about 10:30.'

'I can't go until they play some slow songs. It will be my chance to get close to Brad.'

'I am not hanging around to watch that tosser grind against you. You begged me for two hours. Now keep your side of the bargain and we'll go home together.'

Nina was too busy looking out for Brad to listen to anything Trixie had to say. 'There he is! He's back.'

Brad was returning from the gents'. With a quick glance to make sure no one was looking, he shook his left leg and felt several drips go down. Composing himself by holding in his ample stomach, Brad pondered on what strategy he should use to get Tina into bed. Seduction? Tell her he loved her? Offer her a free gym membership? Taking a sip from his lager-onic, Brad noticed Nina running keenly toward him and decided he would only have to ask her.

Ford had remembered why he never went to clubs. He hated every minute of being in one and was not a fan of repetitive dance music. The Rat Pack were several drinks ahead of him and becoming louder and more boring with every fresh round. On top of their volume, the Rat Pack laughed hysterically at anything that made them feel superior or involved bullying of any kind. *We are the Champions* by Queen began to play. Blake had earlier slipped the DJ a five-pound note to play it. The Rat Pack considered it their theme song, so they all dashed out onto the dance floor to chant along with the lyrics, leaving Ford alone at the bar and very glad of it. Taking a moment to consider what he had learnt from Blake and his cronies, Ford came up with the answer: absolutely nothing. Deciding to finish his drink and go home, he tipped his head back and swallowed his remaining tequila. With a sour grimace, he put the glass down on the bar, and turned to find himself face-to-face with a young woman. She was twenty-something and had long blonde hair, too blonde to be natural, and a curvaceous body that was squeezed into a green micro-mini-dress. Her face was as pretty as any of the young women in the club, but it was hidden by a mask of make-up that made it a different colour to the rest of her flesh.

'My boyfriend dumped me today,' she said with a slight pout of the lips and a sniff.

Ford wasn't sure what to say to that, so just went with, 'I'm sorry.'

'He was seeing some other bitch,' she spat.

'All I can say is, he must be mad to do that.'

The young woman gave a coy smile. 'It's really sweet of you to say that. Would you like to buy me a drink?'

Whatever ego boost he had received from having a woman approach him, at that moment, it stopped boosting. He was annoyed with himself, feeling he had been played for a sucker, but still said, 'Okay, what would you like?'

'What were you drinking?' enquired the young woman, nodding at his empty glass.

'Oh, it was a shot of tequila.'

'Oh, go on then,' said the young woman, as though Ford had been twisting her arm. 'I'll try two of them.'

Ford took out his wallet. 'I was about to go. Can I just give you the money? he said, offering her a twenty-pound note.

'Don't go,' pleaded the young woman, taking his arm. 'I like you, you're nice.'

The word 'nice' triggered a thought in Ford's brain. What was he doing? An attractive young woman wanted him to stay and keep her company. Why not? She was free and available now her boyfriend had dumped her. Now he was no longer nice, he could take advantage of her. 'Okay, I'll stay for a couple of minutes.'

'What's your name?'

'Ford, like the make of car.'

The young woman giggled and held Ford's arm tightly. 'We have something in common. My name's like a make of perfume. It's Channel Number Five. I was going to be called Opium, but my dad said it sounded too much like a drug dealer's name.'

Ford was not very knowledgeable about perfumes, but Channel sounded wrong. 'Do you mean Chanel?'

'My dad spelled it wrong on my birth certificate, so I'm Channel.'

Ford ordered two shots of tequila and handed them over to her. 'There you go, Channel.'

The two tequilas were downed quickly just as a slow song began to play.

'Come on, I want to dance,' said Channel, grabbing his hand and dragging him over to the dance floor.

The Rat Pack were making their way back to the bar, having failed to find anyone stupid enough to dance with them. Blake noticed Ford with the young woman. He rushed over and said loudly enough for Channel to hear, 'How did you pull a hot woman like her?'

Channel gave Blake her coy smile. Clasping Ford to her with the strength of a boa constrictor, she began to slow-dance.

Ford felt like he was in some sort of death grip, but managed to say, 'This is Channel Number Five, she was let down by her boyfriend.'

'The bastard dumped me,' explained Channel, as she ground her hips against Ford. 'And Ford's been nice to me.'

Blake spoke to Ford as though Channel wasn't there. 'If you need condoms and a blue tab, I've got plenty.'

'I'm only having a dance. Then I'm going home,' protested Ford, as Channel's hands began to explore his body.

Blake shook his head in despair at Ford's attitude. 'Even when you're with the Rat Pack, you're still a loser.' Leaning over to Channel, he said, 'If you want revenge sex because you were dumped, I'm your man.' With a final wink to her, he headed back to the bar to continue doing what he did best, which was being loud and arrogant.

'Sorry about my friend,' stuttered Ford, as Channel gazed at him adoringly, rubbing against his penis. It had been weeks since he'd had sex of any kind, and he was not surprised to feel his man-gun, as he secretly called it, being loaded up with ammunition. A few more rubs and he felt a bullet enter the chamber and the safety catch being slipped off. Gritting his teeth, he gazed at the other couples dancing. He spotted Nina, dancing close by with a sun tanned man who was groping her breasts.

'Hold me closer!' whispered Channel.

'I think you'll find that's physically impossible,' groaned Ford, struggling for breath.

Channel took Ford's left hand and held it against her right breast, announcing that, 'All taxi drivers are bastards!'

This statement caught Ford by surprise. 'I'm sure the odd one might be,' was all he could say.

Channel was now definitely getting friendlier than he felt comfortable with, as her left hand found its way under his shirt. Ford closed his eyes and thought of the types of Ford Escort that were manufactured in the 1970s, a technique he had used to bring himself back from the brink on many occasions. Picturing a two-door 1972 1100L soon put the man-gun back in its holster.

When Ford opened his eyes, a large and angry-looking man, unshaven, with tattoos on his arms and neck, stood stone-like, watching them. His teeth were clenched, and a vein in his temple throbbed to the same beat as the music.

'Channel!' shouted the man-mountain. 'I've been searching for you everywhere!'

Channel pressed Ford's hand against her breast even harder. 'That's Val. Ignore the fat pig.'

Ford's adrenaline began to kick in. 'I don't suppose he's a taxi driver by any chance?'

Through his gritted teeth, Val growled, 'I turned around and you were gone?'

Channel broke from Ford to face him, and with her hands on her hips she said, 'Why don't you just go back to that slut you were all over!'

Ford had nearly collapsed when Channel released him. He felt his ribs to make sure they weren't broken.

Val looked to the heavens. 'I just said "hello". She works in the coffee shop by the taxi rank.'

Ford gently nudged Channel toward Val. 'I think I'll just leave you two to sort out this misunderstanding.'

Before Ford could back out of range, Channel had turned around and pounced on him with her boa constrictor grip.

'Take no notice of Val, he's just a bully and a thug. Even the judge said that.'

Alarm bells began to ring in Ford's head. 'Judge?'

'I love you, Channel!' bellowed Val. 'I love only you. I don't even know her name! I just see her when I buy a coffee, you have to believe me!'

His shouting had started to draw a crowd. Even Nina stopped dancing with Brad to take a look at what was happening. When she saw Ford in the middle of it all, she wasn't surprised. Trouble seemed to follow him wherever he went.

Channel glared at Val with a contempt that pierced his heart. As if that had not hurt him enough, she grabbed Ford's unwilling hand and slapped it back onto her breast. 'My new boyfriend said taxi drivers are lying bastards, and he's right!'

Ford desperately tried to untangle himself from Channel. 'I never said that. And I'm not her boyfriend.'

Val burst into tears and sank to his knees. 'Don't listen to him… I never lied!'

Like a matador sensing victory, Channel Number Five, softened him up for the kill. 'You might not think I'm sexy, but my new boyfriend says I am, and he wants to fuck me in every position there is, plus a few new ones.'

'No!' pleaded Val, as his heart was ripped to pieces.

With a sadistic smile, Channel went for the killing blow. 'And he has a friend that's hung like a donkey, so we can have a three up!'

Ford managed to free himself from one of Channel's vice grip arms. 'I don't have any friends that are hung like donkeys. Okay, maybe one, but I haven't seen him for ages, and there has never been any mention of a three up, whatever that is!'

Trixie had been watching events from upstairs and felt some sympathy for the man she had seen looking lost earlier. The young women had spent ten minutes walking up and down the bar area before closing in on him. She'd suckered him for a couple of drinks and was now using him to get back at her boyfriend, who did appear to be a bit of a brute. It was a surprise to see the thug slump to the floor and dissolve into sobs, which she could hear from up above.

Channel's smile of triumph turned to a frown of annoyance, as Val let out a gut-wrenching scream of loss from the very depths of his heart. 'Val! Stop crying and get up! You're embarrassing me.'

Val held Channel's ankle. 'Don't leave me, I'm begging you.'

The commotion had caused the lights to go up and the music to go down. Joe and Leslie, the wide doormen, hurriedly made their way to the cause of the disturbance.

Channel pulled Val up onto his size-twelve feet. 'Val, stop crying this minute, you're showing me up again.'

Nina and Brad were part of the crowd that now circled the lovers' tiff. When Nina heard Channel call the man Val, she laughed out aloud. 'That's the second time tonight I've come across a man with a girl's name!'

The clubbers nearby giggled, just as Joe and Leslie broke through the crowd.

'What's going on?' demanded Joe with menace.

Ford had been trying to slip away, but the crowd kept getting bigger and denser so there was no escape.

Joe took in the visual evidence: a grown man was crying and being consoled by his girlfriend.

Leslie patted Val sympathetically on the back. 'Who made you cry mate?' he asked kindly.

Val sniffed and pointed to Ford.

'I didn't do anything!' protested Ford.

Joe grabbed him by the scruff of the neck. 'We don't want violent hooligans coming in here, making our customers cry.'

Ford searched the crowd, desperately looking for a way out of this mess. He spotted Nina. 'Nina! Tell them I didn't do anything!'

The doormen and crowd turned toward her. Nina glared at Ford, annoyed that he should pick her out when she was getting on so well with Brad. The recollection of the Baby Jane jibes brought revenge to the forefront of her mind. With a sly smile at Ford, she said, 'He kept saying that the man called Val had a girl's name. And he pushed him.'

'No, no, that's not true… Channel! Tell them I didn't do anything.'

Channel was feeling a little bit guilty for turning Val into a sobbing mess, so she opted to lie. 'He's been trying to get off with me all night, and when I told him Val was my boyfriend, he said he had a girl's name and bullied him!'

Leslie gritted his teeth, his head began to throb with anger, as he recalled the hurt of being told he had the same name as a girl. 'Give me five minutes with him! That's all I ask, five minutes!'

Joe had to use his body as a shield to stop his colleague throttling Ford. 'Leslie, be professional, don't take things personal.'

Leslie wiped a tear from the scar tissue around his eye and sniffed. 'I'm okay. Sorry, it's just that these cruel bullies…'

'Don't worry,' Joe assured him. 'The police will deal with this scumbag.'

'Not the police!' protested Ford, as Joe and Leslie manhandled him out of the club.

'Baby Jane says goodbye!' hollered Nina.

Ford glanced back to see Nina, with a big grin on her face, waving goodbye.

Police Sergeant Jackie Osborne and Police Constable Noel Hudson were waiting at the club door, as Ford was roughly led out. Sergeant Jackie hated the night shift. She missed putting the kids to bed and reading them a story. Instead, she was dealing with the lowlifes that only came out at night. She took one look at Ford and sensed trouble. He seemed normal and was still fairly sober. In her book that made him extremely dangerous. With one hand on her taser, she said, 'What have we got here, boys?'

'A hate-crime bully and a thug,' reported Leslie, wiping his damp eyes with his sleeve.

Joe released Ford from his armlock. 'He mentally tortured a customer by accusing him of having a girl's name.'

Ford laughed. 'This is ridiculous.'

Leslie took a handkerchief from his pocket and blew his broken nose. 'I had the same thing happen to me tonight. It's not fair!'

Sergeant Jackie glared at Ford and shook her head in disgust. 'You utter bastard! I know your type, you go through life bullying others.' Her hand clasped the taser on her belt. She recalled being a child at school, surrounded by kids mocking her because she liked to be called Jack, and it was a boy's name. 'Is this how you get your little kicks, is it? Mental torture?'

Ford laughed again more nervously. 'This is a joke, isn't it?'

Sergeant Jackie grabbed Ford by the collar. 'It's no joke, telling someone that their name belongs to the opposite sex. It's hurtful.'

Leslie sniffed and nodded in agreement.

'I've never, ever said anything like that!' protested Ford. 'One of my best friends at school was called Noel, and I never mentioned once that it was a girl's name.'

Police Constable Noel Hudson felt like he had been hit by a thunderbolt. 'What do you mean by saying Noel's a girl's name?'

Ford felt them all staring at him. 'You know, some girls born in December are called Noel.'

Constable Noel Hudson had a flashback to the register being read out at school every morning, and the giggle his name caused suddenly made sense. 'I've got a girl's name?' he muttered.

'You just can't stop bullying, can you?' fumed Sergeant Jackie.

Ford could not believe the way events were turning against him. He found himself laughing nervously yet again. 'I haven't bullied anyone! This is all some mistake!'

Joe had dealt with troublemakers before, but he thought this little bastard was in a different league. 'Bullies like you would even find something about my name being the same as a girl's.'

Ford was puzzled. 'What is your name?'

Joe turned his cauliflower ear toward Ford. 'It's Joe, I dare you to say that's a girl's name.'

Ford was confused. 'It might be short for Josephine or Joanne.'

The scar tissue on Joe's face quivered. 'I've got a girl's name as well?!'

Sergeant Jackie reached for her radio; this evil bastard was going to get the mattress treatment back at the station. 'This is Sergeant Jackie Osborne, I need a police van at the Orifice, right away. Over.'

The radio crackled. 'Vivian and Robin will be with you shortly. Over.'

'They are both male police officers,' said Sergeant Jackie quickly.

Police Constable Noel Hudson had a confused expression on his face. 'They have girls' names as well as me?'

Leslie opened his muscular arms wide. 'I think we need a group hug,' he said with a sob in his quavering voice.

While the doormen and the police officers consoled each other with a supportive hug, Ford turned and did the most manly thing he could think of: he ran away as fast as his legs would go.

Back inside the club, Trixie checked her watch and decided she was going home with or without Nina. The evening had been a bit more entertaining than she expected, thanks to the incident. She found Nina on the dance floor with Brad getting up close and personal. 'Nina, I'm going now. Are you coming?'

'I'm staying a bit longer,' giggled Nina. 'Brad's going to give me a lift.'

Brad gave Trixie a wink and one of his smiles that showed off his dental work, wishing he could give her a lift instead.

Trixie disapproved of Nina's choice, but she had known her friend long enough to know that nothing on earth would change her stubborn mind.

'Make sure you call me later, I mean it!'

'Okay,' agreed Nina, reluctantly. 'I'll call you later.'

Without a backward glance, Trixie strode out of the club, still unable to fathom what Nina saw in that arsehole Brad.

CHAPTER SIX

Nina had the odd ability (or fault, as Trixie saw it) to determinedly put a blinkered optimistic gloss on events, if it suited her fleeting fantasy. The gloss she was applying to Brad was shining so brightly, it would have hurt anyone else's eyes. As far as Nina was concerned, he was turning out to be as perfect as she had hoped. He was good-looking, wealthy and so modest that he only mentioned being the rich owner of a gym half a dozen times. To confirm her belief that Brad was a real catch, he had offered to give her a lift to make sure she got home safely.

The truth behind Brad's chivalrous offer was very different from Nina's glossed perception. He played a numbers game. The more women he hit on, the more chance he had of getting one to sleep with him. Despite his tactics, he was in a three-month barren spell, mainly brought on by word getting around among local women that he was a big-headed, lying twat.

Nina was the third woman he had offered a lift to that evening and obviously the only one to take up his offer. She wasn't really his type; he had a list of specifications, and Nina didn't tick even one. The list actually only had two specifications: One, they should be ten years younger than him; and two, have the body of a lingerie model. Perhaps surprisingly, Brad had never managed to pull a woman with those specifications, but the list was always his starting point. Brad told everyone he was thirty years old, six years younger than he really was. He had worked out that even using his real age, Nina was way over the specification. Still, he needed to end his barren spell, reflecting that a notch is a notch, even if it's an old notch.

Outside in the car park, Brad proudly stood beside his Porsche 911, and waited for Nina to compliment him. Nina did not really know one car from another. She recognised Minis, but that was about it, so she just waited for him to unlock the car.

Brad gave a smug smile and rubbed at a non-existent smudge with his finger. 'How do you like my expensive *Porcha*?'

'Oh, it's nice. I like the colour.'

Brad was a tiny bit underwhelmed by Nina's response, but was confident that he would impress her enough to get her clothes off when she heard the sound of the exhaust. He had had it illegally altered so it sounded like a Formula One racing car. 'Yes, this baby is a classic *Porcha* nine eleven.'

Nina looked very unimpressed. 'I don't think it's nice to name a car after a horrible event.'

'No, this has nothing to do with that nine eleven! It's just called a nine eleven.'

'They should change it to nine twelve or something.'

Brad opened the passenger door for Nina to get in. 'Forget the nine eleven, all you need to know is that it was expensive and it's a *Porcha*.'

Brad's attempts to impress Nina with the engine noise and his driving skills failed miserably. Nina screwed her eyes shut and hugged the seat belt every time he over-revved the engine. It took a while for Brad to drive to Nina's apartment because she screamed in fear every time he went over thirty miles an hour. After pulling up, he said, 'You can open your eyes now, we're here.'

Nina slowly opened one eye and was relieved to see she was home.

'I am coming in for a coffee, right?' asked Brad.

Nina unfastened her seat belt. 'Oh, yes, that's the least I can do for the lift home.'

By the time Nina had managed to clamber out of the car, Brad had grabbed out an overnight bag from the back seat. 'It's best not to leave a bag in a car, it might get stolen,' he explained.

Trixie had just climbed into bed when she heard her phone beep. Guessing it was a text from Nina, she checked the message, and shook her head with disappointment.

Brad was in Nina's apartment, having a cup of coffee, and she had signed off with, *Wish me luck!* Trixie felt like texting her back, advising her not to sleep with him, but thought better of it. It was Nina's life, she was old enough to make her own decisions, but she had some sort of gene missing when it came to men.

Nina nervously fussed about in the kitchen while Brad looked quizzically at the movie posters on the wall. He had never heard of half of them. Brad only ever watched Nicolas Cage movies, so he was pleased to see a poster for *The Wicker Man*.

'*The Wicker Man* is one of my favourite movies!' said Brad with pride. 'I must have seen it a hundred times.'

'You've got good taste,' came the reply from the kitchen. 'Did you ever see the remake? I couldn't watch it all, it was so dreadful. How do you like your coffee?

Brad was sure she must be talking about another movie. 'I only drink decaf. My body is finely tuned because of all the exercise I do in the gym. That's gym that I own.'

Nina searched a kitchen cupboard. 'I don't think I have any decaf,' she said, as she stretched up to move some tins of soup out of the way.

Brad wandered into the kitchen area and stood behind her. He placed his hands on her hips, put his mouth inches from her left ear, and said 'Forget the coffee, Tina…'

'Nina, it's Nina!'

'That's what I meant,' whispered Brad.

Nina turned around to face him.

Brad caressed her hair. 'I don't want coffee. I just want to kiss you gently on the lips.'

Nina wished she had brushed her teeth, but went with the moment.

Brad leant in, opening his mouth wide. His idea of a gentle kiss on the lips involved shoving his flickering tongue right into her mouth. Nina could hardly get her breath. Then Brad began squeezing her breasts as if he was checking the ripeness of melons. He broke off the kiss and attempted to pick her up in his arms. He immediately realised she was a lot heavier than he could manage, so he opted to lead her over to the sofa in the sitting room. Once more, he caressed her hair before shoving his tongue in her mouth and checking to see if her melons had ripened during the journey to the sofa.

'God, I want you so bad, Tina,' croaked Brad, as he did another ripeness check.

'It's Nina!' she managed to say, before Brad shoved his tongue in her mouth again. If Nina thought events were going too fast, Brad now put his foot on the accelerator, and took all his clothes off. 'Oh!' was the only word Nina could think to say, as Brad posed in front of her with his hands on his hips.

He was pleased with her reaction. He was proud of his penis extension and his body. The liposuction to remove ten pounds of fat had cost a fortune in plastic surgery, but it was worth every penny. He could have worked out every day on the gym equipment, which he owned, but long ago, he had decided to fuck that for a game of soldiers, and opted for the knife.

Nina was caught like a rabbit in a car's headlight, as she stared at Brad's clean-shaven, semi-erect penis.

'You can touch it if you want, Tina,' coaxed Brad in a husky voice, giving his hips a shake.

'It's Nina!' She nervously pointed at his circumcised penis. 'Where's his little jumper?'

Brad allowed himself a smirk. 'Where he's going, he won't need a jumper.' Brad gave his penis a slap. 'That's all muscle. Go on, give it a slap. I dare you!'

Nina was curious and nervous at the same time, and gave it a tiny slap.

'Hit it harder than that, go on!' urged Brad.

Nina took another swing, which was a bit firmer.

Brad groaned with pleasure, 'Oh, yes, baby! Keep whacking it.'

Nina had never thought of slapping a man's penis. She had never seen it done in a movie or heard anyone mention it before. With Brad's encouragement, she slapped his several times.

'That feels so good,' panted Brad.

'Are you sure it's not hurting? Because my fingers are stinging!'

'It's all muscle,' he boasted. 'It just makes it harder. If your fingers are hurting, use that to give it a whack.' Brad pointed to a pillow beside her.

'That's a Laura Ashley cushion!' said Nina, as an explanation.

Brad wiggled his hips, making his penis dance about in front of her. 'Go on, Tina, give it a big whack with that.'

Nina was fed up of being called Tina, so she picked up the cushion and violently swung it at Brad's penis several times, punctuating her blows by saying, 'My... name... is... Nina!'

Brad screamed in pain. 'Stop, stop, stop!' He clutched his penis. 'The cushion's got a fucking big zip on it!'

Nina stopped mid-swing. She saw blood on his hands. 'It's bleeding!' she screamed. 'Don't get blood on my carpet!'

'Blood?' exclaimed Brad, a worried expression on his face. 'I can't stand the sight of blood.' Brad moved his claret-covered hands, to see a one-inch gash on his penis that was dripping blood like a very leaky tap. His eyes rolled back in his head, and he slumped to the floor, out cold.

Trixie had just started to drift off to sleep when her phone rang. Pulling the duvet over her head did not block out the persistent ringing. Checking the screen, Trixie saw it was Nina and picked up. 'Nina, are you okay?'

'Trixie, come quick!' sobbed Nina. 'There's blood everywhere and Brad's out cold.'

Trixie hurried out of bed. 'What's happened? Tell me!'

'I was hitting his winkle with a Laura Ashley cushion, and the zip cut it. He saw the blood and fainted.'

Trixie had to cover her mouth to cut off her laughter. After taking several seconds to compose herself, she said, 'I'll be with you in five minutes.' As she hurried to get dressed, Trixie muttered, 'It better not be one of the cushions I bought her for her birthday.'

Nina was waiting at the door when Trixie arrived six minutes later. Inside the apartment, Brad was now clutching a towel to his groin and trying to sit up, but was still looking very pale. Trixie checked the cut on his penis and found it was still bleeding badly. Brad took one gormless look at the blood on his hands and fainted again.

Trixie went over to Nina's house phone. 'I think it's best to call an ambulance.'

'Tell them he fell over!' begged Nina. 'Don't mention the cushion.'

'Don't worry, they're professional people, there is nothing that they haven't seen before.'

It took twenty minutes for two female paramedics to arrive. Vera and Sue had both been as slim as catwalk models when they started their paramedic career. After several years in a job where they work shifts and lived mainly on fast food from lay-by burger vans, they now resembled plus-size models. With fifteen years' experience between them, this was just another day at the office, saving lives. They quickly spotted the casualty slouched on the floor and asked for a cup of tea and a biscuit.

Trixie went to the kitchen to make the tea while Nina nervously looked on.

Vera was the senior paramedic. After examining the wound, she began to giggle.

Sue managed to keep a straight face while she checked Brad's pulse. 'Sir… sir, how do you feel? Can you tell me what happened?'

Brad was still groggy, but managed to mutter, 'She… she just kept swinging it!'

'Swinging what, sir?' Sue quizzed him…'

'He fell over,' lied Nina. 'I don't know how he did it.'

Vera was still giggling as she applied an absorbent pad to the wound.

'It had a fucking big zip,' mumbled Brad.

Sue checked his eyes for signs of concussion. 'What had a fucking big zip, sir?'

Brad peered down just as Vera checked to see if the bleeding had stopped. He felt his head begin to swim. 'Laura… Laura Ashley had a fucking big zip,' he whispered.

'He's talking nonsense. I think he might have concussion,' suggested Vera. 'He must have hit his head when he fell. We need to get him to hospital urgently. Every second counts.'

Trixie came in with two teas on a tray and a plate of biscuits to go with them.

Vera spotted some chocolate digestives on the plate. 'When I say urgently, I mean as soon as we've had our cup of tea and a biscuit.'

Vera and Sue left Brad slumped where he was. Over a cup of tea and a few chocolate biscuits, they explained to Trixie and Nina the best way to get bloodstains out of a carpet.

Ava was surprised, even shocked to see Nina already at work at ten to nine the next morning. 'What's up with you? I don't normally see you until about ten o'clock.'

'I'm fine, everything's fine, things couldn't be more fine,' insisted Nina.

'Are you sure you're fine?'

'Yes! I'm fine.'

Ava took off her 1940s coat and hung it up behind the counter. 'What was that ambulance doing here last night?'

'Who told you about that?'

'One of the neighbours. They said a man was carried out of your apartment.'

'Okay,' conceded Nina. 'If I tell you, you must swear never to tell a soul.'

Ava gave a three-fingered salute, 'Brownie's honour!'

'I met Brad at the Orifice last night.'

'I told you he goes there all the time. Go on!'

'Well, Brad was very interested in me…'

'Why wouldn't he be?'

Nina coughed a couple of times. Ava took a plastic drinks bottle out of her handbag and handed it to Nina. She took a sip. 'Thanks. Anyway, Brad would not leave me alone all night and insisted he give me a lift home…'

'He came in for coffee!' guessed Ava.

'That's right. He came in for coffee, and one thing led to another and…'

'You fucked him!'

Nina glanced at Ava with saintly surprise. 'No, I did not fuck him, as you so bluntly put it.'

Ava was losing patience. 'What happened then?'

'One thing led to another and he suddenly took all his clothes off.'

'Then you fucked him?' ventured Ava.

'No! He took his clothes off and wanted me to slap his winkle.'

'He wanted you to slap his willy?' Ava was puzzled. 'Did you?'

Nina coughed, and took another sip from Ava's water bottle. 'He seemed keen for me to do it, so I obliged.'

Ava began to chuckle. 'You obliged.'

'Yes, I obliged, but when I said my fingers were hurting…' Nina had to stop talking because Ava was laughing too much.

'Go on!' giggled Ava.

Nina continued, 'He said, "If your fingers hurt, use the cushion on the sofa" so, I…'

Ava screamed with laughter.

Nina could not help but smile at Ava's reaction. 'So, I hit his todger with the cushion and the zip cut him to pieces, he then fainted when he saw the blood. Hence the ambulance.'

Ava was still curled up and holding her sides, when she howled. 'I've wet myself!'

Twenty minutes later, Ava was wearing clothes she had borrowed from Nina, and involuntarily giggling at random intervals. 'Are you seeing Brad again?' she managed to say with just a tiny chuckle.

Nina shook her head. 'I doubt he'll ever want to see me again after that little episode.'

Ava regained her composure and declared, 'If he had any sense, he would realise what a catch you are.'

Nina coughed a couple of times, so Ava handed her water bottle over. On Nina's second sip, her phone beeped to indicate a text message. Nina checked the screen and nearly choked. 'It's a message from Brad!'

Ava smiled. 'There you are! He realised what a catch you are. He must have some sense.'

Nina allowed herself a vain smile before reading the text. 'No, no, no…'

'What is it?' demanded Ava.

Nina was, for the first time in many years, speechless. In a daze, she handed the phone over to Ava to read.

Tina, you better get checked out, the doctor just told me I have a STD in my dick. Kind regards Brad.

Ava turned to see Nina in a state of shock. 'Don't worry, you never fucked him.'

Nina pointed to her mouth. 'He shoved his tongue in!' With the memory of last night still etched on her brain, she held up her hand as if it was an alien object. 'I touched it … I TOUCHED IT!'

Ava's eyes drifted over to the water bottle Nina had just drunk from. She promptly picked it up by using two fingers, as if it would explode at any moment, and threw it in the waste bin.

Ford received a frosty reception from Blake when he arrived at work. Before he had time to open his mouth to say good morning, Blake said bluntly, 'You are not welcome to be a member of the Rat Pack, and that means for life.'

Ford was quite pleased about that, but opted to appear disappointed. 'Oh! Not for life.'

'You nearly got the Rat Pack banned from the Orifice,' grumbled Blake. 'I had to tell the doorman that you had a screw loose, and we just let you tag along with us because we felt sorry for you.'

'I can't say I'm not disappointed,' lied Ford. 'I really thought the Rat Pack's greatness was rubbing off on me.'

'Fat chance of that happening,' declared Blake. 'Though I must admit, for someone who's too nice, you pissed off a lot of people last night, so there is a glimmer of hope for you yet.'

Ford took that as a sort of compliment. Maybe the hypnotherapy was working, because he had never had any incidents like this before his visit to Cedric.

'Despite the fact that you are not Rat Pack material, I'll let you watch me today. You might learn something.'

Ford was sure that Blake must be doing something right to sell so many more cars than he did, so he thought this was a good opportunity to see where he had been going wrong.

About an hour later, Blake called out, 'Wilkinson, I see a sale! Watch and learn, watch and learn.'

Ford glanced out of the showroom window. He saw a little old lady with a shopping bag, looking at a small Fiat.

'Stick with me,' commanded Blake, as he rushed to the door. 'Just agree with everything I say.'

By the time Ford had caught up with him outside, Blake had already started his charm offensive. 'Let me guess, madam, don't tell me, the children are getting a bit bigger and you need a car with a bit more room for their school gear. Am I right or am I right?'

The little old lady smiled sweetly. 'Oh, no! My children are all grown-up, so are my grandchildren.'

Blake's jaw dropped in pretend shock. 'Never! Hold on… what is your name?'

'Mildred.'

'Blake gazed all around the car lot. 'Mildred, is this one of those TV prank shows? Because there is no way you have grown-up children. Sorry, I'm not falling for it. Where are the cameras hiding?'

'No, really,' explained Mildred. 'I'm quite old, but I do use a very good face cream.'

Blake still had his mouth wide open in mock disbelief. 'I don't like to swear in front of a young lady, but are you shitting me? You have grown-up children?'

'Three grown-up children over fifty,' confirmed Mildred proudly.

'Ford, be honest,' said Blake. 'how old do you think Mildred is?'

'Eighty-seven?' guessed Ford. He realised his mistake straight away and backtracked. 'I'd say she was born in '87.'

'See?!' exclaimed Blake. 'It's not just me.'

Mildred touched her grey permed hair. 'I've always tried to make myself look nice, even since my poor husband died.'

Blake scrunched his eyes up and very briefly sobbed. 'That's going to upset me all day, knowing that.'

'I'm sorry,' said Mildred, patting him on the back. 'I can see you are a sensitive soul.'

Blake took out a tissue and blew his nose before wiping his eyes. 'Mildred, I don't normally do this, but by hook or by crook, I will get the perfect car for you at cost price.'

'I'm only looking really. My granddaughter said I should buy a little car just to get to the shops. My legs aren't as good as they…'

'Don't waste another breath, Mildred; I have the perfect car for you. Follow me.' Blake didn't risk letting her follow in case she turned and tried to get away, so he led her by the elbow toward a Range Rover that dwarfed the old woman. 'This is the perfect run around for you.'

Mildred had to strain her neck to peer up at it. 'It's very big!'

Blake shook his head. 'No, it's the styling of the bodywork, it's an optical illusion. Isn't that right, Ford?'

Ford was feeling uncomfortable, telling a little old lady of five foot two that the huge Range Rover casting a shadow over her was actually quite small. He hardened himself to the task. 'When you're up close, it looks big, but if you stand back a bit, it's small. As my colleague said, it might be an optical illusion.'

Blake opened the driver's door. 'Carjackers and muggers hate this car because it's so secure. Wait till you see the interior, it's so cosy. Have a sit behind the wheel and see how small it is.'

'It seems quite a big step up,' objected Mildred, with a concerned frown.

'We're not standing on a kerb, that's why,' explained Blake. 'When you're on a pavement, it's like stepping down into it. Here, I'll give you a hand.' Blake spun Mildred to face the driver's seat and lifted her up by the legs, tipping her in head first. Blake turned to Ford, as he strained to push her up. 'Nip round to the passenger seat and drag her in. She's a bit porkier than she looks!'

Ford rushed round and pulled Mildred into the car.

'I only need a small car to go to the shops once a week,' sputtered Mildred.

'With a car like this,' said Blake, patting the bodywork, 'you can go to the shops without getting robbed and having to be a witness in an identity parade every time you need some tea bags. I'll go and get the key fob so we can start her up.'

Mildred was breathing hard. 'I don't care how small it is,' she gasped, 'it still seems very big to me. Oh, I feel all funny…'

'Are you okay, Mildred?' said Ford with concern.

'I feel a bit… a bit faint…' she managed before slumping over the steering wheel.

'Blake! She's passed out!'

Blake thumped the car roof with his fist. 'Not another one. I had three do this on me last year!' Blake had a light bulb moment. 'Try to bring her round and I'll get her to sign a sales agreement while she's still groggy.'

'You can't do that!' protested Ford. 'It's unethical?'

'If you want to keep your job, saint Ford, shut your mouth and wake her up.' With a skip in his step, Blake ran over to the showroom office.

Mildred slowly opened her eyes.

Ford smiled with relief. 'Are you okay, Mildred. You had me worried. Do you want me to call you an ambulance?'

Mildred shook her head and gave Ford a smile. 'I'll be fine. I don't think this is the car for me.'

'I agree. I'll just tell him that your son has power of attorney over your finances. If you want a little runaround. Go to the Fiat garage, you should be able to get a good lease deal.'

Blake appeared with a piece of paper and placed a pen in Mildred's hand. 'Back away from the light, Mildred,' Blake instructed her. 'Sign the paper, then run as quick as you can toward it!'

Whenever Ford thought Blake had hit a new low, he always managed to find a lower level. 'Her son has power of attorney,' said Ford.

Blake snatched his pen back. 'Bollocks! What is up with the world?'

Mildred took hold of the steering wheel. 'It doesn't seem so big now,' she said with a smile.

'Get out,' said Blake curtly. 'You are what we call in the trade a fucking time-waster!' And with that, Blake stormed off, leaving Ford to help Mildred down from the driver's seat.

After a sale-free day, Ford was relieved to be home. He had just hung up his jacket when he heard noises coming from the kitchen. 'Kate! Is that you?' he said hopefully.

The slight hope he had of Kate coming back to him was soon dashed, as Jason's voice called out, 'Hi, honey. Did you have a good day?'

Ford plodded over to the kitchen area, his expressionless face a complete contrast to Jason's.

'I've got you a microwave curry!' Jason said with a beaming smile.

'How did you get in?' asked Ford, with a quick glance of the door to check Jason had not forced it. 'I thought you gave me your key.'

'I had two keys cut. Being the good friend that I am, I knew you'd really want me to have a key.'

'I don't!' argued Ford. 'Why do you think I want you to have a key?'

'Friendship,' said Jason humbly. 'Friendship.'

'You abuse friendships. You take, but you never give.'

'I know what you're saying,' agreed Jason, holding up a latchkey. 'That's why I've got you a key for my place. We'll be key brothers, a bit like blood brothers, but without the risk of infection and dying.'

'You live with your mum. Why would I want a key to your mum's house?'

'It's a gesture, a gesture from one key brother to another.'

'Well, you can shove your gesture up your arse and give me that spare key.'

Jason gave Ford a long, hard stare. 'What's got into you? Why are you being so mean?'

'I'm no longer a sucker nice guy! I did something about it; I went to see that hypnotherapist my mum used to help her stop smoking.'

'Your mum still smokes the odd cigar and vapes.'

'Well, it worked and now he's made me not nice, and that's working as well.' Ford gazed out of the window. 'Who knows, if I'd seen him earlier, I might still be with Kate.'

'It would have made no difference.' Jason went over to the sink and filled the kettle. 'I'll make you a cup of tea. I say this as a friend, Kate was a scatty, loony bitch.'

'Don't talk about the woman I loved like that. I still miss her!'

'You never really loved her. She never really loved you. She was too much up her own arse with her shit paintings to love anyone, but herself.' Jason took two mugs out of a wall cupboard.

'What I think you'll find, you philistine, is that she was just being artistic.'

'Just being mental more like. Who dumps someone because they are the wrong shapes?'

Ford had a thought. 'I wonder if Cedric could stop me being the wrong shapes with hypnotherapy? I might give him a call tomorrow.'

Jason found the tea bags in a cupboard and placed one in each mug. 'You might be shit at your job and unable to maintain long-term relationships, but nobody accuses my best friend of being the wrong shapes.'

'I can't work out if that's a compliment or not.'

When the kettle had boiled, Jason filled the mugs. 'Now I'm living with you for a while, I can have a cup of tea waiting for you when you get home.'

Ford took a couple of seconds to digest this new information. 'You're not living with me. No way!'

'It's only temporary because I'm worried about you,' explained Jason. 'I can't sit back and watch my friend's life be ripped apart after he loses his job and realises that no woman would touch him with a bargepole.'

'I can sell cars! I'm going to keep my job, so you don't need to stay.' Ford pointed at the mugs. 'Put the milk in before any scummy bits appear…'

Jason shook his head with pity. 'You deny it. I don't mind, because when it all goes to shit, I will be here to pick up the pieces. That's what key brothers do.'

'No! I live alone. Never!'

Jason held up his hand to stop Ford. 'I know this is your manly way of saying thank you,' he said with a breaking voice, 'so your thanks are accepted.' He reached for some kitchen towel to blow his nose.

Ford felt like he was losing this battle, but came out with a defiant 'No!' as a last resort.

Jason took the teabags out of the mugs and handed one of the teas to Ford. 'Ushers should stick together and help each other out! It's in the wedding vows or something.'

Ford took a sip of tea and shook his head. 'Okay, you can stay, but only to the end of the month. As soon as you see I've kept my job, you are out of here. What do ushers do anyway?'

'I'm not a hundred percent sure,' confessed Jason. 'I think it's making sure people stay quiet during the ceremony.'

'You're not getting usher and husher mixed up, are you? I thought you'd done research.'

'My God, it's like living with a Nazi interrogator. You weren't kidding when you said you weren't nice any more. I'll find out, don't worry!'

Ford was feeling quite pleased with himself. Even Jason had noticed he was no longer nice.

'Oh, by the way,' added Jason, 'Jenny X is popping round later so if you hear anything odd from my room, just ignore it.'

'What the…'

'Don't worry!' interrupted Jason. 'I've already turned the mattress.' With a friendly pat on Ford's shoulder, he continued, 'I'm lucky to have such a nice friend.'

Ford glanced up to the heavens and shook his head. 'Suckered again.'

Trixie took several steps into the sexual health clinic before turning back and dragging Nina in behind her. Trixie looked fabulous, as she always did, in just jeans and a plain top. In contrast, Nina was wearing a grey cotton leisure suit with sunglasses that even Elizabeth Taylor would have thought too big. She had topped off her inconspicuous look with a black baseball cap.

The young female receptionist told Trixie to take a seat in the adjacent waiting area where several women of various ages were reading the ancient magazines or just checking their phones. Nina was determined not to be recognised so she kept her head down, avoiding any hint of eye contact. Her tactic worked so well that she did not even notice when Trixie sat down in the waiting area. The receptionist called to her, 'Miss, miss! Would you please take a seat?'

Nina glanced up, Trixie was patting the seat next to her in the waiting area, a big smile on her face. Nina tiptoed over and sat down. 'People saw me!'

'So what?' laughed Trixie. 'It's a sexual health clinic. People come here for lots of reasons.'

Nina slowly ran her eyes over other women. 'They don't look like sluts.'

Trixie giggled. 'Where the hell do you get these ideas from?'

'How long do you think it takes?' asked Nina, pulling her hat down and slouching into the chair.

'Seeing as you won't have anything, it won't take long. Stop worrying. Why don't you read your library book?'

Nina took a paperback book out of her handbag. It had a photograph of a young Katharine Hepburn on the cover. Five minutes later, her feet began to nervously tap. 'Oh, God, what if I'm riddled with venereal diseases!'

'Will you calm down?' snapped Trixie, 'I'm annoyed as it is, having to take time off work to hold your hand at a pointless check-up.'

A slim, glamorous nurse in her mid-fifties appeared from a corridor behind the reception desk. 'Hepburn!' she said coldly.

Trixie gave Nina a nudge. 'That's you, Katharine!'

Nina had refused to give her real name in case the hospital computer was ever hacked by Russians, leaving her vulnerable to blackmail. 'Are you coming in with me?'

Trixie shook her head in disbelief. 'You're a big girl, you'll be fine. You don't get infections from slapping cocks. Go on, I'll wait here.'

Nina clasped her book to her chest and moved toward the glamorous nurse.

'Katharine Hepburn?' asked the nurse sceptically.

'Yes, that's me.'

The nurse used her biro to point at Nina's book. 'Your namesake's book, is it any good?'

'I haven't read it yet,' said Nina. 'I've been… busy.'

With no change of expression, the glamorous nurse, barked, 'Follow me!'

Nina accompanied her. 'I'm a bit scared,' she confessed nervously. 'I'm unclean! I slapped a man's knob!'

'Everything is going to be fine,' the nurse assured her with a practised smile.

Nina gave a relieved sigh and smiled back.

The glamorous nurse put a reassuring arm around Nina's shoulder. Under her breath, she muttered. 'You dirty little slut!'

Later that evening Nina was curled up at home on her armchair with a reluctant Petal in her arms. Trixie strolled in from the kitchen with two coffees.

'Here you go, one fat latte!'

Nina took the coffee from her, which allowed Petal to make a run for it. 'Thanks, Trixie. And thanks for coming with me today.'

'No problem. I told you it was a waste of time.'

'I still think I should have a sign around my neck saying, *Unclean*. Ever since I touched his winkle, I keep washing my hands like I'm Lady Macbeth.'

'I don't think I can use the gym again after seeing that gash,' admitted Trixie, with a shiver.

Nina had the urge to wash her hands again. 'I don't think I want sex anymore, I've been put right off men.'

'I'm sure you'll get over it,' smiled Trixie.

Nina gazed at her friend, envious of her self-possession. 'How come you don't have a steady boyfriend by now? You're beautiful, funny and could have any man you wanted.'

Trixie shrugged. 'I don't meet the right men. I only meet twats. I've told you that before.'

Trixie had been out with a number of men and even though she had liked them, she never felt as though she had loved any of them. She had confided in her grandmother on one of her visits to Trinidad. Her grandmother had held her tightly and lovingly laughed. 'You'll know when you feel the destiny-chemistry!' Trixie had asked, 'What is destiny-chemistry?' Her grandmother had pointed to her lips and smiled. 'When you kiss the right one, you will know what it is.'

'They're not all twats,' said Nina seriously. 'I met Edward because he started talking to you at that birthday party.'

Trixie peered at Nina, raising her eyebrows.

'Edward is not a twat!'

Trixie sipped her coffee and picked up a movie magazine from the coffee table. 'I still don't get why you have a thing for him.'

'Ava said that I was too fussy when it came to men, but I think you're fussier than me.'

'Believe me, I'm not as fussy as you.'

Nina gave a wry smile and said, 'I think I might try and be celibate like you.'

Without looking up from the magazine, Trixie calmly said, 'You dirty, cock-slapping slut.'

Nina had just sipped her coffee and spurted it across the room as she burst out laughing. Trixie could no longer keep a straight face, holding her sides, doubled up with the giggles.

CHAPTER SEVEN

Ford was slumped in an armchair in front of his TV, feeling tired and miserable. The late news anchorman seemed to take delight in showing the latest atrocity that yet again proved the human race to be savage, selfish and misguided. 'I can't watch this,' Ford said to himself. 'My own life is depressing enough without being bombarded with bad news.' He was just about to switch the TV off when he heard a key in the latch and a whispering voice. He had forgotten all about Jason and felt his heart sink.

'Oh!' said Jason, as he crept in. 'I thought you might be in bed by now.'

The woman Ford remembered as Jenny X strolled in holding a carpet bag, and sat down on the sofa. 'He's still here then,' she said with a scowl toward Ford.

'Let's just go to my room,' pleaded Jason.

Ford had to look away from Jenny X, whose dress had risen up to reveal the nightmare combination of cellulite and fishnet stockings. 'What does she mean, "still here"?'

'Nothing!' answered Jason. 'Come on, Jenny X, let's go to my room.'

Jenny X glared at Ford as if he were the scum of the earth. 'Free loader!' she said bluntly.

Ford was confused. 'Excuse me?'

Jason attempted to pull Jenny X off the sofa. 'Come on, we'll talk about it in the morning.'

'You are a saint,' she said to Jason. 'There is no way I would let a so-called friend stay rent-free and give him the best bedroom.'

'What is she talking about?' asked Ford.

Jason managed to move Jenny X's bulk off the sofa, and with one more scowl, she headed for the bedroom Jason now occupied.

'What was that all about?' demanded Ford.

'I had to lie to her,' confessed Jason in hushed tones. 'She will only have sex with homeowners after she found out one bloke she went with was living rough in an alley behind 'KFC'. She has ethics.'

'What?! Does she need to see a rent book or mortgage agreement before shagging a complete stranger?!'

'Please!' begged Jason. 'Just go with it for now. This will be the last time I can have sex with her. She only does it twice with strangers. I won't be a stranger anymore.'

'Don't tell me,' said Ford. 'She has ethics.'

Jenny X appeared with a pair of handcuffs in one hand and a ball gag in the other. 'Are we bonking or what?' she said impatiently.

Ford glanced at Jason with raised eyebrows. 'Ethical and ladylike with it.'

'I owe you one,' beamed Jason, as he hurried after Jenny X.

Ford slumped further into his armchair, covered his eyes with his hands, and wondered what he had done to deserve this life of constant nightmares. As he finally made his way to his room, he heard his mother's headboard banging against the wall.

'He had bloody better have turned that mattress,' he thought to himself.

Ford had a broken night's sleep because of Jason and Jenny X's noisy session. He left the apartment early to avoid the embarrassment of being in the same room as them after the things he had heard. A brief recollection of buzzing sounds and Jenny X screaming, 'Shove one in each hole!' sent a shiver down his spine.

Without having breakfast or anything to drink that morning, Ford's normal cycle ride was proving to be hard work. It seemed to take twice as long to put on his cycle helmet, his high-vis jacket and his bicycle clips. As he approached his local Friedfoods R Us takeaway, he noticed a queue of people at the counter. He spotted the drive-thru sign and had a brain wave. He cycled off in the lane behind two builders' vans and waited his turn at the menu board and ordering station.

'Can I take your order?' squawked a female voice from the metal box.

Ford felt under pressure to make a quick decision.

'Can I take your order?' repeated the voice.

Ford did not eat at the Friedfoods R Us, very often so he actually had to read the huge menu.

A rusty red van pulled up behind him and revved its engine as if to say, "Get a move on."

'Can I take your order?' repeated the voice again.

'I'll have a... err... a greasy bacon roll... with a mug full of builder's tea.'

'If you have the breakfast deal, you can have a slice of black pudding and a fried egg for an extra fifty pence!'

'I don't like black pudding; I'll just have the greasy bacon roll and the mug full of builder's tea. Thank you.'

'If you don't like black pudding, we can replace it with a pork sausage?'

'No, I'll stick with the... I forgot what I wanted... Hold on, I'll stick with the greasy bacon roll and the mug full of builder's tea.'

The rusty red van behind him hooted. A bobble-hatted builder, poked his head out of its side window. 'Get a move on, mate; I've got to get to a job by nine!'

'It's not my fault!' protested Ford. 'I keep getting options!'

'Sorry, sir, did you just say you wanted onions?'

'No! Just a greasy bacon roll and a mug full of builder's tea. Please!'

'Drive to the next window.'

Ford duly cycled the twenty feet to the next window, where a bored teenage girl, with make-up covered spots, and dressed in a Friedfoods R Us uniform, was speaking on her headset.

'One all-day breakfast pizza with extra bacon and a cappuccino. Please drive to the next window.'

The bored teenager peered at Ford on his bike and said, 'Oh!'

Ford took his wallet out of the back pocket of his trousers, pulled out a ten-pound note and waited for the amount he had to pay.

The rusty red van pulled up behind him.

Ford offered up his ten-pound note. 'How much do I owe you?'

'You're not in a vehicle?'

'Well, no, but I am using transport.' Ford noticed her name badge. 'How much do I owe, Jackie?'

'I'm Partner Jackie,' the teenage girl informed him. 'The employees of Friedfoods R Us are partners.'

The builder had his bobble-hatted head out of his side window. 'For God's sake, get a move on, I've got to…'

'Get to a job by nine! I know!' fumed Ford. 'I heard you the first time, but it's not me holding things up!'

The builder shook his head, the bobble on his hat jiggling furiously, and checked his watch.

'Please, Partner Jackie,' continued Ford, 'how much do I owe for my greasy bacon roll and my mug full of builder's tea?'

Partner Jackie tapped a keyboard beside her. 'Partner manager to Partner Jackie's window please.'

'Is that necessary?' pleaded Ford.

The rusty red van driver beeped his horn.

Ford turned around. 'It's not me! It's them!'

A young woman dressed in the same uniform as Partner Jackie, but with a tie on, appeared at the window.'

'He's not in a vehicle, partner manager,' Partner Jackie informed her.

The partner manager poked her head out of the window, and peered up and down the lane just to make sure.

'This is a drive-thru window?' she said to Ford.

'And I'm driving thru on a bike! I can't see the problem?'

'Why didn't you just go to the counter?' asked the partner manager.

'There was a queue and I saw the sign for the drive-thru so…'

The bobble-hatted builder combined beeping his horn with sticking his head out of his side window. 'Will you get a fucking move on?! I've got…'

'I know, I know!' shouted Ford, as he climbed off his bike and let it fall to the ground. 'You've got to get to a job by nine, but it's not me! It's them! How many more times do I have to say it?!'

The bobble-hatted builder muttered, 'Wanker,' wound his window up and locked the door.

The partner manager, tapped a button on Partner Jackie's keyboard. 'Partner area manager to Partner Jackie's window to see partner manager.'

Ford picked up his bike and said to Partner Jackie and the partner manager, 'Forget it! Cancel my order.' With a rumble in his stomach, he rode off with as much dignity as he could muster. Next door at the newsagent's, he bought a student special, which consisted of a chocolate bar, a family-size packet of crisps and a tin of cola.

Ford was ten minutes late by the time he got to Frank's Auto Sales. He had just put his bicycle clips in his desk drawer and was rummaging for indigestion tablets when Blake strolled in with a scowl on his face.

'That fucking time-waster's back,' he sniffed. 'Mind you, the girl with him would have got my special attention if he hadn't insisted on talking to you.'

Ford gazed out over the sales lot and saw Aldo standing with a young woman beside the small blue hatchback. The young woman was wearing a tight-fitting black mini skirt with a low-cut top that revealed more cleavage than Ford would have thought possible.

'I bet that fucker wants more balloons,' complained Blake.

Ford straightened his tie and quickly tidied his hair. 'There's only one way to find out.'

Aldo warmly shook Ford's hand and introduced him to his niece Tanya, who smiled shyly and gently shook his hand.

'I was telling Tanya all about the car,' enthused Aldo. 'And I think it would be the right model for her. She needs a reliable car for work.'

Ford thought the word 'model' was a good way to describe Tanya. She was incredibly beautiful. She somehow glowed, radiating beauty.

'All my uncle goes on about,' said Tanya, with a soft European accent, 'is this car, and what Ford had said about it. So, I said to my uncle, "I will see the car for myself", so here I am.'

Ford was not very good with European accents, but it sounded similar to Gina's, his old girlfriend. 'Did he really? Well, what would you like to know about this model?'

'I don't know about engines and things,' confessed Tanya. 'I just go by how it feels to drive.'

Ford smiled. 'Well, that's an easy one to sort out. I'll get the key fob and we'll go for a drive. I'll be back shortly.'

'We're not a fucking taxi service!' snarled Blake, when he saw Ford picking up the key fob for the blue hatchback.

'His niece would like a test drive. Who knows? I might get a sale out of it.'

Blake licked his lips. 'I'll take her for a test drive! All the way to heaven and back on my enormous dick.'

Ford fixed Blake with a look and shook his head in revulsion.

Blake noticed the head shake. 'Are you telling me you wouldn't wanna fuck a woman like that?'

'I don't think about it because the situation will never arise for someone like me.'

'You're right,' agreed Blake. 'A woman like that wouldn't look at you a first time, never mind twice.'

Ford smiled, but felt the knife of truth pierce his heart, as he headed back out to the waiting Tanya.

'Don't give him any balloons!' ordered Blake, as he watched Ford go on his fool's errand.

Ford placed temporary magnetic number plates on the hatchback and opened the driver's door for Tanya to climb inside. Aldo had opted to wait while his niece took the test drive because she was a new driver, and did not want to make her nervous.

Ford sat in the passenger seat and ran through the basics of the controls before they set off. For someone who was new to driving, Tanya pulled away into traffic rather quickly, without any hesitation.

'It might take a little while to get used to the feel of the car, so it would pay to be cautious,' advised Ford.

Tanya turned toward Ford with a smile. 'I feel confident with you beside me.'

Ford missed the smile because his eyes were fixed on the road ahead. 'Take the first left at the roundabout.'

Tanya flashed Ford another smile that he did not see. 'I only just moved here recently, I don't know my way around yet, it would be nice to have someone to show me the area.'

'This car doesn't have a sat nav, but you can buy similar models with one built in... Straight over the traffic lights.'

'I don't think you can beat having someone personally guiding you to interesting places,' hinted Tanya. 'You know, quiet places where you can be alone with someone.'

With his eyes still glued to the road, Ford shook his head. 'Sat navs have come a long way in just a few years and will give you loads of information about an area. You'll be fine.'

Tanya wriggled. 'I think I need to alter the seat.' She pulled over to the kerb. 'How do I adjust the seat Ford? Can you show me?'

'What do you want altered? Height or more leg room?'

'I always like room for my legs, I like to be able to move them.'

'There's a button on the side of the seat, just press it until you have enough room.'

Tanya fiddled with her seat. 'I'm not very good with buttons; can you lean over and show me?'

Ford smiled. 'No need, these seats are made for right and left-hand drives. Here!' Ford pushed a button and Tanya's seat moved back. 'Say when…'

'When!'

'Not much adjustment needed there. Now, if you take the next left that will take us on a route back.'

Tanya pulled away and rejoined the traffic. 'I think I'm wearing the wrong skirt for driving,' she laughed teasingly. 'It keeps riding up!'

Ford still kept his eyes on the road. 'That could be dangerous on a long drive. Just make sure you don't wear it next time you get behind the wheel.'

Five minutes later, Tanya pulled up by her waiting uncle.

Aldo opened the driver's door. 'Well, Tanya, how was the drive?'

'Very business like,' she admitted to her uncle.

'All business?' asked Aldo, as he glanced over at Ford, who was taking the magnetic number plate off the front of the car.

'All business,' said Tanya, grumpily.

Aldo turned toward the large white MPV that was parked across the road, and nodded.

Ford went around to the rear of the car for the other number plate. 'Your niece is a very good driver for someone who has just passed her test. Is there anything I can tell you about the car, Tanya?'

103

'I liked the car, but I'm not sure,' she replied with a half-smile.

'When you're new to driving, choosing the right car is very important, so shop around and look for one with a sat nav. It will help you find your way until you know the area.'

Aldo held his arms up. 'What can I say? Thank you for letting my niece have a test drive.'

'My pleasure.' Ford glanced back toward the showroom and smiled. 'Now, let's get you some more balloons for your grandchildren.'

Blake snapped down the nail clippers and watched the stubborn toenail finally arc toward the showroom window. Following its trajectory with his eyes, he saw Ford giving the time-waster all the forecourt balloons. 'I was right all along! He has got a fucking market stall!' By the time Blake had put his socks and shoes back on, and hurried out to the forecourt, Ford was giving Aldo and Tanya a farewell wave. Blake was red in the face with rage. 'I can't believe you gave him all our balloons! What's wrong with you? I told you not to give him any.'

Ford used his best baffled expression. 'Did you? I could have sworn you said, "Give him all the balloons".'

Blake puts his hands on his hips, and shook his head. 'Well, don't be surprised if we don't get any more customers today, thanks to you!'

'You never know, people might finally realise there isn't a kid's party going on here and come and look at the cars.'

'Balloons and cars go together,' explained Blake, as though he was talking to an idiot, which he was sure he was. 'You know, like ladyboys and margarine.'

Ford had never heard that saying before. 'You must have made that up.'

'Talking about up, I have a hundred balloons in my desk drawer that need blowing up, and seeing as you're the only one giving them away, you can blow the bloody things up.'

'I don't think my job description says, "balloon-blower-upper".'

'Try this job description: "You're sacked if you don't blow the balloons up!" And on top of that, when you want a reference, I'll make sure I mention you giving all the balloons away!'

Ford could not face the humiliation of explaining to future employers that he had lost his job because of his generosity with balloons. 'Okay! I'll blow up the stupid balloons!'

Blake gave a cruel smile. 'By the way, the pump has packed up so you'll have to use your puff.'

Ford watched Blake literally skip back to the showroom, and with a heavy heart, he trudged after him.

Nina and Evie were sitting at the window table in Corks Vino Bar, enjoying the spectacular views of takeaway debris floating past on the river Brid. Nina had known Evie for the last four years. She was a work colleague of Trixie's, and when she had first moved down from Scotland, she had stayed with Trixie for six months until she found her own place. Since that time, they had become close friends, and the three of them had even gone on holidays together until Evie met David. It was obvious straight away that she was in love. They saw a lot less of her, and when they did, no matter what they tried to talk about, the conversation would veer toward how wonderful David was.

'The Yorkshire Dales?!' bawled Nina. 'What happened to Paris?'

The lunchtime patrons of Corks Vino Bar turned their heads and gave disapproving stares.

Evie sipped her white wine. 'David and I had a last-minute change of plan. We decided to do something different; all-girl and all-boy weekends away in Europe are just... you know, too clichéd.'

'I like clichéd!' protested Nina. 'I like Paris!'

'We want to do something that we'll always remember.'

Nina leant forward and clasped Evie's hands. 'I've got a good memory, I'll remember!' With one last desperate plea, she said, 'If we do go... we'll always have Paris!'

'Even I know that line comes from the movie *Casablanca*. Have you ever been to the Yorkshire Dales?'

'No, but it sounds like it doesn't have any shops.'

Evie smiled. 'No, it doesn't have any shops, but you will love the wilderness of it.'

A look of horror came over Nina's face, and she quickly slugged back half a glass of white wine. 'I don't think I like wilderness.'

'David and I have had some of the best times of our lives going for long walks and popping in to cosy pubs.'

'You can have long walks in Paris. They have cosy cafés and shops!'

'Don't be such a misery, it will be fun. Trixie's looking forward to it, she thought it was a great idea.'

'Don't listen to her!' begged Nina. 'I love her to bits, but she's not like a normal person.'

'Don't forget, I have family and friends in Scotland, so I can meet them halfway.'

Nina downed the rest of her wine. 'I suppose it can't be that bad.'

'We'll be taking over a five-star hotel with an award-winning restaurant, we are not camping in a field. And don't worry about having the right clothing, the hotel hires out the boots, the coats, everything.'

'I've been learning French,' said Nina in another desperate attempt to get Evie to change her mind.'

'Okay,' said Evie, calling her bluff. 'Comment tu t'appelles?'

'Oui,' muttered Nina, as she tried to recall some French. 'Les Parapluies de Cherbourg.'

Evie laughed. 'So your name is *The Umbrellas of Cherbourg*, just like the movie poster you have in your shop?'

'Okay, okay. The Yorkshire wilderness, it is.'

'It might be worth bringing one of your Cherbourg umbrellas because it can rain a lot up there.'

Nina's head slumped to the table. 'I hate the rain, it makes my hair go all frizzy.'

Evie laughed again. 'God, you are hard to please. Did I mention that it's our treat, the hotel, the meals, the drinks?'

Nina quickly looked up from the table and smiled. 'I'm looking forward to it already!'

It was Saturday morning. In Nina's apartment, the large, black-framed wall clock showed nine o'clock, as Nina dragged a large suitcase over to her front door. 'Don't help me!' she grunted.

Ava was dressed in 1940s denim dungarees with a floral headscarf. She carefully measured the width of the sitting room with a tape measure, jotting down the result in a notebook. 'I didn't want to patronise you by offering.'

'I wish you wouldn't measure up when I'm here. I wish you wouldn't measure up, full stop, because I'm not going anywhere.'

'It helps me get an idea of the cost for new carpets.'

'There's nothing wrong with the carpets.'

Ava smiled and shook her head. 'They are so 2010.'

'2010 can't be that dated already.'

'Err, grandma, that's like a generation ago.' Ava scratched her chin. 'I could go retro, I suppose.'

'You can suppose as much as you like, I'm not going anywhere.' Nina stood by the front door and looked back. 'Will you be okay until Monday?'

'I'll be fine,' Ava assured her. 'My little sister is helping out in the shop, and Bertie is staying here with me. Have a great weekend, and don't worry about a thing. Where are you going again?'

'A place called Yorkshire, it's somewhere up north. That's why I'm taking a lot of warm clothing with me.' Despite it being July, Nina was dressed in skinny jeans, Ugg boots and a roll-neck sweater under a red, double-breasted pea-coat.

'I think the north has summers as well,' said Ava.

'I've been watching soap operas set in the north for years, and the people are always cold, wet and miserable.'

There was a knock on the door; Trixie strolled in wearing light summer clothes. 'Are you ready to go? The taxi's waiting outside.' She took one look at Nina and said, 'Where are you off to? Mount Everest?'

Ava chuckled. 'That's a good one.'

'I'll have the last laugh when you're freezing cold,' replied Nina, 'because you'll come begging me to borrow a jumper and I'll just say, "Tough".'

'Please don't tell me you're taking that on the train,' groaned Trixie, pointing at the large suitcase. 'We could have just gone in your new car if you were going to take that thing.'

Nina struggled to pick the case up and in a strained voice said, 'You know I panic driving long distances. It's lighter than it looks.'

Trixie tried lifting it by the handle to feel the weight. 'You surely can't need everything in that case. Take something out. It's far too heavy to carry.'

'It's what I need for the weekend.' Nina pointed to the bottom of the case. 'It has wheels, I'll just pull it along.'

'How are you going to get it down the stairs?' asked Trixie.

'Easily! As I said, it's not that heavy.' Nina lifted the case, masking the effort on her face. 'See?!' Nina did a quick check to make sure she had everything with her. 'Ava, look after Petal, and I'll see you Monday. You have my number if you need me.'

108

'I'll manage,' insisted Ava. 'Just go and enjoy yourselves.' She watched Nina drag her case out onto the landing. 'Bye, Trixie. Have a good…'

A tumbling, thumping noise of something heavy falling down the stairs made them both jump.

'What's happened?!' yelped Ava.

Trixie rushed to the landing. 'It's okay, her case fell down the stairs.'

'No damage!' shouted Nina from below. 'It slipped on its wheels.'

Ava followed Trixie down the stairs and stood in the doorway to wave them goodbye.

An overweight, middle-aged cabbie strained himself as he lifted Nina's case into the boot of the taxi. He had to lean against the vehicle to get his breath back before limping round to the driver's door, suspecting that he might now have a hernia again.

Giving Ava a final wave, Nina and Trixie climbed into the back of the cab and set off for their weekend break.

Trixie had arranged for the taxi to take them to King's Cross railway station. The Bridgeford to London line was not running at weekends due to essential repairs that had been going on for several months now. Nina had asked the taxi driver, whose name turned out to be Bill, to use the Costa drive-thru so they could all have a coffee for the journey.

'It's more than my job's worth,' grumbled Bill. 'No beverages are allowed in the vehicle.'

'Oh, come on Bill!' urged Nina. 'I didn't have time for a hot drink this morning. I'll treat you! You can order what you like. Come on Bill, what coffee do you like?'

'I am partial to a flat white,' admitted Bill.

'I'll buy you one, a large one. What do you say?'

Bill grunted, 'Okay, but it's highly irregular.'

There was no queue at the Costa drive-thru, so it was only a couple of minutes before their order was ready.

Passing back two cappuccinos, Bill whimpered a couple of times with pain from his hernia. 'Thanks for the flat white,' he winced, as he took a sip of his hot coffee.

'Aaargh!!!' screeched Nina.

The sudden shriek caused Bill to spill his coffee in his lap.

'It doesn't have sugar!' complained Nina.

'Shit, shit, shit!' screamed Bill, as the scalding liquid soaked straight through his clothing to his man bits. In a panic, he tried to get out of the cab quickly, but his suspected hernia sent shooting pains down his groin, making his exit slow and painful. Unable to run to a bathroom and eager to prevent major scalding, Bill dropped his trousers.

The stunned faces of Nina and Trixie stared out at Bill using a Costa serviette to mop up the coffee spreading across his *Playboy* boxer shorts.

Nina wound down the rear window. 'Bill, while you're out there, can you get me some sugar, please?'

The ride to King's Cross began in a tense atmosphere. After a few minutes, Nina said, 'Has it stopped hurting yet, Bill?'

'No,' whimpered Bill, curtly.

Nina glanced at Trixie, whose head was turned away; her shoulders were shaking with laughter. 'Don't laugh,' Nina whispered, 'You'll make me laugh.'

Trixie had to put her hand over her mouth to stifle her giggles.

'Stop, Trixie,' giggled Nina.

Trixie curled up, her whole body now shaking with laughter. Nina burst out laughing, and for the next ten minutes, they dared not look at each other. With every hint of eye contact, the pair of them burst into laughter again, while Bill's pissed off eyes peered at them from the rear-view mirror.

At King's Cross, Bill made no attempt to get out. He pulled a lever under the steering wheel, and the boot lid lifted up.

Trixie had already paid for the journey in advance, but gave Bill a ten-pound tip out of guilt.

'Thanks,' he muttered grudgingly, with a touch of sarcasm.

Trixie felt like snatching it out of his ungrateful hands. 'My pleasure. Why don't you buy yourself another cup of coffee to wear?'

Bill muttered 'Bitches,' as his scalded testicles and the stabbing pain from his hernia combined to bring tears to his eyes.

Trixie had to help Nina drag her large suitcase out of the boot before pulling out her own small, compact valise.

'I'll get a porter to help with my case,' grunted Nina, as she attempted to pull it along. 'I think one of the wheels has jammed up.'

'A porter? Who do you think you are, Celia Johnson in *Brief Encounter*? You insisted on bringing it, so stop whingeing and hurry up. The train leaves in ten minutes.'

Nina dragged her suitcase behind her, its jammed wheel scraping along noisily. It wasn't long before she was sweating and gasping for breath.

After five minutes of listening to Nina whingeing about the jammed wheel, Trixie finally helped her drag it along the station platform. By the time they were sitting down on the train, they were both hot, bothered and out of breath.

Trixie glared at Nina, as the train pulled away from the station. 'It's not heavy,' she said, in her best Nina voice. 'It's got wheels!'

Nina wiped her brow with the back of her hand. 'It's not my fault the wheel jammed up.'

'Of course it is! You made it too heavy for the wheels to carry. It's bloody summer, you don't need all that stuff. Either get rid of something or manage the case on your own because I am not going to spend my weekend dragging your luggage about.'

'I'll manage on my own,' snapped Nina, 'Just don't come crying to me when you get hypothermia.' Nina had to scrunch her eyes up, as the dazzling sun blinded her.

'I would lend you my spare sunglasses,' laughed Trixie, 'but I'm sure you don't need them.'

Nina shaded her eyes with a hand and wished she had brought some summer clothing with her. 'You're right. I won't need them,' she mumbled stubbornly.

That same morning, Ford and Jason had dressed in shorts and floral short sleeve shirts, as though they were holidaying on a Greek island. They loaded two small suitcases under the hood of a bright orange, 40-year-old VW Beetle.

'It was jolly nice of your Uncle Colin to lend us his car while he's on holiday,' enthused Ford. 'You always said he kept it wrapped in cotton wool and only ever took it out of the garage to polish it.'

Jason shut the bonnet and gave the car keys to Ford. 'That was before he had that funny turn.'

Ford was puzzled. 'Didn't he just have a hip replacement?'

'Yeah, that's why he had a new hip. He had this funny turn when he went around corners.'

'So, why isn't the car his pride and joy anymore?'

'I don't know, do I? Old people go a bit bonkers when they hit sixty.'

Ford took his mobile phone from the back pocket of his chino shorts. 'I'll give him a ring and thank him. What's his number?'

'I've already thanked him. Anyway, the caravan site he's staying at doesn't have a very good signal. Let's just get going.'

The orange Beetle pulled away into the slow-moving traffic of the town. Ten minutes later, the roads were moving freely, as they headed out of the built-up areas.

'Did you remember to bring a map?' asked Ford, as he checked the look of his sunglasses in the rear-view mirror. 'I've never been north of Cambridge before, so I'll need directions.'

Jason could not quite believe his ears and goggled at Ford with disbelief. 'A map? A proper map?'

'A roadmap, you know? You get directions from them.' Ford noticed Jason staring at him. 'What? What did I say?'

'They don't make maps anymore! There's this thing called satnav now!'

'Okay, where's the satnav?'

'It doesn't have one. Just use the map app on your phone.'

'I took that app off. I felt like I was being watched by Big Brother. It kept telling me where I'd been, and the final straw was when it wanted me to review the public toilets I'd used five minutes earlier.'

Jason shook his head in sadness for his friend. 'You can't turn your back on the future, you have to embrace it.' He produced his phone, which was the latest model thanks to his mum's phone contract. 'Leave the technology to me.' Jason deftly used his thumb to slide across the display. 'Here we go, maps… Where is it we're going again?'

'Hawes.'

'Where?' said Jason, scanning the pavements.

Ford gave a half-smile. 'I think it was funnier the third time you did that joke.'

Jason chuckled at his own wit. 'Here we go, head for the M11 and stay on that until we see signs for the A1.'

'Do you know what?' asked Ford. 'I'm looking forward to a relaxing drive and seeing the beautiful British countryside on a rare beautiful day.' He switched on the radio, and The Kinks' *Sunny Afternoon* began to play.

The temperature was climbing and the clouds were dispersing, as the orange Beetle made steady progress north with Ford and Jason singing along to the summer songs.

Forty-year-old traffic officer PC Bernie Blyton had parked up on his favourite slip road, with a good view of the traffic heading north on the A1. He regarded himself as a predator, waiting patiently for his next kill. His nickname at the local police station was Super Cop. A sarcastic nickname for someone who just dished out speeding tickets every day. Every time a fellow officer called him Super Cop, it was like a knife being shoved into his stomach. He had always wanted to be a detective, catching proper villains, but every request for a transfer had been refused. Today, PC Bernie Blyton had decided to prove that he had what it takes to be a proper lawman. He started by tapping into the police mainframe for live criminal updates. The latest crimes scrolled across the computer screen built into the dashboard. Every few minutes, a new alert would appear. PC Blyton stared transfixed at the screen, as he munched his way through a family pack of sausage rolls. The only update that stuck in his mind was an orange-coloured VW Beetle that had been stolen in Essex. While drinking piping hot tea, freshly poured from his two-litre flask, he monitored the traffic. To his amazement, he saw an orange VW Beetle drive past, heading north. He quickly noted the number plate. Bingo! It was the same car. The shock of seeing a stolen car driven by proper criminals made him choke and spit his tea all over the inside of the windscreen.

'Bollocks!' he screamed, as he searched in vain for a tissue or a cloth of some sort. A packet of ring donuts lay unopened on the passenger seat. He quickly split open the pack and used donuts to mop up the tea until he had reasonable visibility.

With blue lights flashing, sirens blaring and tyres screaming, PC Blyton sped off in pursuit of the stolen Beetle.

'I need to go for a piss,' exclaimed Jason, as he squirmed in his seat.

Ford was puzzled. 'We only stopped twenty minutes ago. Have you got a prostate problem or something?'

'I didn't have a proper wee then!'

'What do you mean, you didn't have a proper wee then?'

'There was a queue for the urinals, and I had to stand between two big blokes. I can't go properly when there are big blokes either side!'

'That's odd. When you've had a few beers down the local pub and there's a queue, you're quite happy to piss in the handbasin.'

Jason shrugged. 'I'm relaxed then; maybe I should drink beers in the daytime.'

Ford glanced over to Jason, who was now clutching his groin. 'How urgent is it?'

'Urgent, urgent!'

PC Blyton saw the orange Beetle in the distance. The traffic ahead began to part like the Red Sea, as drivers caught a glimpse of the onrushing blue lights. He felt like he was a god, as he floored the accelerator, taking the patrol car over one hundred and twenty miles an hour. Finally, there in front of him was the orange Beetle. He moved alongside and glared over. The driver was talking to a male passenger who, if he was not mistaken, was going cold turkey, jigging up and down, probably in desperate need of a fix of skag. The driver was probably high as a kite on mama coca, because he wasn't even aware that he was there. All those hours of watching American police dramas were paying off. PC Blyton mentally worked out the list of misdemeanours he could add to the charge sheet: theft, driving a stolen vehicle, driving without due care and attention, no insurance. The driver probably didn't even have a licence, and by the looks of him and his accomplice, they had been taking illegal drugs and most likely selling them outside primary schools. Using all his traffic patrol experience, PC Blyton overtook the stolen car with lights and sirens blaring, ready to use the patrol vehicle to bring these perpetrators to a stop. The smile that sat smugly on his face dropped away as the stolen car turned sharply up the services exit.

'Bollocks, bollocks, bollocks!' he howled at the rear-view mirror. There was no hard shoulder to reverse on, and it was fifteen miles to the next turn-off. By the time he got back, the drug pushers would be well on their way to peddle their filthy wares outside another school. It was no good, he would have to call for armed back-up and get a police helicopter in the air right away.

Ford had turned sharply off the motorway at the last minute as Jason shouted, 'Services! I need to go!'

Ford thought it was just as well because he noticed a police car with its lights on in his wing mirror. He guessed there might have been an accident further on.

The service area was very busy. Cars were queuing for parking spaces, as Ford joined the waiting line.

Jason pointed to several disabled parking bays by the main entrance. 'Park over there!'

'I'm not parking there without a permit, it's against the law for a start off. What if some disabled person turns up?'

'It's an emergency!' pleaded Jason.

'It's against the law!' said Ford, adamantly. 'I'm not getting in trouble with the police because I illegally parked in a disabled parking bay!'

'There's no official law for parking there, trust me. In any case, there's at least eight places. They never ever get used all at once.'

Ford wasn't comfortable breaking any kind of law, legal or moral. 'I'm not breaking the law. I'll just wait here in the queue.'

'I won't be a sec,' said Jason, opening the passenger door. He leapt out, gripping his penis to stop any leaks, and ran into the services building.

All the talk of going for a piss had suddenly made Ford desperate for one, and reluctantly bypassed the waiting cars to drive into a disabled parking space. He felt guilty for parking there and noticed some disapproving glares from a group of cigarette smokers standing by the entrance. His urge to go for a pee became overwhelming, and for the benefit of the onlookers, he grimaced as he clambered out of the car, and uttered, 'Ouch' several times as he limped inside.

By the time Ford had hobbled all the way to the gents' toilet, Jason was already coming out. 'What's up with your leg?'

'Nothing, I parked where you told me and needed a pee. People were watching.'

Jason nodded as though it made perfect sense. 'Oh, well, we might as well have a coffee while we're here.'

A few minutes later, Ford limped out of the toilet and found Jason playing a slot machine in a gaming area. 'I thought you were getting coffee.'

Jason pressed a green button that blinked urgently. 'I didn't know what you wanted.'

'Americano. I always have an Americano. There has not been a single time when we've got coffee and I haven't wanted an Americano.'

Jason spat, 'Shit!' and kicked the machine. He turned to Ford. 'I can't remember Italian words that end in O.'

Ford felt his limping leg begin to ache. 'Forget the coffee; we're only a hundred miles away from the hotel. I wanted to get a newspaper, so I'll just grab a couple of bottles of water as well.'

Jason delved into his pockets for loose change. 'I'll just have another couple of quid on this machine and meet you at the car.'

Ford was waiting at the end of a very long queue at the WH Smith counter when he noticed a group of men and women in the main thoroughfare. They were wearing Invictus Games tee shirts and shorts. Some had blades for legs, others had artificial arms. He quickly paid for his items and tried to hurry past them, but his leg that had never had a limp suddenly hurt like hell, causing him to limp for real. Ford told himself not to make eye contact with any of them. Making eye contact was something he'd tried to stop himself doing on lots of occasions, and he had always failed. He guessed doing it must be hardwired into him.

'This time, I'm looking straight ahead,' he told himself, and immediately caught the eye of a well-built man in his thirties, with regimental tattoos on his arms and his one good leg.

'Did you manage to park your car all right?' the man asked in a north-east accent.

Ford stopped and winced, not sure if it was in real or pretend pain.

'Wey aye, man. I had nee problem,' he muttered, due to a nervous habit he had of copying accents when he felt anxious.

'Some twat has parked in a disabled bay,' moaned the well-built man. 'Can you believe it?! The focker.'

Ford edged away, now limping sideways. 'Aye, the focker! I must nee… get going, I'm doa for me painkillers, like.'

As Ford limped toward the main entrance, he thought it strange that no one was coming in. Pushing open the entrance door, he found out why. Twenty armed police officers had guns pointing at him, as a police helicopter hovered above. Jason was already face down on the ground with his hands cuffed behind his back.

The voice of PC Blyton screeched through a megaphone, 'Put your hands above your head and kneel down.'

Ford did what he was told and was swiftly cuffed and thrown into the back of a police van, along with Jason. It sped off at the head of a convoy of police vehicles, all with blue lights flashing.

Ford turned to Jason accusingly, 'I told you it was illegal to park in a disabled bay!'

PC Blyton was feeling several inches taller due to all the respectful glances from his detective colleagues. They were seeing what this officer could do with limited resources, and

118

probably demanding his immediate transfer to the detective arm of the force. There was a strut in his step, as he followed the detective sergeant into the interview room. The two drug pushers were handcuffed to the table. The one with the limp looked up as they entered.

'I confess!' said Ford, earnestly. 'I'm very sorry.'

'I don't see why you need me,' whined Jason, pointing at Ford. 'He was driving.'

Ford quickly turned on Jason. 'Oh, thanks, mate, but if I remember rightly, it was your idea!'

Detective Sergeant Frank Stone was only weeks away from retirement. He could not wait to get away from the scum he had to deal with on a daily basis, and get to work on his beloved allotment instead. He hated criminal bastards, especially southern criminal bastards like these two.

'You've hit t' jackpot here, Bernie,' he said in his thick Yorkshire accent. 'These two are singing like canaries before we even start.'

PC Blyton felt a surge of pride. In six years, no one had ever called him Bernie.

Frank glared down at Ford and Jason. 'You evil southern bastards!'

Ford was feeling anxious and told himself not to copy the sergeant's accent. 'I've done nowt like this before. Will tha give me three points on me licence?'

Frank leant over the table. 'Three years hard labour, more like. You cheeky focking bastard!'

'Okay, we did a bad thing,' admitted Jason, 'but we promise we won't do it again. Can we go now?'

Ford nodded eagerly in agreement.

Frank Stone picked up the wooden chair nearest to him and threw it against the wall, smashing it to pieces. 'You car-thieving, drug-pushing bastards are going nowhere.'

'Car-thieving?' queried Ford,

'Drug-pushing bastards?' added Jason.

Frank let a smile play across his lips, he had the buggers worried. 'Read out the charges, Bernie.'

PC Blyton took out his notebook, flipped a page open and coughed to clear his throat, only to get a coughing fit.

Jason jumped up and screamed 'BOOO!'

PC Blyton jumped out of his skin, but continued coughing.

Jason had an afterthought. 'Oh, sorry, that's for hiccups, isn't it?'

'Sit down!' ordered Frank. He waited for Jason to sheepishly take his seat. 'When you're ready, Bernie.'

PC Blyton had one last cough before reading from his notebook. 'Car theft, possession of a stolen car, driving without insurance, driving a stolen vehicle, driving without due care and attention, probably driving without a licence. I'm just waiting for confirmation from forensics of the following misdemeanours: drug smuggling, possession of drugs with intent to supply to children.' PC Blyton calmly closed his notebook and placed it back in his shirt pocket.

Frank thumped the desk with his fist. 'What do you smug bastards have to say about that?'

Ford was baffled, confused and bewildered. 'So, this has nothing to do with parking in a disabled bay?'

PC Blyton quickly took out his notebook and added this crime to his notes.

'The car's not stolen,' explained Jason. 'It's my uncle's; I borrowed it.'

'You're the worst kind of lowlife,' growled Frank, 'the kind that steals from his own family.'

The door opened and a female officer entered, holding a file of papers.

Frank held out his hand. 'What have we got, Angie?'

PC Angela Jones handed the file over. 'The car was clean; the dogs didn't find any evidence of drugs. We contacted the car owner, and he said that his nephew had most probably borrowed it again, and if it has so much as a scratch on it, he'll be for it.'

Ford nudged Jason with his elbow. 'You said he'd lent it to us!'

'He did,' insisted Jason. 'I just didn't get around to asking him formally.'

'The only odd thing we found,' continued PC Jones, 'in one of the cases were eighty six condoms.'

'They must be drug mules!' blurted PC Blyton.

Ford gave Jason a puzzled stare. 'Why on earth have you brought eighty six condoms with you?'

Jason shrugged. 'My mum doesn't like to be in the house on her own with them around. She says it gives her the willies.'

'But eighty six? Why do you need eighty six?'

'I had a pack of one hundred sent to me when I signed up with *No-strings-bonking-dot-com*,' explained Jason. 'They were a free gift.'

Frank slumped down on a chair, closed his eyes and rubbed the bridge of his nose. 'Does this mean we have nothing on these two?'

PC Blyton reached for his notebook. 'Driving without due care and attention?'

'Anything else?' groaned Frank.

PC Blyton went back to his notebook and flicked through several pages. 'Parking in a disabled bay?'

Frank stood up slowly, his body felt old and ached. 'That's hardly an offence.'

Jason gave Ford a smug smile. 'I told you it wasn't illegal!'

PC Blyton felt his new career as a detective crumble to pieces. 'We can't let them go. They're car-thieving drug pushers!' he insisted desperately.

'No!' said Frank, who was now trying to come up with an excuse to give to the police commissioner for calling out the armed response unit and the helicopter. 'They're a couple of Essex idiots. Get them out of my sight. And as for you, Blyton, get back to traffic patrol where you belong, before I arrest you for wasting my bloody time.'

It was late morning in Rome. The temperature was twenty-eight degrees Celsius and still climbing. Ennio Rossi sat at a table in the shade of a vine-covered pergola, staring out from the terrace of his villa toward the ancient part of the city. He fondly recalled being a child with all of Rome as his playground. Had it really been more than sixty years ago?

His thoughts were interrupted by a slight cough from the menacing figure of Fredo, his personal assistant. 'Aldo is back,' Fredo whispered. He was ten years younger than Ennio and had played on the very same streets.

Ennio casually waved his hand, Fredo nodded and strode over to the villa's main building. Moments later, he returned with a middle-aged, grey-suited man, who was carrying a sleeved laptop, and hurrying to keep up with Fredo's stride.

Ennio waved his hand for Aldo to sit beside him.

With a nervous smile, Aldo edged past the bulky frame of Fredo and sat down at the table.

'Is he the one?' asked Ennio.

'I think so,' said Aldo, unzipping the laptop. With a few taps of the keyboard, a video began to play. On screen, the balloons and bunting at Frank's Auto Sales waved in the breeze. Aldo was standing with Ford in front of a blue hatchback.

Ennio leant forward and squinted at the scene, his eyes were not as good as they used to be. His stony face gave no clue as to his thoughts. He continued to stare at the screen for several moments after the short film had finished. 'Double-check,' commanded Ennio and, with a wave of his hand, dismissed Aldo from his company.

Fredo bent close to Ennio's ear. 'Do you want me to make arrangements?'

'Wait,' ordered Ennio. 'Let us make sure first.'

With another wave, Ennio commanded his assistant to go. Fredo nodded respectfully, and left Ennio to gaze at his beloved city.

CHAPTER EIGHT

As the train carrying Nina and Trixie travelled north, the bright sunshine gradually turned to dull grey skies. The sweltering temperature in the carriage dropped with each passing hour.

'Is it me or is it getting colder?' asked Nina.

Trixie had goosebumps on her arms and was feeling quite cold. 'Air conditioning,' she said, refusing to accept it was growing colder outside.

Nina glanced out of the window. 'People are wearing coats. We must be in the north now.'

'Just because it's the north, doesn't mean it's cold. It's July, for God's sake!'

'Well, I'm glad I brought my warm clothes with me,' said Nina smugly, as she patted her suitcase, which had its own seat next to her.

Trixie looked out of the window. The few people she did see, seemed to be wearing warm clothing. She shivered.

Nina snuggled up in her coat. 'I'm so cosy in my coat, it's lovely and warm. I wish I was more like you and didn't feel the cold,' she said with a teasing smile.

Trixie stood up and pulled her case down from the overhead rack. 'Bitch!' she said, as she pulled out a cotton cardigan and put it on.

Nina laughed. 'If you promise to help me with my case, I'll lend you one of my hooded sweatshirts.'

Trixie felt a tad warmer, but not warm enough. 'How many did you bring?'

'Only four.'

'Four? It's a weekend break!'

'Hello! We're in the north, we might get snowed in for months.'

Trixie pushed her case back up onto the luggage rack. 'I give up with you sometimes. For someone who is bright, you can be really dumb.'

'Does that mean you don't want a hooded sweatshirt?'

Trixie sighed. 'Okay… Can I borrow one of your tops?'

Nina snickered. 'Say the magic words.'

'Really?! You want me to beg?'

'Say the magic words.'

Trixie sighed again. 'Please, pretty please, please with pink ribbons on it.'

Nina unzipped her case and sorted through some tops. 'You can borrow this one, it's not a nice colour,' she said, handing over a green top.

Trixie took it and put it on straight away.

'No "thank you?"' asked Nina, with a smile.

'I'm not thanking you, because you made me beg!'

Nina giggled. 'I did, didn't I?'

Trixie laughed. 'What a bitch you are.'

'I am, aren't I?' chuckled Nina.

Ford was concentrating hard, as he drove down narrow lanes in the grey mist. For the umpteenth time in the last five minutes, he wiped the mist from the inside of the car windscreen with the flat of his hand.

Jason yawned. 'Can't you go any faster? I'm getting cold. You're only doing twenty miles an hour!'

'I can't see a bloody thing. Are you sure the demister is on?'

'I think it's linked to the heating. They're clever, the Germans.'

Ford wiped the windscreen again. 'They're all very clever when the heating works, but they're not so bloody clever when it packs up. How far is the hotel now?'

'It's hard to say.'

'Roughly how far?'

'I'd say roughly… I don't know because my phone battery's dead.'

'You're joking!'

'No, it died about forty-five minutes ago, but I didn't want to worry you.'

'We passed through a village half an hour ago! Why didn't you say something? I could have bought a map or got directions.'

'Where's the adventure in that? It's more fun to get lost.'

Ford pulled into a dirt lay-by. 'Fun?! This isn't fun! I can't see a bloody thing, I'm freezing cold, I don't know where we are, and I don't know which way to go! Where… explain to me, is the fun in that?'

Jason shrugged. 'We'll laugh about it one day.'

After twenty seconds, Ford managed to move his dropped jaw and speak. 'NO! We won't!'

Just at that moment, the car rocked as a vehicle sped past. Ford could just make out the words *Hotel Shuttle Bus* printed on the rear. 'It must be going to the hotel!' Ford put his foot down on the accelerator pedal and chased after it. 'Wipe the windscreen for me!' he pleaded, as he bent forward to peer through the murky screen.

Jason leant over and frantically wiped at the windscreen. He giggled. 'I told you it was more fun to get lost.'

Ford still hadn't caught sight of the shuttle bus again after a couple of miles. Fortunately, signs began to appear. It was not long after that they saw one for the hotel car park.

To Ford's surprise, the entrance to the car park had locked gates blocking their entry. A cheap-looking wooden shed displaying the words *Car Park Manager* overlooked the gates. Jason reached over and hit the car horn.

'Don't beep,' Ford scolded him. 'Beeps always piss people off.'

'You do talk rubbish sometimes,' groaned Jason, and just to prove his point, he beeped the car horn again.

The shed door opened; a man in his seventies, wearing an ill-fitting grey uniform with a peaked cap and a *Car park manager* badge on his lapel, limped over.

'Why do all car park attendants have a limp?' whispered Jason.

Ford wound down the driver's window. 'Good evening. We're booked in at the hotel.'

Arthur Masham had been the car park manager for the last five years since retiring from driving buses for his whole working life. He had a phobia about the sound of car horns, caused by forty years of daily beeps from impatient car drivers. The sound caused his left knee to lock and gave him a raging headache. 'There's no need to beep, sir. Please don't beep.'

'It wasn't me, it was him,' explained Ford.

'Don't snitch on me!' moaned Jason.

Ford thought 'snitch' was a bit over the top. 'I don't care, I'm not taking the blame for beeping when I didn't beep.'

Arthur rubbed his locked knee. 'It doesn't matter who beeped, just please don't beep again.'

'We're meeting up with our friend for the weekend,' revealed Ford. 'He's getting married soon.'

Jason leant over to the open window. 'What's with the locked gates?'

'The car park was being used in an inappropriate way,' said Arthur, in a hushed voice. 'Some of our hotel guests had an encounter, so to speak, in the carpark.'

'Encounter?' asked Jason, puzzled. 'What sort of encounter?'

'Was it of the third kind?' joked Ford, trying to lighten the mood.

Arthur gave an embarrassed cough. 'It was of the debauched kind. Have you ever heard the term "dogging"?'

Ford glanced at Jason. 'I probably know someone who's done it.'

'Only the once!' said Jason defensively. 'I couldn't see much, it was too dark.'

Ford turned to Arthur. 'So the gate is there to stop people dogging.'

'It's not just dogging,' replied Arthur, producing a small notebook from his jacket pocket and flicking through the pages. 'It's this!' He held up the notebook for Ford and Jason to read. In large capital letters were the words *BUKKAKE BONNET*. 'It's a sick craze sweeping through the country's car parks.'

Jason stifled a giggle.

Arthur shook his head sadly at the memory. 'An elderly couple, in their eighties, arrived at the hotel late at night. Their brand-new Vauxhall Astra was surrounded by masked men with their todgers ready for action. The couple didn't dare leave the car, and the effect of all those men contributing to the bukkake bonnet gave the poor lady a right funny turn.'

Ford put all his effort into keeping a straight face. 'Hence the gates.'

Arthur nodded. 'Carlos down at the car wash had his jet wash on full power for a good ten minutes, trying to get that disgusting mess off the paintwork.'

Ford tried in vain to keep the smile off his face. 'Well, I'll sleep better tonight, knowing that the car's bonnet will be bukkake-free thanks to your diligence.'

'You're a credit to car parking,' added Jason.

Arthur felt a surge of pride, as he opened the gates. 'Have no fear, sirs, there'll be no more bukkake filth on my watch.'

Ford drove in and parked beside a gleaming black BMW saloon car. Jason jumped out and opened the Beetle's front hood. He glanced over to the BMW alongside. 'Ford... is that what I think it is?'

Ford's eyes followed Jason's pointing finger. There on the highly polished black paintwork was a bukkake bonnet.

Arthur had just put the kettle on for a cup of tea when he heard beeping from the car park. He limped to the door and searched for the culprit. The two men who had just entered were waving him over. With his headache starting up again, he hobbled toward them. As he got closer, he had a feeling of rising dread. By the time he reached them, his worst fears were confirmed. 'It can't be,' he stuttered. 'Not in my car park.' He felt faint and stretched out his hand to the car bonnet to steady himself, narrowly avoiding the splattered mess.

'Are you okay?' asked Ford, quickly taking hold of Arthur's arm.

Arthur took a deep breath. '*Car Park Monthly* magazine said it was just an urban myth, but it's... it's true... Bukkake bonnet by stealth!'

Ford whispered in Jason's ear. 'Or they just climbed over the gate.'

Once Nina and Trixie had arrived at Harrogate railway station, it was only a five-minute case drag to the taxi rank. There, a hotel shuttle bus was waiting to take them to the hotel.

The flat-capped burly bus driver, whose name was Maureen, gave them a cheery hello and effortlessly lifted Nina's huge case with one hand and stored it in the rear along with Trixie's sensibly sized valise. Two other passengers were already on board, a snooty couple in their thirties who never looked up once from their mobile phones. Trixie recognised the woman as the head of the Human Resources department at her company. The shuttle bus was soon on its way, with Maureen acting as a tour guide and pointing out places of interest, which mainly seemed to be areas where her family or friends lived.

Thirty-five minutes later, Nina and Trixie were collecting their cases from Maureen, who held out her cap, grateful for any gratuities. The snooty couple barely looked up from their phones, as they grabbed their Louis Vuitton bags without even saying thank you. Nina thanked Maureen very loudly for the benefit of the rude couple and added, 'Here's ten pounds for doing such a good job!'

This generous tipping was not noticed by the snooty couple, as they had walked away quickly. Nina's tip became even more generous because she had nothing smaller than a twenty-pound note, and Maureen was wise enough not to even look to see if she had any change.

It was another short suitcase drag to the reception desk. The snooty couple were demanding an upgrade because they had severe allergic reactions to rooms without a king-size bed. The receptionist, Brenda May, who was in her early sixties and elegantly dressed in grey, took their demands in her stride and assured them that they would not be having any severe allergic reactions because the hotel's standard beds were very big. The snooty couple grumbled something about having only one syringe of adrenaline, before a young porter was ushered over to take the bags up to their room.

'I've stayed here before,' announced Nina, just loud enough for the snooty couple to hear. 'The beds are tiny!'

Brenda had worked at the hotel for forty years and seen many changes. The one thing that never changed was the public; she hated them all. In another life, Brenda could have been an acclaimed actress because her ever-present friendly smile hid her loathing. With the passing of the years, the majority of the public she now saw were younger than her, so she hated them and envied their youth in equal measure.

She gave the two young women at the desk her standard warm smile. She hated them both for being pretty.

'How do you put up with people like that?' asked Nina, pointing toward the departing miserable couple.

Brenda faked another sincere smile. 'We appreciate and respect all our customers. How can I help?' Brenda hated the snooty couple less than these two. At least they had been unhappy.

'Trixie Clarke,' responded Trixie, 'and Nina Summer.'

'We're here as guests of David and Evie,' added Nina.

Brenda checked her computer screen. 'Here we are, rooms twelve and thirteen, they're adjoining rooms.'

Nina turned to Trixie. 'I can't have room thirteen, it's an unlucky number. It's been proved that if you suddenly die in a hotel room, it will be number thirteen. You have it.'

'So, you're quite happy for me to die suddenly in room thirteen?' asked Trixie.

'You're not superstitious, you won't care.'

'That's right, I'm not superstitious,' declared Trixie. With a concerned frown, she turned to Brenda. 'Do you have adjoining rooms with different numbers?'

Brenda smiled. 'Of course, madam, I'll move you to rooms fourteen and fifteen.' After a few taps on the keyboard, Brenda handed over two key cards. A click of her fingers made a doddery old man in a porter's outfit appear.

'Follow me, please,' he said in a feeble voice that suited his frail body, and attempted to pick up Nina's case.

'It's on wheels,' said Nina helpfully, as she watched the old man's face turn a light blue as he struggled with the weight of the case.

Brenda observed Old Jake's face changing colour for the third time that day and smiled because that shade of blue was definitely a new one. She had been trying to kill her ageing husband for years by making him carry heavy luggage. Despite her efforts, he still kept managing to breathe. The doctors had assured her that he only had a year left in him. That had been ten years ago, and the life insurance policies were now costing her a fortune, but Brenda still hoped to be in profit as long as he went soon. Her hopeful smile melted away when the young women offered to help him. Brenda reluctantly clicked her fingers again; a younger porter, in his twenties, bounced over and took the big case away from Old Jake, letting him handle the smaller one.

'Have a lovely stay, ladies,' said Brenda, as she pondered booking room thirteen for Old Jake one night.

'By stealth,' giggled Jason, as he and Ford walked into the hotel reception area with their luggage.

'How weird was that?' exclaimed Ford.

Brenda watched the two young men approach her; she disapproved of their casual attire. 'Good afternoon, gentlemen!'

Ford smiled shyly. 'Hello. Ford Wilkinson and Jason Ross. We have some rooms booked. Hopefully.'

Brenda pretended to laugh at the thin one's remark. She wished she had a pound for every time someone had come out with that. With a quick tap on the keyboard, Brenda said, 'We have two adjoining rooms, twelve and thirteen.'

'I don't want thirteen,' said Jason adamantly. 'It's an unlucky number.'

'It's just a number!' exclaimed Ford. 'It's as unlucky as any other number.'

'You have it then,' insisted Jason, 'if it's not unlucky.'

Ford hesitated, he would rather not have room thirteen just in case it was unlucky. The way his life was going, he did not need any more bad luck.

Brenda coughed gently and said confidently, 'I may be able to put your mind at rest, sir. Room thirteen is the only room in the hotel that I would let my husband stay in.'

Jason immediately said, 'I'll take it!' and held his hand out for the key card.

'Hold on,' grumbled Ford. 'You didn't want it a minute ago. It's unlucky, you said.'

Jason smiled. 'That was before I knew it was the best.'

Ford was sick of life letting him come in last all the time. 'For all we know…' Ford noticed Brenda's name badge. 'For all we know, Brenda might want her husband to have bad luck.'

Brenda pretended to laugh. 'I only want the best for my husband, he's an angel.' She thought about booking him in to the room next week in the hope that he soon would become an angel. A click of her fingers and the young porter dashed over and grabbed their bags.

'I hope you have a pleasant stay,' lied Brenda.

The young porter led them to their rooms, which were connected by an internal door, and gave a quick guide to the facilities available. He must have liked the word 'facilities' because he said it a dozen times.

'Very good facilities,' said Jason with a wry smile in Ford's direction. 'Could you just run through the facilities one more time?'

Ford did not find it as amusing as Jason did, as the young porter explained the facilities once more. After explaining the facilities, the young porter subtly held out his hand to facilitate a gratuity of some sort.

Jason held up empty hands. 'I'm a transcendental beat poet who refuses to be sucked in to the capitalist illusion of life.'

'That means he's a lazy layabout,' explained Ford, taking some change out of his shorts pocket. 'What is the average tip for porters these days?'

The young porter held up the fingers of one hand, less subtly. 'Five pound minimum.'

'Five pound minimum!' whined Jason. 'For carrying two bags up a flight of stairs?'

'I did explain the facilities twice,' pointed out the young porter.

Ford managed to muster five pounds in fifty and twenty pence pieces. The young porter reluctantly took the change in his cupped hands and left without even saying thank you.

'Ungrateful little bastard,' declared Jason.

Ford put his bag on the bed and began to unpack it. 'I'm going to have a hot shower.' Ford glanced at his watch. 'The get-together is down in the bar in an hour, so I'll give you a knock when I'm ready.'

Jason headed to his room through the connecting door. 'I'm going to check out the facilities!'

Forty-five minutes later, Ford was knocking on the connecting door. He was feeling refreshed after his shower and was now dressed in chinos and a casual shirt.

'It's open!' shouted Jason.

Ford found Jason sitting on the bed in his boxer shorts. He looked wet. 'Aren't you ready yet?'

'This is the best hotel I've ever been in!' beamed Jason. 'You can watch TV while you're having a bath.'

Ford was a bit more smugly blasé about TVs in hotel bathrooms, as he'd stayed in quite a few upscale establishments with Kate over the years. 'Well, hurry up or we'll miss the welcome.'

'I love it here,' enthused Jason. 'You can grab booze from the minibar then watch porn while you're having a bath. Brilliant!'

'No, no, no,' protested Ford. 'Please don't tell me you did that. Dave and Evie will get billed.'

'I checked with that young porter, he said it was all-inclusive, so I can watch as much porn as I like. This is going to be the best weekend ever.'

Ten minutes later, Jason was dressed in a similar style to Ford. 'Let's get this party started!' he shouted enthusiastically and held up a hand for Ford to high-five.

'I've never high-fived anyone in my life and I'm not going to start now. Come on, let's go downstairs.'

Jason followed Ford down the hotel corridor. 'You really are a miserable bastard sometimes; I'm beginning to think Kate was right about your shapes being wrong.'

Nina and Trixie had settled in to their adjoining rooms and were able to chat to each other without raising their voices.

'Trixie!' said Nina in her most friendly voice.

Trixie recognised the tone. 'No!'

'You don't know what I was going to say.'

'Let me guess. You want to use my wardrobe because you packed so many clothes, you can't fit them all in yours.'

There was a moment of silence before Nina said, 'I wasn't going to ask, but seeing as you're offering, I'll just hang up a couple of things.'

Before Trixie could protest, Nina sauntered in and took over most of the hanging space. 'What are you wearing tonight?' she asked while staring at the few items Trixie had hanging up.

'One of my little black numbers.'

'Oh!' moaned Nina. 'I was going to wear black. Can't you wear something else?'

'Nina! You've brought a bloody shop's worth of clothes, I only packed two dresses and they're both black. Anyway, you can wear black as well.'

'But we'll match!'

Trixie gazed at Nina with slight annoyance. 'It doesn't matter, nobody will care.'

'I care. I care that everyone will think I'm copying you.'

'You do this every time we go out. Just wear what the hell you like. I'm going to pop down a bit early. It won't hurt my career to flatter my boss before anyone else does.'

'Don't go and leave me on my own all night, you know I can't do small talk and I'll end up drinking too much.'

'Can't do small talk?' laughed Trixie. 'One drink and you can chat to anyone.'

Nina stood back from Trixie's wardrobe. 'Now, decisions, decisions. What to wear?'

An hour later and Trixie was fastening her stud earrings before heading to the get-together, while Nina was walking backward and forward between wardrobes still trying to decide on her outfit.

'I'm going down now,' said Trixie with a last check in the wardrobe mirror.

Nina's bottom lip was pouting. 'I've got nothing to wear.'

Trixie rolled her eyes, and checked both wardrobes before pulling out a deep-red dress. 'You look gorgeous in this, you've had lots of compliments when you've worn it.'

Nina held the dress up. 'I'd forgotten I had this.'

'I'll see you down in the bar,' said Trixie, as she gave a little wave goodbye.

'Have fun creeping around your boss!' shouted Nina to the closing door. She went into her room and opened a side-table drawer. It contained over fifty hues of nail varnish. 'Now, what colour will go with this?'

For that particular evening, the hotel had literally split the building in half. Evie and her party had the west wing bar and restaurant, and Dave's party had the east wing with a separate bar and restaurant.

When Trixie entered the girls' bar, she found she had been outmanoeuvred by several of her colleagues, who were already gushing over Melinda. Nina's words about creeping around the boss pricked her conscience so she decided not to follow the pack. She just acknowledged Melinda with a smile when she accidentally caught her eye. Trixie mingled with the ever-growing group and spent time with Evie's friends and family from Scotland, who confessed to not really knowing anyone.

CHAPTER NINE

Ford and Jason followed the signs in the lobby and headed for the east wing bar. Despite following the signs all the way, Ford and Jason thought they must have gone wrong somewhere because all the men were dressed in formal dinner suits.

'Boys!' shouted Dave from across the room. He strolled over to them with his arms open wide and gave them each a man hug. 'I'm so pleased to have my oldest friends here.'

'Why is everyone dressed up like penguins?' asked Jason.

'You never told us about wearing dinner suits,' added Ford.

Dave laughed. 'Oh, it was just a joke we were having at work. Someone said they were going to wear their new dinner suit, and before we knew it, the whole mad bunch decided to dress up as well. I'll tell you, my work colleagues are nutters, you'll love them.'

'You told me and Jason it was an old hotel, but it's all posh.'

Dave laughed. 'What were you expecting, stone floors and flat caps? You are going to have a great time, and as an extra treat, we have Marie Blanc, the top Michelin chef providing tonight's meal.' Using his thumb and forefinger, Dave blew a loud whistle, a skill that Ford was envious of.

'Guys, guys!' bellowed Dave. The room quietened down. 'This is Ford and Jason, my old school friends. We met in primary school, and still keep in touch. Can you believe it?'

To Ford's alarm, Dave received a round of applause, as if he was doing it out of an act of charity.

Jason smiled shyly and said, 'I'm a transcendental beat poet and number one usher!'

Jason received another round of applause that Ford thought was a bit too sympathetic and could have sworn someone said, 'Aw, bless him'.

The noise level rose once more, as Dave took Ford and Jason aside. 'I've got my bosses here so I need to keep them sweet, but I'll catch up with you later. Just mingle and enjoy yourselves.' After giving them a final pat on the back, Dave rejoined a loud group at the end of the bar.

'Well, if it isn't Laurel and Hardy!' The voice belonged to Dave's brother, Conrad, who was four years older. He was slightly taller, slightly chunkier and, unlike his brother, beginning to thin on top. 'I was hoping you two wouldn't turn up,' he growled.

Even now, Ford struggled to understand how his best friend, who was so fun and open, could be related to a scowling, big-headed bully like Conrad.

'It's a pleasure to see you again, Podgy,' said Ford, using the childhood name they'd given Conrad because he was a fat kid.

Jason had never quite grasped the subtle concept of using childhood nicknames as an adult weapon, so just blurted out, 'Fuck off, Conrad, you fat cunt!'

Conrad gritted his teeth. 'I have a business empire, three houses and a top of the range BMW! What do you two good-for-nothings have? I'll tell you. Nothing!'

Ford found it hard to argue with that, he didn't have anything. 'Oh, just fuck off!' he said, taking himself slightly by surprise. The hypnotherapy was obviously working and he felt like the weight of niceness had been lifted off him.

'Come on, let's get a drink,' said Jason, dragging Ford toward the bar. 'I hope it was his bonnet that was bukakked.'

Brenda was busy behind the reception desk when she heard what she hoped was a death rattle from Old Jake's throat. She was slightly disappointed to find that he wasn't about to pop his clogs, but merely clearing his throat as he watched Nina walk down the wide stairs. Brenda followed his eyeline. The young lady in red looked gorgeous. Her blonde hair, the red of her dress and the light effects from the chandelier created a stunning vision. Brenda felt a twinge of envy. She had been just as pretty at that age and had turned heads when she entered a room. Now, the sight of young women just reminded her of her lost youth. She gave Nina a pretend smile and said, 'Have a lovely evening,' while hating her at the same time.

Old Jake's eyes continued to follow Nina. Brenda caught a glimpse of a smile on his lips and pondered whether it might just push his dodgy ticker over the edge if she persuaded him to watch some hardcore porn.

Nina made her entrance into the bar. She noticed straight away that she was the only one wearing a bright colour and wished she'd put on her black dress after all. As she hesitated, wondering whether to go and change, Evie caught sight of her.

'My God, Nina, you look gorgeous!' Evie rushed over and kissed Nina on both cheeks. 'Everyone! This is Nina, the girl I've been telling you about. She owns the Movie Poster Shop, and I defy any of you to ask a movie question that she will not know the answer to.'

Nina found, to her complete surprise, that she was the centre of attention. She became giddy with the compliments about her choice of dress and soon had an entourage that stayed with her for the rest of evening. Melinda even used her influence to have Nina sit beside her in the restaurant later that evening. Trixie gave up trying to get anywhere near Nina, but was secretly pleased that she was getting lots of attention.

Ford found out pretty quickly that he and Jason were definitely not the centre of attention. Any attempt at mingling with Dave's workmates was a waste of time. He did not know much about rugby union, skiing, golf or the benefits of owning

139

a second home abroad. He did know about cars, but found himself correcting those who bragged about the capability and market value of their sports cars. He gave up trying to mingle and found Jason by the bar. 'What do you think of it so far?'

'They're all fucking boring!' declared Jason. 'It's more like a company bonding weekend.'

'It will get better,' Ford assured him, as Old Jake, now wearing a waiter's outfit, announced in a croaky voice that the restaurant was serving dinner.

Ford and Jason were the last to sit down. They had to share a table with two pasty-faced accountants who debated the pros and cons of a certain spreadsheet program. Wine waiters appeared and Jason persuaded them to leave him bottles of both red and white wine.

'The one thing you get in Yorkshire is proper food and plenty of it,' said Jason, as he grabbed his knife and fork and sat waiting for the food to arrive like a five-year-old.

Ford was feeling hungry and was looking forward to stuffing his face with a hearty northern meal.

Several waiting staff swept into the room and promptly began placing a plate of food in front of each diner. 'Plate of food' was not quite the right term; it was a plate with a piece of food on it.

Jason peered down at a small square of what he guessed was Yorkshire pudding. It had a sliver of beef draped over it and a couple of drops of gravy splattered on top. The accountants enthused over the dish and closed their eyes with pure joy, as they tasted the morsel.

Several diners on other tables broke out in applause.

Jason sat holding his knife and fork, with a baffled expression on his face. 'What the fuck is this?' he said loudly.

'A work of art,' said the lesser pasty-faced accountant. 'Marie Blanc is a genius.'

Ford prodded his sliver of beef with a fork. 'She's got good eyesight, I'll give her that.'

They had to eat their morsel quickly before the dish was whipped away and replaced with another. The accountants clapped their hands on seeing the next work of art. It was a one-inch cube of pork with several peas on a bed of what Jason described as, 'tinned baby food'.

'It's her classic British tasting menu!' enthused the more pasty-faced accountant.

'Where did she learn her craft?' wondered Ford. 'Lilliput?!'

'I'm still hungry,' grumbled Jason, after shoving the latest piece of art into his mouth.

The next dish appeared; it looked to Ford like a fish finger with two burnt chips. That was followed by a chicken wing dabbed with barbecue sauce. The last savoury dish was a sausage on a spoonful of mash with half a dozen baked beans.

The less pasty accountant patted his stomach and proclaimed that he had been to heaven and back.

Jason grabbed Ford's arm. 'Am I sleeping? Am I having a nightmare?'

Ford prodded the sausage. 'No, you're not asleep, but this meal is turning into a nightmare.'

Two dessert dishes followed. A small slice of sticky toffee pudding with a thimble-sized pot of cold custard, and a strawberry sitting on two small cubes of ice cream.

Dave's brother, Conrad, was the first to leap to his feet, calling for the chef to make an appearance. The rest of the party, except Ford and Jason, were immediately on their feet applauding. The noise reached a crescendo when Marie Blanc finally appeared, wiping the sweat from her brow and humbly accepting the adulation.

Marie Blanc had what it took to reach the very top of her profession. She had a fiery temper from her French father and a foul mouth from her north-eastern mother. She was happy to resort to violence if anyone was fool enough to disagree with her, or mad enough to criticise her work. Several months ago, she had been secretly filmed trying to drown a chef de partie in a sink full of dishwater for undercooking a carrot. That had only added to her popularity. Critics praised her food mainly because they were afraid of the consequences of not doing so. Her reputation was so unimpeachable that to fail to appreciate her cooking would be an admission of dumb stupidity. Unfortunately, her shining star had fallen recently after she had been seen kicking a much beloved British theatre actor in the balls after he returned her renowned black pudding pâté uneaten. His excuse being he was a vegetarian.

Since the kicking episode, Marie had hit the five-star hotel circuit until the fuss died down enough for her to return to London.

Marie's contract required her to go round the tables and let the customers take selfies with her. Despite having total disdain for the general public, she did lap up the praise to boost her raging ego.

Ford and Jason had no idea what Marie looked like. They had not leapt to their feet along with the rest of the idiots, as Jason referred to them, and opted to polish off a bottle of wine instead.

Marie had one more table to visit here in the east wing before going over to the ladies' restaurant in the west wing. With a sigh of relief that she was near the end, she went over to the table where Ford and Jason were sitting. 'Did you enjoy your meal?' she asked with a false smile, waiting for the adulation.

'Very nice,' said Jason, handing her his plate. Jason had been brought up with the British way of complimenting meals even if they were terrible.

Previously, Ford had always opted for the 'very nice, thank you' reply as well, but now that he wasn't nice, he decided that he could tell the truth. He handed Marie his empty plate. 'Your chef might be very good, but she would have trouble filling an anorexic up with those helpings.'

Marie stood shell-shocked, holding the two plates.

Jason quickly glanced around the room and said to Marie in a hushed voice. 'Keep it to yourself, love, but is there any chance of ordering some cheese sandwiches? I'm starving.'

'Yer... yer bastard!' blurted Marie.

Jason was puzzled. 'Sorry?'

'You can't go around calling women "love" any more,' explained Ford. 'Women today will mark you down as a misogynist.'

'I don't know what a misogynist is,' confessed Jason. 'Besides, it sounds like the sort of word only a woman could come up with.'

The plates dropped from Marie's hands, leaving her fingers free to close around Jason's neck. 'Yer focking bastard!' she screamed.

'Okay! Forget the cheese sandwich!' croaked Jason.

Ford managed to prise Marie's hands off Jason, only for her to grab at his throat, screaming, 'I'll give you focking anorexic, yer bastard!'

The commotion soon attracted everyone's attention. It was Conrad who managed to pacify Marie by explaining that the two men she was trying to kill were total philistines.

'I'm Church of England!' protested Jason, rubbing his throat.

Dave rushed over just as Conrad led the tearful Marie away. 'Who's upset the chef?' Bodies parted to reveal Ford and Jason. 'What the hell have you done?' he demanded.

'We thought she was a waitress,' said Ford innocently. 'I was being helpful by handing her my plate and happened to mention the helpings were small.'

'And I asked if we could get some cheese sandwiches,' admitted Jason.

'What were you thinking? Marie Blanc is one of the world's top chefs. You could have told your grandchildren that you had actually eaten food prepared by her!'

The surrounding group nodded their agreement.

'Really?!' said Ford, who thought chefs were just glorified cooks at the end of the day.

Dave groaned and shook his head. 'I'm going to apologise to Marie and tell her that you are both retarded and have a drink problem.'

'I don't have a drink problem,' protested Jason.

Dave left to console Marie. The remaining group drifted away to the bar.

Jason grabbed his phone from his trouser pocket. 'I'm still starving.'

Ford peeked over Jason's shoulder and saw that he was looking at a pizza menu. 'Order a large pepperoni for me, I'll pay you back.'

'No need,' said Jason. 'I'll use your credit card like I normally do.'

Nina had started the evening by being tested on her movie knowledge, a test she passed with flying colours. She was now drinking heavily and deliberately doing bad impressions of movie stars to the raucous delight of everyone.

Trixie had witnessed Nina when she was at her funniest and knew without a shadow of doubt that in the morning she would come down to earth with a bump. She'd tried three times to tell Nina to hold back on the wine and eat something, but every time Nina said, 'Okay,' a voice would shout out, 'Hey, Nina! Do Meryl Streep,' or 'Do Tom Cruise,' and she would be off again.

Nina and Trixie were treated to the same Marie Blanc tasting menu as Ford and Jason. When put in front of Evie's party, the artistic morsels of food were enthused over, in the same fashion as with Dave's party.

After the meal, News had filtered through from the east wing that Marie Blanc had tried to kill two men because they thought she was a waitress. Not only that, they had said that the chef's meals were too small. A wave of disappointment swept through the room, followed by a gradual whispering about how shocked they all were, but they could see why someone might perceive the helpings to be small.

Evie's party migrated over to the east wing bar where the plan was for both groups to mingle for the rest of the evening. Once again, Nina attracted lots of attention, this time from Dave and his friends, who were just as enchanted by her movie knowledge and bad impersonations.

Trixie found herself talking to work colleagues she spoke to every day; the droning noise of the combined groups talking and laughing had started to give her a slight headache. After taking a couple of aspirin, she went for a stroll in the manicured gardens of the hotel. They were lit to show off the formal layout and the garden centrepiece, a huge cast-iron Victorian fountain. As Trixie approached the sound of trickling water, she heard male voices murmuring from a bench several metres away and caught a distinct smell of pizza.

Ford glanced up and saw Trixie. She turned and started walking back to the hotel. 'It's okay,' shouted Ford. 'We're friends of Dave and Evie; you don't have to leave because of us.'

Trixie stopped and turned. 'I was just getting some fresh air.'

'Would you like a piece of pizza?' offered Jason.

'You can have some of mine if you want,' said Ford. 'We bought too much,'

'Let me guess, you are the two men Marie Blanc tried to kill.'

'It was a misunderstanding,' said Jason with his mouth full of pizza.

Ford gave a brief description of the events, which made Trixie chuckle.

'I've met you once before,' observed Ford. 'You were dressed as a lion.'

'Were you at the fancy dress party?'

'I'm Ford, I was the Phantom judge.' He put a hand over half of his face.

Trixie smiled as she recalled pulling him and Nina apart. Not only that, she was sure he was the lost-looking man from the Orifice. 'I will have some pizza if that's okay. I'm still hungry after that meal.'

Jason held up his open pizza box. 'I have Hawaiian.'

Ford held up his box. 'Pepperoni! Have a piece of each.'

Trixie gratefully took two pieces and ate them with pure enjoyment. It had been a very long time since she'd eaten any takeaway pizza.

'It's Trixie, isn't it? I'm Jason. I met you once when I popped around to Dave and Morag's... I mean Dave and Evie's new flat.' And as a reminder, he added, 'The transcendental beat poet!'

'Ah, yes. I remember.' Trixie recalled Jason as the layabout friend who Evie moaned about for calling her Morag all the time.

Ford munched on his pepperoni pizza. 'Is your friend Nina here this weekend?'

'Yes, she's entertaining everyone with bad movie impersonations,' answered Trixie.

'It's no good,' said Jason, getting up quickly. 'I need a pee. I'll see you in there.' With that brief statement, he rushed off to the hotel.

Trixie sat beside Ford and they ate in silence apart from the trickle of water from the ornate fountain.

Ford was the first to speak. 'She's quite funny, your friend Nina. She makes me laugh.'

'She still goes on about losing the fancy dress competition,' giggled Trixie.

'I suppose she's here with her boyfriend or partner,' said Ford casually.

'No, no boyfriend.'

'Oh, right!' Ford waited for Trixie to finish eating before collecting up the pizza boxes. 'I might just go and say hello to her, I don't want to be rude.'

'You go,' said Trixie. She smiled as she watched him walk away.

The boys' and girls' groups had fallen back into couples now they were all in the same room. Ford strolled in and heard loud laughter from a group of people at the bar. He spotted Nina, she was standing beside Dave's brother, Conrad, looking as though she was having fun.

Dave was standing with Melinda in the group being entertained by Nina. He spotted Ford at the back of the room. 'Ford knows quite a bit about films!' he said loudly. 'Ford, give Nina a movie question, I bet she can answer it.'

'No, no,' protested Ford shyly.

'Go on!' insisted Dave. 'Any question, and no using Google to help.'

Nina was feeling confident, bordering on being cocky. She recognised the name Ford, and smiled as she recalled him being thrown out of the Orifice nightclub.

'Come on, Ford!' she said teasingly. 'Be a big boy and ask me a question.'

The noise level dropped to a murmur, as everyone waited for Ford's question. He knew lots of offbeat movie trivia, but thought it wouldn't be fair to ask her those, so remembering that Nina had dressed as Dorothy he said, 'What was Dorothy's surname in the movie *The Wizard of Oz?*'

Nina's smile froze on her face, her head went blank. She could not remember.

Trixie had just made her way back in when she heard Ford ask his question. She knew Nina's smile well enough to know that she did not have the answer.

Ford noticed Trixie and as she walked by, he touched her arm and whispered, 'It's Gale! Dorothy Gale.'

'Ask me a harder one!' said Nina, bluffing.

'Just tell him,' urged Conrad, with a leer at her cleavage.

Trixie had managed to take a pen out of her clutch bag and write *GALE* on the palm of her hand while heading toward Nina. With a final push to get in front of Conrad, she tugged the hem of Nina's dress.

Nina glanced down and saw the word on Trixie's palm.

Now, any normal woman would have just given the answer and been grateful not to embarrass herself. Nina, however, was no longer bordering on cocky, but was now one hundred and ten percent cocky.

'Does anyone here know the answer?!' shouted Nina with a hand cupped to her right ear.

'No!' came the mass reply.

Nina looked Ford in the eye and said with a dismissive snarl. 'It's Gale, Dorothy Gale.'

Conrad had googled it and already had the answer on his phone. 'It is Dorothy Gale!' he declared loudly.

A big cheer went up and Nina once again held court.

Ford looked for Jason, but he was nowhere to be seen, and after the escapade with Marie Blanc, Ford was confronted with a lot of cold shoulders. He reflected that not being nice had its drawbacks.

With a final glance back at the happy, smiling faces, Ford decided to call it a night, wishing he'd never been invited. But his departure did not go unnoticed. Nina and Trixie watched him walk away.

Ford trudged back up the main staircase to his room, the sound of laughter gradually diminishing until all he could hear was his footsteps on the smooth stone floor. It took him three attempts to unlock his door with his key card. He wanted to moan about it, but there was no one to moan to. The fact that he wanted to moan about something to someone else saddened him. He used to be fun. Every experience would have an element that would create joy, but the joy of life had been chipped away, day by day, hour by hour and minute by minute. Feeling sorry for himself, he headed straight for the minibar, took out two whiskey miniatures, screwed the tops off, and downed one. His intention was to drink them both, but he was not used to neat whiskey and it felt more like pain than pleasure.

The connecting door between his room and Jason's was locked. He could just make out the sound of splashing and seventies porn music. He envied Jason's ability to just be himself and do what the hell he wanted.

Ford sat on the bed and flicked through the satellite channels for a film to watch. He perked up when he found *Kick-Ass* just beginning. Feeling a lot happier, Ford laid back and enjoyed the next couple of hours. It was way past midnight when Ford was disturbed by a lot of shouting in the hallway. He climbed off the bed and peeked outside the door.

Nina had her shoes in her hands and was dancing in circles. Trixie was trying to coax her to keep moving along the hallway.

'Let's go clubbing, everybody!' shouted Nina. 'Yesss!'

Ford reluctantly opened his door fully. 'Do you need a hand?' he asked Trixie.

Nina stopped dancing. 'If it isn't the Phantom nut face!' she slurred.

Trixie gave a despairing smile. 'We're nearly there, but thanks anyway.'

Nina danced away, with Trixie chasing after her.

Ford closed the door, thinking that Nina might well have a serious drink problem.

CHAPTER TEN

Trixie had a restless night's sleep. She had kept the connecting door open after leaving Nina collapsed on her own bed. Trixie then had to put up with the sound of heavy snoring floating in from the other room. She finally fell asleep exhausted as it was getting light. At eight o'clock, she was woken by more noises from Nina's room. To her amazement, she found Nina sitting up in bed, watching breakfast TV.

'How do you feel?' she asked.

'I feel okay,' Nina assured her. 'In fact, I feel great!'

Trixie could not believe she wasn't suffering any after-effects from the night before. 'You're normally like the living dead after drinking the amount you did last night.'

Nina held up a small packet with *Hangover it gone!* written on it. 'I took two of these and, hey presto, within ten minutes, it really had gone!'

Trixie took the packet from Nina and read the contents. 'It doesn't say what it contains. It just says *may cause acute anxiety*. Where did you buy this?'

'I bought it online; it had very good reviews from some people in China.'

'Nina, what the hell are you thinking, taking dodgy medication? It can be dangerous!'

'They are not dangerous! Can I have them back now?'

'You must be joking! I'm keeping hold of these in case you collapse and the doctors want to know what you've taken.'

'Trixie, you talk to me like I'm some stupid girl!'

'Yes, I do, because you do stupid things!' Trixie examined the packet of *Hangover it gone!* tablets again. 'Are you sure you feel okay?'

'I feel fine, but I don't remember too much about last night. Who did this?' Nina pointed to her left arm. Written on it in ballpoint ink was a room number alongside a phone number.

'It must have been David's brother, Conrad. He was all over you like a rash last night.'

'Conrad? Oh, is he the stinking rich one?'

'Yes, he's the stinking rich one.'

Nina gave a coy smile. 'Conrad's so rich and good-looking, he's perfect for me.'

Trixie sighed. 'He's stinking rich, but an arsehole with it. Even his brother says that.'

Nina climbed out of bed. 'I think you're jealous because he likes me and not you. In any case, from what I do remember, he was perfectly charming.'

'Is being lecherous charming now?'

Nina jumped out of bed and headed for the bathroom. 'I'm scrubbing up and applying my natural make-up so it looks like I'm not wearing any, just in case I see him at breakfast.'

There were quite a few groggy heads in the hotel breakfast room, when Nina swanned in and said to everyone, 'Good morning!' The sight of Nina brought smiles to their washed out faces, as they wished her a good morning in return. Trixie followed her into the dining area, and they sat at a table that had their room numbers chalked on a small blackboard. It took a while for them to order what they wanted because of Nina's constant visitors. They all told her how much they had enjoyed last night and how much they were looking forward to the rest of the day.

Conrad, in jeans and a tee shirt that were snug enough to verge on restricting blood flow, strode over and bent down close to Nina. He said, 'You look ravishing, my dear,' breathing the smell of kippers all over her.

'Why, thank you, Conrad,' she managed, fighting the nausea from the smell of fish.

'I'm looking forward to our little hike today, maybe we could tackle these footpaths together.'

'That would be nice,' said Nina, trying not to look too eager.

He licked a morsel of kipper off his lip and whispered, 'I shall see you later!' before swaggering away.

'What shall we have for breakfast?' asked Trixie, as she perused the menu.

'Anything but kippers,' begged Nina.

Ford was groaning loudly. He was having a recurring nightmare where he was trapped in a large room; there were no walls, just doors, and on every door was a sign that said, *Please knock before entering.* Ford went frantically from door to door, knocking loudly and pleading to be let in. With a feeling of overwhelming dread, Ford banged as hard as he could on the last door in the room. He woke up with a start and sighed with the relief of knowing it had just been a bad dream. But the knocking continued.

'Ford! Are you awake?' Jason's head appeared from the connecting door.

Ford rubbed his eyes. 'I had that bloody dream again, the one with all the doors.'

Jason came in and sat on the edge of the bed. 'The doors have a symbolic meaning.'

Ford rubbed some sleep from his eye. 'What do you think it means?'

'Nine times out of ten, it means you worry about having a small knob.'

'I don't worry about that.' Ford lifted the duvet cover and peered under it. 'I know it's not big, but it's not that small.'

'You obviously think it is, on a subconscious level.'

Ford noticed Jason was already dressed. 'It's unusual for you to be up and about before me.'

'I think it's all these baths I'm having, I feel refreshed.'

'Well, I'll have a quick shower and then we can go down and get some breakfast.'

'I've already had mine,' said Jason, patting his stomach.

Ford, wearing just his boxer shorts, dragged himself out of the bed. 'What do you mean, "already had mine"?'

'I was going to give you a knock earlier, but I heard you groaning. I thought you must have pulled.'

Ford checked his watch. 'Christ! It's half nine!'

'You missed a nice breakfast. If you decide to have breakfast tomorrow, go in late like I did and you can get extra helpings before they close.'

'Oh, don't tell me I've missed out. I was looking forward to a fry-up. Bugger!'

Jason picked a piece of bacon out of his teeth. 'Dave wants us to meet by the entrance at half past for this hike thing.'

Ford went over to the mini bar and found a small packet of biscuits. 'I'm bloody hating this weekend,' he moaned before storming off into the bathroom.

Brenda was in charge of the boot room on the day of the walk, so had Old Jake with her to fetch and carry. He was at the top of a rickety ladder, with Brenda instructing him to lean over more to reach whichever shelf would cause him to lose his balance.

He had just begun to wobble on the shaky ladder when Trixie and Nina turned up.

'Hold on, Old Jake,' said Brenda, when she saw the two women. 'We don't want any accidents just yet. Ah! Ladies, how can we help you today?'

'I'm afraid I don't have any type of clothing for hiking,' said Nina. 'I've only ever walked around cities.'

'Don't you worry, we'll soon have you kitted out. What shoe size are you?'

'Eight and a half,' said Nina.

Brenda took a close look at her throat for signs of an Adam's apple. With feet that size, she could easily be one of those transformers or whatever they called themselves. 'Go along the rails and pick something out.' Brenda pointed to several rows of wet-weather gear on hangers. 'Jake will find you some hiking boots.'

Despite Trixie's recommendations about what to pick from the boot room, Nina opted for designer labels that she knew were very expensive. Fifteen minutes later, Nina admired herself in the dressing room mirror.

'Oh, these clothes make me look adventurous and sexy with it,' beamed Nina. 'I think Conrad will like this look.' The clothing was very stylish. The jacket and waterproof trousers were very flattering and very tight.

Trixie, in comparison, wore dowdy outdoor clothing that she had bought from a market stall when she was a student; along with a small green bobble hat that made her head look very big.

'Those trousers are way too tight,' commented Trixie, pointing to Nina's crotch. 'I'm seeing Camelot.'

Nina wriggled around in her tight trousers. 'I do not have Camelot! I've never, ever had Camelot!' She had once said, 'Camelot' by accident instead of camel toe, and now it was their preferred word. 'We're just walking,' Trixie reminded her. 'It's not a fashion show. It's about being comfortable.'

Nina checked her crotch in the mirror. 'It looks normal!'

'Things can swell up when you're walking; put on something looser.'

'No, I like these! It's not as though we're going to the South Pole, we're only going up and down a few hills.'

Trixie rolled her eyes. 'Okay, but don't say I didn't warn you.'

'Let's have a picture together,' suggested Nina, 'for my Facebook page. Brenda! Do you mind taking a picture?'

Brenda reluctantly took Nina's phone and had to snap several pictures because Nina would say, 'Just one more,' and pose like a fashion model, while Trixie just stood there in her unflattering outfit.

Nina laughed with joy when she saw the images. 'Trixie, I'm going to get these framed, it makes a change for me to look prettier than you.'

Trixie had never been a vain person. She was constantly told that she was very pretty, and that had become a millstone around her neck. She did not feel pretty and had always tried to dress down and not draw attention to herself. She broke into a smile when she saw the pictures, she liked looking dowdy, 'I might frame them as well!'

Brenda assured Nina that her own clothing would be sent to her room, and wished the pair a lovely day while still keeping up her hatred of them and their youth.

The group had begun to assemble outside the hotel, ready for the big walk. The young hotel porter handed out drinks bottles and snacks for the walkers to store in their rucksacks. Conrad had opted to wear shorts with long woollen socks that made him look like a Scoutmaster. He was talking very loudly to Evie and her friends when he caught a glimpse of Nina in her flattering outdoor clothing; he made his excuses and rushed over to her, even shoving Trixie aside to get next to Nina.

'Nina, you must let me walk with you, I insist,' he drooled. 'I'll be your guide.'

The one thing that pleased Nina more than being flattered was being flattered by someone who was very rich and good-looking.

'It would be my pleasure, Conrad,' she said with a flutter of her eyelashes.

The group set off for the big walk at ten thirty. The first part of the trek was fairly open so they walked in large groups. As the path began to climb upward, it was only possible to go two abreast, and Conrad eagerly took up Nina's offer to walk with her. After ten minutes of hiking side by side, he was huffing and puffing kipper breath all over her, as he bragged about how wealthy he was. The group stopped regularly to admire the views of the dales. It was only after the second stop that Trixie realised that Ford and Jason were missing. When she casually mentioned it to Nina, she replied, 'Good, they'll only spoil it anyway,' before rejoining Conrad, who wanted to point out some place of interest in the distance.

To be kitted out for the hike, Ford and Jason had followed the signs for the boot room, which turned out to be situated under their bedrooms. Brenda had managed to get Old Jake to climb to the top of the rickety ladder several times, but to her disappointment, he had never lost his balance, and his pallor never showed any promising, death-in-progress, blue tinge.

A false smile appeared on Brenda's face when Ford and Jason strolled in. 'Ah! You must be the last two for kit hire.'

'Sorry about that, I overslept,' explained Ford.

'Don't worry, we'll soon have you kitted out, won't we, Old Jake?'

'Yes, Brenda,' wheezed Old Jake.

'Let's start with your shoe sizes.'

'Eleven,' said Jason.

'Eight and a half,' sighed Ford.

Jason laughed. 'Small feet, I was right about that dream.'

Brenda sent Old Jake up the wobbly ladder to check the top shelves, while she led Ford and Jason over to the racks to try on some coats for size. After fifteen minutes, they were finally kitted out with the appropriate clothing and comfortable footwear and now at least looked the part of experienced walkers.

'Old Jake will take your possessions up to your rooms,' Brenda informed them. She was very pleased to see a light blue tint appearing at the edges of Old Jake's face and the tip of his nose. 'Just make sure you leave the hire clothing behind when you check out.'

Dave was waiting impatiently by the main entrance. He began tapping his watch when he spotted Ford and Jason sauntering toward him as if they had all the time in the world.

'It had to be you two,' moaned Dave. 'Everyone else made it on time, but oh, no! Not my oldest friends. They just turn up when they want to because they don't give a fuck!'

'We had to be kitted out!' protested Ford. 'The old boy getting the stuff only had one speed, dead slow.'

'I don't want your excuses,' snapped Dave. 'I'm still pissed off at you two for upsetting Marie Blanc. And I'm just pissed off; Evie's absolutely fuming about it.' Dave thrust a map in to Jason's hand. 'The route to the White Lion inn is highlighted, the rest of the group set off a few minutes ago so you should be able to catch them up. I'm going to put a burst on because, guess what? I'm supposed to be walking alongside Evie, seeing as it's our special weekend. Please, please don't fuck anything else up.' With a last glare at them, Dave shook his head and hurried after the main group.

'Is it me,' asked Jason, 'or is he getting more tetchy? He's turned into a right drama queen.'

'I think that's what true love does to some people,' reasoned Ford, feeling quite philosophical. 'It makes them highly strung and nuts.'

The young porter was still waiting to hand out drinks bottles and snacks to the last of the walkers. His smile hid the fact that he was pissed off about being late for his own cooked breakfast because these two were late. He swiftly handed Ford and Jason water bottles and energy snacks then dashed off before his own food got any colder.

'Do you know what?' said Ford. 'I think I'm experiencing what it's like to be unpopular.'

Jason shrugged. 'Feels normal to me.'

Sighing at the thought of walking for miles on end, they set off.

The well-trodden footpath that Ford and Jason were reluctantly traipsing along meandered upwards. After twenty minutes, they caught a glimpse of the main group up ahead in the distance.

Jason stopped to catch his breath. 'Do people really do this for fun?'

Ford halted; he felt a sharp twinge in his calf muscle. 'I know what you mean, I'm not enjoying this one bit.'

Jason spotted a footpath sign up ahead. It said, *Buckbotton ½ mile*. 'Let's have another check of that map!'

'What are you doing?'

Jason spread the map out on the ground. 'The White Lion Inn is just outside Buckbotton.' With his right index finger, he pointed to a section on the map, 'We're here and the village is just over Low Peak, up ahead. It's another seven miles going by Dave's route.'

Ford glanced up at the main group ahead then looked guiltily at the footpath sign. 'No, no, no. It's cheating.'

'What if I told you that we probably haven't even walked a mile yet?'

Ford wrestled with his conscience for several seconds. 'Let's have a look at that map again.' It was true. They could easily cut a lot of mileage off the walk. 'It wouldn't feel right,' insisted Ford.

'All this walking is stuff they like to do. I don't think it's fair to make us do it.'

'They are paying for everything,' Ford reminded him.

'That's why we do it secretly. We'll nip over the top, have a wander around the village and tag on to them when they come

158

through. No one will be any the wiser. Come on, Ford. You said you weren't nice any more. Well, prove it.'

Ford had a feeling of guilt, but that soon went away when he thought about trudging up and down hills for another seven miles, and Jason was right, he was no longer nice. 'Let's go!'

They headed up toward Low Peak with a renewed energy that could only come from knowing that they were cheating and no one would ever, ever find out.

CHAPTER ELEVEN

Fifteen minutes after Ford and Jason had taken the short cut, they were at the top of Low Peak, admiring the panoramic view of the dales landscape. Jason pointed out the distant group. From their vantage point, the walkers looked like multicoloured ants. The two grown men giggled like naughty schoolchildren and watched the hikers for several minutes, until they moved out of sight.

The footpath followed a serpentine route down to the village, with just a few stiles to clamber over. They made their way through a field of grazing sheep without a care in the world till they came to the outskirts of the village. As luck would have it, there was a tearoom close to the path where they entered the main square.

'I think we deserve a cup of tea after all that walking,' declared Jason, smugly.

'And a cake or something,' added Ford. 'I'm starving.'

The tearoom was light and airy with floral wallpaper. Standing behind a small counter was a slim, middle-aged woman wearing an apron that matched the walls.

'Take a seat and I'll come and get your order,' she said bluntly.

They cast off their rucksacks and coats, and sat at a window table overlooking the square. The woman shuffled over, notebook in hand. 'My name is Gracie, I will be your waitress for this table.'

Ford glanced around; there were no other waitresses or customers. 'Thank you.'

Gracie suddenly froze, held her hand up and said, 'Shush!'

A car drove by with a noisy exhaust.

Gracie relaxed and continued as though nothing had happened. She handed them a plastic-coated menu. 'The ginger cake is off today. So is the carrot cake. And the chocolate cake. And I'm not sure about the Victoria sponge. Hold on...' Gracie turned toward a serving hatch by the counter, and shouted, 'Archie!'

The smiling face of a chubby 50-year-old man appeared through the small space. 'Yes, my sweetheart?'

'Victoria sponge,' she said coldly, 'is it on?'

Archie shook his head. 'All out, my rose petal.'

'The Victoria sponge is off,' relayed Gracie, just in case they were both deaf.

Gracie suddenly froze, held her hand up once more and said, 'Shush!' A bus rattled past.

'What would you like?' asked Gracie with one ear cocked to the street noise.

Ford glanced at the menu. 'Well, I'm going for a mug of tea and two toasted teacakes.'

Before jotting the order down, Gracie turned to the serving hatch and shouted, 'Archie!'

Archie's smiling, chubby face appeared. He had crumbs around his mouth. 'Yes, my sweetheart?'

'Teacakes?!'

Archie's head disappeared for several seconds before re-appearing. 'Sorry, my turtle dove, we're out of teacakes.'

Gracie suddenly held her hand up again and said, 'Shush!'

Another car passed by.

Jason decided to get his order in before any more traffic came along. 'Can I have a mug of tea and a jam donut?'

'Archie!' yelled Gracie. 'Jam donuts! Are they on?'

Archie's chubby smiling face emerged again. He had even more crumbs around his mouth. 'Sorry, my sweetness, what was that again?'

'Jam donuts! Are they on?'

Archie disappeared for thirty seconds before returning with a shake of his head. He had sugar and jam around his mouth. 'The jam donuts are all out, my precious angel.'

Gracie suddenly held her hand up yet again and said, 'Shush!'

Ford and Jason glanced at each other with puzzled expressions.

Happy that whatever noise she had heard was not the one she was listening out for, Gracie said, 'The jam donuts are all out.'

Ford was glad that they were not in a hurry. 'Excuse me, Gracie,' he said, in the most charming voice he could muster. 'Would it be possible to tell us what is on?'

Gracie held her hand up for quiet, while she angled an ear toward the window. Content that it was nothing, she shouted, 'Archie! What's on?!'

Archie's smiling face made another appearance at the serving hatch. He had crumbs and icing around his mouth. 'Sorry, my sweetness, what was that?'

'What cakes are on?' she bawled.

Archie's chubby face disappeared for several seconds before reappearing with chocolate crumbs around his mouth. 'Sorry, my loveliness, we only have fruitcake left.'

'I know!' said Ford quickly. 'You only have fruitcake left. Well, I'll order for us both: tea and fruitcake for two, please.'

Gracie wrote down the order on her pad. 'Archie!' she screamed.

Archie's genial chubby face appeared yet again. He was licking his lips. 'Yes, my angel of light?'

'Two teas and two fruitcakes!'

'Coming right up,' beamed Archie.

Gracie held her hand up. 'Shush!' she demanded.

Ford and Jason could just make out the sound of a phone ringing. Gracie dashed out of the tearoom and ran over to the red phone box across the square. Her phone conversation only lasted a few seconds. Ford and Jason watched her march back

162

in with a disgruntled expression on her face. 'Little buggers,' she groused, as she went and stood behind the counter.

'I wonder what that was all about,' whispered Jason.

A door by the serving hatch swung open, pushed by the wide expanse of Archie's fifty-inch waist. He hummed a non-existent tune, as he carried over the tea and cakes on a tray. 'Tea and fruitcake for two!' He grinned good-heartedly, as he placed the tray down and unloaded the items onto the table.

'Thank you,' said Ford and Jason in turn.

'Enjoy!' replied Archie, with a flourish of his right hand.

Jason took a quick bite of the fruitcake. 'It's delicious!'

Archie chortled. 'I'll take your word for that. To be honest, I'm not a great lover of fruitcake.'

'If I was a gambling man,' stated Ford, in pretend deep thought, 'I would have bet my house and my life savings on you not having a liking for fruitcake.'

Archie laughed with surprise. 'Isn't that strange? You must have a sixth sense,' he chuckled, before waddling back to the kitchen.

'No, just two eyes,' smirked Jason.

After two hours of rambling, Trixie noticed Nina was walking oddly. At the next viewpoint, she pulled her to one side. 'Are you okay? You seem to be limping or something.'

'I'm chafing!' muttered Nina, confidentially.

'Chafing?' repeated Trixie. 'Where?'

Nina leant close to Trixie's ear and whispered, 'My bits!'

Trixie whispered back, 'What do you mean by "bits"?'

Nina checked no one was in listening distance. 'Camelot!'

Trixie burst out laughing, which drew the attention of the rest of the group.

Nina was not happy with her friend's outburst. 'It's not funny, I'm in agony.'

'I did say!' giggled Trixie.

'I just hope there's a chemist on the way.'

'Don't worry,' said Trixie with a reassuring smile. 'It's not far to the village now, and we'll find something to soothe the pain.'

Nina gritted her teeth for the last twenty minutes of the walk. Thankfully, she saw rooftops in the near distance. There was just a shallow riverbed to cross before they entered the village.

There was no chemist, but there was a store that sold a bit of everything, going by the window display. Nina muttered, 'Lady things,' to Conrad, 'We'll catch you up!' before grabbing Trixie's hand and leading her into the store.

Donna Thwaite had worked part-time in the store for the last ten years, from when she had just been a Saturday girl. Her schoolteachers had predicted great things for her; she was very intelligent and had the choice to go to Oxford or Cambridge university. Her dreams of leaving the village had been shattered when she became pregnant at 17 years old. Now, she was the mother of two children and married to a sheep farmer. These days, Donna watched the world go by from the shop window, wondering what her life would have been like if events had turned out differently.

An old-fashioned bell above the shop door gently jingled. To keep her mind active, Donna would try to guess what the customers wanted as soon as they walked in. She observed the two women who had just entered together. They were obviously tourists and out on a long walk, so probably with the group that had just passed through. They were of a similar age, so likely to be childhood friends. One had trekked before because her clothing was old and used. The other woman was glamorous and wearing designer clothes that were far too tight for her. Because they did not fit that well, Donna guessed they were staying at, the Hotel; it was the only place that hired out that type of wet-weather clothing. Their boots were wet, which meant they must have walked the dales pass, which was about seven miles. Tight clothes and seven miles of walking up and down dales could have two possible effects for a novice walker: chafing or a blister. Neither of them were limping badly, so Donna stepped out from behind the counter, went straight over to the medical section, and returned just as Nina and Trixie approached the till.

Before Nina could ask about lotions, Donna placed a tube down on the counter and waited to see if she was correct. The surprised expressions on the women's faces as they looked at each other told her she was right.

'That will be three pounds fifty, please,' said Donna.

Nina handed her the money. 'How did you know?'

Trixie was completely baffled. 'There is no way you…'

'A lucky guess,' interrupted Donna. She also guessed they were going to the White Lion Inn. The size of their rucksacks suggested they were only carrying the minimum needed for a seven-mile walk, and the inn catered for large parties. 'Enjoy your meal at the White Lion; the food is very good there.'

Nina and Trixie nervously said, 'Thank you,' at the same time.

Donna's brain had just that second solved a puzzle that she had been pondering over for a while. Now, all the clues had fallen into place. 'Oh, by the way, two friends from your group are hiding down by the bridge.'

Nina and Trixie hurried out of the store, more baffled than ever.

Outside, Trixie gazed back at Donna, standing motionless behind the counter. 'A hundred years ago, they would have burnt a woman like her!'

'I would have burnt her twice just to make sure,' declared Nina.

Ford and Jason spent a leisurely hour in the tearoom watching Gracie suddenly stop what she was doing and order everyone to 'Shush,' whenever she detected a noise from outside in the street. With time on their side, they had treated themselves to another tea and piece of fruitcake, which Archie cheerfully brought out to them. While making small talk, Archie told them that he and Gracie had lived in the village for twenty years since taking over the tearoom business. The next time Gracie ran outside to the red phone box, Ford asked Archie why she kept listening out for the phone ringing. Archie explained that Gracie belonged to the Dales Voluntary Rescue Service. The red phone box was the only reliable phone line in the village, so if the rescue service were needed, it would ring. Unfortunately, the local schoolchildren knew this and would call it quite often.

Gracie stomped back into the tearoom. 'The little buggers,' she said, before running out again to the phone box because it was ringing.

Once they had paid up and left the tearoom, Jason figured they had forty-five minutes to kill before they could tag on to the main group. To fill the time, they took a leisurely stroll around the village. In the middle of Buckbotton was a two-hundred-year-old limestone bridge across the shallow river. They found a quiet spot down by the base of the bridge that was hidden by hedging. They sat on the riverbank watching the glistening water flow past.

'I could quite easily get into this walking,' said Jason, as he threw a pebble into the river. 'It's relaxing.'

'It's definitely relaxing the way you do it.'

There was the sound of chatter and stomping of boots along the road.

Jason began to giggle. 'It's them!' he whispered.

Ford stifled his own laughter and made a shush motion with a finger to his lips. The chatter and the sound of footsteps began to subside. They grabbed their rucksacks and tiptoed back up to the road. They waited a full thirty seconds before raising their heads up to check if it was all clear. Instead of seeing the main group walking through the village, they came face-to-face with Nina and Trixie.

There was a moment of shock for both parties before Nina blurted, 'What are you two doing?'

'I wasn't doing anything!' said Jason, resorting to schoolboy defence mode.

Trixie smiled. 'You two are supposed to be a mile behind us.'

'We walked quickly,' claimed Ford. 'We like to speed walk.'

Nina was not happy to see Ford and his friend Jason. They were nothing but troublemakers. She looked them up and down suspiciously. 'Why aren't your boots wet?'

They both gazed down.

'They're waterproof?' tried Jason, thinking that he should say something.

Nina gasped in shock. 'You haven't done all of the walk!'

Ford held his hand up. 'I confess, we didn't do a tiny bit of the route. We took a wrong turn.'

Nina was enraged. 'I've just chafed myself raw doing that bloody walk.'

'Maybe your clothes are too tight,' suggested Ford, helpfully.

'Maybe your mouth is as big as your fat face!' snapped Nina.

Trixie put her body between them. 'Let's keep things calm, it's just a walk.'

'For some of us,' moaned Nina, 'it was a long one. I'm sure Evie would like to know what cheats David's friends are.'

'It's my fault,' sniffled Jason. 'Only Ford knows it, but I have a heart condition and he was extremely worried that the walk would put undue stress on my weak heart. So, we took a shortcut.'

Nina had a sudden surge of guilt and felt sorry for him; she could feel a tear welling in her eye.

Ford burst out laughing. 'No one is stupid enough to believe a story like that!'

'I liked the little sniffle,' laughed Trixie.

Jason chuckled at his own lame attempt.

Nina did not see the funny side of it at all. 'Cheating! And now making fun of people with heart conditions. Well, I just

167

hope everyone else in the group thinks it's funny because I know for a fact that Evie's dad takes statins!'

Trixie, Ford and Jason glanced at each other and burst out laughing.

Nina stamped her feet in frustration. 'We'll see if David and Evie have a good laugh at my expense when I tell them what you did, shall we?'

Ford held his hands up in submission. 'Okay, if it bothers you that much, I'll tell him in the pub; it's only a walk at the end of the day.'

'So you should,' spluttered Nina in her most righteous voice.

'How far did you walk?' asked Trixie.

'A mile or two,' shrugged Ford.

'Is that all?' whined Nina.

'I don't know about everyone else,' declared Trixie, 'but I'm hungry.'

The four of them set off on the ten-minute walk to the White Lion Inn.

Trixie and Nina walked a little way ahead.

'Why does it bother you that they took a short cut?' asked Trixie. 'It's supposed to be a fun weekend.'

'That Ford deliberately winds me up,' complained Nina. 'I loathe the man.'

Trixie grinned. 'He's okay, you just take him the wrong way.'

Nina winced, as the chafing resumed. 'I hope this lotion works, I can't walk another seven miles like this.'

The White Lion Inn was in an idyllic setting with views of the dales and distant moorland. In front of the picturesque building, a babbling brook ran alongside the large open patio area.

As soon as they entered the inn, Nina rushed past the bar in search of the ladies' toilet. Trixie spotted Evie, who waved her over to the table where she was sitting. A buffet was set out on tables beside a large open fireplace that had one solitary log

168

burning away. The main group were already halfway through their drinks and helping themselves to food.

Ford and Jason attracted no interest apart from a barman who asked what they would like to drink. Jason said, 'Priorities first, let's get the beers in,' and asked for four pints of local bitter just in case the bar got busier later.

Ford surveyed the room for Dave; he saw him chatting merrily away to his work friends. He took his two pints off Jason. 'I'll grab Dave after I've had a pint and tell him what we did.'

Nina entered from the ladies' toilet without the slightest wince. With a sneer at Ford as she passed him, she found Trixie and sat on the empty chair beside her.

The chatter in the bar subsided. Ford glanced up. Dave and Evie were standing in the middle of the room, asking for attention. 'Well done, everyone, for reaching the halfway point!' Dave praised them. Evie applauded everyone. The group applauded Dave and Evie in return.

'We're proud of all of you!' proclaimed Dave.

Evie fidgeted with excitement. 'Seeing as you have all done brilliantly, we have a surprise. Because the walk back is not too strenuous, David and Conrad have found out that we can add another two miles to the route on the way back.' Evie began to weep with joy. 'So we can visit the beautiful church where my Nana had her ashes scattered.'

The news received good-hearted applause from the group, and Evie was given lots of hugs by her family.

Nina leant close to Trixie's ear. There was a sob in her voice, 'I can't walk all those miles, I don't have enough lotion for all those miles.'

Trixie wasn't keen on walking nine miles with Nina whingeing all the way. She had a thought. 'Nina, can you walk a mile or two?'

It took a second for the penny to drop with Nina. She glanced around and saw Ford making his way over to Dave. She made a beeline for him, barging people out of the way, and headed him off.

'I'm just doing it!' said Ford, annoyingly.

'Wait!' pleaded Nina, pulling him by the arm to one side. 'You don't need to say anything. Are you going back to the hotel the short way?'

'I suppose we probably will.'

'Take me with you,' begged Nina.

Ford was puzzled by this sudden change. 'What's come over you? Has it got something to do with the chafing?'

Nina had to fight the urge to raise her voice. 'I am not discussing my chafing with you! Will you take me back or what?'

Ford shrugged his shoulders. 'Okay, but Dave and Evie must never know.'

'I promise I won't say anything,' confirmed Nina. 'But you've got to promise as well.'

'I promise…'

'And your friend!'

Ford sighed. 'I promise me and Jason won't tell a soul. Happy now?'

Nina smiled for the first time since hearing about the extra two miles. 'I'm happy!'

The stop at the inn lasted for an hour and a half. Nina relaxed with the help of three large glasses of white wine and once more became the centre of attention. Ford and Jason shared some time with Dave at the bar, with Ford constantly glancing over at Nina, who was flirting with Conrad for most of the time. Everyone declared the pub lunch a success, and they were all in a great mood for the trek back. Dave and Evie informed the group that it was time to be moving, and ten minutes later, with the extra two miles added to their maps, they were all assembling outside the inn. Conrad once more latched on to Nina and insisted he walk by her side. Nina had to think quickly, otherwise she would have to do the torturous nine miles. 'I don't think it's fair that you have all the leadership qualities and you're not allowed to be the leader.'

Conrad moved in close and breathed tuna fish over her. 'I could be the leader if I wanted, but I want to be with you.'

Nina tried again. She batted her eyelids. 'A man that leads is a real man,' she said coyly. 'And it's not fair on you that I might have to walk at the rear with Trixie.' Nina whispered, 'Between you and me, she's struggling and too proud to ask for help, so I'm going to carry her rucksack for her and inspire her to keep going.'

Conrad glanced at Trixie and shook his head. 'Some people are just lazy.'

'That's why I want you to lead the group back,' insisted Nina. 'You're a natural leader and I don't like it that you're not getting enough respect.'

Conrad pulled his shoulders back. 'You're right, and just for you, I will take the responsibility.'

Nina blew him a kiss; he gave an arrogant smile in return and marched to the front of the group.

'Follow me, everyone!' he ordered. 'I know the route.' Conrad stomped off with the main group trailing behind him like sheep.

After watching the group disappear around a corner, the four conspirators strolled back to the village. After the food and drink, they were all in a relaxed mood. Even Nina had seemed to brighten up, knowing that it was just a mile or so back. As they passed the store where Nina and Trixie had had their unsettling experience, Donna opened the door and called out to them, 'Watch out for the clouds!' before retreating into the shop.

'That was odd,' remarked Ford.

'I think she's some sort of nutcase,' surmised Jason. 'You get lots of 'em around these parts. It's the inbreeding.'

'Oh, well,' joked Ford, 'as long as it's a solid fact and not some wild, sweeping statement.'

Nina quickened her step. 'That woman scares me.'

'We had an encounter with her earlier in that store,' explained Trixie. 'She knew what we wanted to buy, where we were going and even said two friends were hiding by the bridge, and lo and behold, we spotted you two.'

'She did get the bit about friends wrong,' Nina corrected her, walking ahead.

'Don't take any notice of her,' advised Trixie. 'She's in a bit of discomfort.'

'Thank God we're not walking nine miles with her,' laughed Jason.

Ford had estimated it would take them twenty minutes to reach the top of Low Peak. So far, they had been walking for thirty minutes, and there was still a steady climb to go.

'You said it would only take twenty minutes,' carped Nina, for the fifth time since the twenty minutes had elapsed.

Ford was becoming slightly irritated by Nina's constant whingeing. 'It would be closer to twenty minutes if you didn't keep stopping and moaning at me. Like I said, I'm not an expert hiker of the Yorkshire Dales! I guessed twenty minutes and I guessed wrong.'

'You should have guessed better!' Nina suddenly froze like a statue. 'Oh. My. God. I need more lotion!'

They had stopped on an open part of the route with no cover in sight. Trixie found the tube in Nina's rucksack and handed it to her. She quickly took the top off.

Ford and Jason just stood watching her.

'Turn around then!' demanded Nina. 'Trixie, make sure they don't peek. I don't trust either of these perverts.'

Trixie made Ford and Jason face her while Nina unzipped her tight trousers and applied the lotion.

Ford gazed at Trixie's face, her brown eyes were so beautiful that he had to look away.

172

Nina groaned with relief. 'I'm nearly done, just make sure the perverts don't try to catch a glimpse.'

'It's heart-warming to know that a bond of trust and friendship has developed between us,' commented Ford, which made Trixie laugh out loud.

'All done,' gasped Nina, as she managed to zip up her trousers. 'Let's go.'

They set off and ten minutes later they were at the top of Low Peak, admiring the views.

Jason pointed out the hotel in the distance and the path they would be taking down.

'How long will it take to walk?' asked Nina.

Jason turned toward her. 'With breaks for lotion and moaning, about forty minutes.'

With no urgency to move on, they sat on the ruins of an old drystone wall to rest and have a drink. The earlier clear blue sky had been replaced with vast stretches of grey cloud.

'It's a breath-taking view,' said Ford, breaking the silence.

Nina stood up. 'I can only get emergency calls,' she grumbled, as she held her phone up above her head.

'What are you doing?' asked Trixie.

'I want to check my emails.'

Jason was also holding his phone high above his head. 'I did have emergency calls, but even that's gone now.'

'Why don't you just enjoy the fabulous views?' asked Trixie. 'You can check your emails later.'

Nina lifted her eyes from her phone. 'It's landscape, I get it.'

'Landscape?!' blurted Ford incredulously. 'It's the Yorkshire Dales! There is no other landscape like it.'

Nina sighed and took another look. 'I see views and I see some white stuff.'

From the east, a white mist rolled in, erasing the views as it approached.

Ford stood up. 'I think it's low cloud.'

'Here's one for you,' said Jason. 'Is cloud mist or fog? I'm not sure.'

'Whatever it is,' replied Trixie, getting to her feet, 'it appears to be thick.'

'Let's link hands,' suggested Ford. 'We could easily lose each other in dense fog.'

'Or dense mist,' added Jason.

'I'm only holding hands with Trixie,' protested Nina, 'and no one else!'

Ford held Trixie's hand in his left and Jason's in his right. 'It's important that we stay together.'

Within a minute, they were engulfed in thick cloud, giving them visibility of just a few inches.

'There's a strong breeze, so it should thin out soon,' pointed out Ford.

'I don't like it,' gasped Nina. 'I don't like it… I can't breathe!'

'Just stay calm, everything's fine,' Trixie reassured her.

After a few seconds of silence, they heard animal footsteps, followed by a sheep's, 'Baa!'.

'What was that?' screamed Nina.

'It's only sheep,' explained Ford. 'They've probably heard our voices and headed for the sound.'

'Sheep!' shrieked Nina. 'I'm scared of sheep! Make them go away!'

There were more bleats and the sounds of clomping hoofs; the sheep seemed to be surrounding them.

'It's funny,' said Ford, trying to lighten the mood, 'but I don't remember seeing any sheep when we walked up earlier.'

'They must be ghost sheep!' joked Jason. 'Woooo!'

Nina let out a screeching wail, broke free from Trixie and ran away, screaming at the top of her voice, 'Ghost sheep! Help!'

'Come back!' pleaded Trixie.

'Bloody hell, Jason,' moaned Ford. 'Why did you say that?'

'It was a joke. I didn't know she was going to go bonkers.'

Nina stopped running in the dense mist long enough to hold the phone close to her eyes and call 999.

'Help!' she pleaded. 'I'm being attacked by ghost sheep in the fog!' She heard a bleat and ran screaming again.

Gracie had just taken an order for two slices of fruitcake from a pair of elderly ladies when she heard the faint ring of the telephone from the red phone box. By the fifth ring, Gracie had swung the heavy glass door open and picked up the receiver.

'Dales Voluntary Rescue Service! Gracie speaking!'

The voice at the other end of the phone line belonged to Sergeant William Truman, from the police station over in Hawes. 'Gracie, we just had a call from a woman who's lost in the fog. Her phone signal dropped off before she could tell us where she was. According to the weather people, the only fog around here is low cloud up on Low Peak. It should clear soon, but the woman seemed to be hysterical and in fear of being attacked by... hold on, I wrote it down... goats and sheep.'

'Goats?' queried Gracie.

'Southerner,' said Sergeant Truman, as the only explanation needed.

'I'm on it,' snapped Gracie, as she gave the phone a salute. 'Leave it to me, Sarge!'

Before Sergeant Truman could say, 'Keep me updated,' Gracie was out of the door and running back to the tearoom.

The reason for Gracie's enthusiasm was that she was just one rescue away from obtaining the sought-after golden bobble hat: the reward for attending one hundred rescues for the Dales Voluntary Rescue Service. Gracie would be the first woman to reach the milestone in dales history.

She startled the two elderly ladies, as she burst back into the tearoom, flinging her apron through the serving hatch. She grabbed her rescue rucksack from behind the counter. 'Archie! See to the customers! I'm on a shout!' And with those orders echoing around the tearoom, she ran out the door. Archie's smiling, crumb-covered face appeared at the serving hatch. 'Okay, my tulip petal.'

CHAPTER TWELVE

Ford, Trixie and Jason kept their hands linked and their arms spread wide in the hope of catching Nina, as she shrieked in fear, running in random directions.

'Stay where you are!' pleaded Trixie.

'The ghost sheep are after me!' screamed Nina, as she veered off in another direction.

Trixie voiced her concern. 'This is not like her.'

'She's absolutely one hundred and fifty percent nuts!' declared Jason.

'Oh, my God. I just remembered!' said Trixie. 'Nina took some dodgy hangover pills this morning. When I checked the label, it said, *may cause acute anxiety*.'

Nina ran past, screaming, 'Ghoooost sheeeeep!'

'That explains things,' said Ford, while listening intently to figure out which direction she was heading in now.

Nina's screaming was getting louder.

'She's coming this way! Get ready,' warned Ford.

Trixie had seen *The Scream* by Edvard Munch in an exhibition earlier that year, and to her astonishment, the painting appeared out of the mist in the shape of Nina.

'I've got her!' shouted Jason, as he managed to grab Nina's jacket.

They quickly surrounded her in a threesome bear hug.

Nina had a look of terror on her face and was breathing heavily.

Trixie put her face inches from Nina's. 'You're safe, no harm will come to you.'

Nina's breathing slowed at the same time as the mist began to lift, disappearing just as quickly as it had come. 'Back off, you perverts,' snapped Nina, as she pushed Ford and Jason away.

'And she's back!' declared Jason.

The sun came out and distant views reappeared. To their surprise, they were only a short way from where they had been sitting earlier and, oddly, no sheep were in sight. With Nina assuring Trixie that she felt fine, they headed down the path back to the hotel.

In her excitement to save the lost walker, Gracie had broken the golden rule of waiting for a fellow rescuer to buddy up with. As she stomped up to Low Peak, Gracie kept her fingers crossed that the woman who was lost might have really hurt herself by now. With any luck, she might even have a life-threatening injury.

For a woman in her fifties, Gracie was incredibly fit and was striding on to the top of Low Peak in less than fifteen minutes. Gracie was utterly disappointed, to say the very least, when she reached the summit and found no one there; not even any low cloud, nor even a single sheep, never mind a goat. The golden bobble hat had been so close, and now she would have another painful wait for a member of the public to get into difficulties. The waits were getting longer because the selfish public took more notice of the weather and warning signs. Gracie decided to check the lower areas in the desperate hope that someone was fighting for their life and in extreme pain, but there wasn't a sick or healthy person in the area. With all hope of finding anyone to rescue gone, Gracie decided to head back, only to observe a wall of low cloud sweeping toward her. Within seconds, she was blinded, with no way of knowing how far away she was from the main path. The expert advice in weather conditions like this was to stay put, and wait for the cloud to pass. She had given that advice herself on many occasions.

After waiting thirty seconds, she decided that her advice was for amateurs only. Anyway, she knew the terrain like the back of her hand. It only took six steps for Gracie to find an unexpected rabbit hole and break her left ankle. She screamed in pain and vowed to start eating wild rabbits from now on.

As the four visitors made their way down from Low Peak, a piercing scream from up above echoed around the dale. Ford stopped in his tracks and stared back the way they had come. 'What the hell was that?'

'It's probably one of those ghost sheep,' joked Jason, also looking toward the summit.

Trixie stopped and joined them in turning to look back up the path to Low Peak. 'That cloud is back. Do you think someone might have hurt themselves?'

Nina reluctantly halted. She was keen to get back to the hotel as soon as possible. 'Let's keep going, I'm in agony!'

There was another piercing scream from above.

Ford stared into the mist shrouding the summit of Low Peak. 'I think we should go back and check that no one needs our help.'

'I'm the one who needs help,' moaned Nina, as she tugged at different parts of her trousers in a vain attempt to get comfortable.

'Okay,' said Ford, pondering the best option to take. 'Jason and me...'

'Jason and I,' corrected Nina.

'Jason and me,' continued Ford, ignoring her, 'will go back up and have a quick check. You girls can find your own way from here.'

'Be careful!' urged Trixie.

'We'll try not to get attacked by the ghost sheep!' laughed Jason.

Nina glared at Ford and Jason. 'If you tell anyone about that, I'll turn you both into ghosts!'

179

'She's a right barrel of laughs, that one,' said Jason.

The two of them slogged back up to Low Peak. After ten minutes, they had entered the thickening cloud. Worried about getting lost themselves, they kept to the path for fear of losing their way back down again.

'Hello!' shouted Ford. 'Anyone up here?!'

After two seconds of silence, Jason said, 'No one here, let's go.'

'Over here!' sobbed a voice in the distance.

'Keep sobbing!' instructed Ford. 'We'll home in on you!'

'I'm in so much pain!' cried Gracie.

'That's good!' Ford praised her. 'I mean good that we can hear you, not that you're in pain!'

Ford and Jason linked hands, as they slowly edged toward the sobs.

'We're close!' called out Jason. 'What's your name?'

'Gracie!'

'Can you just cry out in pain a bit louder, Gracie?!' asked Ford.

'I'm in bloomin' agony here!' she screamed.

'That's good,' said Jason encouragingly.

'Just over to the right,' suggested Ford.

Jason edged over and accidentally stood on Gracie's broken ankle. She let out a piercing, sobbing scream.

Jason crouched down beside her. 'You can stop screaming now.'

Squatting close to Gracie, Ford recognised her from the tearoom. The Dales Voluntary Rescue Service rucksack was by her side. Ford smiled. 'The dales rescue lady… I'll tell you what, this is great example of irony.'

Gracie sobbed in pain. 'I don't give a damn about irony.' She grabbed Ford's arm. 'We need to contact the rescue services. My ankle's broken in two places. It was just in one place, but then you two turned up.'

'I still don't have a signal,' noted Jason, checking his phone again.

'My walkie-talkie,' sobbed Gracie, 'I dropped it. It should be nearby.'

'Here's a thing,' pondered Ford. 'Is it walkie-talkie or should it be two-way radio?'

'Just bloomin' find it!' screamed Gracie. 'I'm in so much pain.'

Ford and Jason went on their hands and knees in search of the walkie-talkie.

'Found it!' declared Jason, and knelt on Gracie's broken ankle as he passed it to her.

'Not again!' she screamed.

'What are you doing up here on your own?' asked Ford.

'I'm on a rescue mission,' sobbed Gracie. 'A woman is lost and being attacked by goats and sheep.'

'Goats and sheep? The ghost sheep!' chuckled Jason.

'Have you seen her?' pleaded Gracie.

'There is no one up here apart from us,' Ford assured her. 'You were lucky we heard you.'

Gracie raised herself to a sitting position. 'Before I call for help, please can I rescue you both?'

'We don't need rescuing,' insisted Jason.

Gracie clasped hold of Ford's knee. 'Please let me rescue you!'

Ford began to wonder whether she was in shock or something. 'You're in no state to rescue anyone, and with your ankle in that condition, it will be a long time before you do rescue someone again.'

Gracie sobbed inconsolably. 'The golden bobble hat! I'll never get the golden bobble hat.'

'She must be delirious,' guessed Jason. 'Should I try and knock her out with a punch?'

Ford stared at Jason in disbelief. 'Watching all those daytime medical dramas has really paid off; I'm going to have to start calling you "Doctor".'

'Now, was that just sarcasm or was that irony?' wondered Jason.

'Irony!' sobbed Gracie.

'No it wasn't… Or was it?' puzzled Ford. 'Look forget that, what is this golden bobble hat?'

Gracie wiped her snotty nose on her jacket sleeve. 'When you reach one hundred rescues, you are entitled to wear the prestigious golden bobble hat. I'm only one away! I would have been the first woman in dales rescue history to have achieved it.'

'Sorry, we just don't have the time to be rescued,' explained Ford.

'I'm begging you! I might not pass the physical after this injury! Please be rescued!'

Even though Ford was no longer nice, he just knew he it would trouble him if Gracie had to quit at ninety-nine. 'What do you say Jason?'

Jason was very rarely troubled by anything, so said, 'Let's just leave her.'

'Please!' begged Gracie, 'Please be rescued.'

Ford scratched his head. 'If we did get rescued, how long would it take?'

'Less than an hour!' promised Gracie. 'If I make the call now.'

'How about it, Jason?' asked Ford. 'We get rescued and still get back on time to tag on to the others.'

Ford noticed Jason had a faraway look in his eye. Maybe Gracie's desperate plea had touched him in some way. 'Nah! Let's just leave her.'

'Biscuits!' shouted Gracie. 'If you get rescued, you get biscuits.'

'And a hot drink?' asked Ford, who could do with a cup of tea.

'You'll get lots of tea and biscuits!' sobbed Gracie.

Jason shrugged. 'Okay then, as long as they're nice biscuits.'

'That's settled,' said Ford. 'You can rescue us.'

Gracie switched on the walkie-talkie. 'Foxy Lady to base, Foxy Lady to base, over.'

The walkie talkie crackled. 'Come in Foxy Lady, over,' said the voice of Sergeant Truman.

'Foxy Lady is down. Repeat, Foxy Lady is down, over.'

'What does that mean, Gracie? Does that mean you are back down or what? Over.'

'I've broken my ankle up on Low Peak and I'm in bloomin' agony,' sobbed Gracie. 'That's what it means.'

A silence followed.

'You're meant to say, "over" when you finish speaking, over.'

'I've rescued two walkers and broken my ankle. I need urgent medical treatment, please send help right away, over.'

'Are the walkers safe? Can I talk to them? Over.'

Gracie handed Ford the walkie-talkie. 'Press this button to speak.'

'Hello! Ford speaking.'

'Say, "over"!' said Gracie.

Jason snatched the walkie-talkie from Ford's hand. 'For someone who watches a lot of movies, you know nothing.' He pressed the button to speak. 'This is Alpha Centauri, Juliet Bravo, on a ten four, I say again, delta, echo, bear in the air, we are roger to lift off. Over.' He handed the walkie-talkie back to Gracie. 'That's how you do it!'

'Gracie, pick up. Over.'

'Here Sarge, over.'

'It sounds like you've stumbled on a couple of idiots. Just sit tight, Foxy Lady, help is on its way.'

A silence followed.

'You never said, "over", over.'

'I did say, "over". You are the one who didn't say, "over", over.

'No, no, no… After you said, "help is on its way," you never said, "over", over.'

'Okay, Gracie! For Christ's sake, we'll be here all day. Help is on its way. I'm hanging up now.'

'Hurry up, over!' cried Gracie, before collapsing back down on the ground.

'The professionalism in communication is very reassuring,' quipped Ford.

The cloud began to disperse over the thirty-five minutes it took for two other middle-aged members of the Dales Voluntary Rescue Service to reach them. Joyce and Albert were the least experienced of the rescue service and were only sent on a shout when no one else could be found. Gracie was immediately attended to by her colleagues.

'Where does it hurt?' asked Joyce, as she tried to remember her training.

'Where do you bloomin' think? I've broken my ankle,' whimpered Gracie.

Despite her left ankle being at a forty-five degree angle to her leg, Albert asked, 'Which one is it?'

'The bloomin' bent one!'

Joyce peered at the ankle's odd angle, confirmed that it was broken and promptly fainted.

Jason managed to catch her as she slumped over.

Albert instinctively reached for his walkie-talkie. 'Big Daddy to base, Big Daddy to base, over.'

'Come in, Big Daddy, over.'

'We have located Foxy Lady, but now the Iron Lady is down. Repeat, the Iron Lady is down, over.'

'Albert, what the fuck does that mean? What is going on up there? Over.'

'Sarge, Joyce fainted when she saw Gracie's broken ankle, over.'

'Oh, Jesus! The rescue helicopter should be with you shortly, this is one almighty fuck-up.'

Another silence followed.

'Is that, "one almighty fuck up, over", over?'

'For Christ's sake, Albert, just get ready with the flare when you hear it coming. I'm hanging up now.'

Albert noticed Ford and Jason for the first time. 'Don't worry, you'll soon be rescued.'

'They're my one hundredth rescue,' muttered Gracie, with a whimper.

'Well done, Gracie!' said Albert as he patted her broken ankle, causing her to gasp in pain. 'I'm still on number nine.'

'Now we've been rescued, can we go?' asked Jason.

'We can see where we're staying, so we can walk back now. It's only a mile or so,' added Ford.

Albert prodded about in his rucksack and produced a hand-held flare. 'You can't just wander off after being rescued, you might need medical attention, or be in a state of shock!'

Fifteen minutes later, there was the sound of an approaching helicopter. Albert lit the flare and waved its red smoke to attract the pilot's attention. With the visibility now clear, the chopper touched down on a level area nearby. Two paramedics in their mid-twenties jumped down and dashed over with a stretcher. The senior medic, Emily, knelt beside Joyce and felt her ankle, while her colleague, Austin, began to unload the medical kit.

'She's very lucky; the ankle's not broken,' said Emily with authority. 'It's probably just a sprain.'

'You're looking at the wrong ankle on the wrong person,' said Ford, pointing at Gracie's injury.

Emily's eyes followed the line of Ford's finger until they reached Gracie's broken ankle sticking up at an acute angle. Emily began to vomit.

Austin turned around at the sound of vomiting, glanced at Gracie's unnaturally bent ankle and fainted next to Joyce.

Finally, Emily rallied and, with the aid of Albert and the two rescuees, managed to get Gracie on a stretcher and on board the helicopter. The two fainters were picked up and thrown inside like sacks of potatoes. Albert had to be helped into the helicopter because his knee felt funny after the walk up. Ford and Jason were the last to climb in, and were finally rescued.

The helicopter flew straight to the town of Skipington where several ambulances were waiting by the landing field in the hospital grounds. Ford and Jason were the last to be whisked away and soon found themselves in front of a team of doctors. They were checked for dehydration, hypothermia and vertigo. This was followed by a half-hour session with a rescuee psychotherapist who advised them not to get lost for at least six months. If they did find themselves lost, they were advised to try to be found as quickly as possible.

Any hopes of getting away after the medical were dashed when they were taken to attend a press conference held beside Gracie's hospital bed. Gracie was still groggy after having her ankle straightened under anaesthetic. Her Dales Voluntary Rescue Service colleagues had already presented her with the golden bobble hat, which she wore with pride. Her eyes were slightly crossed and her tongue stuck out of her mouth on one side, but Gracie still managed to give a thumbs up to the TV cameras.

The local BBC reporter, Glynis Eccles, was in her early thirties and frustrated that after five years, she was still doing shitty local news, instead of covering major headline stories. Just like on all the other occasions, she had been nominated to interview the rescuees because her partner worked at the hospital and could pull strings. Glynis put on her BBC smile for the benefit of any cameras pointed toward her. 'When did the two of you realise that you were hopelessly lost on top of Low Peak?' she asked.

Jason coughed nervously. 'We weren't lost because we knew where we were.'

Glynis had a rescue script that she had refined over the last five years, and she was fucked if she was going to deviate from

186

it. 'Did you ever give up hope of ever seeing your friends and family ever again? Did you ever give up hope of ever being rescued?'

'One question at a time,' insisted the hospital public relations officer, who was also Glynis's partner. 'Please don't bend the rules, Ms Eccles,' he said, just like she had told him to.

Glynis smiled, hoping that she would be admired by the BBC bosses for breaking the rules and pushing the boundaries of journalism.

'I'll answer them both,' insisted Ford. 'No and no because we knew where we were.'

'One last question,' said Glynis's partner.

'Can you describe the emotion of seeing your rescuer, Gracie, after being completely disoriented and in fear of your life?' asked Glynis.

Jason held his hand up. 'No, because we knew where we were.'

Glynis had one more rehearsed question. 'I insist you tell the taxpayers…'

'I said no more questions, Ms Eccles! You're pushing the boundaries again!' protested her partner, just like she had told him to.

Nina and Trixie made their way back to the hotel without any further incidents. They sneaked past the empty reception desk and rushed up the stairs to Nina's room. Once inside, Nina peeled off the tight trousers and headed for the bathroom to have a shower and apply more lotion.

'I am so relieved to get those off!' shouted Nina from the bathroom.

'Don't get too relieved, you have to put them back on again.'

'I'll talc up, it'll only be for a while.'

'Look, why don't we just come out and say to David and Evie that we took a short cut back because you were in discomfort?'

187

Nina appeared at the bathroom door. 'I don't want people knowing about my Camelot chafing! It's humiliating enough to have those two herberts knowing. I just had a thought… You could tell David and Evie it was you that had chafing.'

'Why should I?'

'Ha! You're happy for me to be the chafed one, but not yourself!'

'Because you are the chafed one! Okay, okay. We wait until we see the group, then we'll tag on at the end, and hopefully, no one will see us.'

One shower, two gins and three hours later, Nina was sitting beside the window, flicking through a magazine, when she noticed figures in the distance. 'They're coming! I recognise Conrad's shorts.'

Trixie rushed in from her connecting room and peered out of the window. 'Right! Get your walking gear back on.' It was a struggle for Nina to put the trousers back on, even with Trixie's help. 'They've either shrunk or you've swollen up,' grunted Trixie, as she tugged at the trousers. 'We need more talc!' With the aid of more talc and brute strength, they managed to pull up the zip. They dashed down the hotel stairs as fast as Nina's trousers would let them, and sneaked out to the rear gardens. Keeping close to the buildings like escaped prisoners avoiding a searchlight, they spotted a sign for the car park and crept along the footpath. The car park was full of cars, but there was no one in sight. They still kept close to the fence and tiptoed toward the main road. They crouched beside a black Range Rover.

'These bloody trousers are cutting me to pieces!' moaned Nina. 'I need to undo the button.'

She stood up and attempted to undo the waist button, when suddenly the uniformed figure of Arthur, the car park manager, appeared from a nearby bush. He pointed a big stick at them.

'I've got you, you disgusting perverts. You picked the wrong car park for your debauched act!' An icy shiver went all the way down his spine. He noticed that they looked like women. He had never read anything about transvestite bukkake bonnet before.

Nina and Trixie gave each other a puzzled look.

'I don't know what you are on about,' protested Trixie.

'We just want to go after the others,' explained Nina, pointing in the general direction the walkers were coming from.

'We're meant to be coming last,' confessed Trixie.

'Have you no shame?!' exclaimed Arthur. He glanced at the black Range Rover bonnet. 'Is it the dark shiny paintwork that attracts you perverts? You people make me sick! Spilling your filth over bonnets is one thing, but to do it dressed as women is depraved beyond belief!'

'Hold on a minute,' said Trixie. 'We are women! What are you going on about?'

'I must admit,' said Arthur, 'you might just get away with being a woman, but your mate needs to try a little bit harder to pull that one off.'

'You cheeky fucker!' spat Nina. She held up her jacket and pointed to her Camelot. 'Well, what do you think that is?'

Arthur lowered his big stick and muttered, 'Oh.'

'Yes. Oh!' snapped Nina.

Arthur took one more glance at the Camelot. 'You need to be careful with trousers that tight, you might get chafing.'

'I don't know what's been going on with car bonnets here, and I don't want to know,' stated Trixie, 'but we need to keep moving.'

'Sorry about the stick,' said Arthur.

'I'm a bit confused,' admitted Nina. 'What filth has been spilled on car bonnets?'

'Gentlemen juice,' whispered Arthur.

Nina remained confused for a moment; then the penny dropped. 'That's disgusting! I've never heard anything like it! You mean men are… All over the car bonnet?'

Arthur sadly nodded. 'Bukkake bonnet.'

Nina's mouth was still wide open in shock when Trixie pulled her away.

Arthur glanced around to make sure no one else had seen him before he hid again in the bushes. As he crouched down on lookout, he heard the two women screaming with laughter as they walked away.

Once they were clear of the car park, Nina and Trixie made their way toward a crossroads, staying low behind a drystone wall. They could not have timed it better, as they heard Conrad's voice on the road side of the wall.

'Nearly there!' he bellowed.

They waited a full ten minutes before deciding it was safe to rejoin the hike. Nina suggested they run on the spot until they were out of breath, just like method actors would do.

Nina stopped after twenty seconds because she was out of breath; Trixie was still going after a minute.

'All right, Trixie!' panted Nina. 'We haven't got all day, you'll just have to act.'

They marched up to the hotel and, with a final check that they looked bedraggled enough, they staggered inside.

In the foyer, Brenda peered up from the reception desk. 'Your party are having drinks in the west bar.'

Nina pretended to be out of breath and just gave an acknowledging wave.

Brenda watched the cheating little bitches walk away. She had seen them earlier, sneaking to the car park.

Before they entered the bar, Nina said, 'Quickly, give me your rucksack.'

'Why?'

'I told Conrad that you were struggling to carry it and that you were too proud to ask anyone else for help.'

190

'Why did you tell him that?'

'I had to think quickly!'

Trixie very reluctantly handed her rucksack over. 'Thanks, all my co-workers will think I'm a wimp.'

'Conrad won't say anything, you worry too much.'

Hot and cold drinks were laid out on tables along with various snacks for the weary returning hikers. The chatter was more subdued than at lunchtime, as the group waited for their energy levels to return.

Nina theatrically stumbled into the bar as loudly as she could and dropped two rucksacks on the floor while taking deep gasping breaths. 'Made it!'

A spontaneous round of applause greeted her arrival. Nina was congratulated and given a comfy chair to sit on in the middle of the group. Conrad was soon at her side, patting her on the back and calling her a saint.

Trixie's arrival was greeted with a few subdued calls of, 'Well done, Trixie.'

All the attention was now concentrated on Nina. Any normal person would have attempted to change the subject when it came to discussing parts of the walk, but she was enjoying the attention and happy to lie her socks off.

'What were your favourite views?' asked Conrad, as he passed her the large glass of white wine she had requested.

'Oh, Conrad, it would be unfair to single out just one when they were all breath-taking.'

'Surely the waterfall must be one of them.'

'Oh, yes… The waterfall, what a sight it was. Water… falling.'

Conrad had found some prawn cocktail crisps among the snacks, and now, Nina was being subjected to his prawn crisp breath.

'Carved mice,' continued Conrad, 'how many did you see?'

Nina gazed around at the faces surrounding her, all waiting for her answer. She did not have a clue what they were on about. 'What carved mice?'

191

Heads turned toward Nina. The noise level dropped to silence.

'The mouse carvings on the church pews?' said Conrad suspiciously.

'Church!' bellowed Nina. 'Of course.'

'Didn't you try to count them?' asked Evie, who had joined Nina's group.

Conrad smiled proudly. 'I must confess, I've been in the church several times so knew where they all were on the pews.'

Nina had to think quickly. 'When I enter one of God's holy houses, I like to light a solitary candle and say a silent prayer for our... for our loved ones, like Evie's Nana, who have only just dropped dea... I mean who have departed this life and joined... joined the baby Jesus. Amen.' With Oscar-winning sadness, Nina made the sign of the cross like she'd seen Al Pacino do in *The Godfather*.

There was a group 'amen' as they all felt slightly guilty for not praying in the church.

Tears were in Evie's eyes as she gave Nina a hug. 'What a lovely thing to do. Thank you so much.'

Dave had spotted Trixie leaning against the bar. 'Are you okay, Trixie? I heard you were struggling. This is not like you.'

Trixie had forgotten that she had been on a twenty-mile charity walk with Dave a few years ago. She wasn't used to telling lies, so used one of Nina's phrases to avoid going into detail. 'Lady things!' she whispered.

'Oh, sorry!' stuttered Dave. He scratched his head in embarrassment. 'I hope you feel... you know... soon.'

'Thanks.'

'I don't suppose you saw my friends Ford and Jason at all? They should have been here by now.'

Trixie shook her head. 'No, but I'm sure they'll turn up very soon.'

Dave could not hide his annoyance. 'It would be them; everyone else is back. I wish I'd never invited them. Evie was right, they're nothing but trouble.'

'I wouldn't be too hard on them. Have you tried phoning them?'

'I tried, but all I got was voice mail.'

The sounds of raucous laughter from the group surrounding Nina drew their attention.

'You and Evie are lucky to have a friend like Nina,' sighed Dave. 'I just wish my friends were more like her… You know, sociable.'

'Dave!' shouted a male voice from the other side of the room. 'You'd better take a look at this.'

Trixie followed Dave over to a corner of the room where a small group of people were watching a large, wall-mounted TV. It was a news channel and there, stepping off a helicopter, were Ford and Jason with foil blankets over their shoulders.

Evie had noticed the drift of people to the TV and joined the watching crowd.

The voice-over described the dramatic events in which a volunteer rescuer with a broken ankle had saved the lives of two lost hikers on Low Peak.

'What were they doing up on Low Peak?' gasped Dave, to no one in particular.

'Taking a fucking short cut!' cursed Evie.

Nina made her way over to the TV and saw the images of Ford and Jason. Knowing that attack is sometimes the best form of defence, she shouted loudly, 'The cheating bastards!'

CHAPTER THIRTEEN

For unexplained health and safety reasons, Ford and Jason were taken back to the hotel in an ambulance with its blue lights flashing and sirens blaring. As if that was not far enough over the top, it was escorted by a police car with its own blue lights flashing and sirens blaring. As the ambulance pulled up outside the hotel, curious faces were peering out of the windows, and some people had even come outside to take a closer look. The jobsworth paramedics insisted that Ford and Jason had to be taken off the ambulance on stretchers because of the latest health and safety memo. The two rescuees then had to sign a disclaimer form in triplicate before the ambulance, again with blue lights flashing and sirens wailing, sped off with its police escort.

Dave stood waiting with his arms crossed. 'It would be you two, wouldn't it? I don't think you could have ruined the weekend more if you'd planned it.'

Ford smiled. 'It's quite a funny story...'

'Stop right there,' demanded Dave. 'I want words with you two before I hear your so-called funny story. I suggest we go to your rooms.'

Dave stomped off. Ford and Jason grabbed their rucksacks and followed him.

Ford led Dave and Jason into his room. 'As I was saying, it's quite a funny story...'

'I don't want to hear it,' said Dave adamantly. 'The walk this afternoon was very special for Evie. She wanted to show everyone the beautiful church where they scattered her Nana's ashes. That special afternoon with her friends will now be the

194

afternoon when Dave's two old school friends took a short cut, got lost and had to be rescued! Why didn't you just do the fucking walk?'

Ford was trying to think of a diplomatic excuse.

Jason was fed up with being moaned at. 'We didn't want to go on a stupid walk and see dead people's ashes! We wanted to spend time with our mate by having a few drinks and having a few laughs before he settles down to married life. Instead of doing that, we've had to mingle with your boring workmates, eat microscopic food and get dragged along on a hike like we were fat girl-guides who need a bit of exercise.'

'I'm guessing you must feel the same way, Ford.'

'I would have said, "like fat Boy Scouts". You have to admit, Dave, this is more like a company bonding weekend. No one wants to talk to us because we don't play golf and can't help their career.'

'That is odd,' mused Dave, 'because Evie's friend Nina doesn't know anyone, yet she's the most popular person here! On top of that, she's never hiked before in her life. Did she complain? Not once. And not only that, she carried Trixie's rucksack all the way back because her friend was finding it difficult. She even had time to say a few prayers for Evie's Nana in the church!'

Ford laughed. 'Did she really?'

Jason chuckled.

'I'm pleased that you think it's all one big joke!' snapped Dave. 'Because of your actions, some brave rescue worker now has a broken ankle. Half of Yorkshire's emergency services were called out on a Sunday! A day they'd rather be spending with their family, rather than risking their lives for you two.'

'There are two sides to every story,' protested Ford.

'With you and Jason, there are three sides!' exclaimed Dave. 'Your version, his version and the real version! Look… I think it's best if you both stay out of Evie's way tonight. She is upset and pissed off with you two. Just order what you like from room service.' Dave gave them one last disappointed glance before leaving, slamming the door behind him.

Ford took off his coat and threw it on the bed. 'I think my mum was the last person to confine me to my bedroom.'

'It's our last night,' pointed out Jason. 'I say fuck them! We're grown-ups. If they don't want us around, we'll go into town, grab a curry, then hit the pubs and try some local beers.'

Now Ford was no longer a pushover nice guy, he felt the thrill of rebellious behaviour. 'Let's do it! Fuck them.' He gave it a bit more thought. 'But let's not stay out too late because I have to drive in the morning.'

They had arranged for a cab to pick them up at the same time as Dave and Evie's evening meal was due to start. They were on their way downstairs to the foyer when they heard Trixie calling to them from behind, 'What happened to you two?'

They waited for Trixie to catch up before continuing downstairs.

'The scream we heard was from a rescue worker,' explained Ford.

'She'd broken her ankle while searching for a woman,' added Jason. 'A woman who was being attacked by goats and sheep. Or as Nina called them "ghost sheep".'

'You mean she was searching for Nina?'

Ford nodded. 'Anyway, the lady was only one rescue away from achieving a golden bobble hat for one hundred rescues and begged us to be rescued, so we were.'

'Why don't you just explain what happened?' urged Trixie.

'I promised Nina we wouldn't say anything, and I don't want to make things difficult for you.'

'I don't care about me,' said Trixie. 'But you're right; Nina would be crushed if the truth came out.'

'We've been confined to our rooms,' laughed Jason, 'so we are sneaking out and going to the nearest town for a curry and a few beers.'

A cab driver wandered into the foyer. 'Taxi for Mr Riff and Mr Raff!'

'That's Jason's idea of a joke,' smiled Ford. 'Anyway, just pretend you never saw us.'

'I never saw a thing,' confirmed Trixie, as she watched them sneak out, secretly wishing she were going with them.

The cab driver dropped them outside the only Indian restaurant in town. It was empty. With low expectations, they ordered food and hoped for the best. To their utter surprise and delight, the food was, in their opinion, the best Indian meal they had ever had. They ate with big smiles on their faces and felt blessed that they had been banned from the party.

Over the next hour, the restaurant began to fill up with people, and word began to go round that they were the two men who had been rescued up on Low Peak. The owner generously told them that the meal was free, and numerous people came to their table and asked to have selfies taken with them. Each time, Jason embellished the story of their daring rescue and how lucky they were to be alive. Unable to eat any more food, the Mountain Survivors, as Jason now called them, went from pub to pub with a growing entourage, who happily pointed out these plucky heroes to those who did not know.

There was a surprise for Dave and Evie on the last evening. It had been organised by Dave's brother and best man, Conrad. Trixie was the last one to enter the hotel restaurant, much to Conrad's annoyance because he was waiting to make his speech. She sat in the only vacant chair, which was with the accountants. She spotted Nina sitting on the same table as Dave and Evie next to Conrad. Nina gave her a smug wave.

The tables had been laid with glasses of white wine already poured. Smartly dressed wine waiters stood on the fringes, ready to top up people's glasses.

To draw attention to his imminent speech, Conrad hit his wine glass with a spoon, which caused it to shatter, spilling white wine all over the table. He continued as though nothing had happened, while the waiting staff rushed over and mopped up the mess.

'Before I begin, will you join me in toasting Dave and Evie for the most enjoyable weekend?' Conrad held a remnant of his broken glass. 'To Dave and Evie!'

'Dave and Evie,' was repeated by the diners, followed by a round of applause.

'Now,' teased Conrad, 'Dave and Evie have no idea of the surprise I have for them tonight, and they look a bit worried.' Warm-hearted laughter echoed around the room.

Nina was taking a big swig of wine when Conrad announced that they would be having award-winning food. It was being created in the hotel kitchen by the top sushi chefs in the north.

Nina choked on her white wine. 'Raw fish!' Excited applause drowned out Nina's exclamation of horror.

Waiters appeared with trays of assorted fish, beautifully displayed. Evie cried with joy and blew Conrad a kiss; sushi was her favourite dish. Nina was crying as well. She was hungry and wasn't even a fan of fish when it was cooked, but raw?! Chopsticks were handed out, and the diners helped themselves to the seemingly never-ending trays of the finest sushi outside Leeds. Nina had to pretend for two hours that she was having one of the most delicious meals of her life. When she finally managed to get away from Conrad and his refuelled fishy breath, she beckoned Trixie to go out to the rear gardens with her. Once outside, Nina checked behind a hedge to make sure they were alone.

'Are you okay? What's with the secrecy?' asked Trixie.

'Fucking fish! Fucking raw fish! I can't stand it!'

Trixie smiled. 'Did you try any?'

'No! Because it's raw fish! I couldn't even eat any rice because Conrad keeps insisting on showing me how to use chopsticks.' Nina gave a dry sob. 'He keeps breathing fish over me.'

'What were your words to me again?' Trixie mimicked Nina's voice. 'Conrad's so rich and good-looking, he's perfect for me.'

'He would be perfect if it wasn't for his fishy breath. I smell fish on my clothes, I can't escape it. I can even taste it and I haven't had any!' At that moment, Nina caught a whiff of a cigarette. 'A ciggy will get rid of the taste, I'll see if I can cadge one.'

'You're not good at smoking.'

Nina was slightly hurt by the remark. 'I'm good at smoking! When I was twenty, I had a real smoker's cough.'

'As I recall, the doctors said it was bronchitis.'

'What do they know?' Nina took a few steps toward the smell of tobacco smoke. 'Come on, they're somewhere over here.'

Trixie reluctantly followed Nina in search of the cigarette smoker.

Old Jake was standing inside the doorway of the boot room building. Brenda had instructed him to smoke at least ten cigarettes every night before she would let him into their rooms. He looked up when he heard two women chatting. They were walking toward him and he knew right away what they wanted. He held out his cigarette packet.

'Oh, I don't mind if I do! Thank you,' smiled Nina.

'Not for me, thanks,' grimaced Trixie.

Old Jake lit Nina's cigarette for her with the lighter Brenda had bought him for Christmas along with five hundred extra-strong cigarettes. He guessed the woman was not a smoker because she constantly pouted and blinked her watering eyes.

Nina puffed away without inhaling any smoke. 'I feel like I'm one of the cool kids in the movies!' she said, as she took a break from puffing.

Trixie took in the scene of Old Jake's ashen, lined face and Nina's watery eyes. 'That's exactly what I was thinking.'

'I can't taste fish any more,' declared Nina.

'Can we go back now?' asked Trixie.

Nina had seen a Tom Hardy movie where he flicked a cigarette away in a very cool way so she decided to do the same. 'Let's go.' Her flicked cigarette flew through the air and hit a downpipe; the burning ember broke off and dropped through the small open window of the boot room, where it landed on a cushion and smouldered away.

By the time Nina and Trixie had made their way back, the group had drifted from the restaurant into the bar. As another surprise, Conrad had arranged for a mobile disco, which had been set up while they were eating. A paunchy, middle-aged deejay wearing sunglasses and a pork-pie hat was encouraging people to, 'Get down,' on a tiny dance floor.

Conrad had been searching for Nina, and his eyes lit up when he spotted her walking in from the garden with Trixie. He rushed over and breathed salmon over her. 'I've been searching for you everywhere. How about a dance?'

'You go ahead, Conrad, I'll be with you in a minute, I just need to visit the ladies' restroom.'

Conrad blew Nina a fishy kiss and danced as though it was the best fun he had ever had in his life. The real reason was that he had organised the disco and now felt obliged to dance for the rest of the evening.

'I hate discos,' groaned Trixie. 'Hours of shit music played too loud. I wish I'd gone with them into town and had a curry instead.'

'Who's gone into town?'

'Ford and Jason. I met them on the stairs earlier.'

Nina looked shocked. 'They were confined to their rooms. They can't just go out!'

'What are you talking about? They're grown men, they can do what they like.'

'They can't just go out and enjoy themselves after what they did. I'm telling Evie.'

Trixie held Nina back. 'Tell her in the morning; don't ruin her last night by winding her up. Anyway, when did you become such a tell-tale?'

'That Ford just gets on my nerves.'

'I noticed.'

'Hurry up, Nina!' shouted Conrad, as the song ended. He was the only one on the dance floor, which was one more than the deejay normally had.

Baggy Trousers by Madness, began to play. Conrad jumped around to the music, trying to encourage others to join the fun. The paunchy, middle-aged deejay made the fatal mistake all deejays make of turning the volume up to get people dancing.

By the time Nina had come back from the restroom, Conrad was sitting down, trying to get his breath back. The dance floor was empty, and people had drifted into the other bar where it was quieter.

The paunchy, middle-aged deejay was undeterred and turned the volume up again to entice them back.

Nina tapped Conrad on the shoulder and pointed to the other bar, he nodded in response, and they left the deejay playing to an empty room.

The rest of the evening was similar to the first night. Nina became the centre of attention and entertained everyone by re-enacting scenes from movies, with Conrad topping her glass up at regular intervals. Conrad's last surprise was a spectacular fireworks display in the grounds of the hotel. Consequently, he never tired of telling anyone who would listen that it was worth every penny of the two thousand pounds it had cost him.

It was getting late when Ford called for a cab to take them back to the hotel. He and Jason had both had far too much to drink, thanks to the generosity of the locals, who had treated them like celebrities.

'We'll get back, and sneak in,' slurred Ford. 'No one will ever know.'

'No one will ever know,' slurred Jason in agreement.

The pub door opened. 'Taxi for the Mountain Survivors!'

Ford yawned and checked his watch. It was midnight; they should be back at the hotel in fifteen minutes.

It was one o'clock in the morning when Dave and Evie reminded everyone still in the bar that they had to be out of their rooms by ten that morning. Just as 'good nights' were being said, the fire alarm went off with a deafening ringing. Brenda, always the complete professional, ran into the room screaming, 'Fire! Save yourselves,' and then headed for the nearest emergency exit. Hotel staff rushed around and led the group out to an assembly point on the front lawn. The party huddled together for reassurance, as they noticed smoke billowing out of the boot room window.

Dave had frantically searched the assembled group for Ford and Jason. They were nowhere to be seen. He gave the worrying news to Evie. 'Ford and Jason are still in their rooms!'

Sirens that sounded far in the distance were soon wailing loudly as two fire engines pulled up outside the hotel. Several firefighters leaped from each engine and set up water hoses.

Deputy Chief Fire Officer Gary Biggins was happy to be attending a proper life-threatening fire. He'd only recently been promoted and had only one previous call-out: a hedge fire started by a group of bored teenagers. With the confidence of knowing this was a big enough fire for him to be interviewed for the TV news, Gary cheerfully informed the staff and guests at the assembly point that, 'Smoke is the real killer in situations like this. Yes, smoke.' He smiled, as he pointed at the black smoke billowing out of the boot room. 'That smoke is what we call in the firefighting trade Black Death. It's lethal. I pity anyone asleep in those rooms above. They would no doubt be unconscious or even dead!' Gary had been given special training to make sure he did not smile when he said the word 'dead' because apparently it gave the public mixed messages.

There was an audible gasp of concern from the evacuees at this news.

'Our friends are still in those rooms,' sobbed Evie. 'You must do something!'

Deputy Chief Fire Officer Gary Biggins had also been given special training in the event of fatalities and was looking forward to putting on his 'upset face' in front of the media. He was slightly pissed off when, just as the hoses were set up, the billowing smoke dwindled to a trickle. A firefighter rushed over and reported that the main source of smoke was a cushion on a chair. It appeared that a stray ember from one of the fireworks had somehow dropped into the boot room through the open window. They had checked the hotel rooms above; all were empty and had not been affected too much by the smoke.

Gary grasped at one last flammable straw. 'Is there a chance that something will suddenly burst into flames?'

The reporting firefighter was confused. 'No, sir. It's out, it was only a cushion. Everything else in the room was flame retardant.'

Gary took off his fire helmet and threw it on the ground in frustration. He stormed off, cursing modern materials and wishing he had a good old-fashioned arsonist in his area.

With all the excitement over, Dave and Evie's guests made their way back to their rooms.

Trixie briefly lost track of Nina until the crowd thinned out and she caught sight of her holding hands with Conrad, walking back into the hotel. Back in her room, the connecting door was locked, and Trixie could faintly hear Conrad's voice from the other side.

When the taxi driver found out that his passengers were the Mountain Survivors, he insisted on taking them on to his local pub in the next village, which stayed open until very late. They had more free beers and more selfies with the locals before they finally begged to be taken back to the hotel. It was after two in the morning when Ford and Jason stumbled out of the taxi and staggered into the hotel foyer.

Dave and Evie stood there waiting for them.

'Oh, fuck! What have we done now?' burped Jason.

Ford was fed up of being treated like a kid. With Dutch courage and the certain knowledge that he was no longer nice, he ranted, 'Moan, moan, moan. Well, you can moan as much as you like. If we're not good enough for your snobby friends with their second homes, then tough! Because we ain't a-changing!'

'That's right!' agreed Jason. 'We ain't a-changing!'

Ford waited for the backlash, but to his and Jason's surprise, a tearful Evie and a misty-eyed Dave gave them each a hug and said they were pleased that they were safe.

Jason turned to Ford. 'The town wasn't that dangerous, was it?'

The next morning, Ford and Jason were suffering from hangovers but fortunately for them, the hotel had extended the departure time until the afternoon for those who needed it. By the time they walked zombie-like into the breakfast room, everyone else had already eaten, packed their suitcases and started on their long journeys home. Ford only managed a few pieces of toast and some orange juice while Jason opted for the fry-up because he wanted to get value for money, even if he wasn't paying for it.

Dave and Evie sat with them for twenty minutes, explaining how worried they had been and that, with hindsight, they realised they had over-reacted to the rescue saga.

Jason nodded wisely. 'I understand, Morag, you just threw a bit of a wee wobbly!'

'I did not have a wee wobbly!' protested Evie. 'And my name is not fucking Morag!'

'It was a wee bit of a wobbly,' said Ford.

'Really!' fumed Evie. 'I wasn't going to mention it because of the events of last night, but…'

'Evie! We said we'd let it go!' insisted Dave.

'No! Not after them saying I threw a wee wobbly!'

'It doesn't matter,' groaned Dave.

'I knew you'd take their side. Well, I think paying for everything is one thing, but having to pay for their use of porn channels as well is taking the piss!'

'One second!' protested Jason, he picked up a sausage and dipped it in his egg before holding it in front of his mouth. The talk of porn channels had brought back memories of the last one he watched, so he put the sausage back down on the plate. 'The young porter told me it was all included. I didn't know the little bastard was lying.'

'What's your excuse, Ford?' asked Evie. 'What was it you watched? Oh, yes… *Banging in Bangkok with a Big Cock.*'

'I must have clicked on it by mistake when I was searching for *Match of the Day*!' said Ford innocently.

Jason chuckled while Dave attempted to hide his smile from Evie.

Evie stood up. 'Well, I'm glad you all find it amusing because I think it's perverted and disgusting. When you're ready, David, I'll be outside, ready to leave.' She stomped off, leaving the three of them alone in the breakfast room.

'The weekend turned out better than I thought,' admitted Jason, as he tucked back in to his fry-up.

'Memorable is what I would say,' reflected Dave, 'for the wrong reasons.'

Ford sipped his orange juice. 'I might be wrong, but I'm pretty sure Morag is getting a soft spot for us.'

Trixie had tried the connecting door before going down to breakfast, only to find it was still locked. It was only later, when she was packing her suitcase, that she heard the lock click, and turned to see a dishevelled Nina still wearing last night's clothes.

'I need my hangover tablets,' she whimpered.

'I've thrown them away.'

Nina began to cry. 'But I need them!'

'Where's Conrad?'

Nina propped herself up against the door. 'He went back to his room, he was really puking up in the bathroom last night; he kept going on about dodgy scallops. Have you got any aspirin?'

'I'll find you some in a minute. I suggest you go and have a shower, you look terrible. We have to catch a train, remember.'

Nina stumbled to her bathroom and promptly stumbled back again. 'Can I use your bathroom? Mine stinks of fish.'

Because of Nina's delicate state, Trixie had to pack her large suitcase for her, giving her friend time to rejoin the land of the living. When they were ready to leave, Brenda was informed that they needed help with the heavy suitcase, and Old Jake was promptly sent up to carry it down. Trixie and Nina followed Old Jake down the stairs one step at a time, with Old Jake taking a breather after every other step.

Ford and Jason were on their way to check out of their rooms and caught up with the slow-moving trio. 'That looks heavy,' said Ford, as he squeezed past and helped Old Jake carry the case down the stairs. Ford let it slip to the floor by the reception desk, causing the one good wheel to break off.

'You've broken my case!' wailed Nina.

Ford picked up the broken wheel. 'I'm not surprised it broke, the case is far too heavy.'

'It's not heavy!' protested Nina.

'If it's not heavy,' reasoned Jason, 'then just carry it.'

'I told her it was too heavy, but she doesn't listen to me,' added Trixie.

A pale-faced Conrad appeared and waved to Nina.

Nina forgot all about her suitcase and her pounding headache, as she skipped over to Conrad. 'I'm glad I saw you before you went.'

Conrad kissed her on the cheek and whispered, 'I'll call you tomorrow and we'll arrange our date.'

Nina felt slightly nauseous when she smelt kippers on his breath. 'I'll look forward to it.'

Conrad glared over at Ford and Jason. 'I hope I never see those two again.'

Ford noticed him glaring at him, so gave him a wave. 'Bye, Podgy!'

After the rooms card keys were handed back, the problem of Nina's suitcase was resolved by Ford.

'We'll take it back in the car, and I'll drop it off at the Movie Poster Shop.'

'That would be great,' exclaimed Trixie. 'It would solve a big problem.'

Nina wasn't keen on the idea, but she was even less keen on the idea of carrying the case. 'Okay, but I'm locking it and keeping the key because I don't want your pervy hands fondling my clothes.'

There was something about Nina that made Ford smile. 'You're very welcome, no need to thank me.'

Trixie gave Ford a big smile. 'I was pleased that you got back to the hotel safe and sound after your night out.'

Surprised, Ford could only manage, 'Thanks.'

Trixie had noticed that Ford only ever made fleeting eye contact with her. 'Well, I'll probably see you back in Bridgeford sometime,' said Trixie.

'The shuttle bus to the railway station is about to leave!' gasped Old Jake from the front entrance.

Nina headed straight for the shuttle bus without even glancing back.

Trixie smiled at Ford, said, 'Bye,' and hurried after her.

'Have a safe journey!' Ford went outside and waited for the shuttle bus to pull away. Nina had her eyes fixed on the road ahead, but Trixie turned her head toward him and gave a small wave goodbye.

CHAPTER FOURTEEN

Ford and Jason strolled out to the car park. All the cars had gone except their orange VW Beetle. Arthur the car park manager poked his head out of the shed door and then ambled over just as Ford lifted the front hood to load in the suitcases.

Jason did a double take at Arthur's face; the old man's eyes were red with dark rings around them. 'Are you okay?'

'I haven't slept in two days,' muttered Arthur, 'because I know they're waiting, waiting to pump their filth over our guests' shiny bonnets.'

Ford closed the front hood. 'It looks like we're the last car, so go home and catch up on your sleep.'

Arthur shook his head. 'As soon as I go, they'll nip in and hide somewhere, waiting, waiting to…'

'Pump their filth over the guests' shiny bonnets?' guessed Jason.

Arthur nodded. 'I know they're waiting, but I won't give in.'

Ford climbed into the orange Beetle and wound down the driver's window. 'Thank you for keeping the bonnet bukkake-free.'

Jason jumped into the passenger side. 'People like you make this country great!' he shouted.

A tear of pride ran down Arthur's cheek. He saluted the car as it drove away and then slowly returned to his shed. Several beeps of the orange Beetle's horn as it sped away gave Arthur a raging headache and made his knee twinge.

As Ford watched the figure of Arthur getting smaller in the rear-view mirror, he said to Jason, 'Do you think I should have said something about the seagulls that are always circling overhead?'

The shuttle bus dropped Nina and Trixie off at the railway station, along with two other couples who were booked on the same train. Without the hindrance of the massive suitcase, they were both relaxed and comfortable as the train pulled out of the station and headed off on its journey south.

'I really enjoyed this weekend,' said Nina, out of the blue.

'I'm not surprised; I'm going to have to start calling you Miss Popular.'

Nina gave a smug smile. 'I was popular, wasn't I?'

'And you have a new admirer. Conrad was all over you like a limpet, and he fits your must-have profile. He's extremely wealthy and good-looking.'

Nina smiled and made two large invisible ticks. 'He wants me to be his date for the wedding.'

'So that's why you've had a little smile on your face since you spoke to him.'

'I would say this weekend was near-perfect. Well, apart from David's friends. How embarrassing were they?'

'Don't be unfair. Anyway, I quite liked them.'

'What is there to like? That Jason is an idiot who has never done a day's work in his life, and Ford is a second-hand car salesman who thinks he's funny, when he's not. He's a nobody and a loser.'

'That's a shame, because he likes you. I've seen the way he looks at you.'

Nina made a shivering motion. 'I can't think of anything worse than being leered at by him.'

'I don't understand why. You two have a lot in common. He likes movies, just like you do, and he's not bad-looking.'

'There! You just said it… Not bad-looking. I don't want not bad-looking, I want very good-looking.'

Trixie gazed out at the passing scenery. A tunnel briefly caused the window to reflect her own face. 'Looks aren't everything.'

Nina's face could not have been smugger if she had tried. 'I'm going to sit back, relax and think of Conrad.'

'Remember to think of his fishy breath.'

Nina closed her eyes. 'You're just jealous.'

She had plenty of time to think of Conrad, because of a points failure outside Peterborough, which halted the train for two hours.

PC Bernie Blyton was still fuming over the orange Beetle escapade. He was now a laughing stock at the station. The humiliation of it all had even affected his appetite. He could now only manage to eat two Cornish pasties and four jam donuts in a single sitting of watching the traffic from the motorway bridge. It was the bright orange paintwork that caught his unbelieving eyes. The very same orange Beetle that had brought on his downfall sped past, heading south. Half of him was saying, 'Bernie, let it go, they're just innocent young men,' but the other half of him was sure they were hiding something, something criminal, something big. He devised a plan to drive alongside them, just to let them know that he knew what they didn't want anyone to know: that they were, in fact, master criminals. He caught up to the Beetle within a mile and pulled alongside it. Something was different: a large suitcase took up most of the back seat, and by the look of the pressure on the rear tyres, it was extremely heavy. He dropped back a few car lengths before he was seen, and put in an urgent call for Detective Stone.

Ford was not aware of the surrounding traffic as he had been trying to guess Jason's I spy letter.

'Sky... scenery... switch? Oh, I give up.'

'Socks,' declared Jason, with a victory fist pump.

'I'm driving? How am I supposed to get socks without taking my eyes off the road?'

'You're just a bad loser.'

'I think being a safe driver and being mindful of potential trouble is more important.'

Detective Sergeant Laura Bruce had gotten where she was by gut instinct. Aged only twenty-five, she was a role model for young policewomen up and down the country. No officer with a fancy university degree had achieved as many commendations as she had in such a short space of time. Promotion after promotion, all down to her gut instinct for crime. When the do-gooders insisted that she needed evidence in a case, she would point to her gut and say, 'I got all the evidence I need.' And after she'd beaten the truth out of her suspect in the interrogation room, she would have it, signed and sealed. Her next promotion, to detective inspector, was just a formality once Frank Stone retired. Laura was in charge this Monday, and that was just the way she liked it. She had no boss to worry about with their constant whingeing about 'proof'. All that morning, her gut instinct had been telling her that a big case was about to break. Her phone rang; it was a transferred call from PC Bernie Blyton. He quickly explained about the men in the orange Beetle. Laura had heard about the incident that happened a few days ago and wished she'd been there. Her gut instinct would have told her if they were hiding something. Bernie updated her on the mysterious heavy suitcase that was now in the back seat of the orange Beetle. Laura's gut instinct was kicking in big time.

'What's your gut instinct say?' she asked, knowing very well what he was going to say because her gut instinct had told her.

'The case is too big to hold the money from the drugs we never found,' reported Bernie, 'so it might be the dead body of a drug dealer who went rogue, double-crossed them, and had to be made an example of.'

'I've got a gut instinct that your gut instinct is right!' said Laura. 'Keep them in sight. I'm getting the whole damn tactical firearms unit in on this one.'

'We also had a helicopter last time,' mentioned Bernie.

'And two goddamn helicopters!'

The return drive down the A1 was going better than Ford expected; there had been no traffic hold-ups, and the road seemed to be getting less busy. He glanced at the rear-view mirror and thought it odd that there were no vehicles behind them. The traffic ahead slowed down and funnelled into one lane.

'Bloody roadworks! I knew it was too good to be true,' moaned Ford. 'There'll be no one working; I've yet to see a road worker do anything!'

Up ahead, a police officer stepped in front of the car and waved Ford over to the exit lane.

He followed the exit slip road. Up ahead, police vehicles with blue lights flashing barricaded the road. In the rear-view mirror, he saw a further barricade of police vehicles had formed up behind them. 'What's going on here?'

Jason had been dozing and opened one eye. 'It's probably one of those random car tax checks.'

The tactical firearms unit surrounded the Beetle and took up positions with their rifles pointing at Ford and Jason's heads.

'I heard they were cracking down on car tax dodgers,' said Ford, 'but this seems a bit over the top.'

'Get out of the vehicle and lay face down on the ground,' crackled the voice of Detective Sergeant Laura Jones through a megaphone. If she could have done exactly as her gut instinct had told her, she would have just had them shot, but the sergeant of the tactical firearms unit insisted they could not just shoot someone based on a gut feeling.

Ford and Jason did as they were ordered and were soon wearing handcuffs and being roughly manhandled to their feet. PC Bernie Blyton jumped out of his squad car, which was part of the rear barricade, and rushed over to the orange Beetle. He proudly pointed out the large suitcase.

As soon as Laura saw it, her gut instinct told her this was going to be a major crime. She stood toe to toe with Jason, and stared into his cold killer eyes. 'What's in the suitcase?'

'Clothes, I think.'

Laura's gut instinct had told her he would lie. She went over to Ford and punched him on the arm. 'Oops, sorry, sir, I just slipped.'

'You just hit me!'

'Are you accusing me, a detective sergeant, of hitting you?'

'I'm not accusing, I'm stating the fact that you did hit me!'

'Did you see anything, Constable?' said Laura, as she stood on tiptoe to go nose to nose with Ford.

Bernie was tingling with excitement, this was proper police work. 'I didn't see a thing.'

Ford recognised the voice and glanced over to where it came from. 'You? Hold on, this isn't still about parking in the disabled spot, is it?'

Laura flicked Ford's left earlobe. 'Let's have a peek in the suitcase, shall we?'

'This is police brutality,' protested Ford. 'Well, if not brutality, mild police bullying.'

Laura smiled. No one had called her a bully for weeks. 'Open the suitcase.'

'We don't have the key, we're just taking the case back with us for a friend,' explained Ford.

'The wheels broke,' added Jason.

Laura sneered, 'Oh, well! With no key, we'll have to let you go.'

Ford was confused. 'Was that sarcasm, or are you letting us go?'

'Shut it!' screamed Laura, spraying spittle over Ford's face. 'Constable, open that case.'

Bernie and two of the tactical firearms officers dragged it out of the car. Bernie used his truncheon to batter the tiny padlock on the zip to pieces. He slowly pulled down the zip and gritted his false teeth in anticipation of a dead body slumping out. The only things that did tumble out were Nina's numerous outfits and a hotel dressing gown.

Laura's gut feeling was beginning to feel more like a gut ache. 'Check the lining for drug money.'

'Drug money?!' exclaimed Ford and Jason at exactly the same time.

Bernie tipped the clothes out on to the road, and used a pocketknife to slash the lining to shreds. 'There's no evidence here.'

Before he had even uttered the words, 'no evidence', Laura had a new gut instinct that the PC's gut instinct had been wrong all along, and she wished she'd listened to her pre-warning gut instinct in the first place. 'Get them out of my sight, let them go!' She nodded to an officer to release the handcuffs. Laura turned to Bernie. 'You've cocked up again big time, but thanks to my gut instinct, I've nipped your error in the bud.'

'You can't just pull us over for no reason, point guns at us, resort to a mild form of police brutality and get away with it!' insisted Ford.

Laura stood on tiptoe again and put her face inches from Ford's. 'I can do what I like, and if you don't pick that case up, I'll have you for fly-tipping! Go on, tell me I can't do that!'

Jason picked up an armful of clothes and threw them in the back of the car. 'Come on, Ford, let's just get out of here.'

Ford helped pick up the remaining clothes and shoved them in the damaged case. With an acute feeling of injustice, he wound down the driver's window as they pulled away. 'I'll be writing a very stiff letter to the Yorkshire tourist board about this!'

Bernie watched the orange Beetle enter the motorway. He felt like crying for the second time in three days. 'But they've broken the law! We only need to find which law they've broken,' he pleaded.

'You just don't have the gut instinct for the job,' advised Laura, as she searched her pockets for indigestion tablets. 'Get back to traffic and leave the real police work to those with real guts.'

The rest of the journey back to Bridgeford was uneventful apart from sitting in traffic just outside Cambridge for twenty minutes. Ford drove straight to the Movie Poster Shop, only to find it had closed at five. Ford noticed the *Closed* sign. 'Oh, great. We're stuck with it for another day.'

Jason shrugged his shoulders. 'Let's just dump it in the doorway.'

'No, I'll leave her a note. Have we got a pen between us?'

After a quick check in the glove department, the answer turned out to be no.

'Give her a call,' suggested Jason, 'and tell her she'll have to come and pick it up.'

'I don't have her number, but I could email her business. Yep, I'll do that.'

The next morning, Ford was still feeling weary from the previous day's drive. By the time he had cycled to Frank's Auto Sales, he was well and truly knackered. He had a notion that his day was going to be bad when he noticed his desk had been moved further into the corner and another one squeezed in alongside it.

Blake was sitting at his desk with his feet up as he normally did. He was showing a video clip on his phone to a sharply dressed, suntanned man in his forties, who craned over his shoulder and drooled.

Ford suspected the man was wearing a wig, but could not be sure. He coughed to announce his arrival.

Blake glanced up. 'Oh, you're back.'

'Thank you for the warm welcome. What's with the desks?'

Blake smiled proudly. 'This is Jezza, one of my Rat Pack buddies. He's your replace… I mean your new colleague. He started yesterday.'

Jezza was chewing gum quicker than a football manager at a penalty shoot-out. He gave a big smile, showing all his whitened teeth, and mimed firing a gun at Ford. 'Right at cha!'

Ford wondered what the fuck that was supposed to mean.

Blake smiled at Jezza like he was in love with him. 'I've known Jezza forever.'

'That's not possible,' said Ford. 'You haven't been around forever.'

'See, Jezza? That's what he's like all the time.'

Jezza shook his head in disgust. It moved a microsecond out of sync with his hair.

Ford took off his bicycle clips. By the time he'd placed them in his desk drawer, Jezza had spotted a man perusing a car on the forecourt and rushed out of the showroom. Within seconds, he had his arm around the customer's shoulder and was leading him over to a more expensive model.

Blake stood up and gazed out of the window. He blew his nose on a tissue. 'It brings a tear to my eye to see a proper car salesman at work,' he sniffled.

'How am I supposed to sell two cars by the end of the week with him competing for the same customers?'

'That's not my problem, my job is to make sure the business sells cars, and now, with me and Jezza teaming up, it will be guaranteed.'

Ford's prediction was correct: Jezza and Blake hogged all the customers. When they were not doing that, they were showing each other porn clips on their phones. Ford's morning did not get any better. A call came in on his desk phone; it was Nina.

'Where's my case!? I need it!'

'Oh, hello, Nina. I went to…'

'I need my case! Where is it?' interrupted Nina.

Ford had a feeling that this conversation was going to be a struggle. 'If you'll just…'

'What have you done with it?' she demanded.

Ford looked to the heavens. 'If you'll just listen for one second…'

'I need my case!' insisted Nina. 'It's got my make-up bag in it, and my hair tongs!'

'I tried to drop it off, but…'

'I need it today!'

Ford raised his voice. 'Just give me a moment to explain and I'll…'

'When am I getting my case back?'

Ford could feel a headache coming on. 'Nina, interrupt again and I'm hanging up! I tried to drop…'

'Well? Where is it?'

Ford hung up and waited for the call back.

'You hung up on me! How dare you!'

'I'm trying to explain what…'

'Where's my case?'

'You're doing it again, I'm trying…'

'When are you bringing it back? I need it!'

Ford hung up once again and waited for the call back.

'You hung up on me again!' screamed Nina. 'I can't believe you just did that!'

'I'll keep hanging up until you stop…'

'I don't know how you have the nerve to hang up on me!'

Ford hung up again. This time, he let the phone ring for twenty seconds before picking up. 'Ford, speaking. How can I help?'

'I hate you. What have you done with my case?'

'Before I speak, do you want to get the interruption out of the way?'

'Just tell me where my case is.'

'We got delayed coming back and the shop was shut by the time we got there, so I have it at my place.'

'Why didn't you drop it off at the flat above the shop?'

'Because I'm not a psychic and you never mentioned anything about a flat above the shop.'

'Well, when are you bringing it back?'

'I haven't got a car; we only borrowed one for the weekend. Look, my apartment's only three or four miles from you. Why don't you just go round and pick it up? Jason will be there.'

'I'm busy!'

'Really? Because you seem to have a lot of time to interrupt…'

'Okay, I'll pick it up tonight around seven.' This time, Nina hung up.

Ford had a smile on his face. The phone rang and he waited for it to ring for twenty seconds. 'Ford speaking. How can I help?'

'I need the address!'

Ford could not stop himself chuckling. 'Who is speaking, please?'

'I can hear you laughing; just give me the fucking address.'

He repeated the address and the postcode twice. He said goodbye, but she had already hung up.

Ford was starting to face up to the fact that he was going to be out of a job by the end of the week, so he spent the rest of the morning searching online for jobs in car sales; he could not find even one within fifty miles. Jezza was pouncing on anyone who walked onto the forecourt even if he was already with a customer, so Ford stopped trying. He had taken the hint, he was now yesterday's man.

Blake took time off from admiring Jezza to pick up a pile of post from his desk. He flicked through the letters. Every time

219

he said, 'rubbish', he threw one in the waste bin. 'Rubbish, rubbish, rubbish, rubbish.' He examined one letter closely and glanced over to Ford before throwing it away. 'Rubbish, rubbish, rubbish.'

Ford had noticed the glance. The next time Blake rushed out onto the forecourt to pursue a customer, Ford checked through the waste bin and found a letter addressed to him, care of Frank's Auto Sales. The envelope and the letter were made of high quality paper. It was an invite for him to the pre-pre-launch of the *Event* in London the following Monday, with a champagne reception. It included a card that had *VIP* embossed on it in gold. Ford re-read the envelope and the letter, wondering where on earth they had got his name from. He'd never even heard of the Event. He quickly checked Google, but none of the results seemed to apply to his invitation.

Blake strutted in from the forecourt, with a beaming smile. 'Jezza's doing a great job; his hard sell is a joy to watch.'

Ford glanced out of the window and noticed Jezza had an elderly man in an armlock. 'He's out of control; he'll give Frank's Auto Sales a bad name!'

Blake just smirked. 'The green-eyed monster has appeared. You're just jealous that he has what it takes and you don't.' He glanced over Ford's shoulder. 'What's that?'

'Well, once I took it out of the waste bin, I found it was an invite.'

Blake peered over to read the details. 'The Event? With a champagne reception? I knew some bloke who went to one of these so-called Events! I saw him one Sunday morning knocking on people's doors holding a Bible in one hand and a cute kid in the other so they wouldn't tell him to fuck off.'

'Do you reckon that's what it is?'

'How come you think you're cleverer than me, but can't see a scam?' Blake pointed at the invite. 'It's all a bit vague.'

Ford's first thought was that he'd never heard Blake say the word 'vague' before. He examined the invite again. There were no more details, and Blake was right, it was vague. Feeling that his time and money would be better spent looking for a job instead, he threw the invite in the bin. At the end of the day, Blake and Jezza had not sold one car between them, but had received three complaints of intimidation, which put a big smile on Ford's face.

Inside the showroom, Blake waited for Ford to cycle away before rushing to the waste-paper bin and retrieving the invitation. He'd heard his fellow Rat Pack members talk about the Event. It was the Holy Grail for car salesmen.

Despite his bad day, Ford was looking forward to seeing Nina that evening and hoped to give her a better impression of himself than the one she obviously had.

Ford had the suitcase ready by the front door, and at seven twenty that evening, the doorbell rang several times in rapid succession.

'That must be misery guts,' said Jason, as he flicked through the TV channels, sprawled on Ford's sofa.

'I'll get the door, shall I?' asked Ford in his most sarcastic voice.

Just as he reached the door, the bell rang again several times. There was a delay on the chimes so Ford waited several seconds for them to stop before opening the door.

'Where's my case?' demanded Nina with a face like thunder.

Ford sensed that he was going to be in for another verbal struggle. 'And a very good evening to you, Nina.'

Trixie smiled and gave Ford a wave. 'Hi, Ford.'

'Hi, Trixie. Did you get back okay yesterday?'

'Not really, we had a two-hour delay…'

'Don't talk to him,' snapped Nina. 'Let's just get my case and go.'

'Now, about the suitcase,' said Ford, 'there was a slight mishap…'

Nina spotted her case and pushed him aside. 'Where's the padlock? What have you been doing with my clothes?'

Ford beckoned Trixie inside. 'It's quite a funny story really…'

'I never packed it like this,' said Nina, opening her case.

Ford turned to Trixie. 'I feel I've had this one-sided conversation with her already today; I had to hang up on her three times.'

'Yes, Nina told me all about it… about four times.'

'Why have you been going through my clothes?' Nina stared accusingly at Ford. 'Have you and your pervert friend been trying them on?'

'I haven't, but I'll check with Jason. JASON! Have you been wearing Nina's clothes?'

'Yes!' shouted Jason.

'Well, it seems you're right, one of us perverts has been wearing your clothes. Happy now?'

Nina had one of her rare moments when she was speechless.

'They're joking with you!' pointed out Trixie.

Ford briefly explained about the police pulling their car over because of the suitcase. 'That is why the padlock is broken and the lining's been slashed.'

Trixie laughed. 'Trouble just seems to follow you around.'

Nina ran her hands over the slashed lining. 'It's ruined!'

'As I said, it's not my fault, but I've managed to buy the exact same suitcase online as a replacement. It should be delivered in a few days. Would you like a tea or coffee while you're here?'

'Tea would be nice,' said Trixie.

'We are not staying,' stormed Nina, as she zipped up her suitcase. 'I've seen enough of you to last a lifetime.'

'I'll help you take it down the stairs,' offered Ford.

'We don't want your help. Me and Trixie can manage.'

'Trixie and I,' said Ford, immediately regretting saying it.

'Whatever!' Nina began heaving the case out of the door.

Trixie gave Ford another wave and said, 'Bye,' before helping Nina drag the case to the car.

Whatever optimism Ford had had about getting Nina to like him, or even reduce the amount she disliked him, evaporated. He slumped down on the sofa next to Jason. 'She is hard work.'

'I don't know why you even bother trying, she's... I don't know, crazy?'

'That's just my luck, I like someone that's crazy.'

'You'd be better off chatting up her friend; at least she's friendly to you.'

'What, Trixie? You're joking, aren't you?'

Jason chuckled. 'Of course I'm joking; she is way out of your league. She only dates millionaires.'

'Really? How come you know that?'

'I heard Dave and his mates talking about her at the weekend. They work with her, so they should know.' Jason spoke in a hushed voice, as though he was imparting secret information. 'Apparently, her last boyfriend had a place in Monte Carlo and she still dumped him.'

On the drive back to Nina's flat, Trixie had to listen to Nina's rant about Ford hanging up on her a further three times, followed by a new rant about her case having a broken lock and a slashed lining.

Trixie was used to seeing Nina lose her short temper, but Ford had, for some reason, a way of winding her up to breaking point. 'He did explain what happened, and he's going to pay for a new suitcase.'

'Huh! I'll believe it when I see it. I don't trust a word that comes out of his big mouth.'

'What's got in to you lately? You're making big dramas out of the most trivial things.'

'Trivial? That man has made my life a misery ever since I clapped eyes on his fat, allergic face.'

223

'He always seems kinda nice.'

'Nice? Nice?! That loser is anything but nice.'

CHAPTER FIFTEEN

Ford figured out that, with the holidays owed to him, he could quit his job at Frank's Auto Sales and, if he was frugal, have enough money for a month or so to find another position. He had arrived at the showroom just as Jezza pulled up in a bright red Ford Mustang with go-faster stripes on the sides. Music was blaring out of the open windows; it was a classical version of an Elvis song, *Heartbreak Hotel*, sung by a third-rate tenor. Ford had no choice but to listen to it while he locked his bicycle up. Jezza waited until the awful version had finished before switching it off. Oozing confidence, he strutted over to Ford. 'I confess! I'm into classical music; arrest me, guilty as charged.'

It was Ford's last day, so he thought what the hell. 'That's not classical music, is it?'

Jezza's arrogant smile dropped. 'It's got real violins and stuff on it.'

'Oh! It's got real violins and stuff on it, so in that case, it must be proper classical music!'

Jezza was not a hundred percent sure whether Ford was taking the piss or not. 'I'll… make you a copy if you want.'

'Thank you, Jezza, but pure classical music like that, with real violins and stuff, goes way over my head.'

They were interrupted by Blake pulling up in his white Mercedes. Like Jezza, he had the windows down with music blaring out. It was a classical version of an Abba song, sung by two tone-deaf sopranos.

By the time Blake swaggered over to open the showroom door, Ford felt his will to live drop down by a notch or two.

'Did you like the music?' asked Blake.

'If I'm not mistaken,' said Ford in his best sarcastic voice, 'that was classical music with real violins and stuff.'

'You better believe it,' said Blake proudly. 'And those two singers on it nearly came third in *Britain's Got Talent*.'

Ford nodded wisely. 'I can honestly believe that.'

As soon as he had taken his bicycle clips off, Ford handed in his notice, informing Blake that, with holidays owed, he would finish at the end of the day. Of course, he hadn't been expecting Blake to break down in tears about the news, but he really was not expecting him to rush over to Jezza, give him a big hug and tell him with tears in his eyes that he was now permanent. Having a whole day with nothing to do but watch Blake and Jezza harass customers, Ford decided to get a printout of his sales records over the years in case any future employer wanted to see them. While he was trying to get the printer to work, Blake marched in from the forecourt.

'That fucking time-waster wants to talk to you!' he said angrily.

Ford glanced out of the showroom window and saw Aldo waiting patiently.

Blake made no attempt to hide his displeasure. 'I told him he was a fucking time-waster and so did Jezza, but he still wants to talk to you.'

Ford went outside, curious to see what the older man wanted.

Aldo gave Ford a huge smile when he spotted him strolling over. He warmly shook Ford's hand. 'I'm still interested in that car you showed me.'

'That's good,' said Ford, 'but you'll have to talk to one of the others, this is my last day.'

Aldo was puzzled. 'I don't understand.'

Ford shrugged. 'I quit before I was sacked.'

At that moment, Jezza ran past, to get to a man who was looking at one of the other cars for sale.

Aldo thought for a moment. 'Maybe a better opportunity will come along. God moves in mysterious ways!'

'Maybe.' Ford held out his hand. 'Good luck with finding the right car. Who knows, I might bump into you again.'

'Did you get the invite?' asked Aldo.

Ford was confused by the remark. 'Sorry?'

'The invite to the Event,' said Aldo.

'So that's where they got my name from!' The part of Ford that was not nice any more was pissed off. The words, 'God moves in mysterious ways' triggered something in him. 'Congratulations, you've taken scams to a new level. This is your job, is it? Finding some sucker who's gullible enough to be brainwashed. What is it? Some sort of cult? I should have guessed once you said you had eight grandchildren.'

'No, no, it's not like that,' insisted Aldo.

'The thing that annoys me most is the fact that you've seen something in me that you and your cult buddies can mould to your own way of thinking.' Ford shook his head in disappointment. 'I suggest you clear off back to your fanatical sect.'

'Let me explain,' protested Aldo, as Ford marched back to the showroom. Aldo glanced over at the waiting white MPV and dreaded having to break the news about what had just happened.

The rest of Ford's last day at Frank's Auto Sales consisted of clearing up unfinished paperwork. There was no point in talking to customers, so he watched the clock tick away the final minutes of his ten-year employment. Part of him was saddened, his father and grandfather had both worked here, and now he felt as though he'd let them down.

It was late afternoon when Ford interrupted Blake and Jezza. They were discussing tactics for getting old ladies to buy expensive cars by frightening them. They had started making a list of the concerns old ladies had. Ford noticed they only had two so far: foreigners and people with ginger hair.

227

'Is it okay if I go now?' he asked, 'There's nothing else for me to do.'

'Go on then.' That was all Blake said. He did not even look up at Ford.

Jezza didn't bother to glance at him either, as he was deep in thought. 'Rats and mice!' he declared. 'Old ladies are scared of rats and mice.'

Blake said, 'Good one,' and added it to the list.

'See you,' called Ford, as he put his bicycle clips on.

The two of them were too wrapped up in thought to answer.

Ford walked out without looking back. The last thing he heard before closing the door behind him was Blake saying, 'A dry minge and dirty net curtains!'

Ford had mixed emotions as he cycled home; he was elated that he did not have to see Blake any more, but petrified of not being able to find another job. The one thing he'd been putting off was telling his mother about what he had just done. Once he got home, he called her straight away to invite her to meet for dinner the next evening in a small bistro that she often frequented.

Every other Wednesday evening, Nina and Trixie would meet up and try a different restaurant. They had an alphabetical system, and had now reached the letter J. The only local eatery they could find online was called Jessica's Bistro, so they booked a table for eight o'clock.

The décor in the bistro had been described by the interior designer as, 'retro classic with attitude'. What that meant was red and white gingham tablecloths, with a candle shoved in an old wine bottle in the middle of each table. A young waitress, chewing bubble-gum, checked Nina and Trixie's reservation before showing them to a table and taking their drinks order. Nina casually surveyed the faces of the other diners. 'It's quite busy for a midweek.'

Trixie picked up the menu. She had missed lunch and was eager to order quickly. 'It either means it's very good or does coupon discounts on Wednesdays.'

Nina took another glance at the diners. 'They don't look hard up.' Her sweeping gaze stopped at a corner table on the other side of the bistro. Ford was sitting there with an older woman.

'Look!' said Nina, in a loud whisper. 'It's that horrible Ford.'

Trixie glanced over. 'I wonder who he's with. She's very stylishly dressed.'

'Some desperate old trollop he managed to get a date with,' muttered Nina.

Trixie took another look at Ford's dining companion. 'I'm sure I've seen her before. She looks familiar.'

Nina tutted. 'Look at her, all glammed up like a dog's dinner. She must be in her late fifties, at least.'

'You should go over and say hello to him. He did bring your suitcase all the way back and bought you a replacement.'

'And hung up on me three times. Don't forget that!' Nina reminded her.

'You've got to say something, he's bound to see us here.'

Nina sighed. 'Okay, but I'll have a swig of wine first.'

The bubble-gum-chewing waitress, right on cue, arrived at their table with a bottle of white wine and two glasses.

At the corner table, with his mother, Tippi, Ford was finishing off his risotto while she picked at a salad. He had held off telling her the reason he wanted to see her, because she had been proud that he'd followed in his father's footsteps.

Tippi, on the other hand, had had enough of watching the signs that her son needed to tell her something that he really did not want to. 'Out with it!' she demanded. 'What is it you're not telling me?'

'What makes you think I have something to tell you? Can't I just share time with my mother?'

Tippi raised her eyebrows. 'You never want to share time with me. Go on, say it!'

'I've got two things to tell you. The first is I've split up with Kate.'

Tippi had always suspected that there was more behind Ford's sensitive and kind nature. 'She wasn't right for you. You can't fight nature's urge.' She reached across the table and held his hand. 'I know you're gay so just come right out and say so, it makes no difference to me. When I was at the convent school, I used to dabble quite a bit with a few of the other girls.'

'What are you saying? I'm not coming out… and… Oh, my God. Why did you tell me about dabbling?'

'Sorry, I judged that wrong.'

'And not just one girl? Quite a bit with a few of the other girls?!'

Tippi shrugged her padded shoulders. 'Don't make a big thing of it; a lot of young people dabble. It's part of growing up.'

'Will you stop saying "dabble"?!' Ford had the look of a rabbit caught in a car's headlights. 'I really think I'm going to need therapy after this.'

'What was it you wanted to tell me if it wasn't about coming out?' asked Tippi.

Ford took a deep breath. 'I quit my job. Mainly because I was going to get the sack anyway for not reaching my sales target.'

Tippi seemed not to care. 'Good, I never thought car sales suited you. You're too nice for a job like that.'

Ford was expecting a bit more of a reaction from his mother than that. 'I've been doing it for ten years. Why didn't you say so?'

'Because ten years ago, we needed money coming in when your father died. What are you going to do now?'

'Find another job before I run out of money,' said Ford dejectedly.

Tippi's face brightened. 'You can always come and live with me and Ronnie, we have a spare room.'

Ford did not get on well with Ronnie, mainly because his mother's new husband wasn't his father, and he would have preferred his mother to be a lonely, weeping widow, rather than having relations with another man. The thought of being in the same space as them smooching like teenagers turned his stomach. 'I'll manage, thanks. Where is Ronnie tonight?'

'He teaches yoga on Wednesday nights.'

Ford nearly choked on his risotto. 'He still teaches yoga?! You're kidding!'

'Don't say it like that! Of course he does.'

Ford wiped some wayward rice from his mouth. 'He's about eighteen stone, with gout in both feet.'

Tippi gave her son a disapproving stare. 'That is weight-ism, I didn't bring you up to talk like that! And it's not gout. The doctor said it was the early stages of rigor mortis or something like that.'

Nina had opted to down the whole glass of wine before going over to Ford's table.

'Go on,' said Trixie. 'Just say, "Thank you, Ford, for replacing the suitcase and have a good evening." That's all there is to it.'

'Will you come with me?' begged Nina.

'You're not five years old. I'll watch from here, just go and do it. Hurry up because I want to order.'

Nina dragged herself over to Ford's table. She coughed to get his attention. Ford immediately stood up and gave her a big smile. 'Hello, Nina, what a small world.'

Nina gave a nervous smile. 'I just popped over to thank you for replacing my suitcase, it turned up this morning. Anyway, enjoy the rest of your evening.'

Tippi glanced up at Nina's face. She'd seen her recently, but could not quite remember where.

'I'm pleased that it turned up,' said Ford. 'Oh, this is my mother, Tippi. Mother, this is Nina; she was at Dave and Evie's weekend bash.'

Tippi snapped her fingers as she recalled where she had seen Nina. 'Katharine Hepburn!'

Nina looked stunned by the words. 'I had better get back, Trixie's waiting.'

Ford looked over at Trixie and acknowledged her with a smile.

When Nina sat back down at her own table, she poured another glass of wine and swigged it back before immediately pouring another.

'Who was the woman?' asked Trixie.

'It's his mother. And guess what? She's the nurse… the nurse from the sexual health clinic.'

Trixie glanced over. 'She does look familiar… What does that matter anyway?'

'It means she'll tell him about the you-know-what, and he'll tell everyone else!'

Trixie shrugged. 'There's nothing to tell.'

Nina lent over the table and tilted her head close to Trixie's ear. 'After she called my name, I told her that I slapped a man's knob. She's bound to tell him!'

Trixie allowed herself a smile. 'She's a professional, it's all confidential.'

Nina peeked over at the corner table, Ford was laughing. 'She's told him, I can see him laughing. That bastard's going to tell everyone now!'

'Calm down, Ford doesn't seem the type who would spread gossip. He likes you, believe it or not.'

'He likes making fun of me! Oh, this will make his day, knowing I slapped a man's knob. I bet he can't wait to tell everyone.'

'Nina, you're sounding like a paranoid nutcase. Look, I will talk to him, he'll tell me if anything was said. How does that sound?'

Nina peered suspiciously over at Ford's table. 'Okay, but he'll just lie.'

Ford was feeling upbeat. The fact that Nina had actually been courteous and even thanked him had cheered him up. Maybe there was a slim chance that she might even like him a little bit after all.

'Do you know her well?' asked Tippi, as she glanced over at Nina polishing off another glass of wine.

'Not that well. I did sell her a car and since then I keep bumping into her.'

'Does she have a drink problem? Because she seems to be knocking it back.'

'Now you mention it,' said Ford, 'she does seem half-cut most of the time. Why did you say "Katharine Hepburn" when you saw her?'

Tippi smiled. 'I can't tell you that. I signed a non-disclosure agreement, I might get the sack.'

Ford laughed. 'That's ridiculous.'

'Some people want to keep their private lives to themselves.'

'I know, but come on, you can tell me, I'm your devoted son.'

'No! And you're anything but devoted.'

Ford laughed out loud and put his hands up as if to surrender. 'Okay, keep your work secrets.'

Nina could not get the Katharine Hepburn remark out of her head. The humiliation of Ford knowing she had slapped a man's knob was too much to bear. She stared blankly at the menu. Unable to stop herself, she turned to look over at Ford's table. He was holding his hands up and laughing. Nina slammed her menu down on the table. 'I bloody knew it!'

Trixie broke off from reading her menu. 'What now?'

'She's told him and he's laughing his head off!'

Trixie glanced over at Ford, he was smiling, deep in conversation with his mother. 'They're just talking... Wait a minute... I recognise her...'

Before Trixie could finish her sentence, Nina stood up and marched over to Ford's table, where she stood defiantly glaring down at him.

A couple at the next table, who preferred their phones to talking each other, instantly began videoing what was happening.

Ford gazed up. 'Hi, Nina. Are you okay?'

'Having a big laugh, are we?' enquired Nina, with venom.

Ford used the standard British response to not knowing what the hell was going on. 'Sorry? I don't know what you mean.'

'You heard! I said, "Having a big laugh, are we?".' Nina wagged her finger at Tippi. 'The glamorous granny here has told you, hasn't she?'

Ford was completely baffled by Nina's outburst. 'I honestly haven't got a clue what you are on about.'

Nina now turned her wagging finger to Ford's nose. 'If you think you can have a laugh at my expense, you are so wrong!'

Trixie rushed over and tried to pull her friend away. 'Nina, I need to tell you something! Now!'

Nina was blinkered by her rage and deaf to any reasoning. The disruption had caused all the other diners to stare over at the fracas.

Ford guessed she had had a few glasses of wine, he could smell it on her. 'Nina, I really think you need help, you need to see a doctor or something.'

'So the glamorous granny has told you!' shouted Nina. 'Well, I'm about to ruin your gossipy fun. You, mister fat face, have picked the wrong girl to mess with!'

Nina grabbed an empty chair from the table of the couple who were recording her, and used it to step up on to Ford and Tippi's table.

'Everyone listen to what I have to say!' yelled Nina. She stood with her hands on her hips and defiantly glared back at the diners, who all stared, gobsmacked, at the woman bestriding the corner table.

'I went to the sexual health clinic for a check-up,' declared Nina, 'because I slapped a man's STD-infected erect knob!'

The whole bistro was deathly silent. 'Only because he asked her to!' added Trixie, in Nina's defence.

The silence of the bistro was broken by a vicar in his late sixties dropping his glass of water, smashing it to pieces.

Nina peered down at Ford with a victorious smile. 'There, I've saved you the trouble of gossipmongering. What do you think about that?!'

Ford stared up at her with a baffled expression. 'I can't think, because my brain just stopped working.'

Trixie tugged at Nina's clothes. 'It's not her!'

'You borrowed the Katharine Hepburn book the other day,' said Tippi, who was shocked and slightly miffed at being called, 'the glamorous granny'.

It was Nina's turn to be confused. 'But you work at the sexual health clinic.'

Tippi shook her head. 'I work at the library.'

Time stood still. No one knew what to do next. Nina's defiant confidence began to ebb away. She noticed for the first time that she was being videoed on twenty or so diners' phones. Her eyes began to redden, a single tear trickled down her cheek, and her bottom lip started to tremble.

Ford was over the initial shock of Nina's outburst and decided on a plan of action to get her out of the situation. He stood up and made a clapperboard motion with his arms, shouting loudly, 'And end scene!' With arms open wide and a beaming smile on his face, he declared, 'Ladies and gentlemen, we are members of the Restaurant Improv Group, bringing live theatre to the eating public. Please give it up for Tippi, the glamorous granny.' With Ford's encouragement, the confused diners began to applaud. Tippi had trodden the boards in amateur productions, and happily stood up to take a bow and blow some kisses.

Ford indicated Trixie. 'The concerned friend was played by the adorable and beautiful Trixie!'

Trixie was relieved that Ford had spared her friend's humiliation and impressed by his quick thinking. She played along with his idea and gave a bow to the diners.

Ford held his arms up to Nina. 'And the girl that slapped a man's knob was played by our leading actress, Nina!'

The bistro diners were now laughing, and along with the noisy applause, there was the odd shout of 'Bravo!'

Ford took a bow. 'My name's Ford, thank you for being part of the live theatre experience. Don't forget to tell your friends!'

It took several minutes for the applause to stop so Nina could clamber down from the table. 'I've never been so embarrassed in all my life. Come on, Trixie. Let's get out of here.'

Nina stomped back over to their own table to collect her things.

Trixie turned to Ford and Tippi. 'Thanks for getting her out of an awkward situation, I hope it hasn't ruined your evening.'

'It made the dinner more interesting,' chuckled Tippi.

'Nina does have a way of making life interesting,' admitted Ford.

Trixie smiled in agreement. 'She should have calmed down in a day or two, so when you see her at the wedding, she won't be so grumpy.' With a final wave, she went in search of Nina, who had made her exit from the stage.

'The young lady who jumped on the table is a bit feisty, isn't she?' said Tippi, as they sat back down.

Ford laughed. 'She is a bit feisty. And for some reason, whatever I do or say just seems to wind her up.'

Tippi smiled. 'You like her, don't you? I can tell.'

Ford laughed. 'Five minutes ago you thought I was gay! Okay, I kind of like her, but I'm pretty sure she hates me even more now.'

Tippi looked straight at her son. 'Her friend likes you more than she does.'

It took a moment for Ford to grasp what his mother had meant. 'Trixie? I'm not her type by a long shot.'

Tippi smiled warmly. 'I wouldn't be so sure.'

CHAPTER SIXTEEN

For the rest of that week, Ford had trouble sleeping after he came to the realisation that finding another job was going to be more difficult than he had imagined. He had called a dozen car sales companies. After he'd told them his work history, they had all promised to get back to him, but none of them had. It was now Saturday, the day of Dave and Evie's wedding, and Ford was on his second cup of coffee to combat the effects of another restless night. He was starting to feel a caffeine kick when Jason entered the kitchen with a large, grey plastic bag and dropped it on the kitchen table in front of Ford.

'What's this?'

'It's a surprise gift from Dave and Evie. Because we're ushers, they've hired suits for us to wear.'

'How do they know my size? What if it doesn't fit?'

'Don't panic. I took your favourite suit with me to the outfitters and they matched the sizes while I was trying mine on.'

'How come I never got to try one on?'

'That's a bit selfish, isn't it? You needed to be out searching for work so we have a roof over our heads, not trying suits on. Anyway, you would have moaned. You've been a right grump since you got the sack.'

'I did not get the sack, I quit!'

'Yeah, yeah, yeah. Whatever you say.'

Ford opened the bag and peered inside. 'It's a tartan rug.'

'Take it out of the bag and have another look.' Jason smiled with eager anticipation.

Ford had a feeling of dread, as he pulled out the bright green tartan material and held it up. It was a three-piece suit. 'They want us to wear bright green tartan suits?'

'Hey! You're being selfish again. It's their big day. If they want us to wear suits and are generous enough to pay to hire them, we should go along with their wishes.'

'If I'd known I would have to wear a tartan suit, I would have refused to be an usher.'

'Whose big day is it?' asked Jason.

'Okay, it's their big day. I'll wear the stupid suit.'

An hour later, Ford was putting on the tartan tie that came with the outfit. He caught a glimpse of himself in his bedroom's full-length mirror, and thought that if he wore a big red nose and a coloured wig, he could get away with being a clown.

Jason burst in without knocking and paraded around in his tartan suit like a catwalk model. 'Morag's going to be as pleased as Punch when she sees us in these outfits.'

'Why do I get the feeling she'll be more pleased to punch us when she sees this tartan?'

Jason did a few more catwalk turns in front of the mirror. 'What's not to like?' He glanced over his shoulder and bent over. 'Does tartan make my bum look big?'

The doorbell rang several times.

'Two minutes!' shouted Jason.

'What's going on? Who was that?'

'That will be the taxi driver,' explained Jason. 'No need to thank me for arranging it.'

Ford glanced at his watch. 'The wedding doesn't get started for another two hours.'

'As number one usher, I've had to do all the planning and the plan is for us to have a beer with Dave before he gets hitched.'

Ford gave one of his rare smiles. 'Where are we meeting him?'

'There's a wine bar down the road from Evie's auntie's pub, Corks Vino Bar. We'll meet him there.'

Fifteen minutes later, a black taxicab pulled away, leaving the two tartan clad figures standing outside Corks Vino bar.

Jason rubbed his hands together and chuckled. 'Let's have a beer to celebrate the day.'

Even though it had only just turned midday, quite a few people were already seated in the wine bar, and every jaw dropped at the sight of the tartan duo.

Jason puffed his chest out. 'I've always wondered what an admiring glance felt like.'

Ford scanned the shocked faces. 'I'm still wondering.'

Jason headed straight for the small bar, where a young man stood posing, wearing a tee shirt that showed off the tattoos on his skinny arms.

'What beers do you do?' asked Jason.

The tattooed young man pointed at a glass chiller cabinet containing one make of European lager.

Jason was unimpressed. 'Lots of choice. We'll have two of those then.'

Ford gazed around the bar. 'Dave's not here yet.'

Two bottles of lager were slammed down on the bar. Jason picked them up. 'You settle and I'll find us a table.'

Ford turned to the tattooed young man. 'How much?'

'Eighteen pounds,' he said bluntly.

Ford had to play the words back in his head in case he had heard wrong. 'Eighteen quid for two bottles of beer?'

The tattooed young man shrugged. 'Yeh.'

'Do I at least get a "please"?'

The tattooed young man rolled his eyes. 'Eighteen pounds… please.'

Ford handed over a twenty-pound note and waited for the change.

The tattooed young man hesitated. 'No tip?'

'A tip? I'll give you a tip, say please and thank you, and you might just get one.'

The tattooed young man scowled as he handed over Ford's change.

'Thank you for robbing me… See? Manners cost nothing. Oh, another thing, I want glasses as well. For eighteen quid, I want glasses with ice in them and a slice of lemon.'

While waiting for his ice-filled glasses, Ford spotted a woman with a professional-looking camera, taking pictures of a group of people. She was shooting at different angles, either on one knee or standing on a chair.

The tattooed young man grunted to indicate the glasses were ready.

Jason was sitting at a four-seater table, fiddling with his phone, when Ford sat down and placed one of the glasses in front of him. 'I don't want a glass.'

'I don't want one either, but after paying eighteen pounds for two beers, I'm happy just to sit and look at them. When do you think Dave will get here?'

Jason placed his phone down on the table between them. 'He's here!'

There was a ringing tone on the phone's speaker. Dave's voice answered. 'Jason, stop calling me! I'm trying to get ready.'

Jason bent over his phone. 'Guess where me and Ford are? We're in Corks Vino Bar, having a beer for you!'

'You're not drinking already, are you? I bet it was Ford's idea, he's been acting strange since he got the sack.'

'I did not get the sack, I quit! And what do you mean about me acting strange?'

'Jason! You should always tell someone if they're on speakerphone.'

'By the way,' Jason told him, 'you're on speakerphone.'

'Please don't drink any more than two beers! I don't want more ammunition for Evie to throw at me about you two. Did you pick up the suits?'

'I only found out about them this morning,' complained Ford.

'What do you think? They were Evie's idea.'

'I love the material!' gushed Jason. 'I can honestly say we're turning heads in these suits.'

'What do you think, Ford?'

'To be honest, it wouldn't have been my choice.'

'Well, it was Evie's choice, she's done all the planning.'

'I want to make a toast to you and your future wife,' announced Jason.

Ford picked up his lager.

'Here's to Dave and wee Morag!'

'Dave and wee Morag!' repeated Ford, before clinking Jason's bottle and taking a swig.

'You're not funny. Look, I have to get ready. It was good to talk to you both. I'll see you later. The one good thing is you can't afford to drink too much in that place.'

Jason switched off the phone.

'He's right,' moaned Ford. 'Eighteen pounds for two small beers!'

'Let it go, it's only money.'

'Yes, my money!'

The woman taking photographs was now standing a few feet away from their table and peering at them through a square frame formed by her hands. 'Interesting,' she remarked.

Ford and Jason gave each other a confused glance.

The woman began standing on chairs and crouching down while still peering at them. 'Very interesting!'

'Excuse me,' said Ford, 'but we can't enjoy our outrageously expensive beer with you saying, "interesting" and staring at us.'

'My name's Bathsheba, I'm a professional photographer. I was just wondering…'

'That's not a real name, is it?' interrupted Ford. 'It sounds like one of those pretentious names arty people give themselves. Your name's probably Janet, or something like that.'

Bathsheba pretended to smile and wished him dead for seeing through her deception; her real name was June. 'No, that is my real name. The reason I was observing you was because the Corks Vino Bar website is being updated and I've been commissioned to take some interesting images.'

'And you want us to be in one!' enthused Jason.

'The suits are intriguing,' said Bathsheba.

Jason swigged his beer back. 'I don't mind you taking a picture, but it might seem a bit odd if I'm holding an empty bottle.'

Bathsheba called over to the tattooed young man. 'Anton, bring two beers over and leave some glasses of wine on the next table.' Bathsheba made adjustments on her camera, as Anton reluctantly did as he had been asked.

'Thank you very much, Anton,' said Ford with exaggerated politeness. 'That, by the way, is an example of manners.'

Bathsheba began to click away with her camera. 'Just relax and smile… Good, very good. Would you mind just swapping the beer for some wine? It is a wine bar after all.'

'I'm willing to do whatever is required in the name of art,' insisted Jason, as he swallowed half a glass of red wine.

Bathsheba asked two young women from the group she had photographed earlier to sit with the tartan duo. She rattled off hundreds of photographs, while the foursome drank glasses of various wines. The two young women, Chloe and Sophie, were tipsy and giggling by the time Ford glanced at his watch. It was twenty-five to two. Jason had just whispered something in Chloe's ear that made her burst out laughing, when Ford tapped him on the shoulder.

'Jason! It's twenty-five to two!'

Jason kept his lecherous, smiling eyes on Chloe. 'Don't worry, the bar stays open all afternoon.'

Ford leapt up and pulled Jason to his feet. 'We're supposed to be ushering in ten minutes!'

Jason's facial expression went from *What?* to *Oh, fuck!* in a nanosecond.

The flight to London from Rome had only taken two and a half hours, yet Ennio Rossi felt travel weary. The skies were grey, as he stepped off the private jet and walked over to a helicopter that would take him and his personal assistant, Fredo, into the city of London. A twelve-minute flight and a final ten-minute limousine journey saw Ennio safely to the Double Luxury Hotel, where an entourage of the hotel's best people chaperoned him to the Double Royal suite. Once they had reached the fifth floor, he requested the sycophantic hotel staff to leave and spent a few minutes taking in the river view before getting to work. 'Fredo, get me Aldo.'

Fredo nodded, took his phone out of his jacket and moved to the other end of the suite so as not to disturb his boss. A few minutes later, he was back. 'Thirty minutes.'

Ennio nodded. 'Excellent.'

'I'll go and supervise the unpacking.'

'Very good. Oh, order some coffee. Let's see if the English can make it better than they did last time.'

Fredo gave a nod and left Ennio wishing he were back under his Italian blue skies. He had just finished his coffee when Fredo approached with Aldo. Ennio indicated for Aldo to sit down. 'I hope you have better news for me.'

Aldo sighed with relief. 'Yes, the news is good, we received the reply an hour ago, he has accepted the invite.'

'How many do we have now?'

'Four.'

Ennio shook his head. With only four people attending, the chances of him finding the person he wanted were slim. The Rossi Superiore showroom in Rome had been, for decades, a Mecca for car lovers. The rich and famous had often passed through its doors, adding to its allure. The opening of a second showroom in London was to be the ultimate experience for the ever-growing number of billionaires gathering in the city from all four corners of the earth. Besides, English was now the planet's tongue, so the move made sense. The word 'showroom' did not do the Rossi Superiore establishment justice. It was an experience that only the very wealthiest would get to know.

The Rome showroom was like a vault, but instead of money or gold, it stored rare cars, ranging from three million to seventy million pounds. Such was the influence Rossi Superiore had over the rare car market that to not sell through them would be folly. There was a three-week waiting list just for an appointment to visit the showroom, and that depended on you having a vast enough bank balance. Hosts and hostesses would meet and greet the clients before handing them over to an adviser, who would answer any questions regarding the wheeled works of art. The advisers were like gatekeepers, they had no incentive to sell a car to just anyone, they had to make sure the priceless vehicles would be looked after. Advisers would even, on occasions, visit clients' estates before approving a sale. Consequently, the advisers were given five-star treatment wherever they went in the world. A car that had been bought from Rossi Superiore always went up in value, it was an investment. It was known that the advisers were chosen by Ennio himself. He had recruiters searching the globe's car showrooms for the right person to be the next adviser. If, on a rare occasion, they found such an individual, it would take months of checking and testing before information on the potential adviser was passed to Ennio. The final test was a face-to-face meeting with Ennio. Nineteen out of twenty would fail Ennio's meeting, and in the last ten years, only a handful had been deemed to have the right qualities for Rossi Superiore.

CHAPTER SEVENTEEN

It took Ford and Jason five minutes to run up the road to the Queen's Head inn. They entered through the front door where a sign said, *Closed for private party*. Inside, they stopped to get their breath back. Sweat poured off them, thanks to the excellent insulation of the woollen tartan suits. The entrance to the oak-beamed inn was decorated with garlands of flowers that led the way to a large bar decked out with numerous bouquets.

Jason gazed in awe at the floral decorations he could see ahead. 'There must be enough flowers to fill at least ten hearses!'

Just as they were about to enter the bar, a large female figure dressed in a lime green wedding outfit stepped into their path.

'Where do you think you two are going?' she demanded.

They found themselves face to face with Jason's Jenny X, his *No-strings-bonking-dot-com* date.

Ford instantly put two and two together. 'You must be Stella, Evie's auntie who is running for mayor.'

Jason was all gooey-eyed. 'You'll always be Jenny X to me.'

Stella angrily beckoned them to a small room just off the entrance. 'What are you two morons doing here dressed like that?'

'We're ushers for Dave and Evie, and we're running late,' explained Ford. 'So if you'll excuse us, we have ushering to do.'

'You're not ushering in those tartan outfits, I'll tell you that now,' stated Stella. 'Evie's Nana died because of tartan!'

Ford was unsure how you could die because of tartan, unless you were strangled with it, so he just had to enquire, 'Tartan?'

Stella stared at him like he was a moron. 'Yes! She tripped over a tartan rug while pouring herself a whisky and whacked her head on an ornament of Brigadoon.'

Ford shook his head. 'I'm really struggling to think of a more Scottish way to die than that.'

Stella made the sign of the cross. 'The last thing Evie wants to see on her wedding day is two walking tartan rugs to remind her.'

'Oh, I think I remember about the rug thing now,' said Jason. 'Yeah, she was pissed, tripped up and hit her head.'

'Really?' groaned Ford. 'How could you not remember that when you were getting the suits?'

Stella pointed in the general direction of the pub's entrance. 'I suggest you two idiots clear off before Evie sees you. No… I'm not suggesting, I'm telling you both to clear off before you ruin my niece's big day.'

There was a time when Ford would have just taken the easy way out and left, but now the nice part of him was gone, he could say what he wanted. 'Look here, Jenny X, we're supposed to be ushers at our friend's wedding, and unless you want the world to know that the mayor elect is having sordid shagging sessions with complete strangers, you'd better make sure we are!'

Stella stood nose to nose with Ford and glared at him. 'You are not a nice person.'

Ford glared back. 'Thank you.'

Stella reluctantly led them through the kitchens, where the Queen's Head chefs were working at a frantic rate, and into a staffroom. She pulled two plastic-wrapped parcels from a shelf above a row of lockers. 'If you want to stay, put these on.'

Ford split open his bag and held up a long black bib apron. 'You're joking!'

Jason was already taking his tartan jacket off. 'I don't know why, but I just love dressing up.'

247

A few moments later, they stood in front of Stella as she appraised their appearance with the long black bib aprons on.

'I think it's watered down the tartan,' said Stella, her glaring undimmed by their new outfits.

'I think black suits me,' enthused Jason, who could not resist giving a twirl. 'What do you think Jenny X?'

'Call me Jenny X one more time and I'll have your balls tied around your neck!'

'We're supposed to be ushers,' pointed out Ford, 'but we look more like waiters.'

'We can be usher-waiters!' suggested Jason. 'And I'm number one usher-waiter.'

'That's settled then,' said Stella brusquely. 'You're usher-waiters, I'm short on staff anyway. Follow me.'

Stella led them down a narrow corridor and into the reception bar. A line of opened bottles stood waiting on a table next to rows of champagne flutes.

Stella explained to Ford and Jason what they had to do. Ford found himself getting annoyed. She was talking to them as if they were a couple of eight-year-olds and a bit slow with it.

After she had finished giving them detailed instructions on how to hand out drinks from a tray, Jason scratched his head. 'Can you just run through that again?'

The actual wedding ceremony was to take place in the adjoining Rose Room, named after a woman called Rose, who had gone mad in the seventeenth century and been locked up in the room for ten years. The Rose Room had been laid out with seating and what Jason would have estimated as a couple of hearsefuls of flowers, filling a huge brick fireplace.

Nina and Trixie arrived at the Queen's Head early, so they could see their friend before the ceremony began. Nina was dressed in a peach outfit, with matching fascinator, that one of the royal duchesses had apparently worn at Ascot, while Trixie had decided to go with a dark blue sleeveless dress that suited her skin tone. Stella had given Evie use of one of the suites in the inn, so they made their way up the Tudor staircase and followed the trail of people bustling back and forth along the corridor. Even though Evie's suite was large, with a four-poster bed at one end, space was limited, as there were also three very young bridesmaids being dressed by three young mothers.

Evie was sitting at a dressing table in an off-white wedding dress that made her look even more beautiful than ever. While a woman put finishing touches to her hair. Evie caught sight of them in the mirror. 'Welcome to the mad house!'

Nina loved weddings. She took one look at Evie, and burst into tears. 'You look so beautiful!'

Trixie was not the type to show her emotions, in fact, she could not remember the last time she had cried, but she agreed that Evie looked stunning.

'I want the day to be perfect,' declared Evie. 'I've dreamt about my wedding day since I was a little girl, so it has to be perfect.'

Evie was assured by everyone that her day would be perfect because she deserved it to be perfect.

Nina and Trixie soon found themselves being edged toward the door as more people turned up, so they decided to join the other guests downstairs. With their good luck wishes and blown kisses out of the way, they headed back down.

Ford and Jason, in their roles as welcoming waiters, stood either side of the entrance to the bar. They were each holding a silver tray laden with glasses of champagne and soft drinks. Ford had realized that being a waiter was like being invisible. No one made eye contact or acknowledged you in any way, so he started saying, 'Please help yourselves to drinks. We are on minimum wage so please feel free to treat us like dirt.'

'Champagne, madam!' said Ford, as Nina approached. Nina grabbed a glass of champagne and continued without noticing him. 'My pleasure, madam, feel free to ignore me.'

Trixie stopped in her tracks and laughed at the sight of both of them. 'What are you two doing? Aren't you ushers or something?'

'Usher-waiters,' Jason informed her, 'and I'm number one usher-waiter.'

'It's a long story,' said Ford, offering Trixie a choice from his tray.

Trixie took an orange juice because it was going to be a long day. 'Come on, tell me. I'm curious now.'

Ford briefly explained about the tartan suits and how Evie's Nana had fatally tripped on a tartan rug.

By the time he'd finished telling the story Trixie had the giggles. 'I didn't know about the tartan rug.'

'That makes two of us.'

More people began to arrive and a queue for drinks started to form.

'I'll see you later,' said Trixie, with a smile, and headed into the bar.

Nina was standing with a group of people, being the centre of attention again, so Trixie just went and mingled with other people she knew.

Dave and Conrad arrived at the inn wearing grey three-piece suits, and began the process of shaking hands and kissing cheeks, as they made their way toward the main bar. Dave's joyful smile dropped from his face when he caught a glimpse of Ford and Jason wearing their black bib aprons and holding trays of drinks. 'What the fuck?!' was all he could manage.

Conrad now saw the culprits responsible for the sudden change in his brother's demeanour. 'I just knew you'd find a way of ruining my brother's day.'

'Where are the grey suits?' asked Dave after the initial shock had subsided.

'Grey suits?' asked Ford, staring daggers at Jason.

'I thought we had a choice of colour,' explained Jason. 'And I knew Evie liked tartan because you told me.' He waggled his tartan trouser leg.

Dave put his head in his hands. 'No! I told you about the tartan rug that Evie's Nana tripped over. The tartan rug that killed her!'

Ford thought about lightening the mood by mentioning it was unfortunate that the incident had happened on the one day in a hundred years when Brigadoon appeared, but decided against it. He would save that for another day.

Dave pulled himself together. 'Now, listen, the two of you, Evie has been planning this day for months and wants it to be perfect, so please just keep out of her way.'

'We'll just watch the ceremony and then nip home to get changed,' suggested Ford.

'Just do it without drawing attention to yourselves,' said Dave, firmly. He gave Ford and Jason a last disapproving glance before entering the bar area to cheers and best wishes.

Conrad glared at them as if they were dog shit on his shoe. 'I knew you two would fuck it up.'

'Fuck off,' mumbled Jason, 'you fat twat.'

Conrad took a few steps before rushing back. 'I heard that!'

Ford and Jason put on their best innocent expressions, while Conrad angrily glared at them. Happy that he had dominated them, Conrad set off after his brother again, only to hear Jason's voice.

'You big eared twat.'

The guests had begun to assemble in the Rose Room, so Ford and Jason kept out of the way until Evie and her bridesmaids had passed by. As the wedding music began to play, they moved to the doorway and watched their friend make his vows. Ford suggested that because wedding photographers just keep taking pictures to justify the amount they charge, they should nip off, get changed, and be back before anyone noticed. They found their way to the staffroom where they had left their tartan jackets and were just about to pick them up when Stella's deep voice boomed out, 'Where do you think you two are going?'

'We're nipping off to get changed,' explained Ford.

'We'll be back later, Jenny X,' added Jason.

'Listen to me, you two halfwits; you'll go when I say you can go.'

Ford laughed. 'You can't stop us, Jenny X, because we will tell the world about your secret bonking life.'

Stella gave a smile a psychopath would have been pleased with. 'One mention of that and I'll take you to court and sue you both. Who do you think a judge will believe? Me, a respectable businesswoman running for mayor, or you and Dopey here, who's never had a proper job in his life?' Stella stood nose to nose with Ford again. 'I dare you to say something! You'll be in miserable debt for the rest of your pathetic lives.'

'Do you fancy meeting up on Wednesday?' asked Jason. There was something about her that excited him.

Stella's glance at Jason confirmed she thought he was a fool. 'No!'

Ford wondered if she was bluffing so just said it. 'You're bluffing!'

'Oh, try me! Not only will I put you both in permanent debt, I'll make sure David and Evie never speak to you again, ever!'

'What are we supposed to say to Dave and Evie if we're serving drinks all day?' queried Ford.

Stella chuckled menacingly. 'My niece believes whatever I tell her. I'll just say that you found out I was short of staff, and because you want her day to be perfect, you volunteered to help.'

'Okay,' grumbled Ford. 'What do you want us to do?'

The restaurant was just a short walk past the Tudor staircase. The wedding guests slowly made their way in and found their seats from the table plans displayed on an easel. Nina was pleased to see she was on the same table as Trixie, but disappointed that it wasn't closer to the top table. She and Trixie sat down together and introduced themselves to the others sharing the table. Trixie knew four of them as work colleagues. The other couple were distant relatives of Dave's who were elderly and turned out to both be a bit deaf. Nina found herself shouting to make herself heard and soon gave up trying.

Nina lent over to Trixie. 'It's not right that I'm stuck up the back with deaf relatives! I should be right near the top table, I'm Conrad's date.'

'Stop fussing, the seating plans were arranged months before you even met Conrad.'

Ford and Jason approached their table, holding opened bottles of wine.

'White wine?' asked Ford.

'Red wine?' enquired Jason.

Trixie said, 'White for me, please.' She gave Ford a big smile as he filled her glass.

Nina did not even glance at him, and just said, 'White.' Ford tilted forward to fill her glass. It took a few seconds for Nina to recognise him. 'You!' she gasped. 'What are you doing? Why are you wearing that apron? Why are you pouring wine?'

'It's the very latest trend, usher-waiters,' replied Ford with a wry smile.

Nina whispered threateningly in his ear, 'Listen up, usher-waiter. If you tell anyone about the other night…'

'The bistro incident?' said Ford innocently.

'Yes! The bistro incident. Tell anyone and I'll… I'll… I'll think of something!'

'Don't worry, I'd never say anything that would embarrass you,' laughed Ford, before moving on to the next table.

Trixie briefly explained to Nina about the tartan suits and why Ford and Jason were wearing aprons. 'It's funny, isn't it?'

Nina wasn't laughing. 'It's not funny, Trixie! It will ruin Evie's wedding day if she finds out. It will crush her... I'm going to tell her right now!'

Trixie had to stop Nina getting up. 'What the hell are you doing?' she said in a loud whisper. 'You just said it would ruin her day.'

'I have to say something! Especially after I lit a candle and prayed for Nana!'

'Go on, tell her, because I'm sure Ford and Jason will be happy to talk about you praying for Nana.'

Nina gritted her teeth. 'All right, but I'll tell her one day when she won't find out about me.'

Evie and Dave received a rapturous welcome, as they entered the restaurant and took their place at the top table. Stella had taken Evie aside while the photographer was changing his camera battery, and woven a tale of Ford and Jason generously stepping in to fill the staff shortage. 'They did it,' she said, 'because they wanted your day to be perfect.' When Evie saw Ford and Jason filling the wine glasses, she burst in to tears and blew them kisses.

Food began to be brought out. All the guests had chosen their courses weeks in advance, except Nina, because she had forgotten. The waitress for her table said it was not a problem, but she would have to have whatever was left after the other dishes had been handed out.

Nina's starter turned out to be pan-fried yellowfin tuna. After one solid minute of whingeing about fish from Nina, Trixie agreed to swap her asparagus and Parma ham with her.

Nina's main course was a cod fillet cooked in a stock. This time, Trixie did not even give her time to start whingeing and just swapped it with her chargrilled chicken.

When it came to the dessert, Nina was given a baked chocolate fondant while Trixie had chosen a banoffee cheesecake. Trixie said she'd recently gone off cheesecake and asked if they could swap. Nina pretended not to hear and shoved the fondant down her throat as quickly as possible.

'Really!' said Trixie. 'I swapped two courses with you.'

Nina still had her mouth full of chocolate fondant. 'I never heard you. Did you say you wanted to swap?'

Trixie stared into Nina's eyes and waited for the tell-tale twinkle that meant she was lying. Nina burst out laughing. 'Oh, you know I love chocolate, I promise I'll make it up to you.'

'I'll get my own back, don't worry.' Trixie thought she would start by not telling Nina she had chocolate fondant all over her chin.

The wedding breakfast went smoothly, followed by speeches that Ford thought were way too long. Not only that, but as Conrad interminably rambled through his boring speech, Nina cackled loudly at every pathetic pun he came out with. Ford and Jason decided serving tea and coffee must mark the end of the shift they had been coerced into working, so they went to see Stella. They found her in the main bar beside the till.

'We're done!' said Ford. 'We've done what you asked, and now we're going to go and get changed. Oh, just one more thing, you treat your staff like shit. We never had a break and we're both starving.'

'I agree with that,' said Jason, 'but I'm still willing to meet up for a bonking session.'

Stella stopped reading the itinerary for the day and glared at them. 'You are not going anywhere. You are mine until it's all over.'

The one thing that Ford hated in the world was injustice, especially if he was the victim. 'You can tell Evie what you want now; she's had her perfect wedding, so we don't care.'

Stella switched on her psychopathic smile. 'If you leave, I'll tell the police you stole money from this till.' Stella pushed one of the till's buttons, a draw slid out, and she stuffed a handful of notes down her cleavage. 'Oh! It looks like I've been robbed. I wonder who could have been in here on their own. Oh, yes, I remember now, the two halfwits who tried to ruin my niece's wedding!'

'Now, that is proper blackmail,' acknowledged Jason.

'I don't care if it is proper blackmail, I'll take my chances,' said Ford.

Stella went back to checking her list. 'Go on then, and have fun trying to find a job with a police record.'

'How did you know?'

'A little bird told me.'

Ford was not a happy bunny. Stella not only had them by the nuts, she was twisting them as well. 'I can understand now why they call you a power-crazy-psycho-bitch-maniac!'

Stella pondered the term for a moment. 'I've been called worse.'

Ford had to come to terms with their fate. 'If you're going to blackmail us, at least have the decency to feed us!'

'Go to the kitchen, they're making sandwiches for the evening. You've got half an hour break.'

'Half an hour,' enthused Jason, 'that's very generous. Thanks.'

Stella wondered if he was being sarcastic, but remembered he was an idiot, so she said, 'It's my pleasure.'

One of the chefs in the kitchen pointed to a tray of squashed sandwich rejects and told them to help themselves. Jason set about gorging himself because it was free, but Ford only managed a couple of crushed cheese sandwiches. Being blackmailed had ruined his appetite. He took himself for a stroll in the gardens behind the pub. From the large patio area, he peered in through the French doors. The wedding guests were mingling, as the tables were cleared. He caught a glimpse of Nina swooning over Conrad, and felt nauseous. He had always thought that he'd reached a point where he could not feel any lower, but after seeing her acting like a besotted schoolgirl, he knew he was still heading downward. After their half-hour break was up, Ford and Jason were told to offer canapés and drinks to the early evening guests. Their several hours of service were evenly split between being totally ignored and treated like dirt. Ford concluded that Dave and Evie's professional friends were complete self-absorbed twats.

Jason had decided he liked being a wine waiter because he could drink what he liked. He caught Ford at the bar when he went to fill his tray up. 'Guess what!' giggled Jason.

'When you giggle and say, "Guess what!", I know it's going to be rude.'

'Because these aprons wrap right around, I've had my knob out for the last ten minutes and those snobby bastards haven't got a clue.'

Ford looked vacantly at Jason. 'What do you expect me to say to that? "Oh, what a great idea, Jason! I think I'll get my knob out as well, just to teach them a lesson"?'

'Does that mean you're getting it out or not?'

'Not! I wish you hadn't told me. I can't look at you now, knowing what's lurking underneath there.'

The final straw that broke Ford came when a section of the room that had been curtained off was opened up to reveal a dance floor and a stage. A four-piece band of middle-aged men with mod haircuts started playing a set of cover songs.

Just in time to stop Ford breaking down completely, Stella appeared and beckoned the two of them over. 'I've got good news for you two idiots. It's only the Stewart tartan that upsets Evie, and God knows what the tartan is you've been wearing.'

'You are joking!' groaned Ford. He took off his apron and threw it across the room. 'Thanks for blackmailing me. If ever I feel the need to be coerced into doing something against my will, I know where to come. Now, if you don't mind, I'm getting my jacket and getting out of here.' Ford angrily stomped off.

Stella peered at Jason. 'I suppose you're going to throw a tantrum as well.'

'No, I was just wondering if I can have a job here with you.'

Stella gazed down at a distinct bulge in his apron. 'Let's see if you pass the strict interview first!'

Ford found his way back to the storeroom and said goodbye to the few staff he'd had a nodding acquaintance with over the past few hours. He'd been looking forward to this day in the hope that he might have been able to show himself in a better light, and that Nina might have noticed him in a positive way. Instead, he had been invisible. Taking a route to the exit that avoided the wedding guests, he spotted Stella leading Jason by his apron strings up the Tudor stairs. He shuddered at the thought of them together.

Trixie was searching for Nina when she spotted Ford heading for the exit. 'Hey, Ford!'

He stopped at the sound of his name and gave Trixie a smile. 'Hi.'

'When you said tartan, you really meant tartan,' she giggled, feeling the material of his lapel.

'It is a bit tartan. The tartan of all tartans... It's my own fault for trusting Jason... Anyway, I was just going.'

Trixie glanced at her watch. 'Going? It's only eight o'clock?'

Ford shrugged. 'If you'd had the day that I've just had, you'd be going home as well.'

'I thought you were having fun being an usher-waiter.'

'I was until Evie's auntie started to blackmail us.'

Trixie smiled sympathetically. 'I did hear she was a bitch.'

Ford nodded. 'I think she's affectionately known by her friends and family as a power-crazy-psycho-bitch-maniac.'

'You shouldn't let her ruin the day for you,' declared Trixie. 'I thought you'd be looking forward to dancing later.'

'I've got two left feet and no sense of rhythm.'

Trixie noticed that Ford was barely making eye contact with her again. 'You really know how to sell yourself. Anyway, it doesn't matter about having two left feet when you do a slow dance.'

Ford laughed. 'They're nearly all couples here, so I don't think there's much chance of that.'

'You could always ask me to dance.'

Ford fleetingly looked her in the eye, and with a wry smile said, 'The queue would be too long.'

Nina staggered from the bar with Conrad holding her around the waist to keep her upright. 'Trixie!' she giggled. 'David and Evie are just about to have their first slow dance, and Conrad's got a handsome friend who wants to dance with you. Come on!'

'Hold on.' Trixie turned around. Ford was gone.

Ford stepped out into the warm evening air, it was twilight, and the surrounding buildings looked slightly surreal.

'Hey! No goodbye?' said Trixie, as she followed him out.

'I didn't want to get in the way of you dancing with a handsome man.'

'Are you really going to leave me to dance with one of Conrad's friends? You know the old saying: any friend of Conrad's is a twat just like him.'

Ford chuckled.

'Was it that funny?'

'It just seems so wrong, hearing you say that word.'

'Why is it wrong?'

'Because… because you're… Okay, I'll have one dance, so you don't have to dance with a twat.'

Dave and Evie were in the middle of the dance floor. The band began to play Aerosmith's *I Don't Want to Miss a Thing*.

The newlyweds received warm-hearted applause for their first dance as man and wife. After a minute, other couples joined them, led by Nina, who dragged Conrad out with her and danced with him in just one spot. Trixie took Ford's hand and led him past the watching guests and on to the dance floor. To her complete surprise, he could actually dance.

'For someone with two left feet, you dance pretty well.'

'My mum was a ballroom dance teacher,' explained Ford. 'When my dad died, I used to drive her to the dance school and wait around. Then, one day someone needed a partner, so I stepped in and prayed my friends would never find out.'

'I think it's impressive, you're probably the only man here who can properly dance.'

'Maybe, but I don't think they will be playing any foxtrots tonight.'

'Oh! I thought of you the other day,' said Trixie, noticing that he still would not look at her for more than a second.

'Really?'

'I'm working on a promotion for a showroom that sells rare cars.'

'I don't think cars are my thing any more. I'm currently unemployed.'

'What are you going to do?'

'I haven't figured that out yet.'

'Maybe I could help you…'

The song came to an end. Nina staggered over and pushed herself between them. 'Trixie! I need to talk to you urgently.'

Ford stepped back and gave Trixie a wave before making his way off the dance floor.

Nina watched Ford walk away and smiled to herself.

'What's so urgent?' asked Trixie.

Nina shrugged. 'Nothing. I just helped you get rid of that creep.'

'I didn't want your help.'

Conrad called out to Nina. 'Tell Trixie Tristrum's waiting for his dance!'

'You're not going to meet anyone decent with that loser hanging around you. Have a dance with Tristrum, he's got a

260

yacht. Well, it's not his, but his dad lets him use it whenever he wants.'

'Nina! Just go and... Just go back to Conrad and leave me alone.'

Another slow song had started and Conrad was over like a shot, taking Nina in his arms and breathing pan-fried yellowfin tuna all over her, as they swayed to the music.

CHAPTER EIGHTEEN

Ford was in a melancholy mood, so he walked the three miles home. He strolled into his apartment at nine twenty-five and considered drowning his sorrows with whisky, but the thought of Evie's Nana put him off; he opted for a large gin and tonic instead. He stood gazing out of the kitchen window, deep in thought. He was not far off thirty years of age and he was drinking alone on a Saturday night. A lot of men his age were already settled down with a partner and a family. Why was it that everyone had a better life than him? Was he the only one thinking that, or was it human nature to feel this way? Deciding he needed to watch something to improve his mood, he scanned the comedy section of his video cassettes. He smiled when he saw the title of a 1969 Mel Brooks film, *The Producers.*
'Just what I need!'

While Ford tried to cheer himself up, Nina was hitting the wine, hitting the dance floor and hitting Conrad's hands to stop him groping her body. Nina's initial feeling of being flattered by having Conrad besotted with her had turned to intense irritation. He was like her shadow, never leaving her side for a second. Even when she went to the ladies' toilets, he was waiting outside, ready to wrap her in his arms and fishy aromas.

Trixie had spent some of her evening talking shop with Melinda and discussing a new project. She did take to the dance floor a couple of times when Evie collared her to be part of synchronised dance routines. When it came to Nina, Trixie had deliberately kept her distance. The episode with Nina pushing herself between her and Ford still annoyed her, but for some reason, Trixie couldn't help feeling compelled to protect Nina from herself.

Blake had tried to find out more about the Event over the last few days, but it was still a bit of a mystery. All he knew was that to get a sales job at Rossi Superiore was to win the lottery. He still could not figure out how Ford had been sent an invite when Blake was clearly the best car salesman in the area, but he never gave it more than a passing thought. The invite was meant for him, and he had it now. Blake was a bit disappointed to find that the showroom for the Event was anything, but showy. The whole front of the building was plain black. Two men wearing black designer suits guarded the double doors of the entrance. Blake handed over his invitation and was escorted into a large reception area by one of the men. A stylish woman in her forties, also dressed in a black designer suit, took the card.

'Mr Wilkinson, we've been expecting you. My name is Ingrid, please follow me.'

Blake followed her and wondered if wanting to have sex with a woman wearing a suit meant he might be gay.

Ingrid led him into a large lounge with a wall-size photograph of a 1962 Ferrari 250 GTO that had recently sold for seventy million dollars. Blake could only identify it as being red and old-looking.

Dark grey leather sofas and armchairs stood on the Brazilian walnut flooring.

'Please take a seat,' Ingrid urged him. 'I'll inform Mr Rossi that you are here. In the meantime, help yourself to refreshments.' Ingrid clapped her hands twice and a team of serving staff appeared with trays of drinks and canapés.

'This is more like it,' thought Blake, as he took a glass of champagne. Despite being an impostor, Blake wallowed in the attention and felt his arrogant ego soar to new heights. 'This champagne glass is dirty, get me another one,' he demanded. Even though there was nothing wrong with it. Blake wanted it known that he was no stranger to having the very best.

The glass was hurriedly replaced. He glanced at the exquisitely made canapés.

'No crisps and no salted peanuts? What sort of hospitality do you call this?' He took a sip of the champagne. 'And this should be at least three degrees cooler.'

The serving staff nervously glanced at each other.

'Well, don't stand around, looking like idiots. Get it sorted.'

The champagne waiter scurried off, wondering where he was going to find a thermometer.

Trixie was going over the final details of the press day with Ennio in his luxurious office. She used a remote control to change the images on a screen that filled one wall. All the leading car journalists had been invited to the preview, which would be the motoring event of the year. The rarest cars on the planet were to be assembled in one place, a spectacle that might never be seen again.

Ingrid knocked on the open office door, and waited for eye contact from Ennio before entering. 'Mr Wilkinson is in reception.' She handed him the invitation.

'Thank you, Ingrid.' Ennio turned to Trixie. 'Please excuse me.'

'No problem, I'll make the changes you suggested and catch up with you later.'

Ennio trusted Aldo's opinion; even though the other candidate had been excellent, they did not have what Ennio called *abbastanza umiltà*, enough humility. He was praying that this person would have the qualities he was looking for.

Ingrid led the way back to the lounge area and introduced Ennio to Blake.

Blake gave him his best false smile and shook his hand very firmly to show he was assertive. 'Just call me Ford.'

'I hope you helped yourself to champagne, Ford.'

'I did,' said Blake, 'even if it wasn't cold enough.' And to prove to the old git standing in front of him that he was used to drinking it, he went on to say, 'But I prefer Dan Perry-non, it's got more bubbles.'

Ennio turned to Ingrid. 'Please escort Mr Wilkinson off the premises.'

'Of course,' said Ingrid. She smiled to herself. Things had turned out better than she could ever have anticipated.

'Hold on!' gasped Blake. He pointed to his lapel badge. 'I got this for being top salesman for four months in a row and that's still an official record! You're making a big mistake!'

Ennio looked puzzled by the remark. 'I'm not making a mistake. You are an idiot!'

Blake was proud of the fact that he did not have any pride, and threw himself down at Ennio's feet. 'I will do whatever you say, just give me a chance! I'm good at what I do... I could even flog that old banger in the photo on the wall, if the right sucker came along!'

Trixie was on her way to see Ingrid when she came across Ennio and a man on the floor clutching at his feet.

Ennio gazed down at the prone figure. 'Ford, please go.'

The two designer-suited doormen dashed in and started to gently drag him out to the street, with Blake still calling out, 'I'll give you one more chance to change your mind!'

'Excuse me, Ennio,' said Trixie. 'Did you call this Mr Wilkinson by the name of Ford?'

Ennio held up the invitation to show her.

'I know a Ford Wilkinson, and that wasn't him. There can't be that many people with the same name.'

'I believe it's a very common name,' announced Ingrid.

Ennio made a quick call on his mobile phone. Trixie's Italian wasn't great, but she picked out the words *moron* and *fuck-up*.

'Does the Ford Wilkinson you know live in Bridgeford?' asked Ennio.

Ford had spent most of the day either on the phone or filling out countless job application forms. The monotony was briefly broken when Jason turned up to pack his bags.

'Stella wants me to be live-in staff!' he said excitedly. 'I get to have dirty sex, drink as much as I like and get paid as well. I think I've found my dream career!'

Ford was pleased for his friend, but at the same time, he had come to like having him around because it was nice to know that his life wasn't quite as shit as Jason's. Now, it was Ford who was in the gutter and not even looking up at the stars, but down a rancid drain.

It was five o'clock in the afternoon when Ford quit job hunting for the day and checked the fridge to see what he could eat later. The doorbell rang.

Ford spoke to himself. 'I wonder who that is.' He opened the door. Two smartly dressed men stood there smiling. One was in his sixties and the other ten years younger.

'Mr Ford Wilkinson?' asked the younger man.

'Yes?' Ford thought the man had sounded French or Italian.

Fredo took a step back to indicate that Ennio was the main person to talk to.

Ennio held out his hand. 'My name is Ennio.'

Ford shook his hand and offered to shake Fredo's hand. Fredo was not sure what to do, so just let him shake it.

'What can I do for you gentlemen?'

Ennio held up the invitation to the Event. 'I think you may have mislaid this.'

Ford looked to the heavens and laughed. 'You fanatics don't give up, do you? Are you that desperate to get new members that you have to do home visits?'

Ennio was confused. 'Sorry, I don't understand.'

'Blake was right all along, it's just one big scam. What loony sect are you with?'

Ennio paused for a moment. 'Does this person you call Blake have a little Monopoly car badge?'

'Yes, he does.'

'Would you say he was an idiot?'

'Well, yes, he's quite a big idiot, really.'

'Ah! Please let me explain… Do you mind if I call you Ford?'

'Go ahead.'

'Would you mind if we take a walk? I don't get much opportunity these days.'

Ford was curious. 'Okay, but if you mention God or aliens, the conversation is over.'

Once they were down on the street, Ennio instructed Fredo to wait with the chauffeured limousine. He sauntered with Ford along a path that led to an open park area.

'Have you ever heard of Rossi Superiore?' asked Ennio.

'I should think most people interested in cars have heard the name. It deals in rare cars for rich people.'

'I would say it deals in cars for discerning people who just happen to be wealthy.'

Ennio stopped walking and partially closed his eyes. 'I forget the quiet; I've lived in a busy city all my life.' At that moment, there was no traffic noise, just the coo of a lone woodpigeon in the distance.

Ford patiently waited thirty seconds for Ennio to open his eyes. 'What has all this to do with me?'

'You have come to my attention, because you may have qualities that would suit that particular company.'

Ford laughed. 'I think there's been a huge mistake. I don't have any qualities.'

267

'I disagree; you have been observed and tested for many months. The man you know as Aldo has spoken with you many times and was impressed by your vast knowledge of classic motor vehicles. His attractive niece could not distract you on a test drive, which showed professionalism. The older lady that passed out in the car…'

'She was testing me?'

'She proved that you had integrity.'

'I may have those things, but it doesn't help when it comes to selling cars.'

Ennio smiled. 'However, you try to find the right car for the right person, even if they buy it from somewhere else. That, my friend, is the most important quality you can have. At Rossi Superiore, the cars sell themselves. The adviser's role is to make sure the right car goes to the right customer.'

Ennio took out the invitation from his jacket pocket and handed it to him. 'Come and see. There is no guarantee of a position because the demands are very high, but I promise you it will be an experience that you will enjoy.'

Ford took the invite. 'I'm not sure. It all seems a bit odd.'

'If you have doubts, speak to your friend Ms Clarke,' said Ennio reassuringly.

Ford had never heard of her. 'Ms Clarke?'

Ennio smiled. 'She has the lovely name Trixie.'

Ford was taken by surprise. 'Oh, Trixie! I believe she did mention something about a showroom the other day.'

'It is thanks to her that I found you.'

They ambled back to the limousine with no more talk about Rossi Superiore, enjoying the simple pleasure of walking along in shared silence.

After saying their farewells, Ford watched the limousine drive away, not knowing what to think.

Later that evening, Ford decided that he needed to contact Trixie. The only way he knew of doing that was to call Dave, but he was now on honeymoon and unlikely to be helpful after recent events. He had a thought and checked the website for the Movie Poster Shop. It had a mobile phone number, so he gave it a try.

Nina had climbed out of the shower and was drying her hair with a towel when she heard her phone ringing. Nina was always too curious to let a call ring without answering it. 'Hello!'

'Nina, it's Ford… The car salesman and usher-waiter.'

'Don't forget the fat red face.'

'And with the fat red face. Which, by the way, was brought on by a long-term skin allergy, so you're treading very close to insulting the disabled.'

'Don't ramble on! What do you want? I've just washed my hair and it goes funny if I don't dry it straight away.'

'Have you got a contact number for Trixie? I need to speak to her.'

'What about?'

'Look, I just need to…'

'I'm not passing on a number without knowing what it's about.'

'It's just something to do with the corporate event she's working on, I now have an invitation for tomorrow and just wanted some more information.'

'Text me your number and I'll pass it on to her, but there is no way I'm giving you her number. In fact, I'm not keen on you having my number!'

'I promise I'll never call you again. Can you just pass her the number I'm calling on? Please.'

'Okay, but don't be surprised if she doesn't call you back.'

The conversation ended there as Nina hung up.

Nina had to dry her hair properly before calling Trixie. After blow-drying it for forty-five minutes to make sure every last drop of water had been dealt with, she phoned Trixie and explained Ford's odd phone call.

Trixie was pleased that Ford wanted to talk to her. That meant Ennio had managed to contact him. She explained to Nina how rare in invitation to Rossi Superiore was and that a chance to go inside on a personal tour was a fantastic opportunity. When Nina mentioned Ford having been invited for tomorrow, Trixie gave a heavy sigh. She had to visit clients in Manchester and would not be able to meet him there. Nina read out Ford's phone number, which she had scribbled down, not realising she had swapped around two numbers.

Ten minutes after the call, Nina began to ponder on what Trixie had said about Ford being given a fantastic opportunity. She wondered if she had been too hasty in classifying him as a loser.

Ford waited by his phone for two hours. As soon as it rang, he picked up. 'Trixie?'

'It's me, Nina.'

'Oh!'

'Has Trixie not called you?'

'No. I was hoping she would.'

'She's busy and a very popular lady, so she might not have had the time.'

'Well, thanks for passing my number on anyway.'

'I just wanted to wish you good luck for tomorrow.'

Ford was a bit taken back by Nina saying something pleasant. 'Thanks. I'm a little bit apprehensive. It's an odd way of doing business, sending out invitations.'

'Is it just for you or can you take a guest?'

Ford checked the invite. 'It says *and guest*.'

'If you don't want to go up to the city on your own, I'll come with you. Trixie says the showroom is unbelievable.'

Ford broke out into a big smile. 'That would be great, thanks.'

They arranged to meet up at the railway station in the morning. At the end of the call, Ford's face was aching from smiling so much.

The next morning he was surprised to see Nina at the railway station with two return tickets already in her hand.

'It's the least I can do to thank you for taking me with you,' said Nina, as she handed him his ticket.

'Oh, okay. Thanks.'

'Come on, the next train is due in five minutes.'

Before he could reply, Nina was already through the gate and heading up the stairs to the station platform. Ford fed his ticket into the automatic gate and had it instantly rejected. He made the assumption that he had put the ticket in the wrong way and tried again. Once more, his ticket was spat out. Despite there being three entry gates, a queue began to form behind him. He became more agitated as he heard moans and shouts of, 'I need to catch that train!' With no staff about to assist him, he stepped to one side and let the mob through.

'It's not my fault,' he explained. 'The ticket's faulty!'

A bored member of station staff, who could not have looked scruffier in a uniform if he had tried, slowly slouched over and held his hand out.

Ford interpreted the hand gesture and handed him his ticket.

The bored staff member sniffed and said, 'That's the return, you want the out ticket.' He pointed to the printing. 'It says two-part return.'

'My friend has given me the wrong ticket! Can't you just let me through?'

The station employee shook his head. 'People try this on all the time. Buy a ticket.' With a final sniff, he traipsed off with his hands in his pockets.

Ford still had Nina's number on his phone so called her. It went straight to voice mail. He had no choice but to buy a ticket. With a distrust of machines, he opted to queue for the window, only to be stuck behind a group of mature women from the Townswomen's Guild attempting to buy a dozen train tickets, with the number of pensioners in the group changing after every consultation between them.

271

Ford had to use every last penny he had to buy a ticket because the credit card machine was, as the ticket seller said, 'throwing a bit of a wobbly'.

Two London-bound trains had gone through before he finally managed to make it to the platform. He was hoping Nina had waited for him, but she obviously had not cared enough to do that. The information board flashed up five minutes till the next train, and was followed by an immediate tannoy announcement that there was a technical problem further down the line and consequently all trains were delayed by an hour.

CHAPTER NINETEEN

Ingrid had been writing a shopping list in anticipation of the money being transferred into her account. She was only a day away from being a wealthy woman. Even though Rossi Superiore paid well, they did not pay well enough for the lifestyle she desired. The chance to change her life had come from a man called Lorenzo Folco, who had been a candidate for an adviser role. Even though he had never made the grade, he learnt from other failed candidates what Ennio was looking for, and had trained a woman named Joanne Kemp to fit the profile that would lead to an invite. He had purposely stayed friends with Aldo and over the last six months had drip-fed him information about her and how highly regarded she was. The adviser role at Rossi Superiore was well known to pay handsomely. Not only that; the adviser decided on who the cars would be sold to. It was a power that could easily be exploited for gain. A ten thousand pound payment into Ingrid's bank account as a goodwill gesture had fired her lust for more money. Her role was simple; all she had to do was make sure that the candidate Joanne Kemp had no serious competition. The deal was irresistible. Fifty thousand pounds would be paid once the contract was signed and five percent of any bonus Joanne Kemp received every subsequent year.

Ingrid had already mentally spent fifty thousand pounds, when she received the bad news; Ford Wilkinson had been given another opportunity and was expected to arrive late in the morning. She began to form a plan of action. She would make this Wilkinson feel unwelcome, question his ability and sow seeds of doubt in Ennio's mind. Ingrid summoned the designer-suited doormen and told them that fake invitations were being circulated, so they needed to be on their guard. As luck would have it, at that moment, a young woman was heard making a fuss at the entrance, so she went to investigate. The young woman, named Nina, was Mr Wilkinson's guest. He had been mysteriously delayed and she did not have the invite to get in. Ingrid allowed her into the building and over the next hour questioned her about this man Ennio had gone out of his way to invite back. The more Nina told her about him, the more she realised that he was a loser who had somehow struck lucky.

Two and a half hours later, Ford jumped off the jam-packed train at Liverpool Street station and ran for the crowded underground. Another twenty minutes later, feeling as squashed as a sardine from both the overground and underground trains, he dashed out of Covent Garden tube station, hot, sweaty and bedraggled.

When he finally reached the Rossi Superiore showroom, he was out of breath. One of the designer-suited guards took one look at him and told him to move on.

Ford handed over his invitation, which was no longer crisp and new after being handled so much. The guards debated openly in front of him whether it was a fake. They eyed him up and down before giving it back to him and politely asking him to push off and get lost.

Ford was now feeling hot, bothered, humiliated and annoyed. 'Hold on! You're not employed to be forgery experts! I suggest you take this and show it to Ennio, who personally placed it in my hand, and tell him it's a fake!'

The designer-suited guards gave each other a confused stare.

'There's no point just looking dumbly at each other,' added Ford. 'Check with someone!'

'There's no need to be rude,' said the slightly shorter of the two.

The slightly taller one snatched the invite out of Ford's hand and entered the building. Ford thought it was a different person who came back out because he was all smiles and apologies. 'Please follow me!'

He led Ford into the reception area, where Ingrid stood with a welcoming smile that definitely was a fake. The smile gradually became real, when she saw the scruffy state Ford was in. 'Mr Wilkinson? You were expected earlier.' Ingrid glanced at her watch and shook her head, hoping to unsettle him. 'Come this way.' She led Ford into the lounge.

Nina was sitting in an armchair, having a pedicure and a manicure done by two overly made-up young women. She was drinking something that could have been orange juice, through a straw.

'Where have you been?' demanded Nina 'I've been waiting for ages.'

Ford wanted to ask some questions of his own, but could not work out which one to put first. 'How come they let you in without an invite, when I was more or less told I was a forger?'

Nina sipped her drink. 'I just said I was waiting for you.'

'Waiting? I didn't see much waiting at the railway station.'

Nina swapped her drink over to her right hand, so the manicurist could work on her left. 'I thought you were with the rush that came up the stairs as the train pulled in.'

'I wasn't rushing because you only gave me the return part of the ticket and had your phone switched off, so I couldn't tell you.'

Nina giggled. 'What am I like!'

Ingrid was confident that her money was going to be safe; she peered at Ford and wondered how on earth he had even been given an invitation. There must have been an error. That was the moment when the idea came to her. He was a clerical error. Ingrid made the decision not to offer any refreshments

275

because she did not want him to relax. 'Wait one moment, Mr Rossi is very busy. I will let him know that you are waiting.' If it had not been for the security cameras in the building, she would have told him he was too late and sent him on his way.

'Thanks,' said Ford, feeling sweat drip from under his arms.

Ennio was deep in thought, as he looked vacantly out at the London skyline. He felt saddened that the young man Ford had not taken up the opportunity to visit.

Ingrid gave a gentle cough to attract his attention. 'Sorry to interrupt, Ennio, but we have a Ford Wilkinson in reception. I think he might be another impostor, he's less convincing than the other one! Should I call security?'

Ennio sighed and took a deep breath. 'Show me.'

Ford was thirsty after all his rushing about. 'Nina, can I have a sip of your drink?'

'No! It's my Buck's Fizz.' Nina deliberately sucked on her straw while looking at him. 'Get your own drink.'

'I would, but nobody's offered me one. Come on, just a sip.'

'No way! I don't want your saliva all over my straw.'

Ingrid led Ennio into the lounge. 'There, see what I mean? I'll get him removed.'

Despite Ford looking as if he had been dragged in by a wildcat, Ennio smiled. 'Ford, how are you?' They shook hands.

'Considering I've had the journey from hell, well, not hell, it wasn't that bad, but bad enough to be annoying; I'm okay,' answered Ford.

'Have you had some refreshments?'

'No, I think I must have been too late getting here. I wouldn't mind a drink of water.'

Ennio flashed an accusing glance at Ingrid, who promptly said, 'I'll get that for you Mr Wilkinson.' She rushed over to a table in the corner of the room and returned with a large glass of water.

Ford introduced Ennio to Nina, who was now free of her manicurist and pedicurist.

'How do you do?' gushed Nina, in a voice so posh, she sounded like the 'after' version of Eliza Doolittle.

Ennio smiled. 'It pleases my heart to see a young couple together.'

'We're not a couple,' explained Nina. 'I have a rich boyfriend; he has his own successful business.'

'We're more like friends,' said Ford.

'We are not friends,' Nina corrected him. 'We're more like acquaintances.'

'Nina is a good friend of Trixie's though,' explained Ford. 'She volunteered to keep me company.'

'I suggest,' said Ennio, 'that Ingrid takes your acquaintance on a tour, and you and I can have a talk while I show you around.'

Even though the frontage of the Rossi Superiore showroom was wider than the showrooms in the vicinity, it gave no indication of the vast interior that stretched over four floors. Ennio led Ford through the first section of the first floor. Rare cars that Ford had only ever seen in pictures posed on either side of a four-metre-wide red carpet. Each car had a screen backdrop showing its part in motoring history.

Ford stopped in his tracks. To his right was a 1964 Aston Martin DBR1 and on his left a 1964 Ford GT40. He knew the combined value must be at least twenty million pounds, but that wasn't what astounded him, it was the sheer beauty of the cars. He felt a tear slide down his cheek.

Ennio glanced at Ford and spotted the tear. He smiled. He had never seen that reaction before. They went on without saying a word. Around every corner, Ford saw the beauty that car designers had achieved over the decades. The final, top floor was dedicated to recently built cars from luxury car makers that were limited in number.

Nina's tour with Ingrid took the same route, but at a much quicker rate. Nina spent most of the tour saying, 'How much?!'

When she asked Ingrid what type of job Ford was being interviewed for, she learnt that the adviser role was the most coveted job in the car industry, with a seven-figure income. Nina tried to picture what a seven-figure sum was. 'A million pounds? For selling cars?'

Ingrid smiled. 'It's not really selling, and one million would be a minimum.'

Nina was visibly shocked to hear that such a large amount could be earned. 'So, if Ford is the right person for the role, he can expect to earn a lot of money?'

Ingrid smiled sympathetically. 'Between me and you,' she whispered, 'Ennio has already chosen someone who is perfect for the position.'

'Why is Ford being given a tour if you already have the perfect person?' asked Nina.

'I believe there has been a clerical error,' muttered Ingrid. 'Please don't tell your friend.'

Ennio's walk through the building with Ford lasted an hour longer than the tour usually took. They eventually dawdled back toward the lounge. There was no talk about figures or contracts. Ennio simply told Ford that he must communicate his decision about whether he wanted to put his name forward for consideration by midday the following day. Ford was feeling overwhelmed by the experience. As a child he had put together plastic kits of a number of the cars he had seen today. It all seemed so surreal. They met up with Nina and Ingrid in the lounge; the women were sitting on one of the leather sofas, chatting away.

'Let's celebrate the finish of the tour,' declared Ennio, ushering over a wine waiter. Four glasses of champagne were poured and handed out.

Ennio held up his glass. '*Salute!*'

'*Salute!*' echoed the other three.

After some general small talk, Ford and Nina made their farewells. Ennio gave Ford his business card and reminded him to call him with his final decision either way by midday tomorrow.

On the way out, Ford hurried over to the wine waiter and whispered something in his ear before leaving with Nina. On the street outside the showroom, the two of them set off in the direction of the underground station. Ingrid came rushing out of the showroom door.

'Nina! One moment, please.'

They stopped in their tracks and turned around to face her. Ingrid went up to Nina, took her aside and whispered softly in her ear, 'Please don't mention the clerical error, it would embarrass Ennio and I could lose my job.'

'I won't,' replied Nina, who thought it was a bit odd.

Ingrid chuckled to herself as she watched them walk away. The one thing she had gleaned about Nina was that the bitch could not keep her big mouth shut.

Ford's return train journey from Liverpool Street station was going to be a lot less stressful than the one out, mainly because there was a train this time. Five minutes after they pulled away from the platform, the inner-city suburbs came into view.

Nina glanced over at Ford, who seemed lost in thought. 'What did you think of the tour? Was it what you expected?'

Ford was still in a daze. 'It was pretty amazing. Not a lot impresses me, but that was pretty impressive and exceeded any notion I had of what to expect.'

'Ford,' said Nina hesitantly, 'I want to tell you something, but I don't want to hurt your feelings.'

'That's an odd thing for you to say. You've never worried about hurting my feelings before… Go on. Say it.'

'Ingrid told me they already have the perfect person for the role as adviser and you were a clerical error.'

Ford let the news sink in. He sat silent, looking out of the window for several minutes. 'What was I thinking? I can't get a job selling budget cars in the real world, so my chances of selling rare cars are going to be less than zero.'

'I'm sorry,' said Nina. She genuinely felt sorry for him.

'I've lived with disappointment all my life,' sighed Ford, with a shrug of his shoulders. 'One more isn't going to make any difference.'

'It's a shame because whoever takes the position will get very wealthy.'

'Money changes people. Most of the wealthy people I've met have been selfish arseholes.'

'Conrad's rich and he's not a selfish arsehole!' protested Nina. 'My ex-boyfriend was extremely rich and he wasn't a selfish arsehole either, so you're wrong.'

Ford regarded Conrad as the biggest selfish arsehole he'd ever met, but just to avoid an argument, he said, 'You're right. That was a sweeping statement.' He stared out at the passing scenery and cursed his own vanity for even wanting to be considered for a position.

They sat in silence for a moment longer until Nina said, 'What's the first film you think of with a train in?'

'I bet yours is *Brief Encounter*,' guessed Ford, and going by Nina's miffed expression, he was right.

Nina stared at Ford, trying to read his mind. 'I bet yours is… *Harry Potter*!'

Ford gave her a puzzled look. 'Do I look like the sort of person who'd have *Harry Potter* down on a list?'

'What is it then?'

'*Once Upon a Time in the West*, the Sergio Leone film.'

Nina scowled. 'I don't like westerns. Has that got a train in it?'

'Have you never seen it? Of course it's got a train. It's got more train scenes than *Brief Encounter*!'

280

'Let's have a bet,' said Nina. 'Who can name the most films with trains in them, in two minutes.'

'What is the bet?' asked Ford.

'If I win,' said Nina, 'you promise to never, ever mention the knob-slapping episode as long as you live.'

'Okay, but I never would have mentioned it anyway. What if I win?'

'Think of something, but don't make it dirty or smutty.'

Ford knew exactly what he wanted. 'Have one date with me.'

Nina hadn't been expecting him to say that. 'A date?'

'One date,' suggested Ford, 'so I can prove that I'm not the person you think I am.' Nina thought about it a bit longer than he would have wanted. 'Make it a date in public,' he added.

'Okay, a date in public if you win. Right, two minutes from... now!' Using their phones as notepads, they each made a list. 'How many?' asked Nina after the two minutes were up.

'You first!' insisted Ford, with a confident smile.

'We'll say it together. Ready... Fourteen!'

'Fifteen,' said Ford, showing her his list.

Nina suspiciously checked Ford's answers. 'Hold on, you've got *Murder on the Orient Express* twice.'

'You said name films with trains in them,' reminded Ford. 'I just included two versions with the same title.'

'Okay, but I still think it's cheating a bit,' complained Nina.

'Let's have this date tomorrow night,' said Ford.

'Where?'

'You name a place.'

Nina gave it some thought. 'The Regent Cinema; they are having a seventies season. *Chinatown* is showing tomorrow night at eight.'

'Great, I love *Chinatown*. I'll meet you there at seven thirty.'

When they reached Bridgeford, Ford waited with Nina at the taxi rank. After seeing her off safely in a cab, he remembered he had used all his money up, so he had to walk home. After just one minute of walking, the darkening clouds burst and heavy rain began to fall. Thirty minutes of squelching later, he stood dripping on his front doormat, feeling miserable. He had changed his clothes and was drying his hair with a towel when the doorbell rang. When he opened it, the last person he expected to see there was Frank, his ex-employer, standing under an umbrella.

'Ford, thank God you're in. I need to speak to you.'

Ford invited him in. 'How are you feeling?'

'My heart's still beating, so I'm fine. Ford, you need to know that I knew nothing about the ultimatum Blake had given you. You've always been an important part of the business.'

'I think Blake might have been right, I'm not good at selling cars. You'll make more money now he's brought his friend in.'

'Those two jokers have nearly ruined me in a week! The local paper has a two-page spread on aggressive selling, and photographs of my business with them two idiots keeping an old lady as a hostage, until her son bought the car he was looking at!'

'It sounds terrible, but I can't say I'm that shocked by what Blake does.'

'Ford, I need you to come back and steady the ship. I want you to have your old job back.'

Ford shook his head. 'I appreciate the offer, but I don't know if I want to do that anymore.'

'The showroom means as much to you as it does to me. We're practically family. Your father and I bought that business from the previous owner.'

'Yeah, that's true, but I also remember you bought my dad's half for peanuts after he died. My mum just about had enough money to pay for his funeral with what you paid her for it.'

'The business was going through a rough patch. It was a fair price. I kept you employed, remember that!'

Ford's head flooded with memories from the past. 'That's right, you employed me, all right, and kept me on low wages even though I was selling the same number of cars as the older salesmen. When I think about it, you used me for years. All those extra hours and days because… we're practically family.'

'Are you feeling okay? Because you're acting strange.'

'I'm acting normal for someone who has been shit on for most of his life. You took on Blake. You put him in charge even though I'd worked for you for ten years longer than him. That was your decision, now act like a boss and take responsibility.'

Frank was stunned by Ford's outburst. In all the years Frank had known him, Ford had been meek and mild. Frank briefly wondered whether Ford might have a brain tumour pushing on something in his head.

'Now if you don't mind,' said Ford, opening the front door, 'I'd like you to leave.'

Frank turned to Ford before he stepped out into the rain. 'Don't come crying to me when no one will employ you.'

Ford slammed the door shut, and had a sudden realisation of what burning your bridges meant. He really was up a creek without a paddle.

CHAPTER TWENTY

Nina called Trixie later that evening and told her about the tour of Rossi Superiore. She went into detail about how Ingrid had welcomed her in, and how she was treated to food and drinks before being provided with a manicurist and pedicurist.

'How did Ford get on with his visit?' asked Trixie.

'That Ingrid was very nice. Have you met Ingrid?'

'Yes, I met her… How did Ford…'

'Ingrid told me about the adviser role and that it pays a fortune! Did you see how pricey those cars were? Unbelievable. A lot of the cars weren't even new!'

'How did Ford get on?'

'He enjoyed the tour, but it turned out to be a waste of time.'

'What are you talking about?'

'Ingrid told me he was a clerical error and Ennio had already chosen someone. Oh, guess what? I'm having a date with Ford tomorrow night. We had a bet and he wanted to take me out if he won. That's quite romantic when I think about it. Who knows, if we click, it might be the start of something new!'

'A date? But you don't like him. What about Conrad?'

'Conrad keeps breathing fish over me, I can't bear it. Anyway, you were the one who said that Ford and I had things in common.'

Despite being in one of the most comfortable king-size beds ever made, Ennio was having trouble sleeping. His meeting with Ford had unsettled him.

Fredo stirred beside him. 'What's troubling you, Ennio?'

'The young man I met today… I worry whether he has the right qualities. Are my standards set too high?'

'You must have more faith in people,' yawned Fredo. 'Do you remember when we called at his home? Did you know he was the first person to offer to shake my hand? It's a little thing, but it was a nice thing to do.'

'He did an odd little thing today,' remembered Ennio. 'When he was about to go, he went over to the young wine waiter and whispered something in his ear. I asked the waiter what Ford had whispered to him.'

'What was it?'

'He said that he had done a great job and he would have given him a tip, but he had spent all his money on the train fare.'

Fredo grinned. 'Really?'

Ennio smiled at an even earlier memory. 'That day he shook your hand… when we went for a walk, he let me stop and enjoy the quietness without feeling the need to say anything.'

Fredo glanced over at Ennio. 'It's those little things that make them reach the standard.'

Ennio kissed Fredo's head. 'I don't know what I would do without you.'

The next day at midday, Ennio was sitting at his desk. No call had come through; he checked his watch and waited twenty more minutes. After the time was up, he picked up a pen and reluctantly drew a line through Ford's name.

Ford heard a key in the lock, he expected it to be Jason, but Tippi hurried in. 'You're here, good. I thought you'd be home now that you're jobless.'

'Hi, Mum, thanks for the self-esteem boost,' said Ford as he shuffled into the kitchen and topped the electric kettle up with water. 'I'll put the kettle on.'

Tippi was flustered. 'I can't stop; I've got too much bad news. I need to spread the bad news while I feel strong enough.'

'Bad news?' asked Ford.

'Oh! It's terrible news! Terribly bad.' Tippi had to blow her nose because the news was so terrible.

Ford had always known the day would come when he would have to deal with a sick, elderly parent. 'Tell me, I can take it, how long have you got left?'

'What do you mean, how long have I got left?' asked Tippi.

Ford held his mother's hand. 'You're dying, aren't you?'

Tippi swung her handbag and caught Ford on the back of his head. 'I'm not dying! What makes you think that?'

Ford rubbed the back of his head. 'Because you came in going, "It's terrible news, it's bad news!" What am I supposed to think?'

Tippi felt like swinging her handbag at him again. 'Do you want the terrible news or what?'

'Come on then,' demanded Ford. 'What is the terrible news?'

Tippi sniffed. 'Poor Cedric's been arrested.'

'Cedric? What's he been arrested for?'

Tippi gave a half-sob. 'For impersonating a hypnotherapist and defrauding people.'

'Impersonating a hypnotherapist… Does that mean he's got no qualifications?'

'The police said he learnt it all from a second-hand book.'

Ford was confused. 'Hold on… That means I might still be nice! How can that be?'

Tippi took out a compact mirror from her handbag and checked her make-up. 'That man is a saint.'

Ford was still trying to digest the news. 'What did he say when the police confronted him?'

Tippi sniffed. 'The only thing he said when they bundled him into the police car was, "I'm just a patsy!" It was an odd thing to say because he's a vegetarian.' She rummaged in her handbag and took out a packet of small cigars. 'Right, I'd better be off, I have to spread the terrible news before someone beats me to it. That poor man's been falsely accused; he helped me

286

stop smoking cigarettes.' Lighting her cigar as she waved goodbye, Tippi hurried out to spread the terrible news.

Ford changed his clothes three times before deciding on a casual outfit that gave the appearance of him not having given his clothing that much thought. He arrived at the cinema early because he thought it unfair to make someone wait around. He positioned himself outside the cinema so he would be able to see Nina whichever direction she came from. After thirty-five minutes, with the film due to start shortly, he checked the foyer in case he had missed her somehow. He tried calling her number, but there was no answer. He waited another thirty minutes, which felt like several hours, before facing the brutal truth that he had been stood up. He had been let down before, but this time it hurt more. It felt like this final straw had broken his spirit. Ford trudged home, trying to think of a comedy film that would cheer him up. He decided they had not made a film funny enough for how he was feeling tonight.

After her conversation with Nina, Trixie was feeling unsettled, not because Ford had failed to get the position at Rossi Superiore, but because he was having a date with Nina. A long, hot soak in the bath just made her feel hot and unsettled, and her stomach ached just thinking about Ford with Nina. For the first time in many years, Trixie felt tears flow from her eyes.

Nina's name flashed up on her ringing phone as she climbed out of the bath. She wiped her eyes, took a deep breath and answered it. 'Hi, Nina.'

'Guess who I'm with? Go on, guess!'

Trixie switched on the speaker so she could dry herself off. 'You told me. You're on a date with Ford.'

'Oh, forget him. I'll tell you, shall I? It's Edward! He called me out of the blue.'

Trixie wrapped herself in a towel. 'Edward?! What does he want?'

'He wants us to get back together!' screamed Nina in excitement. 'He saw me on social media and thought my acting was brilliant!'

Trixie went into her bedroom and sat on the bed. 'Slow down. Saw what on social media?'

'The restaurant! The restaurant improv group video.'

'Are you saying someone stuck it on social media?'

'Edward showed me. It's gone viral and had over a million hits. I'm a star!'

Trixie grabbed her iPad from the bedside table. 'What did Ford say when you told him?'

'Who cares about him? I'm going to be famous!'

Trixie began searching for the video of Nina. 'Please say you called Ford to cancel your date.'

'I have to go. Edward's taking me to a fancy restaurant to meet up with a friend of his who's an agent!'

Before Trixie could respond, Nina had hung up. It did not take Trixie long to find the video. It had gone viral. The numbers of views were increasing by the second.

Ford climbed up the steps to his apartment. To his surprise, Trixie stood waiting at the door. 'Trixie?'

'Hello, Ford,' she said nervously.

'If you wanted Nina…'

'No, I don't want Nina,' interrupted Trixie. 'I wanted to talk to you.'

Ford unlocked his front door. 'Come in.'

Trixie followed him in and waited while he switched the lights on.

'Can I get you a drink? Tea, coffee?' asked Ford. 'Or I could do you something stronger?'

'What are you having?'

'Well, Trixie, after the worst two days I've ever had in my life, I'm having something stronger.'

Trixie had never seen him looking vulnerable. 'I'll join you. It's not good to drink alone.'

'Take a seat… Whisky or gin?'

Trixie half-smiled. 'Gin, please. I can't drink whisky without thinking of Scottish Nana with bits of Brigadoon in her head.'

Ford smiled for the first time. 'I have the same problem, I'll join you.' He opened the fridge door and took out half a lime and two bottles of tonic water. 'What did you want to talk about?'

'I just wanted to say I'm sorry about the Rossi Superiore thing, I genuinely thought you were in with a shout.'

'I have a long list of my failings, so I'll just add clerical error to it. Thanks, by the way, for telling Ennio they had the wrong man. Or should I say the wrong clerical error.' He fetched ice from the freezer and dropped the cubes into the two glasses.

'The reason I'm here is because I know why Nina didn't turn up on your date.'

Ford shrugged, pretending this was water off a duck's back. 'I've been stood up more times than I care to remember. When you're an ordinary bloke, you get used to it.' He finished making the drinks, handed one to Trixie and sat on the armchair opposite her.

Trixie took a sip. 'Her ex-boyfriend spotted her in a video on social media.'

'A video on social media?'

'Remember the improv thing in the restaurant? It's gone viral apparently.'

'The improv thing? Oh! I think I do remember people videoing us, now you mention it.'

Trixie produced her phone and played the video for him. 'It's started a craze for copying it in bars and restaurants. There's hundreds of copycat videos now, doing exactly the same thing, word for word.'

Ford watched the two-minute video, followed by a two-minute copycat. 'That is unbelievable.'

Trixie gazed at Ford. 'In that video, you said I was adorable.'

'Did I really? I never noticed.' Ford avoided eye contact and took a sip of his drink.

Trixie smiled. 'Did you mean it?'

Ford went on the defensive. 'I'm sorry if I offended you, I just blurted out the first words I could think of.'

Trixie took another sip of her gin and tonic; the mix was perfect. 'Do you mind if I ask you something?'

'Ask away.'

'Why do you only look at me for a fleeting second before looking away?'

Ford glanced at her briefly. 'Do I?'

'You just did it again,' Trixie assured him.

Ford smiled shyly. 'I don't think so.'

'Look at me and don't look away.'

Ford turned and gazed at Trixie's face for three seconds before turning away. 'There, I looked.'

Trixie put her drink down on a side table and stood up. 'If you're not going to be honest, I'd better just go.'

Ford also stood up and gazed straight into her brown eyes. 'What am I supposed to say that doesn't make me sound like a twat, like every other arsehole? You're very pretty… You are so pretty, I find it intimidating. There, I've said it.'

'Is that all you see? A pretty face?'

'No, of course not.'

'What else do you see? Be honest with me.'

'I see someone who has probably broken a thousand hearts and could easily break another and not even realise it.'

'A thousand hearts?' laughed Trixie.

'Okay, I got carried away with the number,' confessed Ford.

'Right, stand there and look at my face,' demanded Trixie. 'Go on, just look at it.'

Ford looked in to Trixie's eyes. 'I'm looking.'

'Keep looking.'

'What am I looking at?'

'Just keep looking.'

'What am I supposed to see?'

Trixie pointed to her face. 'Look and find faults.'

'There are no faults.'

'Everyone has faults. Keep looking.'

Ford scrutinised her face. After thirty seconds he said, 'One of your eyebrows is higher than the other.'

'Good!' said Trixie. 'What else? Say what you see.'

Ford took a closer look. 'One nostril is different than the other. One cheekbone is more angular. One ear sticks out more. You have one long stray hair sticking out of the bottom of your chin. You have...'

'Okay, Ford, that's enough! So, after seeing I'm not that pretty, what do you think now?'

'That you desperately need plastic surgery and a shave?'

Trixie chuckled. 'Thanks for the compliment.'

'Okay, your turn. What do you see?'

Trixie stepped closer to Ford. 'I see someone who is caring, funny and a genuine nice guy.'

Ford felt himself blush. 'I've always hated being a nice guy, but when you say it, I quite like it.'

The sound of a key in the front door made them step apart and turn towards it. A young woman wearing paint-splattered overalls let herself in, carrying a large easel and a paint-covered bag slung over her shoulder.

Ford could not quite believe what he was seeing. 'Kate?'

Kate flung the bag down and propped the easel against a wall. 'I made a big mistake. Ford, you're not the wrong shapes after all!' Kate took a long look at Trixie. 'And you have really good shapes; I would love to catch them on canvas.'

'You'll have to catch them another time,' said Trixie. 'I was just going. Bye, Ford.'

'Hold on!' pleaded Ford. 'Can I see you tomorrow? I can explain this!'

'I have a busy day tomorrow. I had better go. I have an early start in the morning.'

Trixie was out of the door before Ford could stop her. He hurried after her, only to see her dash down the street and disappear around the corner of the building.

CHAPTER TWENTY-ONE

It was Trixie's last day at Rossi Superiore; her role was to ensure that the world's leading automobile journalists were treated like royalty before being given the freedom to discover the cars by themselves. It had been Trixie's idea. She had suggested the plan to Ennio, who approved it one hundred percent. Nothing had been leaked about the vehicles in the Event, and as Trixie had said, the range of rare cars needed no introduction.

Lanyards with press passes were given to the journalists on arrival, along with refreshments in the lounge prior to a welcome speech from Ennio in front of the curtained off first floor.

Trixie was standing at the back of the room as Ennio started his speech. Fredo tiptoed quietly toward her.

'You've done an excellent job, Ms Clarke,' he whispered.

Most of her colleagues were afraid of him, but she had always found him polite and pleasant. 'Thank you, Fredo.'

Fredo waited for some gentle applause to stop. 'It's a shame about your friend Ford.'

'These things happen.'

'Ennio would not say it, but he was disappointed that Ford did not even call to say he was not interested in a position.'

'I think that's what happens when you waste someone's time and call them a clerical error.'

'I'm sorry? Please explain,' replied Fredo.

'No, I'm sorry,' apologised Trixie. 'I shouldn't have said anything. It was unprofessional of me.'

Ennio had come to the end of his speech, and the huge curtains were drawn open to reveal the treasures beyond. There were gasps of delight and wild applause, as the auto press enthusiastically started their tour of the vast area.

Fredo was puzzled by Trixie's words. A clerical error? He waited while Trixie gave instructions to several members of her staff. 'Ms Clarke! Please, just one moment.'

'Yes, Fredo?'

'Please explain to me once more about the clerical error,' said Fredo seriously.

Trixie gave a big sigh. 'I just think it would have been kinder of Ennio to tell Ford that he already had someone for the position.'

'I'm confused. Ennio never discusses his choices and has still not made a decision.'

'Well, Ingrid told my friend Nina that Ford was a clerical error and the choice had already been made.'

Fredo digested the information. 'Thank you for explaining it to me.' He hurried off in the direction of the offices.

Rossi Superiore had numerous security cameras with built-in microphones that covered every inch of the building. Fredo went to the security hub and asked for footage of Ingrid on the day Ford had taken his tour with Ennio. Footage from several angles was found and played on fast-forward.

Ingrid had waited nervously all that morning for Ennio to confirm that Joanne Kemp would be given the role of adviser. The call for her to go to his office at one thirty was expected; she hoped she could keep her emotions in check, knowing that she would now be wealthy. It was no surprise to see Fredo sitting beside Ennio; it was common knowledge they were lovers.

Ennio smiled as she entered. 'Ah! Ingrid, take a seat.'

Ingrid sat down on a cream leather swivel chair opposite Ennio.

Ennio casually sat back in his chair. 'You'll be pleased to know a decision has been made on my new adviser.'

'I'm sure you have made the right one,' said Ingrid, wondering how long she should wait before booking her holiday.

'I just have one question,' continued Ennio. 'Can you explain this?'

The screen filling the far wall lit up. A video image of Ingrid standing with Nina appeared. Ingrid was smiling sympathetically, as she said, 'Between me and you, Ennio has already chosen someone who is perfect for the position.'

'Why is Ford being given a tour if you already have the perfect person?' asked Nina.

'I believe there has been a clerical error,' muttered Ingrid. 'Please don't tell your friend.' The image froze.

Ingrid's immediate reaction was to run, but a glance at the two-designer suited guards at the office door dissuaded her.

'You disappoint me, Ingrid,' said Ennio, sadly.

'I was forced to do it,' confessed Ingrid. 'I had no choice!'

The image on the screen changed. This time, it showed Joanne Kemp. She was in tears. 'And it was Ingrid's job to ensure the other candidates were hindered. In exchange, she was given a lump sum and a percentage of any future bonuses I would have received.' The screen froze again.

Ingrid was stunned. 'I can explain...'

'We don't want your explanation,' said Fredo. 'We just want you to confirm the name of the man who transferred money into your bank account.'

'Lorenzo Folco... What will happen to me now?'

'That will be up to the police.' Fredo nodded to the doormen, who escorted her off the premises.

When Aldo was informed about the plot, he was distraught, and immediately offered his resignation. Ennio had known Aldo for over twenty years and trusted him implicitly, so assured him that his resignation was not necessary. The problem Ennio had was contacting Ford to apologise to him. He could not be reached.

At the end of a long day, Trixie had a debriefing with her team after completing the contract at Rossi Superiore. Ennio was more than happy with the way the Event had turned out and promised to use her company again. As he shook her hand, he asked her if she had a way of contacting Ford. Trixie said she would find out his phone number from Nina or her colleague David and let him know.

When she finally walked out of the showroom, it was raining heavily, so she groped around in her bag to retrieve her mini umbrella. It took a few seconds for it to open. When she lifted it up, Ford was standing in front of her, getting very wet.

'Can I share your brolly?' he asked.

Trixie held it over his head. 'What are you doing here?'

'I need to explain about the other night,' declared Ford.

Trixie saw the sincerity in his face. 'There's a wine bar around the corner, tell me in the dry.'

Even though it was not yet six o'clock, the wine bar was quite busy, but they managed to find a vacant table by the window. A waiter came over and promptly took their order for two glasses of white wine.

Trixie took her raincoat off. 'Ennio's been trying to get in touch with you.'

Ford wiped water droplets from his forehead. 'I don't care about him. I wanted to talk to you.'

Trixie was puzzled. 'What do you have to talk to me about?'

'The woman who turned up last night out of the blue was my ex-girlfriend Kate. She still is an ex-girlfriend.'

The waiter returned and placed their drinks on the table.

Trixie took a sip. 'What did she mean by saying you were not the wrong shapes after all?'

Ford put his head in his hands in embarrassment and briefly explained the reason Kate had dumped him.

Trixie's smile gradually turned into a chuckle. 'She dumped you for being the wrong shapes?!'

Ford smiled shyly. 'Yes, it's true.'

'Well, I think you have nice shapes,' said Trixie, patting his hand.

'Trixie,' said Ford nervously, 'I also wanted to ask you something.'

Trixie sipped her wine, she noticed he was looking uncomfortable. 'What is it?'

'I know I'm not a millionaire…' stuttered Ford.

Trixie giggled. 'The millionaire story is what I tell work colleagues to stop them pestering me for a date. I'm not that much of a bitch.'

'So… If you're not that much of a bitch and I asked you out, you might consider it?'

Trixie looked into his eyes. 'I might do. I would need you to pass the test first.'

Ford frowned. 'Test? What sort of test? I'm no good at tests.'

'A kiss. A kiss on the lips.'

Ford pecked her on the lips. 'Did I pass the test?'

'What do you call that?' Trixie chided him. 'I meant a proper kiss on the lips.'

Ford smiled at Trixie's smirk. 'A proper kiss… You will have to stand up for me to do my proper kiss.'

'Okay!' Trixie stood up.

Ford walked around the table, nervously took her in his arms and kissed her slowly and gently on the lips. Trixie pulled him in closer. They kissed each other for a full thirty seconds before reluctantly parting.

'Destiny-chemistry,' smiled Trixie.

'Is that good or bad?' asked Ford.

Trixie beamed him a smile. 'It means you passed the test and can now ask me for a date!'

On the next table, a young man was sitting with an older lady. They were laughing very loudly.

A fiery young woman marched over to their table. 'Having a big laugh, are we?!' she shouted.

The young man at the table said, 'Sorry? I don't know what you mean.'

'You heard!' yelled the young woman. 'I said, "Having a big laugh are we?!" The glamorous granny here has told you, hasn't she?' The young woman took a chair from Ford and Trixie's table and used it to climb onto the couple's table.

Ford and Trixie sat back with big grins on their faces as they watched the rest of the scene play out. They stood and applauded along with the rest of the wine bar after the young man had said, 'My name's Ford, thank you for being part of the live theatre experience, and don't forget to tell your friends.'

They were still laughing when they sat down together side by side. Trixie turned Ford's face toward her and kissed him on the lips. 'See? You said I was adorable.'

Three Months Later

It was getting dark by the time Ford strolled out of the Rossi Superiore showroom and said goodnight to the designer-suited guards. He was now an adviser and living in London. He spotted her across the road; she was watching the tourists and commuters file past to the nearest underground station. He dodged the busy traffic to get over to her. 'I thought I was meeting you at home.'

Trixie turned and melted his heart with a smile. 'I just fancied walking with my wrongly shaped boyfriend.' They kissed as if they had been apart for weeks.

'How is my ugly girlfriend?' asked Ford as he put his arm around her.

Trixie laughed. 'Better for seeing you.'

Ford glanced at his watch. 'What time do we have to be at this film premiere?'

'It's not till eight thirty. We have plenty of time.' Trixie spotted the smile on his face. 'We don't have time for that. I meant time to get something to eat.'

'I don't care where we eat as long as we don't have to watch another "girl on the table" re-enactment. Especially since we're seeing the film later.'

They headed toward the heart of the West End. 'Nina's really looking forward to meeting us there,' said Trixie.

Ford had seen Nina several times since the video went viral. On the last occasion, she had taken him to one side and thanked him for coming up with the improv idea.

'I still can't believe she's in this film,' he said.

'Be honest,' laughed Trixie. 'Who else is going to play the lead part? She is the girl on the table. The girl seen by millions of people!'

Ford shook his head. 'It will go straight to DVD and be in a charity shop a week later. I just know it.'

Trixie gave him a playful shove. 'Don't be negative. It might be brilliant.'

'Really? They could have come up with a better title than that?'

Trixie laughed loudly. 'It's a good title!'

He chuckled. '*The Girl Who Stood on a Table* is not a good title!'

'It's lovely, much better than the one you came up with,' sniggered Trixie.

Ford chuckled. 'Mine was so much better.'

'*The Girl Who Slapped a Man's Knob* is not a good title!' Trixie was sure she'd never laughed so much before her time with Ford. She loved his sense of humour and she truly loved him.

They stopped in the middle of the street and kissed.

Ford had never been so happy now that he had Trixie in his life, and despite being a nice guy, he had not finished last. Not by a long shot.

Epilogue

Jason and Stella are now a couple. He accompanies her on official engagements as the mayor. In their free time, they attend the local swingers' club and have become popular members, as they are pretty much up for anything.

Dave and Evie had a wonderful two-week honeymoon in the Caribbean. Along with the honeymoon memories, Evie brought back a positive pregnancy test.

The Movie Poster Shop is now being run by Ava, who lives with Bertie and adopted cat Petal in Nina's old apartment with its carefully measured new carpets and curtains.

Frank's Auto Sales no longer exists on the 1980s industrial park on the outskirts of Bridgeford. The criticism the business received from the town's newspaper and the local BBC news contributed to Frank having another heart attack. It took heart bypass surgery to get him back on his feet. Well, not on his feet. He had so many veins taken out of his leg to use for the bypass, his feet became numb. Consequently, he keeps falling over. Frank's caring son-in-law was by his bedside after the operation. While Frank was still groggy from the anaesthetic, Blake made him sign a document that handed the entire business over to him. Now on the 1980s industrial park on the edge of town is a huge sign above the renamed car sales lot. The sign has the words *Blake's Autos (As seen on TV)* with Blake's smiling face looking down as though butter would not melt in his mouth.

Nina's life had been a whirlwind of meetings and appointments ever since Edward had turned up unannounced at her apartment. The 'girl on the table' video had made her instantly famous, and thanks to Edward's agent friend, she appeared in newspapers and on TV. Her movie knowledge and bad impressions made her popular with the public, who found her to be a breath of fresh air. The 'girl on the table' video and its copycats have now been viral for months, with combined views of over five hundred million. It was only a question of time before a screenplay was developed with Nina in mind to play the lead role. The critics did not rave about the film, but they did rave about Nina's performance and her star is still shining brightly.

Nina never did get back with Edward, despite his insistence that he loved her. Conrad was now fishy-smelling history, and she never found her rich, good-looking man. Instead, on a train journey to Manchester to see a producer, she met someone. He was a London GP, returning home for his father's sixtieth birthday, and after two hours on the train together, they both instinctively knew they wanted to keep on spending time with each other. Nina called it her two-hour *Brief Encounter*.

Trixie still keeps in daily contact and recently asked Nina if she was happy.

Nina simply said, 'I've never been happier.'

The end.

Made in the USA
Middletown, DE
21 April 2020